One brave and beautiful woman, her life was touched
by four very different men. . . .

*Slade Cavanaugh*—Hungry for fame, his career came before everything—including his wife.

*Zakarov*—A Bolshevik determined to turn Dr. Sun's army into an
organized machine, he is a giant among men—in his dreams, his
dedication to freedom . . . and in his love for Chlöe.

*General Lu-tang*—A bandit chieftain turned self-styled warlord, he
embarks on a journey of self discovery and passionate awakening
that begins the day he abducts Chlöe.

*Cass Monaghan*—Chlöe's mentor, he's the newspaper editor who
shaped her thinking in her early years, who urged her to dare—and
who will bring her destiny full circle.

## DISTANT STAR

Also by Barbara Bickmore
Published by Ballantine Books

EAST OF THE SUN
THE MOON BELOW

# DISTANT STAR

## BARBARA BICKMORE

BALLANTINE BOOKS
NEW YORK

Library of Congress Catalog Card Number: 92-90386

ISBN: 0-345-36109-1

Cover design by James R. Harris
Cover painting by Jim Griffin

Text design by Holly Johnson

Manufactured in the United States of America

First Edition: March 1993

10  9  8  7  6  5  4  3

Dedicated to

*friendships that have stood the test of time*

*Diane Browning, for all these thirty years*
*of uninterrupted friendship and love,*

*Ilene Pascal who, among other important things,*
*named my heroine and my dog,*

*Dorothy Milbank Butler, whom I met on my first day*
*of second grade and still cherish.*

# ACKNOWLEDGMENTS

I wish to thank

Bill and Mary Ann Miller, who have gone above and beyond friendship's expectations and who have rescued me when I was stuck,
Bill and Barbara Bruce, for their friendship and Bill's editorial suggestions,
Brigid and Malcolm Delano, who have made a difference,
Debra Clapp, my older daughter, for taking me on a two-month, 3600-mile journey through China (and for much else),
Lisa Clapp, my younger daughter, for keeping the home fires burning during that time and making that trip, and so many other things in my life, possible,
Sarah Flynn, for being the kind of editor writers dream about,
Meg Ruley, my agent, always responsible for making dreams come true.

# DISTANT
# STAR

# PART I

# 1923–1925

# CHAPTER 1

Chlöe hugged herself as she leaned against the railing and watched San Francisco's white skyline grow even smaller against the horizon. A soft ocean breeze blew a strand of her black hair across her face.

She could hardly believe the last two months. Could scarcely have imagined that at twenty-one she'd be on her way to the Orient. Even in May she could never have predicted the present, much less the future that stretched so tantalizingly ahead of her.

She was just where she wanted to be—a far cry from Oneonta, New York.

Turning her head, she studied her new husband. Slade was staring back at their last view of the United States. Though he didn't turn to look at her, he must have felt her gaze, for he reached out and put an arm around her shoulders, pulling her close to him.

She loved to look at him. Certainly he wasn't handsome; his facial features were too average to be striking. But he stood out in any crowd. There was a gracefulness about him, especially his hands. And the way he walked. But most of all, she thought, it was his eyes. Clear gray. Unusual only in that one could tell by looking into them that he was listening. Maybe it was this intense listening ability that had made him one of the *Chicago Times*'s most famous correspondents by the age of twenty-eight.

She hadn't seen his eyes when she'd first observed him across the Monaghan living room in Chicago just four months before. Yet the moment she saw him, a dark shadow silhouetted against the sinking sun, her heart began to beat like a gypsy moth's wings.

Now, with Slade's arm around her, with the whitecaps bouncing between them and the diminishing San Francisco skyline, it was Cass Monaghan she thought of, not Slade Cavanaugh. Cass Monaghan, who'd so often shaped her thinking these past four years, Cass Monaghan who—with his daughter, Suzi—had played Pygmalion with her, fashioning her into someone she'd only vaguely been aware was within her, urging her to dare. Cass had warned her, to be true, telling her life would not be easy as the wife of a foreign correspondent, and that China would be hard on a woman, but he *had* introduced her to Slade. For this and for all else he had done for her over the years—for this she would be forever grateful.

Her family itself was more exciting than anything else in Oneonta. Chlöe was the fifth of seven children and spent much of her growing-up years hitting baseballs, riding horseback, and tinkering with her father's Model T with her four brothers.

When she was fifteen, her mother insisted she stop playing touch football and put her hair up.

"Start being a lady."

Chlöe found acting like a lady boring. The older she became, it seemed, the less interesting life was allowed to be. She determined to escape the strictures small-town life placed on her. Someday she would escape to the city. Binghamton or Albany or even New York City.

It wasn't that she didn't love her family. Her parents, "Doc" Shepherd, the town's pharmacist, and Louise, always had time for their brood. Chlöe couldn't remember a night at the dinner table without laughter. The family, all of them crammed on top of each other in the Ford, would take Sunday picnics up to Otsego Lake in Cooperstown—the lake made famous in James Fenimore Cooper's Leatherstocking Tales as Glimmerglass. Here they'd fish and swim and pretend they were Indians.

Chlöe never seemed satisfied. She had always been filled with what her mother called "divine discontent." She never quite understood what that meant, but she did know that she bored quickly, that she searched for excitement, and if, as her father said, there wasn't any, she invented it. She didn't know what she wanted, but it wasn't what Oneonta could offer her.

In Oneonta—which lies pretty near the middle of New York State—daily life was about as unstimulating as it could be. Chlöe in later years would describe her upbringing as "apple pie, American flag, Methodist, and Republican." In other words, what was supposed to be a typical middle-class American upbringing in the early decades of this century.

Whenever anyone new moved to town and entered her class at school, Chlöe always befriended them, mainly because she wanted new blood in her life, wanted to hear of life outside her small town, where life—like the seasons—was all too regular. She loved blizzards because they broke the routine.

Chlöe and her best friend, Dorothy, taught themselves how to type on Doc Shepherd's typewriter at the pharmacy, and during the winter of their junior year put out a two-page newspaper each month. The next year they talked Mr. Edgerton, the principal, into letting them start Oneonta High's first newspaper, with Chlöe as editor. She liked being in charge. When reporters failed to meet deadlines, she wrote their articles too.

There had never been any doubt that she would go to college. All the Shepherd children were expected to go to college. The boys were the first to leave. Walt had gone to RPI and Jeff went to Northwestern. But Mrs. Shepherd thought Lorna should stay right in town and go to the normal school so she could live at home. Then Richard went to the University at Buffalo. Her parents took it for granted that Chlöe, as a girl, would follow Lorna into teaching, and attend the local college, living at home while she did so. But Chlöe had other ideas.

She dreamed of doing things, she didn't know what. But as she looked around her own family, and the other families she knew in Oneonta, she thought women spent their lives reacting. They kept houses for men, they picked up and moved to a new town wherever the men's jobs took them, they waited for men to make decisions, and then went along with them (or argued). They sewed and cleaned and gossiped and were active in charities and the PTA. Chlöe thought a woman's lot in life seemed pretty dull. She dreamed of traveling in Europe, not of playing bridge. She daydreamed about discovering a new planet or of becoming another Marie Curie and making some wonderful contribution to mankind. She thought of Queen Victoria, ruling a nation. Of Sarah Bernhardt onstage. Of Emily and Charlotte Brontë and Emily Dickinson, though she never dreamed of not marrying.

She knew she wanted to get out of her small town and didn't want to be doomed to shapeless cotton housedresses, dusting, gossiping over the fence with neighbors each day. Primping her hair each night at five, so she'd be attractive for her husband when he came home from a hard (or stimulating) day's work, when all he wanted was to spend the evening reading the paper or listening to the radio. Or taking Frisky for a walk. Or shoveling snow. Chlöe wanted more than that.

Chlöe wanted to get away. Go to a city. Feel her heart beat with excitement, with something awful and wonderful. She wanted to feel kisses that aroused passion or fear, or something. She was stimulated by ideas she had to wrestle with, ideas like those she discovered in eleventh-grade American literature class, where she fell in love with Thoreau and wished that, as he had, she could come to believe in something so strongly that she would be willing to go to jail for that principle. Admittedly, he had stayed there only one night before a relative bailed him out, but the idea of being willing to sacrifice one's comfort and freedom for a greater cause galvanized all her mental energies. She would sit before her bedroom window, staring out at the bare branches of the gnarled pear trees, and try to think of noble causes—ones with which she could involve herself and, if necessary, sacrifice herself to. But none ever came to mind. She couldn't refuse to pay her poll tax, like Thoreau had, because there was no such thing nowadays.

So, it was really no surprise when her English teacher suggested she apply to colleges other than the state normal school right in town. "Why not Cornell?" the teacher suggested to Doc and Mrs. Shepherd. "I think she could get a scholarship." The thought of Chlöe's going away to school had never entered their minds, and they didn't much like the idea. Their vision for all three of their daughters included graduation from the normal school and perhaps a year or two of teaching until each girl married and settled down and had children and lived no more than a few blocks away.

But they gave in gracefully, particularly after she *was* awarded a scholarship, and hoped she wouldn't fall in love with someone who lived farther away, like in Syracuse or Buffalo or, God forbid, New York City. Their very fear was Chlöe's hope.

# CHAPTER 2

Her roommate was Suzi Monaghan. Five feet seven—about the same height as Chlöe—cool-looking, elegant. Dressed in clothes like none Chlöe had ever seen in Oneonta. And hair as blond as Chlöe's was black. Not beautiful—her cheekbones were too prominent, her eyes too widely spaced, her shoulders too broad. But so striking-looking, so arresting, few ever discovered she wasn't beautiful. At first Chlöe was intimidated. This sophisticated big-city girl was seemingly un-flappable.

However, they remained roommates during all four years at Cornell, and, whenever they entered a room or walked down the street together, heads turned.

Suzi was from a different world. Chicago. She and her widowed father, publisher of the *Chicago Times*, lived in a Lake Shore Drive penthouse overlooking Lake Michigan, and Suzi was well known to the governor of Illinois, had met Gloria Swanson, and dined at the White House. Her voice was well modulated and her eyes were blue-green flecked with gold.

The two girls both enjoyed tennis and agreed they were modern women who wanted careers before marriage, though, of course, they admitted, after marriage their careers would be their husbands and children. But they'd like to wait to get married until they'd done some things, though their definition of just what this might mean remained vague.

Together they joined Pi Beta Phi and double-dated whenever possible. They went through nearly all the Lambda Chis, Chlöe sidestepping for a few months with a Sigma Chi who taught her to ski and pinned her for a month.

"I think you did that just to get serenaded." Suzi grinned at her friend on a snowy Saturday night after the entire fraternity had sung "The girl of my dreams is the sweetest girl . . ." to Chlöe. Brent was the first boy Chlöe had let touch her breast, though only through her sweater.

In May the girls figured they'd dated every single weekend of their freshman year. "Home's going to be a letdown after this," sighed Chlöe.

"So come to Chicago for a couple of weeks," Suzi suggested, not for the first time.

It was Chlöe's first taste of big-city life and her first introduction to someone who wielded real power. The Monaghans' world was so unlike the structured small-town life in upstate New York, so different from knowing everyone all your life, a life that never yielded surprises. Chlöe had never known anyone wealthy before and certainly no one as influential as Suzi's father, Cass Monaghan.

Cass Monaghan seemed a giant to Chlöe as well as to most others who met him, yet he was only five feet ten, a stocky man with broad shoulders and thick, crinkly red hair and a rusty mustache. Chlöe guessed he was in his early forties, a dozen years younger than her own father. Like Suzi, he dressed elegantly, and just seeing him walk down a street you knew he was powerful and important. He was the most interesting person Chlöe had ever met. He took her on a tour of his paper and she was in awe that she was standing in one of the places that helped influence American thought. He was a hard taskmaster, and Chlöe could see what Suzi had already told her. To work for Cass Monaghan, you damn well better perform your job to the best of your ability.

Big-city life invigorated Chlöe. She was sorry when the Monaghans chose to visit their summer home far up the Michigan peninsula for the second week of her visit. She wanted to see more of Chicago, to visit more museums, attend more plays, do more window-shopping, and dine in elegant restaurants.

It took all day to drive up the Michigan peninsula to Big Sable Point. Cass dismissed the chauffeur and drove them himself in his sleek open car. By late afternoon, with the scent of pine forests and glimpses of Lake Michigan off to the left, Chlöe decided maybe she didn't mind leaving the city after all.

Besides, together Cass and Suzi were the most delightful company in the whole world. She laughed so hard that her cheeks ached, and she felt a stitch in her side. It was obvious that Cass adored Suzi, and anything she wanted was hers. Chlöe was amazed how much they hugged each other and looked at each other with affection, and how Suzi kissed her father not only good night but good morning. Even when she left briefly for a walk, his eyes followed her fondly. Before long Chlöe too wished for Cass's arm around her shoulders, for a good-night kiss from him. He did hug her before the trip was over, and she basked in the warmth of his acceptance.

She had expected something sumptuous after the elegance of the Lake Shore Drive apartment, but what she found in upper Michigan was a small, rustic log cabin with two bedrooms and a large, cozy living room with a fireplace on one wall and windows overlooking the lake through birch trees on the other. There was no electricity, but the glow from the oil lanterns was cheerful and made Chlöe feel snug evenings. Cass caught fish and cooked for them and wore an old shirt with a hole in it and brown corduroy pants that he left at the cabin. Visibly, he relaxed.

They swam in the lake and canoed along coves where deer drank. Chlöe heard loon cries that sent shivers through her, so lonely did they sound. Canada geese, green-winged teal, and mergansers populated the water. Cass went out each dawn when mist shrouded everything and, quiet as an Indian, paddled across the lake so he could see the ducks and splashing, high-jumping fish, their silver sprays dancing on the water, so mirrorlike at that hour of the morning. One day Chlöe arose early too and asked if she could accompany him. Cass looked at her and said, "If you promise not to say a word."

It was wonderful. Like the dawn of creation. She sat hunched over in the canoe, holding the paddle in her hand while they just sat, scarcely gliding through the calm water, surrounded by the fog, hearing the croaks of the early-morning frogs and the cries of those loons.

Cass reached out for a thermos and poured two cups of hot coffee, handing one to Chlöe. His hand brushed hers and fleetingly she thought, I want a man like Mr. Monaghan. It was not only his luxurious way of living that appealed to her. Nor his power. She found him easy to talk with, easy to be silent with. She found him admirable.

"What do you want to do with your life?" she heard him ask.

Her hands wound around the warm cup, her elbows resting on her knees, and she looked into the mist. "I guess I want what every woman wants," she answered.

His laugh echoed across the water. "So every woman is supposed to find fulfillment in exactly the same way?" He stared at her. "Are men all supposed to have one thing that will bring each of us universal happiness, then?"

Chlöe thought for a moment. "Women don't have the choices men have. I guess our choices are whether we'll marry a plumber . . . or a doctor . . . or"—she smiled at him—"a newspaper publisher."

"And what? If you've a publisher for a husband, or a president, you're more successful than if you marry a plumber?"

Well, certainly, she thought. But she didn't say it. She wondered if he was making fun of her.

"Oh, my dear." Cass picked up his paddle and slid it slowly into the water. "It hurts me to see the limitations you're putting on yourself. Chlöe, you're capable of doing anything you want, except perhaps becoming president."

Chlöe didn't know what to say.

When they returned to the dock and Cass reached out a hand to help Chlöe out of the canoe, he said, not looking at her as he tied the rope around a post, "A word of advice, Chlöe, from someone who has a penchant for giving it. Don't do what the world tells you to do. Not that I mean you have to reject suggestions. But have the courage to follow your heart. Have the courage to dare. To be different. Don't settle for anything you don't have to work your guts out for." Then he looked at her, and his clear blue eyes beamed a smile at her.

What was also wonderful about Cass as a father was his questioning. He asked Suzi more questions than he told her things. "Daddy's always forced me to think," Suzi told Chlöe once. "He's never just let me follow in his beliefs even if it's something I agree with him about."

And Suzi performed that task for Chlöe. In their first year together, with Suzi for a roommate, Chlöe'd had to question everything she'd ever believed. And everything she was just learning. Even about her appearance.

Suzi told her, "Use your looks, Chlöe. You might not be responsible for your beauty, but, my God! Use it to your advantage. No one looks like you. Who in the world has violet eyes? Men are going to drown in them. Don't just take them for granted."

"Your father acts like it's what's inside that matters."

Suzi thought for a minute. "Daddy's not like other men."

Later, lying in bed, she relived Cass's conversation out on the lake. If men had so many choices, she wondered, why didn't women? He'd told her she could do anything she wanted. But she couldn't think of anything specific she wanted. There were really only two choices for women: marriage or not. She couldn't even envision the latter, couldn't imagine a life without a man at the center of it. The worst thing to happen to a woman was to be alone. Everyone knew that. Yet she was aware of vague yearnings, ones that had nothing to do with a man.

Chlöe did not realize her conversations with Suzi and with Cass added so much to her consciousness that the boys she met seemed superficial, if not downright dull. Chlöe never had conversations with others like those she had with Suzi and her father. What Chlöe and Suzi talked about was whether or not there was a God, was there absolute good or evil, did power corrupt or were those who sought power intrinsically corrupt to begin with. Were poor people happy because they didn't bear the rich man's responsibilities or were poor people ever happy? Was Margaret Sanger and her revolutionary new ideas immoral or a savior of women?

On this last they spent hours of discussion, not just in their freshman year but through all four years of college. Margaret Sanger had been repeatedly arrested and sent to jail for espousing birth control methods. Suzi ventured that Mrs. Sanger wanted to end bondage for women. "It doesn't seem fair, does it?" she asked. "I mean, men can do it anytime and not be afraid of repercussions, but we can't. Only Puritans thought men and women went to bed together to purposely make babies. Only they thought it shouldn't be fun."

Chlöe couldn't imagine having sex outside of marriage and then, of course, it would lead to babies, and that was one of the main purposes for marriage, wasn't it? She knew sex should be reserved for marriage. Any woman who did it without benefit of marriage was, of course, loose, immoral.

Suzi laughed at this. "What? The night before marriage it's sinful and disgusting and the night of marriage it miraculously becomes beautiful? C'mon, Chlöe, where do you get your ideas?"

Chlöe stared at Suzi with awe. She wasn't like *anyone* in Oneonta.

In her junior year Chlöe reigned as queen of the Winter Ice Carnival and became fascinated with history, sharing her sense of injustice with Suzi. Her outrage was directed at the Congo and the inhuman treatment of natives by slave traders and King Leopold. The next term her sensibilities were assaulted by the fate of the American Indians, their annihilation by her own countrymen. She'd already gone through slavery and the Civil War, trying not to hate southerners for their attitude toward this segment of mankind.

"I mean," she said to Suzi, "I realize it's the poor and illiterate, the people who aren't white, who have been taken advantage of. But shouldn't it be that those of us who *are* superior should then be kind and compassionate to ones of less intelligence?"

Suzi, who was filing a nail, looked over at Chlöe. "Why do you say less intelligence? Do you mean every person who isn't white has less intelligence?" Her voice had a hard edge to it, and Chlöe knew her well enough to realize Suzi thought she had just made an outrageous statement.

Suzi's needling began to change Chlöe's perception of the universe. In her Asian history class she found a healthy respect for the Japanese but very little for the Chinese. As they studied Japan, she would lie in bed at night and picture lotus pools and precise Japanese flower arrangements and wonder what she would look like with eyes that slanted. She visualized herself in a kimono staring at mist-shrouded Mount Fuji.

But when they turned to China, her professor, a young man in his thirties who could have made garbage-collecting sound exciting, told the class, "Americans may confuse Japanese and Chinese because they are both the yellow race, but they are very different peoples. While the Japanese are racing to catch up with the twentieth century, China is still in the dark ages. It's a country that has made no significant contribution to mankind since the Ming Dynasty. In the twelfth century, when Marco Polo traveled there, it was a highly civilized country filled with wonders. But for the past six hundred years it has been going downhill. More populous than any country in the world, it has nearly 450 million people, 99 percent of whom are illiterate. China is really not an organized country but is controlled by warlords who tax the peasants and control by threats of violence. China remains largely as it was two thousand years ago, resenting the Western powers for trying to bring it into this century. It has little to offer—silk . . . tea . . . little more to recommend it. Only its size and population make it of any importance.

"It's nearly as large as the United States, with five times the population. The Chinese are unsophisticated, backward, labor as animals do in this country, unappreciative of what we and other European powers do for them. They resent us for the Versailles Treaty."

The summer between her junior and senior years, when Chlöe paid her annual pilgrimage to the Monaghans, she and Cass and Suzi paddled out to one of the tiny islands for a picnic supper. She asked Cass what he knew about China. He was the only person she knew who traveled around the world. He went to Europe every winter, she knew that. She wasn't sure whether she brought up the topic hoping to impress him with what she'd learned or if she was searching for answers to questions her teacher had left unanswered.

Suzi stood up. "If you two are going to talk politics, I'm going to go skip stones in the water."

Chlöe, sitting cross-legged, looked intently at Cass, waiting for a response. "I haven't been to China," he said. "Hong Kong, but not the Chinese mainland." He picked a blade of grass and rubbed it between his fingers, thinking. "Be more specific, Chlöe. You don't want an evening-long discourse, I'm sure."

"Tell me about the Versailles Treaty and why that angered the Chinese. Why do they think it was unfair to them?" She knew more about treaties in 1796 than about such recent history as 1919.

Cass leaned back against a tree trunk. The early-evening sun threw golden rays on his ruddy face. He drew up a knee and put his hands around it. Chlöe suddenly wondered what he had been like as a young man. Had he been like any of the boys she knew? Would any of them grow into Cass Monaghans? Somehow, she doubted it.

"Well, to begin with, China has never really been unified and it has no real armies. When China entered the Great War against Germany, America assured her a place at the peace talks. Hundreds of thousands of Chinese were sent to Europe to help our side in the war, so China took for granted that once Germany was defeated, it would get back the land, the large province called Shantung, that Germany had taken control of."

"That seems fair," Chlöe thought aloud.

"You'd think so, wouldn't you?" Cass's smile was grim. "But Japan had come to the aid of the Allies because England and France had promised to reward the Japanese with Shantung. President Wilson supposedly didn't know this. When he insisted that Shantung should be given back to China, Japan threatened to refuse to participate in the League of Nations. Since this was Wilson's pet dream, he gave in. I think that was wrong, myself. And so did Chinese students and other intellectuals who then demanded that China refuse to sign the treaty. Thousands marched in Tian An Men Square in Peking, and down the streets of Shanghai and Canton, with anti-American placards and shouts of 'Down with Yankees.' From all I've learned, it was the great unifying force in China, though China today is still anything but unified. Factions are still fighting for control. There really is no one central government in that gigantic land."

"Well, perhaps it served Wilson right," said Chlöe. "I mean, his own country wouldn't sign it either. Maybe that's poetic justice?"

Cass nodded and reached out to put a hand over Chlöe's. "My dear, I have never understood why America rejected the League of Nations. I predict that someday we shall rue that decision. Things like that are why I run a newspaper."

Chlöe looked at him. "What do you mean?"

Suzi, having returned, listened to the latter part of their exchange. She walked over to her father, putting her arms around his neck, and leaned down to kiss his cheek. "He thinks he can help save the world."

Cass laughed, reaching up to pat Suzi's hand. "Well, I'd be satisfied with helping to save a small part of it."

Yes, thought Chlöe, that would be enough.

# CHAPTER 3

Every day a copy of the *Chicago Times* arrived for Suzi. Chlöe didn't begin perusing it until their junior year, and it wasn't until their final year at Cornell that she began to devour it.

This was how she first met Slade Cavanaugh. He was the *Times* Paris correspondent and, though he wrote with clarity and seeming insight about the politics of postwar Europe, it was an article about a trip to Spain with his friend Ernie that caught her attention. The bullfights at Pamplona, fishing in the ice-cold streams of the Pyrenees, descriptions of the peasants and the countryside. Chlöe could see it all.

She smelled the freshly brewed coffee and salivated at the flaky croissants when he wrote of the outdoor cafés in Paris. In a sentence he evoked an image that others could not capture in a page.

When Chlöe mentioned his writing, Suzi said, "Daddy thinks he's the best political analyst in Europe even though he's just twenty-eight."

"Téll me more about him," Chlöe urged Suzi.

"He's not like his writing. I met him when Daddy hired him right out of Columbia. He was sort of awkward then, but remember, I've been used to Daddy's friends. He came to dinner a lot that first year he worked in Chicago. I was a sophomore in high school. He was quiet and polite and Daddy told me he had a great future. Then he sent him off to cover the war. After the war Daddy kept him in France, and now he's become as famous as the people he writes about.

"I've met him a couple of times since. He's no longer quiet." Suzi laughed. "In fact, he's become a little arrogant about his fame, I think. He likes being important. On the other hand, he can charm you to pieces. I admit I made a play for him last August when Daddy and I went to Europe, but he kissed my cheek after we'd danced all evening and that was that."

Chlöe wished she knew some famous people. And her chance came sooner than she'd expected.

The spring of her senior year, when Chlöe was wondering what she was going to do with her life come graduation, the Monaghans invited her to Chicago at Easter break. Suzi was urging Chlöe to come work in Chicago.

"We can live with Daddy until we find jobs and then we can get an apartment." Career women. It sounded faintly bohemian and appealed to Chlöe. But she was afraid the only jobs open to her would be as a secretary. She wished there were something in particular she wanted to do—some dream to pursue.

The weekend they arrived in Chicago, in late March, Cass was having a small black-tie dinner party, and it was there that Chlöe met Slade Cavanaugh. She and Suzi had just finished dressing and entered the Monaghans' immense living room filled with perhaps a dozen people. Across the room, silhouetted against the sinking sun, there he was.

Chlöe poked Suzi with her elbow and whispered, "Who's that?"

Suzi looked across the room and answered, "Slade Cavanaugh. Daddy didn't tell me he'd be here. Wonder what he's doing back from Europe."

Chlöe couldn't take her eyes off him. Not that he was handsome. He wasn't. His brown hair curled a bit too long, and he was thin in a rangy way. Actually there was no single outstanding feature about him. He held a cigarette in long, slender fingers and listened intently to what someone was saying. With the sun behind him, Chlöe couldn't see his facial features distinctly, but there was something about the way he stood and the way he gestured and his flashing smile that riveted her.

Shaking his head in response to the man with whom he was talking, Slade threw back his head and laughed and, in that second, saw Chlöe. She was intensely aware of the moment he did, for his eyes stopped moving and rested on her. Chlöe gazed back at him, a half smile playing on her lips.

Chlöe felt an excitement, a challenge that was new to her. Though he continued his conversation, Slade's eyes did not leave her.

In a minute he began to thread his way gracefully across the room toward them.

His eyes moved from her and centered on Suzi. He leaned forward, kissing her on the cheek. "I've been looking forward to seeing you again." He grinned, and it was as though Chlöe ceased to exist for a minute. All his intensity was focused on Suzi.

Suzi smiled. "You came over to have me introduce you to my best friend, and I know it."

Slade turned to face Chlöe. "That says something very good about you." His hand reached out to shake hers. From somewhere

far away Chlöe heard Suzi's voice introducing them. She looked into
his clear gray eyes and heard herself saying, "I've never met anyone
famous before."

His hand held hers and she heard him say, "I've a feeling this
was worth coming home for."

Suzi moved away.

"You've been roommates all these years at Cornell? Then you
know the Monaghans, and let me tell you, there's no human being
on this planet more important to me than Cass Monaghan. I'd go
to the ends of the earth for him. You're fortunate to be a friend of
Suzi's."

Chlöe could never remember what she said to him. She tried
not to gush, tried not to sound like a simpering fan, but recalled
quoting something he'd written, and his eyes lit up.

One of the most fascinating qualities of Slade Cavanaugh was
that he talked as interestingly as he wrote. He answered Chlöe's
questions with a refreshing openness, a quality she was unaccus-
tomed to in men. He already had crow's-feet, and Chlöe could sense
that beneath his amusing stories and his considerable charm was an
essentially serious man. Toward the evening's end, impressed by his
spontaneity, Chlöe dared express this observation.

He laughed, saying, "I doubt that anyone else would agree with
you."

"I'm not talking about anyone else. I'm talking about the real
you," she said, longing to reach out and place her hand on his arm,
hoping to feel the pulse of blood beating underneath his wool jacket.

His silence was as deliberate as his gaze. He didn't directly answer her but stared into her. "I think," he finally said, reaching out
for her hand, "that I want to get out of here and go stand on a
street corner or someplace where no one's watching so I can kiss
you."

His hand enfolded hers as they silently rode the elevator behind
the elderly operator. Holding hands tightly, they ran through the
lobby, unable to stop laughing, until they were halfway down the
block. It was chilly, and a breeze off the lake whipped empty cigarette wrappers around their legs as Slade halted. While Chlöe leaned
against the cold building, he bent over and touched her lips with
his, a gentle, soft kiss until she threw her arms around him. The
tension that had crackled between them all night released itself in
their kisses, and at that moment Chlöe found what she had never
found with anyone else.

They spent the next five afternoons and evenings together.

Late one night Chlöe asked Cass about Slade. She approached him when she'd come in still feeling Slade's kisses on her lips. Cass was sitting in the library, even though it was past midnight, concentrating, papers scattered over his desk. "May I interrupt?" she asked.

He looked up, his face crinkled in a smile, and said, "Anytime." He slowly laid down the pencil he held.

She tossed her coat on a chair and walked over to his desk to sit in the leather armchair opposite him.

"Talk to me," she said, "about Slade."

He looked at her, his elbows resting on his desk, his fingers forming a pyramid in front of his face. Finally, he took his rimless glasses off and laid them in the circle of light from the lamp, and looked at her again. "What do you want to know?"

"Anything. Everything."

He waited another minute and then leaned back in his swivel chair. He didn't look at her now. "I've tried to keep my mouth shut all week. But since you've asked me. . . ." He tugged at his mustache. "Slade's one of my top men. Accurate, reliable, readable, daring. He'll go anyplace, do anything for a story. I don't know what kind of husband he'd be, but I'd be proud to have him for a son."

"Well," Chlöe laughed, "it hasn't gotten that far."

"Yet."

"Yet." She nodded.

Cass grinned. "He's someone I'm proud to have work for me, and whom I trust implicitly in his job. I'm not sure he'd make a woman happy. He's married to that job."

Chlöe stood up, putting her hands behind her back, and walked over to the window. Lake Michigan stretched gray far below her. "Cass, I'm going to be twenty-one years old next month and I've never felt what he makes me feel." She turned to face him.

Cass shrugged his shoulders. "Maybe we're thinking of different things. He's a top-notch reporter. He's tough, my dear. He'll do *anything* to get a good story. He'll sacrifice comfort, undertake tedious journeys, and he seeks out dangerous confrontations. He's also famous, and he likes fame. What kind of life is that for a woman?"

Chlöe thought it sounded exciting. She smiled at Cass.

She dreamed of Slade. For the first time in her life she dreamed of hands touching her, a tongue feathering along her neck, of lying naked next to him—not touching but breathing in unison, their hands entwined, whispering in the dark.

At the end of the week, returning to Ithaca on the train, Chlöe was a woman in love.

The first night back in Ithaca, Chlöe wanted to write to him, telling him she missed him and loved him. They had not mentioned the word.

Instead, she wrote to her parents, extolling the pleasures of her Chicago visit and telling them she'd met such a nice young man, never mentioning that he was a foreign correspondent. For all she knew, his next assignment could be Chicago, or Washington, or even San Francisco. Well, any of them sounded exhilarating, and Chlöe didn't care where she'd wind up. Those places were all far more cosmopolitan than upstate New York.

As she continued seeing the boys she had been dating before the Easter vacation, she waited every day for a letter from Slade. But none came the first week, or the second, or the third.

By the end of a month, she tried to block him out of her mind, tried not to remember the touch of his lips, the look in his eyes, the sound of his laughter. But every boy she dated, every night she went out, she compared them to her remembrances of Slade. Yet, she told herself, he could have any woman in the world. She must seem like such a schoolgirl to him after the continental women he was used to. Her heart ached.

When forget-me-nots were replaced by forsythia and tulips and daffodils, she told herself to stop thinking of him. Think of pleasanter things. The pear tree at home would be a mass of white blossoms, she thought with an aching loneliness she had never known before.

May passed.

She arranged to join Suzi in Chicago after graduation, not yet informing her parents of that plan. She was furious with herself that nothing seemed to matter.

Two days before their June tenth graduation, a voice hollered up the dorm stairs, "Chlöe, someone's here to see you."

It never dawned on her. Not here in Ithaca. She and Suzi, finished with their exams, had just come in from playing tennis, and perspiration dripped down the side of her face. Brushing her thick hair back with a twist of her hand, she ran down the long stairs, wishing she were in the shower. Standing in the center of the large lobby, holding out what must have been at least five dozen yellow roses, was Slade Cavanaugh in white ducks and a slightly rumpled white shirt. He grinned as Chlöe stopped mid-step, her hand rushing to her throat, her breath stopping.

He made a mock solemn face and knelt on his right knee, still clutching the roses in his left arm and said, his voice ringing up the stairs and down the hallways, "I have come, beloved, to ask you to marry me."

For just a moment, irritation stopped any response. How sure of himself he was! He'd wooed her for a week, and then two months and ten days of silence. What made him think she'd be waiting for him, wanting him, ready to marry him? What made him think she wasn't involved with someone else? How dare he take her for granted!

Heads peeked out of doors down a maze of hallways as Chlöe began to run down the stairs. He was up and bolting toward the stairs, his open arms awaiting her. Engulfed by flowers, he embraced her, kissing her and murmuring over and over, "Chlöe, Chlöe, Chlöe. What a goddamned name to try to make sound romantic."

She laughed, inhaling the attar of roses, which for years thereafter she would consider the most romantic aroma in the world. "What took you so long?" she whispered.

"I had some dragons to slay, some phantoms to get rid of." He held the flowers out to her, taking a step back so he could look at her. "How quickly can we get married?" he asked. "We leave for China in early August."

"China?" She stared at him.

His lips were on hers again, and she heard him laughing as they smothered in all the roses. Chlöe knew that no matter when or where he was going, she would be along.

# CHAPTER 4

Cass had never had a man in China before. He told both of them, "The world thinks of China as a dull backwater. I've a hunch it's where a lot of action's going to take place. China's been in turmoil since the Manchus were overthrown in 1911. Since then, no one's been in charge. Factions are fighting among themselves. They want to rush headlong into democracy before the people know the first thing about self-rule. For thousands of years these people have been told what to do. Now they think they can suddenly blossom forth and make their own decisions."

"But you believe in democracy, don't you?" Chlöe asked him.

He'd come to Oneonta for the wedding and was briefing the soon-to-be newlyweds about their assignment. "Of course I believe in democracy." Cass pulled at his mustache. He and Slade sat in the big slatted-wooden chairs on the Shepherds' front porch while Chlöe sat on the arm of Slade's, draping a hand on his shoulder.

Cass continued. "But I also believe it should be given a chance. It has to be worked toward rather than thrust on an unprepared, uneducated, and unknowledgeable population. The Chinese—the educated ones, the ones who are aware of more than their own geographical boundaries—want to rush from feudal times smack into the twentieth century."

"What's wrong with that?" Chlöe asked.

"One doesn't go from the middle ages to the advanced stages of the industrial revolution in one fell swoop. China, of course, doesn't know it's backward. It has always been the center of the universe."

Slade smiled. "And, of course, they're not. We are."

Cass looked at him and laughed. "That did sound arrogant, didn't it? It's just that I'm afraid, at this time, China isn't quite ready for democracy as we know it. I'm afraid that the forces fighting for it don't stand—as they say—a Chinaman's chance."

"What interests me," said Slade, who had already done some homework, "is how they choose a leader when they're given a chance. I mean, they don't have elections."

Cass nodded. "China's so divided. Partly, I guess from all I've read, it's because peasants from one village don't even know what's happening in the next. News travels just as far as a man can walk. So what's happening a hundred or a thousand miles away is of no interest. It's beyond comprehension. The people who try to gain power are in cities and don't even take peasants into consideration, yet peasants are ninety percent of the population."

Cass took his glasses off, blew on them, wiped them with the handkerchief in his jacket pocket. "Sun Yat-sen's still hoping to be president. I don't know what kind of man he is, really. I'd guess not terribly effective if he hasn't achieved his goal in all these years." He looked at Slade. "That's one of the things I'll expect from you. What's Dr. Sun like? And I want to know about these others who are trying to unite China, whether for their own aggrandizement or for patriotic reasons."

Chlöe put a hand over Slade's, feeling a part of him already, though the wedding wasn't until the following day. At the same time, she realized they knew next to nothing of each other. The thought excited her. A lifetime to get to know each other.

She knew her parents were crushed. She was leaving them for three years. But she would have been gone anyhow . . . to Chicago or New York or someplace. It was just that she'd known it, and they hadn't wanted to recognize it. In their hearts, she was sure, they'd told themselves she'd return home and find a job until she fell in love and married and raised their grandchildren in Oneonta.

But they liked Slade. If Cass vouched for Slade, the young man must be all right. After all, Cass Monaghan was famous.

The wedding would be in the Methodist church, though Slade had told Chlöe, "I'll go through with it for your sake, but I have to warn you, I don't have much patience with organized religion."

Cass and Suzi had arrived with Slade the day before, and the previous evening, after dinner, Cass said, "Chlöe, can we take a stroll?"

They walked down the tree-shaded Oneonta street on which the Shepherds lived, the street lamps creating patterns, dancing and shining through the maple leaves. He put an arm around her and said, "It's not too late, you know."

She knew what he was talking about. "Cass, I've never felt this way before. I'm in love."

"Glandular," he said. "My advice is to go to bed with him." This shocked her and she looked over at him. "Run away to Tahiti with him for a month. Get to know him before vowing to spend your life with him."

She smiled at him and said, "Don't worry. I'm going to be very happy."

He sighed. "My God, I hope so. I feel responsible for this."

"Cass, you're his best man! You must like him!"

"Of course I like him. He's a terrific reporter. Best one I have, but I worry for you."

"I'll probably spend the rest of my life being grateful to you. I don't know why you're so worried. He's your favorite employee and you've said for years that I'm a second daughter to you. I've been suspecting you got us together on purpose."

"That's just it." He stopped, taking his arm from around her, and turned her to face him, his hands on her shoulders. "Chlöe, I assigned him to China not only because he's so good and I need a top-notch man over there, but so you could experience and grow. Yet now I'm nervous about what I've helped set in motion."

"I'm a big girl, Cass. I know what I'm doing."

"I want you to be right. If you won't be dissuaded, I'll root for you. If I prayed, I'd pray for you. I suspect you'll need it. If I were a magician, I'd wave a magic wand over you. I love you, my dear, and I shall worry about you every day and every night."

Finally, every pew in the church was filled and Chlöe was perhaps the most beautiful bride Oneonta had ever seen. Her gown had a long satin train and a veil that reached to her waist. She had always anticipated her wedding day, knowing what a thrill it would be. But none of the plans for the wedding, or the ceremony itself, affected her as she'd thought they would. Her mind was centered on Slade, on their future together, on spending her life with him, and going to China. Those thoughts preoccupied her far more than the ceremony that would tie them together.

The night of the rehearsal Suzi shared Chlöe's bedroom. Lying on the bed, kicking her feet in the air, she said, "I envy you in many ways. Yet somehow I wouldn't want to be going to China. I think you'll be really lonely there. Slade out getting stories and you alone with no one to talk to."

"For heaven's sake, Suzi," Chlöe said. "Don't do that to me. I can travel with Slade, and your father tells us there are lots of other foreigners, British and Americans, already in Shanghai. It's only for three years. I don't care where I go for three years as long as it's with Slade."

Suzi reflected, "I wish Daddy were as gracious about Grant." Cass rebelled at the idea of a son-in-law closer to his age than to his daughter's.

"You going to marry him?" Chlöe stood in front of the mirror, catching her hair up in a ribbon, pulling it off her neck in the humidity of New York in July.

"Oh, God, I don't know. I'm crazy head-over-heels in love. And I think he is too, but he keeps telling me he's too old for me."

In June, Suzi had gone with her father—as she had for years— to the annual publishers' convention held at White Sulphur Springs. She'd been going for so many years that a number of the men recalled times she'd sat on their laps when she was seven, eight, and nine. It was here, at Cass's table one night, that Suzi met Grant

Moore, managing editor of the *St. Louis Dispatch*. Before dinner was over Suzi had fallen in love with the only man she would ever love.

But Grant was thirty-nine, eighteen years older. Though he spent the week dancing with Suzi, playing tennis with her, swimming in the oversize pool with her, walking through the rose gardens with her, he didn't get around to kissing her until the last night. Then he broke away, whispering, "Suzi, this is all wrong. I've got two kids, an ex-wife, and I'm too jaded for you!"

He told her it had been a great week but they shouldn't see each other again. He'd phoned the next Sunday and the next, though. Then he'd stopped calling.

Cass admitted Grant was a fine man, but he said, "He's *my* friend. He's old enough to be your father! He's only three years younger than I am, for God's sake!"

Suzi didn't see what age had to do with love.

Suzi had known ever since she was little that she wanted to work for the *Times*, not as a reporter, but in the financial end. "Someday," she vowed, "I'm going to be the first woman publisher of a first-rate American newspaper."

Chlöe laughed. "You're going to get married and have kids and forget all that. We may have had dreams of grandeur, but once you fall in love . . ."

Suzi was firm. "I can be in love *and* have a career."

Chlöe smiled to herself. All she wanted now was to be Mrs. Slade Cavanaugh.

"Are you scared?" Suzi asked.

"Scared? You mean of China?"

"No. Of sex. I mean, here you've been a virgin for twenty-one years and tomorrow night you'll—well—be a married woman."

Chlöe smiled into the mirror. "A little nervous maybe. What if I disappoint him? I don't really know what to do. I asked Mom, but . . ."

"But what? I wish I had a mother to ask."

"When I asked her what I was supposed to do, she gave me this funny look and said, 'Honey, you don't have to do anything. You just lie there.' "

Chlöe and Suzi looked at each other. And then Suzi began to giggle before both of them broke into uncontrollable laughter. No matter what anyone said in the next few hours, the girls would look across the room at each other and begin to laugh until they had tears in their eyes.

For as long as she lived, Chlöe never remembered anything about her wedding day. She didn't remember putting on the blue garter, or her father driving her and Suzi and Dorothy and Lorna and Marian to the church. Couldn't remember Slade's face being there when she said "I do" to him. Years later, when she looked at the snapshots, she wondered where her mind had been that day she became Chlöe Cavanaugh.

She did remember arriving at Pennsylvania Station in New York City at one-thirty in the morning, her pink linen traveling suit already wrinkled. She was hot and sticky from the six-hour train ride. And she remembered the lobby of the hotel, whose name she never did know. It was gold and dark red. In their room were dozens of yellow roses and a bottle of champagne. After drinking half of that, she did remember that no matter what her mother had told her, she was completely unable to lie still. Slade's kisses, and the way his hands touched her, and the length of their naked bodies touching in the darkness brought her to life despite the exhaustion she felt. In fact, she wanted him never to stop touching her, never to take his lips from her breasts, never to leave her. But he did. Far too quickly. While her nerve ends were still raw with desire, with yearning, he murmured, "I do love you, Mrs. Cavanaugh." Throwing an arm around her, he lay still. In a minute she could tell from the regularity of his breathing that he was asleep. And she was alive, electric, wild with . . . She didn't know what.

Lying there in the darkness, hearing city noises even at three in the morning, she feathered her fingers down the arm that Slade had thrown across her and wanted to feel his kisses upon her again. Wanted the yearnings he had awakened within her to be satisfied. Wanted . . . And then she felt ashamed. She watched the wall where the neon sign's reflection flashed on and off and thought, This is my wedding night and I'm really happy.

That happiness lasted as the train sped across the country for five days. She would lie alone in her berth in the sleeping car at night and yearn for her husband, in the bunk above her, denied any privacy in the crowded car. So when they did arrive in San Francisco, before seeing the shining white city that nestled on hills above blue water, despite the fact that when they were shown their hotel room it was only ten in the morning, they fell on the bed, wrestling their clothes off, mad with desire for each other's bodies. Yet their lovemaking was over so quickly, Chlöe's yearning body again felt suspended, in limbo.

While waiting for their ship to sail, they spent a great deal of time sightseeing, holding hands, and smiling, literally running sometimes, filled with happiness so great it welled out of them and spilled over onto passersby, who smiled at the sight of two young people so obviously in love.

The happiness continued all the way across the Pacific. There was no cloud on the horizon. Every new thing she learned about Slade fascinated and delighted her.

"You know," he said. They were standing at the rail, where, it seemed to Chlöe, they had spent half the voyage. "England has always done China a great disservice. In the early 1800s, in order to balance its trade, England introduced opium to China. Did you know that?"

Yes, Cass had told her. Her history professor had simply dismissed opium in China as being the habit of lazy, immoral pagans. Slade went on. "The poor peasants, hoping to free themselves from their hopeless fate, escaped into dreamland with opium, able to forget their misery for a while. But it also dissipated their energies and morality and made Englishmen very rich."

"It'd be funny, wouldn't it," mused Chlöe, staring out at the horizon, "if someday China or some other countries that the British and we ourselves have corrupted were to do it in reverse? If sometime the Orient grew so much opium and sent it to England and America and we lost our morality and ability to achieve because of it? Would just serve us right."

"That *would* be poetic justice, wouldn't it? But not likely." He continued talking but shifted the vein of their conversation. "Well, I don't always think these imperialistic countries, us included, are very humane. After all, for years Chinese have been excluded from becoming American citizens. They were fine for building our railroads and being our cooks and washing clothes, but not for being recognized as real people."

She turned and leaned her back against the railing, looking at his clear gray eyes, at his straight nose profiled against the sky, at his thick dark hair that she loved to run her hand through, at the mouth she thought was the sexiest in the world, and she thought there was much she could learn under his tutelage. Maybe her real education was just beginning.

———

Chlöe's first intimation that complete happiness was temporary occurred six miles off the China coast, where the brown mud from the
Yangtze River, carrying along with it the stench of China—the smell
of a public outhouse—swelled into the Pacific. Like a giant mudslide,
its thick effluvia slowed down the ship. Rotted orange peels floated
on it, as though it had a life of its own.

"Like the rest of China," muttered a Standard Oil salesman,
bitter about being reassigned to this land where he'd spent five years
already. "Rotten. Stinks. Not just in odor, though that most notice-
ably. Filthy. Uncivilized. Goddamned most backward country in the
world. They're not even people there. They're animals . . . beasts of
burden. And they don't even know what the word *clean* means. In
less'n your three years you'll be begging to come home. I wouldn't
bring a wife here, not for all the tea in China." He laughed at his
own joke. "No life here for a nice civilized American woman."

Chlöe's hand reached out for Slade's. She wanted to feel his
security. The smell *was* awful, yet in no way did she see it as an
omen.

Six miles west they pulled out of the Pacific, up the Yangtze's
tributary, the Hwang Pu River that led to Shanghai. Most of the
passengers were on deck despite the sweltering sun. From nowhere
sampans appeared, being poled hard with easy strength by thin men
in blue cotton trousers and bare chests.

Throngs of Chinese on either side of the river labored at work
that horses and machines did in America. A shiver passed through
Chlöe. It's only for three years, she told herself. Certainly I can
stand anything for three years. Especially with Slade at my side.

Looking over at him, she saw his eyes dancing with excitement.
He put his arm around her shoulders. "God," he said, his voice
throbbing with exhilaration. "Look at it, Chlöe! Just look at it!"

She did. But all she could think of was the smell. Putting a
handkerchief to her nose, she tried to keep herself from throwing
up. While she watched, a man cracked a whip through the air, and
she heard the sickening sound as it lacerated a peasant's skin. The
coolie fell, blood bubbling from the red streak on his back. No one
paid any attention, but her fingers dug into the flesh of Slade's arm.

Men, bent double under loads on their backs, shuffled along.
Shouts and a cacophony of noises nearly deafened her, noises that
would be with her all the years she spent in China.

As the ship moved slowly up the muddied yellow river toward
the city itself, she saw men urinating against a wall, watched as

young children—boys no older than nine or ten, she was sure—ran back and forth, obeying orders screamed at them, sometimes being cuffed on the side of the head, running away crying. But it was the smells that besieged her senses the most. She had used an outhouse at her aunt's farm, and this was what it smelled like, only ten times stronger. She tasted the rotten smell of the Orient as it coated the insides of her nostrils and the top of her tongue.

Looking at her husband, she wondered if he could be oblivious of the odor of excrement and urine. Seeing his shining eyes, a terrible premonition that China would not be good for them swept through her. For the first time in her life, she experienced raw fear, fear so sharp that she tasted it. And it tasted just like it smelled.

# CHAPTER 5

On Slade's expense account and salary they could not afford the Hotel Cathay, so—like nearly every other journalist in Shanghai—they stayed at the Astor Hotel.

Already known as one of the world's leading seaports, Shanghai resembled no American city at all. There were no tall buildings, and it spread out for miles. Most of the ocean-borne goods crossing its wharves were carried not by seagoing vessels but by Chinese junks, which plied the seas from Singapore in Malaysia to Vladivostok in easternmost Siberia. It had over a million and a half people but not a single streetlight, boasting only a small electric-light plant of erratic output. A primitive telephone system, which was cumbersome and needed cranking, was owned by the subscribers and there were not many of them.

As soon as they arrived at the hotel, Slade kissed Chlöe goodbye and left to present himself to the U.S. consul. The *Chicago Times* was never to be taken lightly. Only the *New York Times* and the *Times* of London carried more prestige in Shanghai, or in the world, for that matter. And Slade knew the consulate should be his first stop in town.

Chlöe, who didn't even begin to unpack, napped while Slade was gone. The awful humidity enervated her. Hanging at the head of the bed was mosquito netting. The manager, whose clientele were all foreigners, had warned them that they should always enclose themselves within the netting while they slept, for the bite of a malaria-infected mosquito could be deadly.

When Slade returned, it was nearly four, and he awakened Chlöe, touching her. "What's wrong?" he asked, noticing her unease. "Nothing," she lied. She did not want to tell him she hadn't been sure how to go to the bathroom; there was no toilet. Though they had been married six weeks, she couldn't quite talk to him about her bodily functions and ablutions. In the shabby tiled bathroom there was a sink, but it had only a thin stream of cold water which leaked continually, and a slit in the narrow floor. While Slade was out she had studied the slit for a long time and decided it *must* be the Oriental equivalent of a toilet. One must squat over it and, since there was nothing to hold on to, hope that you didn't fall head over heels into it. She pulled the chain next to it and a slow trickle of water poured out of the wall, along the groove around the slit, washing away any residue. Chlöe's nose had puckered with distaste.

"Find something pretty in your trunk," Slade said, his voice filled with enthusiasm. "We're dining at the consulate, but not until eight. C'mon, honey, get up. Let's go explore this city." Laughing, he grabbed her and pulled her from bed.

He waved away the few rickshaw coolies and reached out for Chlöe's hand. "We'll walk." He couldn't keep from grinning.

Here, where the foreigners lived, there weren't the hordes of people who had crowded around them at the dock, smelling of sweat and strange odors. The streets in this section weren't jammed with coolies vying for passengers in their dirty rickshaws. Along the street was a gravel walk and behind the high walls Chlöe glimpsed mansions with beautifully manicured lawns.

"This part of the city is called the Bund," Slade told her. "It's where most of the consulates—not the American one, which is only a few blocks away—and homes of wealthy foreigners are. You won't believe this, but no Chinese are allowed here except as servants and delivery boys. I mean, can you imagine? Chinese not being allowed on their own soil?"

Chlöe found a tranquility here that was absent when surrounded by multitudes of jabbering Chinese who talked in nothing but the highest decibels. "That park over there"—Slade pointed across the road—"is where the Europeans and Americans stroll of an evening and listen to band concerts and catch the evening breeze. Maybe it's the social event of the day. We'll probably live near here."

She put her hand through Slade's arm.

They passed immense Victorian buildings, stolid, solid, the products of enormous wealth. They read the brass signs on the high walls. The Asian Petroleum Building, the Shanghai Club, the Bank of Japan, several steamship lines, bank after bank, one with a white dome looking quite like a capitol except that it had two enormous lions on either side of its entrance. Building after building, including the British consulate, which resembled a palace, bespoke power. And all of them looking over the squalid, noisy river—quieter here than a few blocks up.

They walked out of the Bund, through whose gates there was a sign that she did not then see, saying in both English and Chinese, NO DOGS OR CHINESE ALLOWED WITHOUT A PERMIT. They walked into China's largest city, thrust into it, she would say later.

Narrow two-story buildings ran together. Chlöe noticed the steep roofs overhanging the streets, the buildings sitting right against the street, mile after mile of gray walls. In the center of the city, which Chlöe thought resembled a crazy quilt with its narrow winding alleys and laundry hanging across the streets, were windowless dark shops hardly as large as the bathroom at home. Children laughed and ran around uninhibitedly. Chlöe watched as one little boy squatted in the middle of the sidewalk and relieved himself. His trousers, she noted, were simply open, a slit dividing the two halves of the pants. No wonder Shanghai smelled as it did.

From a little round podium in the middle of an intersection a bearded, white-turbanned Indian directed traffic. "Did you know policemen in the foreign-occupied cities are Sikhs?" Chlöe asked Slade.

"No," he laughed. "I didn't know that. Do you know why?"

"Nope," she murmured.

Wherever people walked, they spat into the street or on the sidewalk, or blew their noses—holding their noses in their fingers and just blowing, phlegm scattering into the breeze or onto the ground or onto the back of the jacket of the person in front of them.

"Oh," she said, her voice faint, her mouth scrunching up in distaste. Slade didn't even seem to notice.

The noise was unbelievable. At the top of their lungs people spoke with each other. These were city people, and only a few wore the blue cotton jacket and trousers that were the uniform of Chinese peasants. The city men often wore long gowns cut simply. Most were cotton, but here and there the elegance of silk indicated wealth.

A few still wore queues, long, shining neat braids hanging down their backs. Chlöe pointed at them. "I read that pigtails were a symbol of subjugation for centuries. The Manchus required them of all Chinese men for hundreds of years. Then in 1911, when the Manchu dynasty was overthrown, Chinese men cut off their pigtails to declare they were no longer under domination.''

Slade squeezed her hand. ''From the number of those who are wearing them, I imagine some became attached to them. I suppose in the countryside there are probably millions who've never heard of the revolution.''

''Not heard of it?'' Chlöe asked. ''It started a dozen years ago.''

''Honey, I understand there are millions of peasants who have no idea China's even a country or who rules it. Not that anyone does now.''

There were no well-dressed or attractive women in sight. The ones they saw had hair askew or cut in straight, uneven shingled bobs or tied in buns on their necks, and they all wore trousers.

''I gather,'' said Chlöe, ''that Chinese women try to look as plain as possible outside their homes. Maybe they're afraid if they're too attractive, jealous gods will seek vengeance. Or, more likely, some man will look at them and desire them. I bet that whole thing was invented by men to keep other men from their women.''

Slade looked down at her. ''Where'd you hear that?''

''You know I've been reading up on China too.'' She smiled, feeling rather proud of her limited knowledge.

Old women with homemade, archaic-looking brooms hobbled around on tiny feet, sweeping the sidewalks and streets. A vain attempt. All they did was raise the dust, which settled.

''Look at those crippled women! Those tiny feet. They can't be more than three or four inches at the most! I could get sick just looking at them.''

When Slade didn't say anything, Chlöe continued. ''Probably another idea thought up by men so their women couldn't run away. God, imagine how painful!''

''Where do you get your ideas?'' Slade asked. ''You sound like men dream up barbaric ideas to keep women in their places.''

Chlöe, busy surveying the scene, thought, Yes. In our places.

She wondered how anyone ever crossed the streets, which were thronged with rickshaws, and pedestrians. Most everyone stared at Chlöe and Slade, nudging their neighbors and pointing.

Sitting on street corners, old men played Chinese Chess or Mahjongg, and old women smoked pipes. ''Probably opium,'' Slade whispered. Small children ran around with no supervision, and Chlöe ventured that it looked like a gigantic Woolworth's. Everything was so gaudy.

She clung tightly to Slade's hand. The sheer number of people awed her. Compared to Shanghai, Chicago and New York City seemed like sparsely settled towns. Now and then Slade would turn to look at her and squeeze her hand. She could scarcely believe that she, who had always yearned for the exotic, for different things, for escape from small-town America, was in an environment more alien than she'd ever imagined, on a continent half a world away from home, surrounded by unfamiliar people and things.

Suddenly they came upon an enormous gate, several stories high, its doors wide open, and beyond it she saw greenery, a park. "Oh, Slade," she said, "let's go in there. There's a bench under those bamboo trees, and it's not crowded. . . ."

He looked at her, his head cocked. "Of course, darling." His voice was solicitous.

She could tell, once they were seated on the bench just on the other side of the giant gates, that Slade was impatient to go on, but she wanted just a moment of tranquility.

A group of soldiers noisily halted before the gate. Their commander, astride a horse, shouted to a man on foot, dressed in an ill-fitting uniform, who shoved five other men into a straight line, directly under the gates. The quintet, standing next to each other, were dressed in a motley array of clothes, three in the blue outfits of Chinese peasants, one in rags, and one in a wrinkled but very white shirt and well-pressed black pants held up with a tie.

Oh, my God, Chlöe thought, reaching for Slade's hand. They're going to shoot these men. But there were no raised guns, and she began to breathe a bit easier as the commander dismounted, throwing the reins to one of his men. He spoke quietly to one of the soldiers, who walked toward the five men standing in a row and straightened them out, until they stood next to each other precisely aligned. Chlöe felt sure something macabre and gruesome was about to happen, but no guns were evident. She and Slade remained seated, paralyzed.

The commander walked back and forth in front of the prisoners, exhorting them to do or be something, she thought. Then he strode to the end of the line and, squinting as an artist might to get a perspective, he pulled a wide silver sword from a long sheath in his belt. Oh, no, Chlöe thought, feeling she must be in a nightmare, willing herself to awaken. Though her hand clutched her throat, she could not move.

The commander touched the blade with his thumb, running it back and forth against the edge, and a smile crept onto his face. With a loud cry he raised his arm, holding the sword high above his head, and began to run. Lowering his arm to a right angle and keeping it stiff, with precision and neatness he lopped off all five heads without breaking his running stride. The heads flew helter-skelter into the air. The bodies jerked like puppets, collapsing in awkward positions, crumpling onto the ground. As Chlöe stared, frozen, one of the heads rolled across the path until it stopped by her feet, right side up, staring at her with pleading and astonished eyes.

Blood began to ooze from it and form a pool around the severed neck.

As she looked up, she saw drops of ruby blood, like carmine tears, shining on the end of the sword that sparkled in the sunlight. The commander took a cloth from his pocket and wiped the sword clean, then sheathed it and mounted his horse. Gesturing, he turned his horse and rode away, while his men gathered the still-jerking bodies onto a cart. A soldier ran over, smiled at Chlöe and Slade, and leaned over to pick up the head that stared with such surprise at Chlöe.

Within five minutes it was all over, except for the pools of blood where the slain men had fallen and where the rolling heads had spattered a trail before stopping. Neither Chlöe nor Slade had moved.

She felt Slade's cold fingers rigid around hers.

"Let's get the hell outta here," he said. "Let me get to a type-writer."

Still seated on the bench, she leaned over and vomited until nothing was left, until only dry heaves took over her trembling body.

# CHAPTER 6

"First of all," said Ann Leighton, "you'll have to get a rickshaw boy of your own."

Chlöe, unused to servants, smiled. A far cry from Oneonta.

The consul's wife continued. "White women don't walk the streets alone here, my dear."

The memory of the afternoon clung to Chlöe. She had lain shivering in Slade's arms for an hour, telling him she absolutely couldn't dine at the consulate that night. But he had insisted, pawing through her unpacked trunk and pulling out the green linen, wrinkled from being packed for so long. He sent it for a pressing.

"You can't just lie here and dwell on that scene," he said, his voice stern. "Get up now. Bathe and dress and wear those long earrings and let the American consul know that the most beautiful woman in the Orient is the wife of the *Chicago Times* China hand."

So she had.

Get the adrenaline flowing, she told herself. Take a deep breath. Square those shoulders. Show them what you're made of.

During cocktails before dinner at the consulate, she had attracted all the attention: first, because of her fresh beauty, and, second, because of her afternoon's harrowing experience. Once she had talked out the episode, however, she relaxed, smiling effervescently through dinner with the Leightons and their other guests, British businessman Edward Blake, known as Ted, and his blond wife, Kitty. Lou Sidney, correspondent for the *Times* of London, was also there.

Chlöe enjoyed the dinner partner on her left, Lou Sidney. A tall, angular man in a rumpled linen suit, he looked out of place around the formal table, yet he also seemed, Chlöe thought, to have an inner security that she found both unsettling and irresistible. She wanted to know him better.

At that moment she also felt Slade's eyes burn into her, flashing an all-too-familiar look. She recognized a date's look of jealousy when she saw it. She also knew how to handle that look. She cocked her head, smiled at Slade, and winked.

The waiters cleared away the soup bowls and Chlöe felt the attention of the other men and, consequently, the women. This was not a new experience for her. As the dinner progressed, Chlöe found herself more and more the center of attention. She brought news of a different kind. Slade's concerned the "big picture," the hard news that hit newspapers. Her news, most of it gleaned from her talks with Cass, concerned the *people* in the "big picture." She told about the New York and Paris showings, where a woman named Chanel had set the fashion world on its ear with simple yet incredibly stylish designs and had also created a scandal with Igor Stravinsky. Picasso too was creating scandals as well as abstract paintings. A newcomer to Russian politics, someone named Stalin, was in a struggle for power with the Trotskyites.

As Chlöe continued to talk to an eager audience, she noticed a new look in Slade's eyes. This was a look *not* familiar to her—the look of a show's star being upstaged by his supporting actress.

But as the diners finished their rack of lamb, the topic of conversation shifted back to China.

"You know," said Ted Blake, "the Chinese have never had any *real* morality."

From childhood, Chlöe had often tempered her comments but had never compromised her principles, a trait that had annoyed a few friends but won others, such as Cass. She now decided to challenge Ted Blake, saying, "Don't you think we—I mean Britons and Americans—are so arrogant? You *do* mean morality as *we* understand it, don't you?"

Dead silence. Everyone stared at her. She plowed on, despite new warning signals from Slade's eyes. "I mean, it's impossible to judge one culture's morality against another's, isn't it?" From somewhere she thought she heard her husband's voice trying to interrupt, but she persisted. "After all, how do we know what we consider morality is a gauge for the rest of the world?"

She then acknowledged the annoyance flashing in her husband's eyes. Cease and desist, clear as day.

"At least," Chlöe said as she beamed one of her most glorious smiles on each diner in turn, "at least, that's what I think. But then, I'm just fresh out of college."

Nervous *ha-has* tittered around the table.

Into the silence rushed Ann Leighton, saying, "Shall we ladies retire to the drawing room while the men light up cigars and have their brandy? We can solve the really important problems of life. And I do want to hear more of this Chanel . . . and Igor!"

Politely, everyone laughed.

Lou Sidney immediately lit up a long, thin brown cigarette as his eyes met Chlöe's with a delighted twinkle.

The two women, Ann and Kitty, wore evening clothes more formal than Chlöe had ever known. Slade had warned her that in government circles people dressed formally and behaved with strict propriety—and never more so than when abroad.

She realized she'd plunged into a new life. She'd always wanted adventure. She'd always wanted something more exotic than One-onta. And now, by God, she had it.

Ann and Kitty apparently felt they should set Chlöe's priorities straight: first, orient her to their way of life in Shanghai, and, second, help her find a suitable house.

"I'm afraid," said Kitty, "you'll find living conditions here leave much to be desired."

Chlöe could have spent all evening listening to Kitty's clipped British accent. "Of course, Ann's lucky to live in the consulate and never has to worry about that. Actually, I should talk. We live in lovely apartments just down the boulevard."

"Even," Ann agreed, "if the American consulate isn't quite in the Bund, you'll want, of course, to get as close to the Bund and a civilized way of living as possible. Most of the Europeans and Americans live there."

Kitty interrupted. "This is your first foreign assignment, isn't it? I can tell. You've probably just got married." She reached out a hand and patted Chlöe's arm. "I remember what it's like. Trying to adjust to marriage and a foreign country at the same time. So very different from home."

They seemed so sure of themselves, so . . . so well adjusted, thought Chlöe. She was slightly intimidated by the two women, both so accustomed to living abroad, both so knowledgeable.

"It's our third assignment," Kitty continued. "We spent several years in Portugal. Lovely place, in comparison, even if it is under the Pope's influence. Then Egypt. Ah, Cairo. Shepheard's, moonlight sails on the Nile, the mysterious Sphinx. I could have stayed there forever."

"Isn't it dirty too?" The words popped out before Chlöe thought.

"Oh, my, rather!" Kitty leaned forward. "All these heathen countries are. But really quite different. So many British, you know. Made such a difference. Other people with the same values. That is *so* important."

Chlöe didn't know what to say.

Kitty went on. "There *is*, of course, a large British and American contingent here too, but it's not quite the same. The Chinese are sooo different. Not quite . . ." She hesitated. "Oh, Egypt's not a'tall the same as here."

Ann looked at Kitty for a moment and then said to Chlöe,

"You'll find China rather noisy, I'm afraid. There's no place in China that isn't noisier than Times Square on New Year's Eve. And privacy? Forget it. That's something Chinese don't understand. I hear there's not even a word for privacy in their language!"

Chlöe thought she must be exaggerating. Certainly within the confines of one's own home.

"And you must remember. I can't stress this too strongly. Always"—Ann shook her finger—"sleep with mosquito netting around you. Malaria, cholera, typhoid, plagues of all kinds, it seems. Don't ever"—and she leveled her stern gaze upon Chlöe—"drink unboiled water or buy food from those dirty little street vendors."

Kitty stopped gazing into space and rejoined the conversation. "You'll need a number one boy, and he'll do the rest of the hiring, probably relatives. A cook. A woman to clean. A man to wait on table and run errands. Rickshaw boys. There's a protocol. If you have problems with any of them, do not complain directly. Talk to your number one boy."

Chlöe smiled. "And what does the number one boy do?" She couldn't imagine having so many servants for just her and Slade.

Kitty smiled, seeing the humor in Chlöe's question. She placed the tips of her fingers together and squinted her eyes in the stereotypical Chinese pose. "Ah so. I've never quite figured that out. Makes sure the other Chinee work, perhaps." She relaxed her pose and smiled. "All I know is he's necessary and loses face if you approach any of the others directly. Face is of utmost importance in the Orient. Never let them lose face in front of others or you will have inestimable trouble. They'll seek scrutable revenge in some inscrutable way."

Chlöe felt as though she were caught in the flickering unreality of a motion picture, as though this conversation, much less all else that had happened to her today, would end as soon as the lights went on. "Face? What does that mean?"

Ann jumped in to answer. Chlöe sensed that these two women were close friends, that their dialogue moved back and forth from one to the other as easily as two tennis champions in a warm-up rally. "Let me explain face this way. A Chinaman never says 'I don't know.' If you ask someone directions, he will point you in any direction, even though he has no idea where it is you want to go, and tell you how to get there. You'll find yourself lost many times. But if he told you that he really didn't know how to get to wherever you want to get to, he'd lose face."

"I don't understand it," Kitty interrupted. "It seems essentially silly to me. But it is one of the motivating forces of the Orient. Little things that bother us not a'tall matter to them most keenly."

"Conversely"—Ann smiled at Chlöe—"things that matter greatly to us are to them of utterly no import. In other words, you can go nearly batty."

Both women laughed, and Ann raised her eyes heavenward. "Can one take seriously any nation that is so incredibly inefficient?"

It was Kitty's turn to interrupt. "Things that should have been done yesterday might get done next year. Might. And, in the long run, it doesn't seem to matter. Life slows down, and there's a pleasantness to that. So if it doesn't get done today, maybe they'll do it tomorrow. Or the next day . . ."

A waiter stole into their presence, silent in his cotton shoes, but Ann noticed him immediately. "Would you prefer after-dinner coffee," she asked Chlöe, "or a liqueur?" Chlöe had never had a liqueur in her life.

"Whatever you're having," she murmured.

Ann turned to her servant and said, "Cointreau."

Kitty smiled. "Yes, you never have any doubts about me, do you?"

"Oh," laughed Ann, "I often harbor grave doubts about you, darling. But not about your preference for Cointreau."

The two women smiled at each other. A comfortable relationship, thought Chlöe. I hope that will happen to me. That I'll find some friends. Someone to smile to across the table, who understands what I'm feeling without forcing me to say it. She'd never felt that way with anyone other than Suzi. Not even Slade. And somehow that surprised her. She had thought when she married, something automatic would happen, that she'd become one with her husband. But then, she reminded herself, she had built that relationship with Suzi over the years and she had known Slade five months. And had seen him for only a month and a half of that time.

Funny, wasn't it, to think they could be so intimate physically yet in so many ways still scarcely know each other.

"Your first week here will be busy," said Ann. "Tomorrow there's the rose garden tour, and Polly Akins's tea. Of course, you should attend that too," she said to Chlöe. "Meet everyone worth meeting, of the women at least. That's Thursday afternoon, day after tomorrow. We'll wangle you an invitation. And dinner at the German consulate—"

"If there's one group to beware of," Kitty broke in, "it's the Huns. Fortunately they lost a lot of influence in the war, but they're always so damn right. So positive they know the *only* way to do things."

Ann laughed, a silvery laugh that trailed across the room. "Not at all like the British, my dear."

"Touché." Kitty raised her glass and smiled over the rim of it. "Serves me right. Only difference is, *we* are right."

"Actually, the most depressing ones are the White Russians," Ann continued. "Shanghai, Peking, Tientsin, Harbin, are all crowded with the former nobility—and those who claim to be—who fled before the Red terror. They're broken people. Those who escaped with any of the family's jewels have opened Russian restaurants or teahouses. Others have become servants, maids to wealthy Americans, butlers. . . . I wouldn't hire one of them for a minute. So haughty. Others—well." She shrugged her shoulders.

Kitty nodded. "You won't find too many young women your age, I'm afraid. Most of the vice consuls are young, unmarried men. I guess married men don't want to risk their families in the Orient. Filthy place, you know. If it weren't for the money to be made here, I don't know why any civilized people would subject themselves to the Orient. They're not Christians, even the ones the missionaries think they convert."

She stopped to sip her liqueur, and Chlöe asked, "Is it so important that they believe as we do?"

She noticed the swift look the two women exchanged. Ann said, "My dear, they're heathens. Pagans. Barbarians. They have few redeeming graces. One or two of them, a sprinkling, are educated, or what passes for education here. But even they're hard to understand. Their English is quite minimal and they do speak it with the funniest accents."

Why shouldn't they? wondered Chlöe. It is *their* country. But something advised her not to say that aloud. "Don't you try to learn Chinese?" she did ask.

Kitty laughed. "Oh, my dear, it's an impossible language. Perhaps one could learn its ideographs. That's the pictures they draw in place of words. But just listen to their singsong. You'll soon see. It's really quite impossible to learn."

The two women laughed.

Chlöe sipped the Cointreau, finding it burned her throat.

In the morning Slade announced, "Lou Sidney's offered to show me the ropes. Introduce me to the other journalists. He says he has an office I can share." He finished tying his tie and glanced from his own reflection in the mirror to her. "You created quite a sensation last night, it seems. They all went ga-ga over you."

"Ga-ga?" she giggled.

"Well, no man there could keep his eyes off you. And after you told them about our experience in the afternoon, each one of them seemed to want to protect you."

She was surprised at the sharpness in his voice. Ah, jealousy. She'd hoped Slade would be one man who wouldn't suffer from it. "Would you rather I wore drab clothes?" she asked. "You were the one who chose my dress, you know." Her voice became defensive.

"Jesus, Chlöe, I'm proud of your looks. It's the way you acted. Like you needed to be the center of attention. I didn't think it was terribly feminine."

She glanced up at him and noticed the thin, straight line of his lips, disapproving.

Ah, she thought. So it wasn't Slade Cavanaugh, famous correspondent, who was center stage. She made a mental note to be more aware of that in the future.

Then, as though to show he wasn't angry, Slade leaned down and kissed her forehead. "Find us a house. I hate hotels. I've lived too many years in hotels." And then he was off for the day.

How do I go about finding a house? Chlöe wondered. Ann and Kitty had advised her to find a place close to the Bund, where most foreigners lived. Perhaps one of the consular officials . . . And, at just that moment, there was a knock on the door. When she opened it, Chlöe found a young woman with disheveled bright red hair. She was smiling and her freckles accentuated the paleness of her skin. "I'm Daisy Maxwell," she said. "Mrs. Leighton sent me over. She thought you could use some help in finding a place to live, not knowing Chinese and all."

She walked in and sat down, making herself at home. "Would you like that?" She smiled again.

"Oh, yes," Chlöe said, happy to find a woman close to her age. "I was wondering how in the world to go about it."

"Well, here I am, ready to help. It's what I'm very good at.

Showing newcomers to Shanghai. Though, really, I'm a secretary at the consulate.''

"You've lived here long?'' Chlöe still stood, wondering whether the tailored skirt and blouse she was wearing were all right. Daisy wore a navy cotton dress and a white seersucker jacket.

"I've been here five years," Daisy answered. Her eyes were doe-soft and there was a hesitancy, a breathless quality, to the way she talked. "My parents gave me a round-the-world tour upon gradua-tion and I never got any farther than here. First stop after Honolulu. Well, are you ready? I have two rickshaw boys waiting.''

Chlöe grabbed her purse and followed Daisy down the wide stairway to the genteelly shabby hotel lobby. All buildings, Daisy informed her, were less than four stories tall because that meant elevators weren't required. Chlöe should consider herself lucky to have a room on the second floor.

Self-consciously Chlöe stepped into the rickshaw. She wasn't used to having someone carry her around. The rickshaw coolies, with their bare chests and conical hats, jogged along at a steady pace. Chlöe had never seen tropical trees like the ones that lined the wide avenues. Stunted palms and banyans were gray rather than green. "Everything in China's dusty," Daisy called from her rick-shaw. "It's the dirt. That's the predominant color of China. Dirt. Gray or dust color.''

Soon Daisy called out to the rickshaw boys, who stopped in front of a high wall. Daisy pushed open the wide wooden door. The courtyard was sweltering in the late summer heat.

The dark two-story house was filled with enormous overstuffed horsehair sofas and chairs and thick wool carpets. In the courtyard there was only a bamboo tree. The kitchen behind the house was small and dirty, airless in the heat. Chlöe couldn't imagine any cook being assigned to spend his days there.

Involuntarily, she shook her head. Daisy laughed. "Well, it's near the Bund, and close to the social life of Americans. If you don't like this, I have several more I can show you.''

But Chlöe hated them all. Though in walled courtyards, they were right on main thoroughfares and the noise of the city and its dust drifted across the walls. "I don't think I could stand to live with all the noise," Chlöe apologized. She felt ungrateful not to like at least one of them. "Where do you live?'' she asked Daisy.

"Oh, I wouldn't recommend that part of the city," the young

woman said. "It's not a section where nice young American families live."

"We're not a family," Chlöe said. "There's just my husband and me." Well, that *is* a family, isn't it?

"Yes, but you'll be entertaining and . . . Well, come on, I'll offer you a cup of tea. You can see it."

Daisy had been right. Chlöe couldn't have stood to live in her apartment. From its perch on the second floor, above a bank, all the bedlam of the street below reverberated. The narrow stairway was dark, even at noon. The unpainted gray cement walls added to the gloomy uneasiness. At the top of the stairs they entered one of the dreariest rooms Chlöe had ever seen. What Daisy called the living room measured twelve feet square, all painted a lime green—lime-green floor, lime-green walls, and lime-green ceiling. In the center stood a table with four stark wooden chairs and two other semi-upholstered ones. That was all aside from a chocolate-brown cupboard. But the bedroom . . . ah, the bedroom!

"Wow!" Chlöe gasped.

Daisy smiled, pleased.

Here, Chlöe thought, Daisy spent most of her time.

Though the same size as the living room, this room focused on the biggest bed Chlöe had ever seen. It left enough room for only a bookcase that entirely lined one wall. On the bed were at least fifteen brightly colored cushions. All Chlöe could think of was what a job it must be to move them at night and replace them in the morning. It looked quite as she imagined a brothel must look, except for the books. There were hundreds of them. On the dark blue ceiling, as opposed to the whitewashed walls, Daisy had stuck hundreds of little silver stars everywhere, the kind of stars Chlöe's grade-school teachers had stuck at the top of her papers next to an "excellent" comment.

Chlöe was aware of Daisy's eyes pinned to hers, waiting for her reaction. She laughed. "It's certainly different. Did you do all this?"

"Indeed I did." And now Daisy smiled again. "Come into the kitchen while I fix us tea." The kitchen was through a narrow hallway and was no larger than the tiny bathroom next door. The dark, airless, cramped kitchen was even more depressing than the houses they had looked at.

"What I love," said Daisy, lighting a match to a burner, "is that no one for blocks speaks English."

"Mrs. Blake told me Chinese is impossible to learn."

Daisy looked over at her, and her eyes narrowed. "But we expect even the most illiterate of them to learn enough English to clean our houses and understand us, huh? I've been studying Chinese since I arrived. I won't deny it's difficult, but I also won't insult the people whose land I'm living in by not learning their language."

"My husband feels that way. He wants to learn the language, but I don't know if I'm up to it."

Daisy nodded. "What's the point of living in a foreign country if you're not going to know anyone but other Americans, or English? And often, despite their horrible arrogance, I prefer the English. They're at home anyplace. Though, of course, unless you're white and speak the King's English, you're really not quite . . . not quite human, I guess is the word. But they're so much more relaxed about everything. They take inefficiency in the Orient for granted and they're really rather grand about accepting it. Americans, on the other hand, are driven absolutely nutty by inefficiency and lack of sanitation. I don't know which is worse for them."

"But not you?" Chlöe asked, accepting the cup and saucer Daisy handed her. She followed her hostess into the lime-green living room to the scratched wooden table.

"I was at first," Daisy admitted. "But I'm having a wonderful time. I'm letting myself flow. My secretarial duties at the consulate are really not all that demanding, except for now and then. I do most of the translating . . . I've learned to read and write as well as speak Chinese fairly well." There was pride in her tone.

"There's always hours off for lunch, and I manage to find terribly interesting people to dine with. At least once a week there's the races. Heavens, I'd never been interested in horses before, but it's quite jolly. I feel far luckier than if I had to entertain the kinds of people the Leightons do. And keep up that kind of front, though I'm sure they're used to living that way. I'd be bored silly if I had to attend all the teas Mrs. Leighton does or always be on her uppers, making sure that she represents Uncle Sam, so to speak."

"So you manage to keep busy?" Chlöe found the young woman quite irrepressible and, in her own way, charming.

"Oh, my dear." Daisy bubbled. "Shanghai is filled with single men. And the single men are all looking for women to dance with and to dine with and to drink with and to take on picnics, or drive out into the country—that is, as far as roads go. There's a dearth of young women, fortunately. I was never so popular at home. And I have first crack at all the new young vice consuls. The world's journalists have suddenly discovered China's worth writing about. All the young Standard Oil employees are coming over straight out of college, and though they just pass through Shanghai on their way into the interior, I show them the sights of Shanghai before they leave to spend their years here walking throughout China selling oil to light its millions of lamps. As they trickle through, I live it up with them for a few days of fun. It's a change of pace and a change of people."

Chlöe, who had at first thought Daisy plain, now found her extremely attractive. She liked her élan, her honesty, her gregariousness. In the long run, she thought Daisy might wear better than either Ann Leighton or Kitty Blake. At least, she thought, her energy and her thirst for adventure more closely matches mine.

Sensing Chlöe's mood, Daisy suggested lunch in "a typical Chinese restaurant. Not that it's one where you'll find other Americans. Not, at least, the kind who live in the Bund."

It was a large, crowded, noisy place. The noise rose decibels above even the street clamor. "The people here," said Daisy, "don't understand how to talk without yelling. I wonder if it's endemic to the whole country."

They found two seats together at an already crowded table and watched their neighbors dig into various dishes on the table, lean out to grab something. Eventually, a waiter appeared, slapping down bowls in front of them. The chopsticks looked none too clean. Their neighbors passed heaping serving bowls to them.

Daisy laughed and put a hand on Chlöe's arm. "You should see your nose, all scrunched up. Get used to it. This is China."

There were bowls of rice and pork rolls and beef concoctions and thousand-year-old eggs and raw fish strips, and . . . and . . . and . . . fish eyes. Fish *eyes*! But the food kept coming: bowls with green stuff and black goo.

Daisy enthusiastically elbowed her way into them—leaning and grabbing. She devoured all the strange and awful-smelling dishes passed to her, describing their contents to Chlöe as she did.

After spitting chicken bones on the floor between them, the woman next to Chlöe began a lively discussion. The man across the table began shouting at them.

Daisy pointed to a dish near them. "That's fried eel."

Chlöe's jaw dropped, and Daisy laughed. All right, Chlöe thought. All right, by heavens! She took a deep breath, paused, then reached for the eel and helped herself to a small portion.

With trembling bravado she gulped it down. She took rice in her bowl and reached for a small but very sweet and juicy orange. There were, she thought, worse things to have for lunch than rice and an orange, although most of her rice dropped through her chopsticks back into her bowl. She reached out her hand for some peanuts in a bowl next to her. The woman beside her burst into gales of laughter and, shaking her head, elbowed Chlöe's arm.

The jovial-looking woman had merry eyes and, smiling in a kindly fashion, deftly wielded her chopsticks, rapidly picking up the peanuts one at a time. The man next to the woman leaned forward, smiling through a gap in his teeth. Chlöe clasped her chopsticks and could feel the couple staring at her, willing her to success. The woman nodded again and demonstrated. Chlöe reached out for a peanut, struggling to hold it between her chopsticks, and felt the flush of success when the peanut did not drop before arriving at her mouth. The couple grinned and the woman, apparently taking this small success as a sign that Chlöe was now Chinese, began a stream of rapid conversation.

Though Chlöe smiled inanely back at her, there was no way she could talk with her. But the woman communicated with Chlöe. Throughout the entire meal she included Chlöe in her conversation. Her husband said little but nodded his head and smiled at Chlöe too. Chlöe followed the woman's directions on how to eat each dish. The woman demonstrated that Chlöe was not even eating her rice correctly.

"Bring the bowl up to your chin and shovel it into your mouth with the chopsticks as rapidly as possible," Daisy shouted. Each time Chlöe succeeded in following directions, the woman patted her hand.

When the meal was over and they were ready to depart, Chlöe, who had heard Daisy saying "*ni hau*" upon meeting people, thought the least she could do was say that in Chinese.

More gales of laughter. The woman again reached out to Chlöe and clasped her hand. Not letting go of it, she somehow conveyed that "*ni hau*" was said only upon greeting and that she should say "*zai jian*" as good-bye.

As they left the café, Daisy grinned. "Your first Chinese lesson."

"Are they all that friendly?" Chlöe asked, warmed by her first interaction with a Chinese.

"No, most of them call us foreign dogs and think of us as imperialists. Which we are, of course. But on a one-to-one basis I've made some very good friends among the Chinese."

In their day of searching they found no house Chlöe would even consider living in. She'd rather stay in the Astor Hotel than be forced to live in those dark, noisy depressing places that Daisy had shown her. And all of them furnished with such—such Teutonic-looking pieces. It reminded her of her grandmother's house, with the little lace antimacassars on the heavy prickly horsehair fabric that always rubbed Chlöe the wrong way.

Back at the hotel, Chlöe lay down, exhausted from her day of house-hunting, and from the noise and the heat. But she felt an energizing thrill from the novelty, from her new friend, and from her interaction with the "real" China.

It was after four when Slade returned. "God, you spend more time napping! C'mon, Lou's going to show us a house." They'd already heard that Chlöe had rejected out of hand everything Daisy had shown her.

The sweltering heat of the day had diminished and a softness had rolled into the air. Lou Sidney was waiting for them outside the hotel entrance in a rickshaw. Chlöe and Slade climbed into a double one. Slade reached over to hold her hand. His eyes danced and Chlöe noticed his absorption with the city around them, the way his arm rested along the back of the rickshaw, sensed by his body that he was excited.

Half an hour later, after their rickshaw boys had run through the city, they came to a dirty wall whose entrance was an enormous, intricately carved oaken door. Lou jumped out of his rickshaw and groped in his pocket for the keys. Chlöe looked down the narrow cobblestone street and saw only walls on both sides. She stepped to the massive carved door, and as soon as she entered she knew this was meant to be their first home. A large whitewashed bungalow overlooking the river, it stood on a slight hill high enough that the evening breeze blew gently through her long hair. Bamboo trees and willows leaned into the water. A huge verandah wrapped itself around the front and along one side of the house. Lou said a government official who, for unknown reasons, had been beheaded, had owned the house and no Chinese wanted to live there and suffer the same fate.

It had no furniture in it. Chlöe loved that feature as much as anything. She particularly loved the bathroom, which—to her delight—contained a Western-style toilet, but the pièce de résistance was a claw-footed tub. Though small, with a green glaze interior, the tub wore a coat of yellow paint on the outside, and a fiery dragon in shades of dark and emerald green wound itself around the entire tub and eventually stared out the window.

Lou led the way through the large living room, whose wide doors opened onto the verandah, and from there they could look down the lawns through the willows to the sluggishly flowing river. Across the lawn at that moment a peacock strutted, fanning its phosphorescent feathers and cackling loudly.

"I suspected when I met you last night that you'd like this," Lou said, his sallow face wreathed in a grin. Chlöe studied him and thought he looked like a horse neighing, with his high forehead and long chin, and his large, slightly yellowed teeth. "I thought then that this was the house for you." Chlöe thought he had quite the warmest eyes she'd ever seen.

Behind them, from the river, she heard distant shouting, heard a bell ring faintly, felt the tropical breeze wrap itself around her, and knew she had found a home in China. But whether China would ever feel like home, she doubted.

# *CHAPTER 7*

Cass had given them a thousand dollars "to get yourselves situated in a place where you'll be happy to live." So Chlöe—asking for Daisy's assistance in finding her way around the city—went shopping. The only pieces of American furniture that she insisted on were mattresses, refusing to consider the one-inch layer of cotton on wooden slats that the Chinese slept on. Aside from that, she filled the house with bamboo furniture and cotton-covered pillows in bright yellow and white, with accents here and there of a vibrant blue or emerald. She hung oil lamps everywhere and placed lamps on tables so that in the evenings theirs was the brightest house in this part of Shanghai.

She immediately asked Gao Hu, the number one boy whom Ann Leighton's number one boy had recommended, to hire a gardener, who set to work creating a serene area of beauty centering around a small oval pool that he filled with goldfish and one lily pad that bore huge fragrant white blossoms.

Chlöe loved it. She thought it quite the most beautiful of houses. She loved her and Slade's room overlooking the river under the weeping willow that constantly shed its leaves. She found a Wedgwood-blue fabric and had it made into a bedspread and drapes, which she thought looked rather dramatic against the stark white walls. Outside their window the peacock screeched from high up in a tree.

She particularly loved the bathroom, with its dragon twisting around the yellow tub. Whenever they bathed, the servants made innumerable trips, bringing hot steaming water from the kettles out back behind the kitchen. Slade rigged up a rubber hose so that the bath water could be drained directly out the window and sluice down the walls to keep the lawns green. Aside from within the Bund and at the consulates, theirs was the only grass Chlöe saw in Shanghai. China was not a country that placed a high priority on aesthetics. Any patch of arable land was not for beauty but for food. Or, certainly not to require further work, work like mowing a lawn that brought no tangible result.

Everyone told her it was foolish to live so far from the Bund, but she adored the house. She savored lying in bed at night, listening to the river sounds, letting the moonlight that filtered through the leaves of the willow dance upon her naked body after she and Slade made love.

She smiled to herself, knowing that in the next room there was a green dragon that wound itself around a yellow porcelain tub and stared out the window, warding off dangers.

The cook came not from Gao Hu's suggestions but from Lou, who said, "He's been the cook of someone I know up north, where there's a famine now. I think he'll serve you well."

He did more than that.

Her entertaining began with inviting Lou and Daisy to dinner. The dinner had been divine: steamed young pigeon, Hopei chestnuts, imported bamboo shoots and mushrooms she and the cook found in the market, lotus root, and lichee nuts. For dessert the wonderful red and white dates of Te-chow in Shantung province and T'ang-shan pears soaked in the Shao-hsing wine of Chekiang.

"I bet," Daisy said, "you're the first foreigners to serve Chinese food to your guests. I'm always getting roast beef and Yorkshire pudding or, if I'm lucky, French food in the French Concession, but no one ever serves a meal like this."

That gave Chlöe the idea of never serving anything but the Chinese food for which she was rapidly acquiring such a fondness.

Slade, though, rebelled. "Once in a while, honey, just once in a while something I recognize."

But just once in a while.

How it happened, Chlöe didn't remember. But before they'd been more than a few months in Shanghai it became the thing to do to drop in at the Cavanaughs' for Sunday evening buffet.

Lou said, "What's such fun is you never know who you'll see here." Pretty soon one saw everyone. Lou told her, "It never seems like the same crowd I see at the consulate dinners, yet they're all here."

"That's because," Chlöe said, "all the others come too. The ones the consulates seldom entertain."

Dozens showed up every Sunday. People found it fun to ride in rickshaws to the quaint part of the city, arriving with bowls of food, and always it was a Chinese delicacy, which on their own they'd never have had their cooks prepare.

One afternoon Slade and Lou appeared with strings of Chinese lanterns they twined around the yard. So, on Sunday evenings the Cavanaughs' was the most lit-up place, in more ways than one, in Shanghai.

Another afternoon Lou came in, grinning. "Come here," he said, pulling Chlöe by the hand. Outside the big wooden gate, in a cart pulled by two oxen, was a scratched upright piano. "Just the thing for Sunday nights."

Chlöe looked at it with a jaded eye. It was ugly. "Who plays?" she asked.

"I do. And I've got a man who's coming to tune it."

Chlöe painted it a bright blue to match the peacock that strutted around the porch amid all the company, and Lou wasn't the only one to play it. People gathered around and sang songs of home, the old standbys. "It's three o'clock in the morning . . ." "Come on and hear, come on and hear, Alexander's ragtime band," "Shine on, shine on, harvest moon." But the favorite was when Lou sat down and began to play Cole Porter . . . "When they begin the beguine," or "Night and Day."

On such evenings Chlöe would kick up her heels and dance the Charleston, which inspired someone to donate a Victrola and all his records. People began to dance on the grass as well as on the verandah. The Cavanaughs' Sunday nights and Chlöe's uninhibited laughter, her delight in everything that came her way, made Chlöe famous in Shanghai. Her knack of greeting each person as though he or she were the most welcome guest in the world further enhanced Chlöe's popularity. They never extended invitations—people just came. Soon nothing else was planned for Sunday evenings. Out of the way as it was for all Westerners, the Cavanaugh house, their verandah, and lawn were filled to overflowing.

But it was something else that made her famous and led to a rift between her and Slade. Perhaps it began when he overheard someone say, "You're coming to Chlöe's Sunday night, aren't you?"

Slade cabled stories home, articles that had to do with the Kuomintang, the revolutionary party headed by Dr. Sun, articles that told of the disorganization and lack of unity and direction in China, that factually reflected events in the country.

But three months after they'd arrived, near the end of 1923, they received a letter from Cass.

"I didn't realize that in paying Slade to be my eyes and ears in China, I was getting two reporters. I hope—take for granted—you won't object, Chlöe, but that letter you sent us of your first day in Shanghai, that one describing your trip up the Hwang Pu and those beheadings as a normal part of Chinese life . . . well, I published it. Am enclosing copy of it from the Sunday magazine section and hope you'll be pleased. Even gave you a *big* byline, as you'll see. It touches the *human* part of the Orient. Keep it up!"

## CHLÖE CAVANAUGH

Her name stared at her in half-inch-high letters. She'd barely begun to think of herself by her married name. "Look," she said, smiling with delight and pride.

Slade shook his head. "Don't get too excited. It won't keep up. One letter does not a journalist make. Very nice, honey. But it's a fluke. Being in the Sunday section isn't like hard reporting. It's nice of Cass, but certainly your letter wouldn't have made it if you didn't have an in with him. Bask in it, it's fun, sure. But . . ." His voice trailed off.

Chlöe's excitement dwindled. He was right. He'd studied journalism for four years, worked hard at his craft these past seven years. Of course if Cass didn't care for her it wouldn't have been printed. Yet, it was nice. Awfully nice. Chlöe Cavanaugh in big black letters.

As for Shanghai, she had a love-hate relationship with it. It frightened and exhilarated her. Once, while shopping in the main shopping area, she was sure her ribs were about to be crushed, so she gave up and fled for the safety of home. Ann Leighton had been right. Use your own rickshaw. Don't mingle with the masses. For the first time she had a sense of what "the masses" meant. They smelled. They were deafening. They lived in dark, airless holes, and one could never tell, from their eyes, what they were thinking, or if they were thinking. They all looked alike with their slanted black eyes and straight black hair.

At the same time, she was fascinated by both Shanghai and its people. She spent days exploring the city, sometimes by herself, sometimes with either Daisy or Lou, sometimes with the two of them together. Women like Ann and Kitty turned up their noses at the very thought.

In the early 1920s, the *Times* of London was the only international paper with a long-time correspondent in the Far East. Slade was the second full-time foreign correspondent. Within six months the *New York Times* would assign a permanent correspondent, but right now it depended on stringers, or Lou Sidney, whose stories other papers bought via his. Lou was pleased to have another newspaperman with whom he could talk and drink. There were a number of journalists, actually, but they free-lanced and had no permanent bases and never knew whether they'd be paid for the stories they sent back to the States or Paris or Berlin.

Lou Sidney, having represented the London *Times* for more than five years, was the dean of all foreign correspondents. Despite his considerable talent, despite having the ear and often the confidences of the "important" Westerners at the consulates and foreign banks and the head of Standard Oil, Lou, thought Chlöe, was an anomaly. She looked at him, shoulders in a perpetual hunch, fingers as well as teeth stained yellow from his omnipresent cigarette. His long, gentle face, the pale blue eyes alternately sad, laughing, terribly serious, amused . . . depending on which moment you caught him. He couldn't have been more than thirty-five, but his forehead already was wrinkled, accentuated when he raised his eyebrows.

"I like Lou," she said on a Sunday evening after the last guest had left.

"Who doesn't?" Slade responded.

Chlöe walked out onto the verandah into the cool evening air. Slade followed, enveloping her in his arms. She leaned her head back against his shoulder, watching the bamboo leaves as they rustled in the breeze, hearing muffled sounds in the distance, watching the crescent moon reflected on the river. His hand moved from her waist, cradling her breast.

Turning her head toward him, she ran her tongue across his neck and heard his low laugh. His lips against her ear, Slade unzipped the back of her dress and reached out for her, pulling her to him. "Don't go in." She could tell he was smiling in the dark. "Stay here." His hands touched the shoulders of her dress, slipping it down her arms, his fingers brushing against her. She stepped out of the dress as it fell to the stone floor. From afar came the wailing cry of a lute, its dissonant chords floating in the soft air.

Slade's arms reached around her, and she felt her breasts swelling, wanting him, as they stood with the rustling willows overhead. She felt beautiful and alive with desire that burnt every nerve in her body. As he slipped out of his shirt, she reached out for him, their naked bodies touching. He picked her up, his lips upon hers, and carried her over to the chaise. She twisted her legs around him, never wanting to let him go, and he whispered, "Oh, God, darling," as she opened herself to him, hoping he would go more slowly than usual, wanting this moment to last into infinity, wanting to absorb him into her body and into her skin, wanting the mounting tension to shoot through her, to enter her bloodstream and charge her until she would have to lie still, replete and exhausted with the act of love.

But it was over. Far too soon. She heard Slade moan, his body slumping against her. She lay on the chaise in the darkness, waiting for the yearning and urgency to dissipate itself so that she would no longer feel the hunger that somehow was never satisfied. She ran her fingers through Slade's hair and kissed his cheek. Soon they arose and picked up their clothes and walked, naked—hand in hand—to their bedroom, where he fell asleep.

Chlöe lay staring into the darkness, wondering if garden parties, croquet, the races, Sunday-night buffets, Slade's body quickly meeting hers, were what life was all about. And, if so, why she wasn't more satisfied.

She felt guilty wanting more. She had, she told herself, more than she'd ever dreamed of having: an exotic country—a country that fascinated and repelled her anew each day, a famous loving husband, a carefree life so unlike any she'd ever known or imagined. But it didn't seem like more. Just different.

"I think I'll learn Chinese," she said aloud, wondering if that would add a dimension to her life.

Slade had already learned a few phrases, and perhaps it was time for her to be able to relate to this country.

# CHAPTER 8

She had met no Chinese but her servants, with whom she could barely communicate. Gao Hu knew enough pidgin English that he was able to pretty nearly decipher what she wanted done and could instruct the other servants. Though he treated both Chlöe and Slade with obsequious respect, Chlöe suspected that in his mind he was the boss. She never felt entirely comfortable with him, often feeling like a retarded child in his presence.

Then Mr. Yang entered her life. Slade hired him, at Chlöe's request, to come to the house three afternoons a week at two o'clock to teach them Chinese. On those days Slade conscientiously tried to come home for lunch, but he did not always make it.

The first day Mr. Yang appeared, a medium-tall slender man in a gray silk robe that reached to his white-socked, black cotton–shoed feet, Chlöe liked him. He was very erect and very formal, clasping a book between his hands, bowing when she entered the dining room, where their class was held. He wore a small round black satin hat that fit his head snugly; he never took it off. His eyes were bottomless black. Before Chlöe learned that scholars were the most esteemed people in China, he had already won her respect, not only with his patience in trying to teach them his language, but when he rose to leave, he always left with a bit of drama. The first day his exit line was "A thought upon which to meditate until we meet again is something that the great philosopher, Confucius, taught: 'It is in the fulfillment of the social responsibilities that the individual realizes his complete personal fulfillment.' "

Chlöe wrote these words down as soon as he left so she would not forget them.

Mr. Yang taught Chlöe much more than his language. Although

he had been hired to come for two hours each session, many days—particularly when Slade left early or couldn't attend at all—he stayed until five, partaking of tea and a sweet with Chlöe. Mr. Yang was a Confucianist and inculcated Chlöe with his version of Confucian philosophy. Years later, when she heard that the great philosopher considered women as less than slaves and that there was a class hierarchy to Confucianism, she did not understand, for those were not the aspects of Confucianism that Mr. Yang taught her.

Chlöe learned Chinese far more quickly than Slade did, perhaps because he was busier than she, or perhaps it was her greater enthusiasm and determination. She spent hours each day studying the language, saying the words aloud over and over to herself as she drew ideograms and tried to connect the word with the picture.

Many mornings she arose early and went to the market with the cook, although she could tell he would have far preferred to do his shopping alone. She loved this part of the day. It was so vastly different from the United States. Along the convoluted alleyways people hawked their wares, literally grabbing potential buyers, shouting at them to purchase their products. Gorgeous large, fresh vegetables lined baskets or were nestled in newspapers—broccoli, rape, lettuce, taro, bok choy, carrots, pickled and salted greens, cabbage. There were huge white peaches and tight-skinned oranges sweeter than any she'd ever tasted; indeed, more fruits than she had ever seen: bright yellow succulent loquats, cherries, bananas—small, dark ones unlike those sold in America. Watermelons—tight but sound and very green; pineapples that were smaller and browner than ones imported into America; sweet greengold muskmelons. Arrowroot, pumelos, big red dates. Gigantic pink-brown mushrooms and lichee nuts, persimmons filled with sweet juices. Big brown eggs spilled out of boxes and baskets. Chickens wandered in and out of the dirt-floored shops. Bean curd and meat dumplings were sold from stalls. In washtubs or wrapped in wet newspapers, still alive, were enormous carp and sometimes eels. Ducks and chickens were sold squawking, their feet tied together with string. The air was pungent with the spicy aroma of fresh ground ginger and bright red peppers.

Her senses had never been so alive in America.

Nearly every evening there was some dinner to attend, some ball at which to dance, some party that glittered. Chlöe soon learned that she needed more formal dresses for a week in Shanghai than she'd needed in all her life. She set Shanghai on its ear by ordering several traditional Chinese silk gowns, in emerald, in royal blue, and in a bloodred. She began wearing them, with their mandarin collars and long slits above the knee, to the Sunday evening buffets.

"For God's sake, honey," Slade exclaimed when she donned the first one, "what the hell are people going to say?"

She grinned at him. "That I'm a Chink lover?"

He looked at her reflection in the mirror, before which she sat screwing in long earrings. "Maybe I'll get my ears pierced," she said. "That would be a nice touch, don't you think?"

He shook his head and then he began to laugh. "Chlöe, you do beat all," he said. But he didn't object.

Saturday afternoons the foreigners in Shanghai spent at the races, and Sundays—after church and after heavy noon meals and naps—there was a band concert by the navy band in the Bund park along the river before their informal, though increasingly elaborate, buffets.

Chlöe yearned for an evening alone with Slade, with just the two of them dining by the fireplace, but it seldom happened.

Slade usually managed to come home for their Chinese lessons, but he rushed away immediately at four even though Chlöe would have liked him to stay. She wanted to hear of the day's events, to have a glass of golden Chinese wine with him, to hold his hand while he told her what was happening in the rest of China.

Instead, she spent some of those late afternoon hours with Mr. Yang, learning the ways of China. One day, sitting primly, with folded arms, waiting for their tea, Mr. Yang told her, "In China, the *human* world is primary. The world of *things* is of secondary importance." He kept these Confucian homilies until after the lesson itself.

"Does this mean," Chlöe asked as number two boy brought in tea, not on the silver tray with the silver tea set Chlöe and Slade had received for a wedding present, but in a tall, slender green and blue porcelain jar. She hesitated as she poured the tea into the matching cups, so dainty and fragile they looked as though they might break if touched. ". . . I should not enjoy a time like Christmas?"

Mr. Yang did not understand. When Chlöe explained about Christmas and the practice of giving and receiving presents, Mr. Yang shook his head in rapid back and forth motions. "The superior man understands what is righteous. The inferior man understands what is profitable."

Chlöe suspected this was his indirect answer to her question.

As always, she would have to think about their conversation after Mr. Yang left.

She persisted. "Does that mean making money is bad?"

"Wealth and honor," said Mr. Yang, his fathomless eyes focused on something far away, "are what every man desires. But if they have been obtained in violation of moral principles, they must not be kept."

"You mean"—Chlöe ran her hand down her leg, feeling the silkiness of her stockings, luxuriating in what money could buy—"that if someone steals something, he should give it back?"

Sometimes she got the idea Mr. Yang thought of her as a naïve child or a barbarian who asked direct questions even though she knew this was not the way of the Orient. This time he permitted himself the trace of a smile.

"He should not have taken it in the first place, of course. Poverty and humble stations are what every man dislikes. But if they can be avoided only in violation of moral principles, they must not be avoided."

"Do you mean"—she settled back in her chair, enjoying her conversation with this Chinese scholar, wondering why she and Slade never talked of such things—"it's better to be poor and good because rich is necessarily evil?"

"Not exactly." He reached out and set his empty teacup on the table, leaning back and letting his hands flow into their opposite sleeves, sitting in what she surmised was his favorite position, his hands hidden and lying flat against his stomach. "Wealth is evil in itself only if it has been obtained in violation of a moral principle. A superior man never abandons humanity even for a moment." Chlöe assumed the same applied to superior women. Or was there no such thing in Confucian ideology?

Mr. Yang continued. "Jen—one of the precepts of Confucianism—jen is our ability to love, and that constitutes the core of our humanity. If one becomes wealthy at the expense of someone else, *that* is evil. Jen is precisely what makes us truly human. To abandon our love of humanity is to give up a fully human life. Love of mankind is worth sacrificing one's life for. It is the basis of all human value and worth."

They were silent for a few minutes as Chlöe absorbed this concept. Then she asked, her fingers clasped together on her knees as she leaned forward, "It's what makes life worth living. Is that what jen is?"

With his eyes never wavering, Mr. Yang looked at Chlöe for a long time. She did not blink either, staring into his bottomless eyes as though perhaps she could find his core there. At last she did see the flicker of a smile, a warmth she had sensed but not seen before.

Then, he drew a piece of silk across the table to his book and opened it, placing the cloth bookmark carefully so that it would not wrinkle along the spine of his book, and closed it, holding it in both hands. Then he stood, bowing slightly, and said, "Madame, you are a pleasure."

Chlöe felt a thrill as she sensed the difference between what he so often said upon leaving: It has been a pleasure. This time he said "you." You are a pleasure.

"Ah, sir." She bowed her head. "You are an excellent teacher." She knew by then that she could say nothing more complimentary to him.

For the first time, she felt she might be on her way to some semblance of understanding. For just a moment she felt incredibly close to Mr. Yang, whose world was so different from hers. She looked at him and wondered if he had a wife and if he had children and, if so, what kind of father was he. What did he do in those hours he was not here, in her dining room, trying to educate her in the ways he believed and thought?

The moment of warmth lasted, and she controlled herself not to reach out to touch his arm, not to say thank you. After he left, his words, "Madame, you are a pleasure," lasted so long that she felt no resentment when Slade did not arrive for dinner. She dined by herself, and smiled throughout her solitary meal. She kept repeating it over and over until she thought that perhaps not even Slade's saying I love you sent such a feeling of satisfaction through her.

She found herself wondering why the wives of Americans and British and French in China were consumed with irrelevant matters like who had pinched whom or who might be sleeping with whom or how unreliable the help was or how stupid the Chinese were and how your help robbed you blind. She played tennis three mornings a week. She attended galas at least one afternoon a week and nearly every evening. She had more pretty dresses than she thought she'd have in a lifetime. Her dance card was always filled.

Yet the happiness that she supposed came with such a life escaped her.

She felt the restlessness that had been part of her all her life. The sense of not doing anything. She felt useless. The novelty of China—though it had not worn off—did not provide her with what she'd hoped it would. Parties, seeing the same people day after day after day, were no more exhilarating than they had been in Oneonta or Ithaca. She wanted more . . . much more . . . out of life. But she still didn't know what.

She and Slade, along with Lou Sidney, were the only journalists invited to the British consulate dinner for the new ambassador stationed in Peking. Since there was no central Chinese government as such, a posting to Peking meant only a duller life than in Shanghai. There was not nearly as large a foreign population in that northern city. It was far colder and darker in the long winter, there were not the number of social events that Shanghai offered, yet since it was considered the capital of a country that was in no way unified, ambassadors were stationed there, presenting their credentials to the local warlord, who had no control over the rest of China and could not speak for it.

As with so many dinner parties, the talk soon turned to Sun Yat-sen and his perennial bid for the presidency of a united China.

"He seems like a dreamer to me," Slade said. Chlöe looked across at him, watched his left hand resting casually on the table, his long, slender fingers tapping lightly on the white cloth. "He never has taken over the reins. He's spent more time out of the country than in it."

"But no one's more revered by the Chinese. China for the Chinese. Democracy. Equality. Freedom."

Chlöe looked at the man who spoke. "Don't you believe in all that?" she asked.

The man coughed behind his hand. "Of course, of course."

"But not in China?" she asked.

There was silence. Chlöe could hear it, it was so loud.

Yes, she thought, the foreign community is so dedicated to democracy in their own countries but are scared to death of democracy in the country they're helping to awaken. They like the status quo, Slade told her, where they demand and receive preferential treatment. They want nothing to upset the balance of trade. Chlöe listened carefully those evenings when Lou and Slade sat in their living room, smoking cigarettes and drinking gin and tonics, philosophizing about this country in which they were all now living.

The next afternoon Chlöe brought the subject into her conver-

sation with Mr. Yang. He had assigned her a simple translation from
the Chinese into English. When they finished the translation and
sat waiting for Mr. Yang's favorite jasmine tea, for which she too
had developed a fondness, she asked the scholar, "What kind of
man is Dr. Sun?"

Mr. Yang shook his head as though he couldn't give her a de-
finitive answer. "I believe," he began, "that Dr. Sun and his followers felt a new breed of people would emerge once the Manchu
dynasty was overthrown. But that is not possible all at once. I per-
sonally think the Manchus were overthrown too speedily and too
easily. Before anyone had time to think what to do about it. No one
made plans how to govern the people. The warlords of the various
provinces have not been willing to give up their autonomy."

"Aren't there many kinds of warlords?" she asked.

Mr. Yang nodded. "They can range from local bandits who
terrorize villages to those who protect large cities the size of Peking.
It depends on their military might. Those who cut out large provinces for themselves or swear to protect cities and towns earn their
moneys from taxes. They fight off any intruders. Some, with great
military might, rule an entire province."

Chlöe thought of protection rackets in the United States.

"In villages, warlords pay taxes to warlords of their province or
of the nearest large city. The city warlords paid taxes to the Manchus. Now there is no central government, so perhaps they keep the
moneys themselves."

"*Warlord* is such a sinister word."

"In China," Mr. Yang nodded his head in agreement, "soldiering is not an honorable profession. Only rabble join armies. They
rape and pillage, they use people, they are careless and cruel. One
hopes one's son never falls into such an abyss. Warlords, however,
serve a useful purpose. If you pay taxes to a warlord, he swears to
fight off any other warlords or bandits who come to your village and
you are safe. But it is not an honorable profession."

"Why do people put up with them?"

"Because the common people cannot protect themselves. Because it has been a way of life in China since 1850."

"But what of Dr. Sun?" Chlöe asked again.

Mr. Yang shrugged his slender shoulders, indicating he did not
really know. "I think because there was no other plan of what to
do with millions of people after the overthrow of the Manchus, Dr.
Sun succeeded in his idea of a republic. Peasants and shopkeepers

were never happy to pay taxes for the extravagance of the dowager empress. Supposedly, if the country is ever united, they think they will no longer be taxed for the luxuries when they themselves have scarcely enough to eat.''

Chlöe could tell by his tone of voice that he was skeptical. "You don't believe it?'' she asked.

A thin smile played along the teacher's face. "Human nature is not taken into consideration. Someone will have to collect the taxes. Someone will have that power. And power breeds corruption.''

Chlöe thought of her own government. Certainly it was not corrupt. "Always?'' she asked. "Do you think that power *always* corrupts?''

Mr. Yang folded his hands into their opposite sleeves, sitting erect with his now-hidden hands in front of him. "I know of few exceptions. Confucius, perhaps Buddha, your Christ. But their followers who tried to wrest power into their own hands became corrupt. Only when one keeps his eyes on a distant star is ideology pure. Once it is close, taken into one's hands, it corrupts.''

"So you think all religions are corrupt?''

"Confucianism is not a religion,'' he said, his eyes staring out the window into the peach tree whose branches were now bare. "It is a code of ethics. A way upon which to base one's life.''

"Isn't that basically what religion is, a code of ethics?'' Chlöe asked.

Mr. Yang then laughed one of his rare laughs, a small, squeezed sound, but Chlöe could tell from the curve of his lips that it was a laugh.

Chlöe came back to her original question. "Is Dr. Sun a good man?''

"I know little of him.'' Mr. Yang shook his head, folding his piece of silk between the pages of his book, signifying he was ready to leave. "He is a Christian.'' That did not make him particularly estimable in Mr. Yang's mind. "He spent part of his youth in Hawaii and much of his adult life in America. I understand he is a doctor but I do not think he has much practiced medicine. He had a wife and two children but has abandoned them, it seems, to seek money for his cause. He has taken a second wife. I do not know much more about him, though China is rife with stories and expectations. He is very respected. They are calling him 'the father of modern China.' '' He stood up and bowed slightly.

Chlöe returned the courtesy and accompanied him to the gate.

———

"I think I'd like to go on a trip for ten days to two weeks," Slade announced as they dressed for dinner. "Want to come?" he asked.

"Yes," she answered immediately, not even knowing where he was going. It didn't matter where.

"I want to go down to Canton and see if I can set up an interview with Dr. Sun so I can try to get a handle on him. It looks like he's going to be president of China again, if he can achieve unification. If anyone can, it's Dr. Sun. He's the only hero China has right now."

"What fun," Chlöe said as she screwed in her earring, studying her reflection in the mirror. "When are we going?"

"How about later this week? He and his wife are both Americanized, so they should be willing to see someone from the American press."

Chlöe walked over to him. "I'll love to see new parts of China."

Slade leaned down to kiss her cheek. "Well, let's hope it'll be fun. Maybe you can meet Madame Sun and get a feeling for what she's like. She went to college in America."

Chlöe raised her eyebrows. "An American-educated Chinese woman?"

"Her sisters too," said Slade. "First American-educated Chinese women ever. For all I know, first educated Chinese women anyplace."

"How unusual. I didn't know Chinese women were educated at all."

"Maybe you can get her story." He put his arms around her waist and laughed down at her. "See, a real helpmate."

"Oh, I like that." She smiled, thinking, I *really* like that.

# CHAPTER 9

"Madame Sun," said Slade, entering the hotel room, "invites you to tea while I'm interviewing Dr. Sun."

Chlöe was looking out the window at the garden behind the waving bamboo. She thought the garden unkempt. But then, she thought, so was everything else she'd seen in the ten months she'd been in China.

The three-day train ride from Shanghai had been uncomfortable. It was not only crowded, but she decided ninety percent of Chinese men must smoke, and she had trouble breathing throughout the trip. The floor had obviously been urinated on, and she stuck her head out the window most of the time, hoping to be able to breathe without regurgitating. The quilts on the bunks were filthy, obviously not changed since the previous occupants. Or within the last year, she thought. There were no sheets. She'd hoped whoever had lain there before, any of the dozens of them, hadn't had TB. If she slept, it was only fitfully, wrestling with the lack of sanitation, with the smells, with the noises of hundreds of unclean people.

At times like these she hated China. She remembered her bathroom at home. Remembered the bathrooms in Risley Hall. Remembered the bathrooms at the Monaghans' in Chicago and even the crude though clean one up at the cabin in Michigan. She remembered her grandparents' bathroom and conjured up every clean, neat bathroom she'd ever known. She lay in her dirty quilt and remembered with longing being able to brush her teeth with water straight from the tap.

In Canton, dust tanned the leaves of trees lining the streets. The city might not be as crowded as Shanghai, but that was a relative matter, she decided. When Slade left her alone, she ventured forth to see the city. Now, having a minimal amount of Chinese at her command, she was not nervous about getting lost. She had heard of white slave rings where foreign women were abducted and sent to work in the brothels of Macao or Peking or Canton or Shanghai. They were never heard of again, these white women. But she refused to allow these tales to frighten her.

Having her own rickshaw boy in Shanghai had given her the freedom to tour the city or to travel to the Bund to parties or to call on other women. She was proud to have chosen a home away from the sector of the city where most of the Westerners lived. She never felt unsafe, but then, she was never alone. Though the cook went home at night, and so did the laundress and the young girl who did the housework, Gao Hu lived in a little room behind the kitchen and Chlöe suspected that the rickshaw boy slept behind the pampas grass, down by the river under the willows. She never asked, because having the servants there at night when Slade was not home gave her a sense of security. She was less frightened than intrigued by China. And now, after the incident that morning, she was also infuriated.

"Did you hear me?" Slade asked, a slight edge to his voice.

Turning to look at him, wanting to share with him what had happened, she answered, "I was just thinking."

"Well, stop thinking and get ready."

"This morning something happ—"

"C'mon," he said, irritation in his voice. "You haven't even begun to dress. I don't want to be late."

She could tell he wasn't listening to her. Reaching for a new silk blouse, she decided to tell him later. "Madame Sun . . . What do you know about her?"

"She comes from one of China's more influential families," he said, untying his tie.

"By that you mean. . . ?" Chlöe walked over and picked up his shirt where he'd tossed it on the bed.

Slade ambled over to the wash basin and began rinsing his hands. "Interesting father, from all I can gather, who somehow or other got to Boston when he was just a young kid, like ten or so. Missionaries latched on to him there and converted him. They even sent him through a Baptist college in Georgia or South Carolina or someplace down there. He became an ordained minister," Slade laughed, drying his hands on a towel, "and came back here to teach his people about our God!"

"When was this?" Chlöe smoothed out Slade's tie, which had dropped to the floor.

"I dunno. In the 1880s, maybe forty some years ago. And as they say of the missionaries who went to Hawaii: They went to do good and did very well indeed."

"You mean he ended up making a lot of money!" She slipped into a black skirt.

"By, of all things, publishing Bibles. He became the biggest Bible publisher in China. From all I've heard, he and Dr. Sun were two of those largely responsible for the overthrow of the Manchus and for trying to make China a republic. . . ."

"Ah," said Chlöe, listening carefully, "then Madame Sun's father . . ."

"Charlie Soong," said Slade.

"He was a good friend of her husband's? She must be much younger, then."

Slade nodded. "Charlie sent his three daughters, Ai-ling, Ching-ling—which is Madame Sun's given name—and Mei-ling to America when they were young. I mean, the two younger ones must've been about ten or eleven when they were sent all the way across the world. They stayed till they graduated from college. The sons went too. T.V., the oldest boy, went to Harvard. He's Dr. Sun's financial adviser."

"How do you know all this?" Chlöe asked him.

He walked over to the bed and sat on it, reaching for his shoes.

"Go on, tell me more about Madame Sun," she urged.

"I've heard, true or not, that her father—her whole family—stopped speaking to her when she married Dr. Sun. He's old enough to be her father. She's what, in her early thirties now. And he's fifty-eight."

Chlöe wondered how a woman could go to bed with a man old enough to be her father. It reeked slightly of incest, she thought. She pictured pale, wrinkled skin compared to the golden tautness of Slade, whose athletic physique and leanness so appealed to her. She thought of lying naked in bed next to an old man, and shivered.

"They've been married nine or ten years now. He was in Japan, as were her parents, when she came home with a B.A. in 1913. She replaced her sister, Ai-ling, as his secretary and then married him. Rumor has it that he still had a wife. I've heard claims that Dr. Sun divorced his first wife, to whom he'd been married for thirty years or more, for he has a son older than Madame Sun. Maybe they considered his first marriage, not being Christian, was null and void."

"Maybe they have a Ph.D. in rationalization," said Chlöe.

Slade looked at her and laughed out loud. "Come on." He reached out a hand to grasp her arm. "Let's go. I want you to discover the real Madame Sun, the real Soong Ching-ling."

When they arrived at the Suns' home, high on a hill overlooking Canton, a servant showed Slade to a door through which he vanished. Then the man led Chlöe down a long hall and to a drawing room that contained American-style furniture. There were, here and there, objets d'art that Chlöe could tell were from China's past, but mostly it was a room that could have been in America.

Just then a door opened and, moving like a symphony, a petite figure gracefully entered the room. She wore a long gown of shimmering green silk, and she glided rather than walked. Her shoes were American, black patent leather high heels. Her hair was pulled back on her neck, revealing long jade earrings that matched her dress.

Her large, luminous eyes shone with clarity and with what seemed to Chlöe was complete purity.

Chlöe thought she looked fragile, with exquisite features. She had never seen anyone lovelier. When the woman spoke, her voice was gentle.

"I am Madame Sun Yat-sen." She held out her right hand in the American fashion, while her left hand clutched a white lace handkerchief.

Gesturing that they should seat themselves, she lowered herself into a large chair facing Chlöe. The bulk of the chair accentuated her delicacy. A tea tray arrived, and Madame Sun poured tea, passing it to Chlöe in fine, brightly painted china.

"I understand you've recently graduated from college. I thought I would permit myself a trip into nostalgia and that it might be far more fun to talk with you than sit in there with the men."

Chlöe could not keep her eyes from this woman. For the first time in her life she felt in the presence of royalty. She didn't even realize she'd spoken until Madame Sun answered, "Yes, at last we are going to have a united China. It's about time, don't you think?" Her English was impeccable. "But I talk politics every day and night. Tell me about America. I haven't seen it in, oh, it must be ten years. Those were happy years I spent in your great country. I went there when I was twelve and stayed until I was twenty-one."

"Didn't you see your family in all that time?" asked Chlöe, wondering what it would be like to grow up among strangers, wondering how one could stay in exile from all that was familiar for so many years.

Madame Sun smiled at her, and Chlöe was dazzled. "I did not see my parents, but my sisters were with me. My elder sister, Ai-ling, was attending college in Macon, Georgia, when Mei-ling, my younger sister, and I were sent there. Mei-ling was the one who really did not grow up in China at all. When our father sent us there, Mei-ling wasn't more than eight years old. She didn't see our parents until she too graduated from college. She had a completely American upbringing and has only recently returned. But Ai-ling and I are of two cultures. When I came back, I felt more American than Chinese. I am," she smiled obliquely, "still fighting that. Yet I wouldn't give up those years in America for anything. They broadened my horizons fantastically."

"Didn't you miss your family?"

"I never felt estranged from them. Half of them were with me."

Then she leaned forward, one hand resting on her knee, and said, "Tell me what New York City is like now. Has it changed so much? I didn't know cities could be so clean until I saw your Washington and New York."

Chlöe laughed aloud. No one had ever called New York City clean. Yet she understood Madame Sun. It was clean compared to cities of the Orient.

Madame Sun asked Chlöe if she was enjoying living in Shanghai and volunteered that she had grown up there in a large home on the outskirts of the city. "We were one of the first homes to have American plumbing." She smiled. "I do miss that most of all in China."

"So I'm not alone?" Chlöe said.

"I hope you are not alone in any way. I hope that your marriage will be as fortunate as mine has been." Her eyes glowed and her voice intensified. "The dreams of all my childhood years have a chance of coming true. My husband and I share the same dream, a free China, where there can be a chance for all. Where no one starves," her eyes were fastened on some ideal in the distance, and it was as though she were talking not just to Chlöe, "and people do not die from famines or rampaging diseases or in wars. Where the rich do not get richer off the poor and the poor do not live like animals. Where my people can be free, where education will be available to all who want it. Where my fellow countrymen will not live in the dark ages."

She twisted the lacy handkerchief in her hands and leaned forward, her eyes penetrating into Chlöe now. "Do you know that we have had no Chinese doctors until recently, when some have been educated in England and America? Do you know how few engineers we have, so few men with dreams for the future of our country, so few industrialists, so few men who even understand international banking? It is time for us! The world thinks we're not capable, I know, but we will prove them wrong."

Though her black eyes were locked with Chlöe's, Chlöe thought Madame Sun was talking more to herself. The energy she exuded caught Chlöe up in its power. Madame Sun's eyes were bright, with a feverish glow to them. "It's not that Chinese do not work hard. They do. At unending tasks, like donkeys. They have not had the opportunity to do much more than be beasts of burden. My husband will lead them out of darkness and into the twentieth century!"

Chlöe felt her heart beating hard. What fire! What sense of

mission. What idealism. And to think it was all in the realm of possibility for this woman. For her husband. For this country. She felt tears gather in her eyes and blinked wildly to control them.

Madame Sun sat back in the big chair and visibly relaxed. Now her smile was serene. "I can't imagine a life not married to Dr. Sun. Marriage is the avenue to the fulfillment of dreams." Her voice now held a tender quality.

When Slade was finished with Dr. Sun, a servant led him to the drawing room and Madame Sun rose to greet him, holding her hand out before he was halfway across the long room. As he approached her, she said, "It is an honor to meet the husband of a woman whose fame has preceded her."

Slade's hand halted in midair for a few seconds.

"It's my husband, not I . . . ," protested Chlöe. She thought Madame Sun's laughter as musical as she imagined a lute would sound.

"Your husband is famous in America," Madame Sun smiled directly at Slade, "but what you did this morning is famous in Canton."

Slade cocked an eyebrow.

Oh, thought Chlöe, how could she have heard?

"What did my wife do this morning?"

"She beat what would be the equivalent of a mayor in your country, Ch'en, the warlord of Canton, over the head with her parasol." Madame Sun's laughter pealed like bells.

She doesn't sound upset, thought Chlöe. Then she said aloud, "The mayor? The warlord?"

"My God, Chlöe." Slade stared at her, open-mouthed. "You did what?"

"I tried to tell you . . ."

Madame Sun put her hand through Chlöe's arm and smiled. "My dear, Canton has laughed all day on hearing of an American woman beating the arrogant Ch'en. And with a parasol!"

"It was the only thing I had," Chlöe said. "He was beating a coolie so cruelly I thought the poor man might die. He was bleeding, and I got him to the hospital."

"Chlöe, my God! Stay out of these things. You're—"

"She's wonderful." Madame Sun was still laughing. "We are all delighted."

Slade was silent in the rickshaw all the way back to the hotel and remained so for several hours. At dinner Chlöe tried to draw him out. "How was your interview?" she asked.

"Fine," he said, picking shrimp up with his chopsticks. "Sun had a Russian adviser, Nikolai Zakarov. Big guy. He just sat there and didn't speak until the interview was over and tea was brought in. I'll meet with him again tomorrow. This Russian's immense, got black hair, wild bushy beard. I liked him, even if he is a Communist. He exudes charm."

"Doesn't it make you nervous, one of the leaders of China having a Communist for an adviser?" Chlöe wanted Slade to go on talking, to get over the snit he'd been in.

"Apparently this Zakarov started the Whampoa Military Academy for Dr. Sun. These Chinese know nothing of modern war tactics, and Zakarov has whipped an effective army into shape, under a young leader named Chiang Kai-shek."

"Isn't that all the more alarming, if China's building an army based on the Bolsheviks?"

"I doubt that the KMT is that powerful," said Slade, putting down his chopsticks and reaching for the warm Chinese beer.

Chlöe knew the KMT was short for the Kuomintang, the political party that led the revolution in 1911 and had built up slowly over the years. It was the largest and strongest party in China, the *only* unified and cohesive one, with Dr. Sun as its leader.

"I've a feeling that for all his idealism, Dr. Sun's an ineffective leader," Slade went on. "A man filled with dreams of glory who doesn't know how to put them into practice. I suspect this Zakarov knows how."

"Is China going Communist?" Chlöe asked. All she really knew of communism was that her father found it brutal, cruel, enslaving, and eminently dangerous. It robbed one of individual freedom and was the diametric opposite of democracy, even though publicly it espoused equality for all. Her father blamed the Russian Revolution and communism for all the strikes in America.

"I doubt that one Russian means all of China will be Communist. What I gather is that this Zakarov is an organizer extraordinaire. And he has Sun's ear. I suspect he's negotiating to have Sun reinstated as president, whether in reality or as a puppet."

Chlöe said, "Madame Sun wouldn't believe her husband would be a puppet."

Slade said, "Women always like to think their men are strong."

Chlöe looked at him. Did all men, she wondered, like to think their women were weak? "She's strong, Madame Sun is."

"I thought her quite fragile and feminine as well as good-looking."

Chlöe thought good-looking was an understatement for Madame Sun.

When they were getting ready for bed, Slade said, "You know, we're guests in this country. For God's sake, don't go beating someone up or interfering with what anyone is doing to a servant! The mayor! Jesus Christ! There could be frightening repercussions!"

"Well, I didn't know he was the warlord or mayor or whatever. . . ."

"Chlöe, it matters a great deal what people think of me in China." He turned to frown at her.

"He was beating a young boy who was cowering in the gutter, blood pouring from his ear and eye. The only way I could get him to stop . . ."

Slade pulled on his pajamas. "I hope I never hear of you doing such a thing again. Their habits here are not ours. And you're in *their* country. I don't want to hear any such thing again. Understand?" He crawled under the covers and pulled the cord that released the mosquito netting, separating them through the gauze.

She stood outside the netting, looking at her husband.

"Chlöe, do you hear me?" he asked again.

She didn't answer, angry at him for treating her like a naughty child. Her hands were balled into fists.

Into his pillow he muttered, "Your wife's fame precedes her!"

She let him fall asleep before she crawled into bed.

While the city's noises drifted through the hotel windows, as the sound of firecrackers exploded unexpectedly, Chlöe lay awake, irritated at Slade. How dare he speak to her like that!

Then, unable to control her mind, she began to think of the woman she'd met today, on the verge of fulfilling her childhood dreams. She tried to think of her own childhood dreams. Owning a horse. Being kissed by Will Hendrix. What a silly girl I was, Chlöe thought, wondering if she was still silly, playing tennis and going to parties day after day, night after night. Playing at housekeeping with five servants in China. She was so empty compared to Madame Sun.

————

Two days later Chlöe received a note from Madame Sun, who invited her, since it was such a beautiful day, to join her for a walk in Liuhua Park. Madame Sun's rickshaw boy would be waiting on the other side of the bridge at two o'clock.

Chlöe and Slade were staying at the Guangzhou Hotel on Sha Mien Island in the Pearl River. Slade told her the island had originally been nothing more than a sand bank and now, like the Shanghai Bund, it was where foreigners lived and where Chinese were prohibited. Magnificent villas edged the river. There were two bridges connecting the island to the city itself and, at night, they were closed by iron gates.

The island had broad avenues lined with palms and banyan trees, lush tropical gardens, tennis courts, a soccer field, and a sailing club.

Madame Sun waited on the other side of the river, in her rickshaw, for Chlöe, who was embarrassed. "I'm sure *you* could get permission to come across," she said as she climbed into the rickshaw.

"My dear," said the Chinese woman, "I have no desire to. I do not wish to be any different from my countrymen. I prefer to let the authorities try to humiliate me so that I can keep clear in front of me the idea that we must rid ourselves of foreign domination. We must not let ourselves be intimidated or taken advantage of."

Chlöe wanted to apologize for all the Western powers.

Madame Sun chatted on, pointing out landmarks to Chlöe as they headed toward the park on Liwan Road. The rickshaw boy jogged among bicyclists and pedestrians by the thousands. Chlöe was still overwhelmed, even after all these months, at the crowds in China.

Liuhua Park, which Madame Sun told Chlöe meant Park of the Stream of Flowers, was lovely. It had a number of lakes and bamboo groves. Covered walks and paths wound along the lake. Arched stone bridges crossed other smaller ponds. Madame Sun suggested they sit and rest under a covered pavilion. The lake was green with algae and smelled like a public latrine. Madame Sun either did not notice or ignored it. Perhaps living in China eventually inured one to its odors.

"I understand your introduction to China came as a shock."

Chlöe looked at Madame Sun in bewilderment.

"A school friend from New York sent me a copy of the article you wrote about your first day in China."

"New York?" Chlöe exclaimed. "It was published in Chicago."

"Nevertheless," Madame Sun smiled, "the copy she sent me

was from the *New York Herald-Tribune*. It made me remember how I felt, accustomed to American ways after nearly ten years, when I returned home to such practices as beheadings and garrotings."

"Garrotings?"

"It is a typical and time-honored Chinese method for meting out death sentences. A wire is wound around the victim's neck and—quarter inch by quarter inch—is tightened ever so slowly, working itself into the flesh. I imagine soldiers and warlords get intense pleasure from witnessing the fright and pain of the victim. And satisfaction from the agonizing strangulation of an enemy."

Chlöe stared at her in stupefaction, finding it difficult to believe that such words came from a face with such gentle eyes.

"But all this is beside the point. Yours was a very human story. I saw the head rolling at your feet, smelled what you smelled as you came up the Hwang Pu. You wrote of my people and of your emotions. It touched me."

Chlöe felt a thrill of pride at the same time she was embarrassed.

"I ask you," Madame Sun put a hand out to cover Chlöe's, "to write in such a way of my husband and of our cause."

Chlöe's hand flew to her chest. "I'm not a journalist. My husband is."

Madame Sun nodded. "He writes facts. He is a good writer of facts. But all that has been written of us is facts. Often erroneous ones, to be sure." Her smile dazzled Chlöe. "Think about it, won't you?"

I can't, Chlöe thought. I know how Slade reacted last time. "I wouldn't know what to say." But she felt inordinately pleased.

The Chinese woman gazed over the small lake. It was peaceful and the sounds of the city were muted. Then she turned her gaze directly on Chlöe and blurted out, "I wish you would stay in Canton awhile."

Chlöe stared at her.

"This may indeed sound silly. But there are times when I feel so alone. It is not that I am without people always around me, but I have no one who understands me except my husband. And he is often too busy. He needs me, I know. I am important to him and his cause. But in those other times, I have no one. No woman friend. Having a background like no other Chinese woman, I have no one who understands me. I have no one to talk and laugh with, no one to share my thoughts with the way I had in the United States."

She turned to look at Chlöe and placed a hand on her arm. "I know. I know what it is like to be apart from one's husband. It is selfish of me to even ask. But perhaps for just a few weeks, a month? We would be honored to have you stay with us." Her smile turned into a laugh. "We have Western plumbing. It's the one concession to America I insist upon.

"And then you can take your time to study us, *feel* us . . ."

Slade wouldn't approve, Chlöe was sure. Writing was *his* forte. He'd made it clear that this area was his bailiwick.

Yet her story had been picked up by the *New York Herald Tribune*! Madame Sun was making her an offer any foreign correspondent would give his eyeteeth for! Certainly Slade could appreciate that. And this woman fascinated her as no one had ever done. Oh, how exciting it would be to spend time with her and write about her. Tell the world what this woman and her husband were trying to do. Tell the world? Oh, my.

"Let me ask my husband," she said. "I am flattered, Madame Sun."

"My friends call me Ching-ling."

When Chlöe told Slade of the invitation, she omitted the part about Madame Sun's request that she write mainly about her husband. To her surprise, Slade did not react as she imagined he would. "My God, Chlöe, how fantastic. You can get an insider's view of the Sun Yat-sens. What a break! Of course, stay a month, if that's what she wants." He slapped his forehead with the palm of his hand. "Can you imagine? An insider's view into the Suns! Boy, what I can do with this!"

Three days later he left and Chlöe's bags were moved from the hotel on Shah Mien Island to a room in the home of Dr. and Madame Sun Yat-sen.

# CHAPTER 10

Nikolai Zakarov was the largest man Chlöe had ever encountered. His curly hair was as black as his eyes and there was a swarthiness to his skin. His face was dominated both by his fiery eyes and his thick beard, so different from the neat Vandykes Chlöe had seen on a few other men. His eyes—alive and curious, questioning—were not almond-shaped, but Chlöe thought he had an indefinable Oriental cast to his features. As he walked into the Suns' drawing room he seemed, to Chlöe, as though he were holding his energy on a leash, so vital and overpowering was he.

Here was a forceful man who was used to giving orders and who had a strong sense of self, a sense almost—she was surprised the word even came to her mind—of mission, without a doubt of the rightness of his goals.

She didn't realize she'd thought all this until later, when she remembered how he'd overwhelmed her. He wore a slightly wrinkled white linen Western-style suit, and bowed before Madame Sun, taking the hand that she stretched out.

"Nikolai," she said in that soft, sweet voice Chlöe loved to hear, "I'm so glad you could come. It's just us tonight, us and our guest." She turned toward Chlöe. "Mrs. Cavanaugh." Ching-ling's smile lit up the room. "The doctor will be down a bit later. This will give you two a chance to get acquainted. We've all spent many years in the United States."

Chlöe watched as the big Russian smiled across the room at her, not diverting his eyes as Chinese men did but looking directly at her, walking with leonine grace toward her. He reached out a hand that seemed more of a paw, and Chlöe was not surprised at its strength but at its gentleness. So this was a Russian Bolshevik. Slade had liked him.

"I met your husband," said the Russian in English, with hardly a trace of an accent.

Madame Sun walked over to the large sofa and sank into it. "Nikolai," she said, smiling up at him, "is helping us in our dreams for China. Nikki, tell Chlöe," she gestured to show that that was Mrs. Cavanaugh's given name, "about your years in America."

Chlöe walked over and sat down at the other end of the sofa from her hostess while Nikolai strode over to the large wing chair opposite them. He sat down and crossed his legs, his enormous booted foot jiggling in the air. "They were happy years," he said.

Chlöe asked, "Where were you?"

"Detroit," he answered.

"Did you attend school there, like Madame Sun?" Chlöe asked.

He threw back his head and laughed. "The only class I took in a school was in order to learn to read and write Russian."

Madame Sun reached across the sofa and touched Chlöe's arm.

"Nikolai was escaping the czarists. Tell her about it, Nikki. I'm su Chlöe would like to hear your story."

"Ching-ling, don't you get tired of making me repeat my life's story to everyone who comes to visit you?"

She smiled, flashing her luminous eyes. "Never." She turned to Chlöe. "He was captured by the czarists and given a choice. . . ." Her voice was silver. "Siberia or exile to the West."

Chlöe sipped her drink and said, "I'm afraid my knowledge of Russia is sketchier even than it is of China."

Ching-ling arose and, with her hands clenched in front of her, walked back and forth across the room. "The czarists were like the Manchus. Caring not at all for their citizens, keeping them peasants without education, without food, letting them starve and freeze to death, letting them live like desperate animals, as so many of ours still do."

"And as many Russians still do," Zakarov admitted. "But that is changing." He looked at Chlöe, but she did not think he saw her. His eyes were focused on something beyond the immediate present. She noticed a scar on the left side of his face, a fine white line that zagged along his cheekbone, beginning close to his eye, descending, hidden, into his beard. "I grew up in the village of Yanovichi, forest country, very cold, very dark in winter, where all the men were loggers."

"By the time he was twelve he was breaking log jams on the frozen rivers," Ching-ling interrupted, "a very dangerous job."

Looking at him, his eyes now angry with remembrance of things past, Chlöe could imagine he was more than capable of dangerous work.

Nikolai Ivanovich Zakarov was the middle of five children born to Olga and Josef Zakarov, in the year 1892. He remembered how he was forced to sit weaving straw into shoes so that his toes would not freeze. But they seemed always frozen and, because the straw pricked his tender young skin, he limped and his sandals were bloody. By the time he was five years old, the calluses on the soles of his feet grew so thick that forever after he seldom felt any sensation there.

Dinner, always soup and heavy dark bread, was eaten at four-thirty in the afternoon in winter. In summer they ate later, sometimes as late as nine o'clock, when it was still light. He remembered laughter those summer evenings, but never any other time. Women

gathered in front of the Davidoviches, and children played at kicking a can or found round stones that they rolled in the dirt, always
laughing with each other. The unmarried girls, those over fourteen,
sat sedately with their own sex and longingly eyed the young men
who pretended to ignore them.

All day, every day, from before dawn until time for dinner,
everyone labored. The women carried wood on their backs, like
donkeys, and walked, bent over, up and down the mountainsides.
At the end of the day, while their husbands sat smoking corn husks
and discussing politics, the women cleaned their homes—nothing
more than hovels—and prepared dinner, taking care of their families. They died early.

There was no school and only one or two people Nikolai knew
learned to read and write. There were no books to read, no hope
or thought of leaving Yanovichi. The only ones who left were those
unfortunate enough to be standing in the street when the czar's
cavalry rode through, conscripting all the young men who happened to be outside that day. Young wives never saw husbands
again; sons disappeared. Too frequently, bleeding young girls were
found alongside the dusty road after the soldiers on horseback swept
through.

Even when there was not enough money for meat bone for the
soup, they had to pay taxes. If there was no money for taxes, one of
the boys in the family was conscripted for work at the czar's sawmill
on the edge of town two days a month.

Once when Nikolai was ten or eleven, the year before he began
working the log jams on the river, he saw a sleigh pulled by six large
horses. Few people in Yanovichi owned horses, and he had never
seen six together. The sleigh sped along as though skimming over
ice, sparkling silver in the sun. A man sat in front, his long whip
whistling near the horses, and he grinned as he zinged it through
the air.

In the seat behind him, cushioned under bearskin rugs, were a
man and woman with high fur hats, huddled close together and
laughing. The woman looked over at Nikolai and, scrunching up
her face in distaste, pointed at him. He was ashamed. Embarrassed.
He felt dirty. Not that he had ever been truly clean, but he felt
there was dirt deep inside him.

The sleigh flew on, leaving a trail where its runners tamped
down the snow, creating icy sparkles in the bright sunlight. It left
an invisible mark on the boy. This was the first time he'd realized

there was a different life, that he wasn't as good as others. That there were comforts in the world and people who owned more than his fellow villagers did.

When he was twelve Nikolai was sent out to do a man's work. Breaking log jams on the river was one of the most dangerous jobs available, but it also paid better than most others. His parents tried to fight it, but the manager of the mill took one look at Nikolai's height—he was already almost six feet tall—and at the brawn he exhibited and offered his parents such a high wage for him that they couldn't refuse.

He was sent up and down the river. When the ice broke up in the spring and the swirling waters hurtled toward the sea, then the log jams could crush a man in a second. Nikolai, by the time he was fourteen, had become expert under the tutelage of Ivan Leonovich.

Ivan knew how to read and had worked all over Russia. He filled Nikolai's head with tales of what cities were like and how royalty lived off the sweat of peasants, whom they considered on a level with their dogs. He told Nikolai of such spectacular balls and other extravagances that Nikolai, looking at his own people, felt bile rise inside him.

Ivan told the boy about Lenin and Trotsky and their dreams. These dreams became Nikolai's. For two years Nikolai worked every day with his friend and then, when Nikolai was sixteen, Ivan said, "I have enough money. I'm going to St. Petersburg to join Lenin. Come with me."

Nikolai did. It was 1910. He dared not say good-bye to his family. It was critical that they could truthfully say they did not know what had happened to him. By the time he returned to Ya- novichi they were all dead. . . . But that was many years later.

In St. Petersburg Lenin was pleased with the young man. His quick intelligence and physical brawn were put to use. He was six feet four and Lenin suggested he grow a beard to hide his youth. Nikolai joined more experienced men in their efforts to rouse the workers, make them aware that there could be a better life. He was instructed how to organize strikes. Nothing frightened the young man. Nothing could be worse than the life he had been born into. As he strode through the coal mining towns, through the cities where factories belched smoke into the air and a gray film covered everything, as he urged loggers to refuse to break the log jams unless their lot in life improved, as he sat in cold, dark rooms with his hands jammed into his pockets, listening to Lenin and others talk of a new world where human beings would no longer be treated as animals, where no one would starve or freeze to death, he watched and listened and felt his spirit uplifted.

He helped the homeless he saw huddled against buildings, covering themselves with newspapers only to be frozen stiff by morning. He became infected with the idea of salvation, with equality for all peoples. He watched in furious silence when he saw a poor wretch being beaten, when he saw hunger in the eyes of children, when he saw trails of blood left through the snow, remembering his own bloody feet as a child.

One cold afternoon, when he was not quite nineteen years old, Nikolai watched from outside the barbed wire fence as the manager of a boot factory screamed at a line of hunched-over shoulders, exhorting the workers until in some unfathomable rage he grabbed for a whip and, raising it, whistled it through the air onto the backs of three men, slashing their coarse shirts and bringing streaks of blood to the surface. Nikolai heard their cries and saw the manager raise the whip again.

He climbed over the fence, jumping to the ground and reaching out his arm as the manager was ready to lash the men again, two of whom had already fallen to the ground. Nikolai grabbed the whip from the startled manager's hand and, turning it on him, beat him, exulting in the man's cries, listening with joy in his heart to the man's whimpering pleas. But he could not stop. Over and over he felt the whip slash, felt pulp at the end of it, heard bones crush, and not until two workers pulled him away did he realize what he had done. Nikolai Zakarov had killed a man.

Although, or because, his star had been rising in Lenin's firmament, the revolutionary leader called Zakarov to him that night, ordering him to leave Russia. "I have plans for you," said the leader. "I do not want you dead. Go—go to America and stay until the revolution is ready for you. I need you in the future and will not let you be killed or sent to Siberia. You are too valuable. I will send for you when it is safe."

America? Leave Russia? How, then, could he help in the revolution?

"Learn all you can," Lenin ordered. "Study English. Study the American idea of egalitarianism. Become part of the American workers."

Nikolai stared at the man he so revered, his mouth open in

dismay—in amazement and puzzlement. How could he do that? How could he go to a foreign country where he knew none of the language and study it? How would he live? Where should he go?

He went to Detroit, where he found a room in a dingy boardinghouse that he thought the most luxurious room he'd ever slept in. There was an indoor bathroom on the same floor, just two doors away, and brilliant light bulbs overhead and in the lamp next to his bed. His bed was changed each week and he marveled at the clean sheets. He had his own towels. Breakfast came with the rent. He roamed the streets, wondering how to find work, until he discovered a Russian teahouse, which was not really a teahouse at all but a small restaurant and gathering place on a corner near a factory. They served hearty borscht and the heavy brown bread Nikolai loved so well for lunch, and American beer and Russian vodka in the evening. Here he met other Russians, ones who had jobs in the factory, who told him how good life was in America, who invited him to their three-room apartments for dinner and who spoke of him to the Irishman, Mr. O'Toole, who ran the union.

O'Toole sent word that he'd see Nikolai. After lunch one day, Dmitri Yostakovich took him to the plant and to the little shack where Mr. O'Toole headquartered. Dmitri waited with him.

The broad-shouldered Irishman looked at Nikolai, pushing back his chair until it teetered on its two back legs and Nikolai thought it would fall over. The union boss said something that Dmitri translated. "Hold out your hands. He wants to see them."

Nikolai did, his big hands shooting out from the too-short sleeves. O'Toole kept looking at him but speaking to Dmitri, who answered in English.

"He wants to know if you understand English. I tell him no, you just got here, but are eager to learn. I tell him you want to be American. On our shift is Russian boss. Most all of us are Russians or Latvians. We all belong union. He likes because we all hard workers. Never cause trouble."

O'Toole said something again, which Dmitri translated. "He say you come work tomorrow. He try you."

Nikolai looked directly at O'Toole, who was smiling at him, a blue-eyed wide-open smile. He held out his hand. Nikolai shook it, being careful not to press too hard. He had never shaken hands with a boss before.

Daniel O'Toole was the foreman of the foundry, a wide-shouldered, heavily muscled, cussing, beer-drinking family man who sang tenor like an angel. He became the most important American in Nikolai's life.

Nikolai Zakarov learned his job quickly and well, studying the men with whom he worked, looking around him all the time. When he'd been there a month, O'Toole grabbed Dmitri out of the production line and walked him over to Nikolai.

Dmitri tapped Nikolai's shoulder. "He ask if you learn English yet. You study?"

Nikolai did not know how to read Russian, much less know how to go about studying English. He shook his head, wondering if O'Toole was going to fire him.

He and Dmitri conversed some more before O'Toole wrote something out on a scrap of paper and, turning on his heel, left.

Dmitri handed the penciled paper to Nikolai and said, "Mr. O'Toole say his daughter is English teacher. You go to his house for Sunday dinner after church and he have daughter teach you English."

Nikolai studied the paper. He had no idea what it said. It was O'Toole's address. On Thursday Nikolai found someone who walked with him and pointed the house out to him. Nikolai was astonished that a factory worker could live in a house like that. It must have at least five rooms, maybe six, and there was a front porch to it, and behind it a carriage house or garage. The plot of ground on which it stood was not large, but flowers grew along the front pavement and in pots on the porch. He walked there the next night alone, to make sure he could find it. On Saturday he tested himself again to make sure he would not get lost or be late. He didn't know when "after church" was, so he arrived at ten o'clock and stayed down the block until he saw the family arrive home from what he guessed might be church, and then he waited another half hour.

Nikolai sat silent around the O'Toole's dinner table, where more food was piled than he'd ever seen in one place. There was ham with boiled potatoes and string beans, homemade applesauce and cole slaw, freshly baked Parker House rolls with sweet butter and homemade jams. For dessert there was a large slab of apple pie topped with a wedge of sharp cheddar and on top of that homemade vanilla ice cream, something Nikolai had never tasted. It was the best meal he'd ever eaten.

After the table had been cleared and he could hear Mrs. O'Toole washing dishes in the kitchen, O'Toole motioned for Nikolai to stay seated, and drew out a book, beckoning to his daughter, Paula. She came and sat opposite Nikolai. He couldn't tell whether or not she was afraid of him, so timid was she.

It was on that afternoon in April, when the days were lengthening and there was the hint of spring in the air and the first tulips were poking above the still-cool earth that Nikolai's American education began. He remembered the first word he learned. It was *hand*. Paula pointed to her own hand and said the word. Then she pointed to his and he stared at her blankly. She reached out and took his hand and pointed to it and repeated the word. He grinned like a young boy in kindergarten, repeating it aloud. "Hand."

He was also thinking what a warm, small hand she had, as the smell of spring came in through the window on the slightly billowing curtain. A feeling of well-being surged through him as he realized O'Toole was extending the hand of friendship to him.

By June, Nikolai understood sufficient English that he could say a few words of it, though he understood more than he could speak. He understood enough that he could laugh with his coworkers. He drank beer after work with the other Russians and sometimes with O'Toole and his friends. They could hardly believe he had never played baseball, so on Saturday afternoons, when they got together after work, they invited Nikolai to the park with them and showed him how the game was played.

Paula was an excellent and patient teacher, and as the heat of the Detroit summer advanced, she suggested they go canoeing on the lake in the park. She showed him how to paddle, laughing when he stood up and fell over the side, his feet stuck in the muddy bottom.

He was twenty years old and then twenty-one, and it was a long time since he'd had a woman. He received a promotion at the factory, having nothing to do with O'Toole, who told him he was a good worker and sat around drinking beer with him, discussing unions and their future. Here Nikolai learned of the American workingman. O'Toole and his friends thought they still had a long way to go. Nikolai thought they had come a long way. He would be satisfied if his country's revolution resulted in this for the workingman.

Nikolai liked O'Toole and appreciated his Sunday dinners at the O'Tooles, which became part of the rhythm of his life. With Daniel O'Toole and his fellow workers at the foundry Nikolai felt a camaraderie such as he'd never known. He loved playing baseball and being a part of something so friendly. He enjoyed his job, which required no mental energy, and he liked the physical exhaustion that followed a hard day's work. Compared to the work he'd done in Russia, this was easy. Then he would take a bath, something he had seldom been able to do in Russia, and slick his unruly wiry hair down as best he could, put on clean clothes, and either go out to the bar, where he basked in the warmth of newfound friendships, or walk around the streets of Detroit or go to the O'Tooles' three nights a week for his lessons with Paula.

Her soft voice caressed him, and when he looked at her she met his glance steadily and smiled with increasing assurance. Soon they were swimming at the lake and, later, walking along the lakeshore admiring the autumn colors. That winter, he learned to ice skate and guessed he'd never known what laughter meant before he met the O'Tooles and his other new friends. But it was Paula mostly. She was shy, and he watched her unfold like a flower. He felt stirrings of desire for this quiet, rather colorless girl who seemed to become more vibrant each time he saw her.

He remembered still their first kiss. It was over a year after they'd met, over a year since their English lessons had begun, and she reached out to him, putting her fingers on his wrist and said, "Your English has hardly any Russian accent." While she smiled at him he put his large hand over hers and they sat staring across the table at each other until he pulled her to him, until his lips met hers and he could tell she had never been kissed, could tell she was not quite sure what to do. He held her in his arms, melting her lips until they responded to him. He heard her little soft moans and wanted her as he'd never wanted the few girls he'd had as a youth.

The next day he asked Daniel if he could marry his daughter and that generous man put a hand on Nikolai's arm, his eyes genial and shining, and said, "I've been hoping for this all along. I'd be proud to have you for a son, to have you be the father of my grandchildren."

And that's what he became. Within two and a half years Nikolai and Paula had two children. Nikolai was rising not only in the company but in the union. He still spent his evenings with his father-in-law learning all he could, not only about the union but about the men in it, and about the American way of life. Paula, while she didn't whine, gave him reproachful looks when he came home late, beer-breathed.

She thought that after Michael was born, Nikolai would stay

home more, but that was not a way of life Nikolai understood. He found far more challenge and excitement in the company of the men with whom he worked. Paula was for bedtimes, for tenderness, and he did feel for her a gentleness he had not known was within him.

His English, within four years, was so proficient that he was reading books, devouring one after another of what Paula told him were the classics. He would read them in bed, after Paula had fallen asleep. It was in this way, through English, that he was introduced to Tolstoy and Dostoevski and Chekhov.

He then decided he should learn to read and write his native language. He enrolled in an English language class for Russian immigrants and studied in reverse. He laboriously learned his mother tongue, writing it and trying to read it, though he could not do that nearly as well as he read English.

He knew what Paula wanted, but he was not willing to give her as much of his time as she desired. As a way to keep him home, she began to teach him arithmetic, and he became fascinated. Afterward, whether to show his pleasure or because they had done something together, they made love, always on Tuesday nights. There was some fragility about Paula that brought out affection in him. He wanted to please her. The few times he had had girls in Russia, they had been there for the taking and he had taken them, with no thought to their pleasure, with no real desire for them as individuals, but just because he felt the need for a woman. With Paula it was different.

He knew he did not love Paula as Americans thought of love. He knew that because she kept asking him, "Do you love me?" He had never thought of love before. He loved Russia, he knew that. And loved his vision of equality the world over. He thought perhaps he loved Daniel O'Toole. Sometimes, too, he loved this wonderful country from which he was waiting to be recalled. He never thought of America as his. He knew it was a resting place. He knew, even after America's involvement in the war and when the Russian Revolution began, that he was waiting. Never for a moment did he imagine spending his life in America.

He had told Paula that before they married. But he could tell she never believed him. She'd shake her head and smile as if to say yes, that's what you think now. But wait. Wait until you've been here awhile, until you have American sons and an American wife and a good American job. No one leaves the good life of America to go back to the old country. They come to America to escape those conditions. You'll see. You're becoming more and more American each day.

Even Daniel spoke against "the damn Bolsheviks." Hardly any Americans were sympathetic with communism. Even the laborers didn't trust the Communists, the "Reds." Daniel said over and over, "Thank God you're not one of them Commies. Glad you got out when you did." Nikolai couldn't bring himself to tell the O'Tooles otherwise.

But the day came—his sons Paul and Mikey were four and five—when a stranger knocked on the door of the house that never ceased to amaze Nikolai. Five rooms, with central heating and an indoor bathroom and electric lights. The stranger—Nikolai never even remembered what he looked like—asked, "Nikolai Zakarov?"

Americans, in their free and easy informality, called him Nick Zakaroff, so he knew that this man was from Russia. He nodded. The man handed him a long white envelope, soiled but intact. Then he turned his back to Nikolai and disappeared into the night. It was August 1918.

Nikolai turned the envelope over in his hands and heard Paula call out, "What is it?"

He turned to look at the lamplight shining on her pale brown hair, at the socks she was mending in her lap, at the little basket in which she kept her darning, and he thought, this is the end of this life. He tore the envelope open.

"Come back," he read in Russian, "to Moscow. I need you. Russia needs you." The scrawled signature read "Lenin."

He looked at his wife across the room and told her, said that she should pack, that they were all going to Russia.

Paula's hand flew to her throat and she dropped the basket with the darning egg and her needles and thread, but the gray sock stuck to her skirt.

"No," she said in a strangled voice. "We're Americans. The boys and I are Americans."

"And I," he said, "am Russian. I am going home."

"Can you leave us, the boys and me?" At that moment he felt a part of all mankind, a part of the great equality he dreamed of for everyone, for men the world over and for men and women together.

He didn't want to hurt her, this daughter of his great and good friend, the mother of his sons. He walked across the room and knelt beside her, taking her face in his hands, saying, "I am going back.

I would like you to come too," and he knew if he made love to her, if he showed her how much he cared and wanted her, she would come too. But even as he did so, he knew it didn't matter at all whether she came or not. The person he would miss most was his father-in-law, who threw a temper tantrum when Nikolai told him the news.

Paula did not accompany him. Her father insisted that if Nikolai could not be dissuaded from this insane step, then he should return to Russia and see what it had become in the eight years he had been gone. If it was suitable for Paula and the boys, he, Daniel, would pay their passage, much as he hated the whole idea. He did, however, believe in the sanctity of marriage.

Nikolai did not send for Paula in the next two years. Lenin, who had always been fond of the young man, sent him to a Prussian military academy. It was there that his ability for organization became evident.

Then Nikolai returned to Detroit for Paula and the children. But Paula never adjusted to the lack of central heating, to the smell of cabbage that always permeated their three cement-block rooms in one of the newer apartment houses. Nikolai tried to explain to her how lucky they were to have three rooms for the four of them, but Paula wasn't convinced.

She couldn't, or wouldn't, learn Russian. She said it was an impossible language to learn and isolated herself, unable to communicate with her neighbors. Her sons, sent to school, learned Russian immediately and even in the apartment talked to each other in the language of their schoolmates and their father. Paula became more and more isolated, particularly after Nikolai was sent to England as a strike agitator during the British coal miners' strike.

Here he was arrested and sent to prison in Scotland for six months, while Paula, frenzied, wondered where he was and how to cope with life in a country whose language she couldn't speak. Nikolai did not resent one moment of his prison experience. He used it for learning. He never doubted he would be released, for he already knew that Western justice was different from that of Russia.

When he was released he was deported with the proviso that he would never again set foot on British soil. By the time he returned to Moscow, Paula had become a total recluse, even sending the children out to purchase food. He looked at her, her hair bedraggled, her face thin and pale, and was disgusted with what had originally appealed to him. She begged him to return to Detroit.

But Lenin asked him to go to China. China was in chaos. It had never, in its thousands of years of history, had an organized army. Western powers had turned down Dr. Sun Yat-sen's pleas for help, and this created Russia's opportunity to spread its form of democracy in the most populated country on earth.

Nikolai's orders were to assist Dr. Sun in whatever way necessary, set up a military academy outside Canton, where Dr. Sun resided, and unify the workers of China.

Nikolai Zakarov was thirty years old and realized this was where all his life had been heading. There would be no one in all of China to tell him what to do. He would be given the chance to try to accomplish single-handedly what it had taken the whole Russian Revolution to do.

He looked at Paula and knew the answer before he asked. Would not she and the boys come to China with him? And so he sent them back to Detroit.

It would be his job to turn the confused Kuomintang into an organized political party, one of his discipline and vision. He was to free the Chinese from warlords so that the KMT would be the guiding force behind a mass movement so powerful that it would change China forever. Zakarov's job was not to make Communists of the Chinese so much as to instill the Kuomintang with Communist goals and ideals. As soon as he founded a military academy, Russian army advisers and experts would follow, with the military hardware necessary. Nikolai could hardly contain his sense of mission as he traveled on the Trans-Siberian Railroad for eight days and nights. He exulted in the role he was to play in history, of helping to foster brotherhood among all men.

# CHAPTER 11

Chlöe had lain in bed for the longest time, unable to sleep. She groped in the dark for the flashlight and aimed it at her wristwatch. Only one-thirty. She could have sworn she'd been lying there much longer than that. Maybe it was sleeping alone. No body next to her. No Slade.

But she knew that wasn't the only thing keeping her awake. It was Nikolai Zakarov, for one thing. Larger than life. Like no one she'd ever met before. He had the charismatic leadership qualities she thought Dr. Sun lacked. But a Russian would never be permitted to lead China. She wondered if Nikolai, and even Madame Sun, sensed that if Dr. Sun became president, he couldn't govern competently without his Russian.

Chlöe had been sorely disappointed with Dr. Sun. His wife and Nikolai had far more effective personalities. Certainly Ching-ling, fragile and feminine as she seemed, was made of steel. She wondered what Ching-ling had ever seen in this old man to attract her. Of course, Ching-ling had known Dr. Sun as her father's best friend all her life. He'd been twenty-six when she was born. Probably her godfather, Chlöe thought. When Ching-ling was young, perhaps Sun Yat-sen had had the fire and the energy that ignited the little girl. Perhaps she had carried his vision of what China could be to America with her and could not separate the dream from the man.

To Chlöe, Dr. Sun seemed worn out and always complaining of aches and agues. She suspected he'd had dreams of glory for more than thirty years but no knowledge of how to carry them out. Perhaps he was a prophet more than a man of action. But he wanted to be the latter, and that Chlöe saw as his fatal flaw. She admired that he dared to dream beyond himself, that he was filled with hope and optimism for the future of nearly half a billion people. But it was obvious he really had no idea how to accomplish these visions. His mercurial temperament kept everyone off balance, everyone but his wife, it seemed.

At the dinner table, while Ching-ling and Nikolai had debated the merits of who should be appointed commander of the Whampoa Military Academy, which Nikolai had founded the previous year, Dr. Sun said little, concentrating on his food, and staring at it more than participating in any discussion. Nikolai said care must be taken with the appointment of a commandant; he must be not only a capable military man but share their vision of the future. He suggested Chiang Kai-shek, who had spent several months in Moscow the previous year, observing military operations there.

Ching-ling had shrugged her pretty shoulders and in her soft voice said that she did not trust him. She didn't know why. "Perhaps it seems that he's more dedicated to his own aggrandizement than to helping China."

"Well," Nikolai said, raising his rice bowl to his mouth in the Chinese fashion, "isn't that true of all of us? Don't we each have our own agendas?"

Chlöe, before even thinking, asked, "Don't you care about China? Isn't that your primary goal?"

Nikolai, looking at Ching-ling, answered, "What I dedicate my life to is worldwide equality for all peoples, all men and," now he turned and smiled at Chlöe, "all women."

"I suspect," said Ching-ling, her slender fingers tapering around the stem of her wineglass, "that this is a way station for Nikolai. When China achieves its goals, then he can go on to the next country. But for now we share the same dream. Dr. Sun's and my limits are the boundaries of China."

Dr. Sun didn't even seem to be listening, he was toying with his chicken te-chow.

Suddenly Dr. Sun spoke, almost as though he were musing to himself. "Chiang's had military training and he has vision."

Nikolai looked over at him. The older man had gone back to his chicken.

"There are even those in Canton who do not desire unification," Ching-ling explained to Chlöe. "Warlords are afraid they will no longer have power. And that is true. Once we," Chlöe noticed the accent on the *we*, "are in power, they will no longer be able to do that. Peasants will rise and it will be the people who have the power."

"What will be done to warlords or people who defy you?" Chlöe asked.

"They will be converted or exterminated." There had not been even a moment's hesitation.

Later Chlöe couldn't remember who had said that. Whether it was a man's or a woman's voice.

"Chinese justice is swift and Chinese—according to American standards—are cruel," admitted Ching-ling. "It is the way of the Orient."

Nikolai looked at Chlöe then and said, "This is not America. Your country is violent too, but in different ways. More hidden ways, though you and the other Western powers look the other way at your own cruelty and arrogance here in the East." He hesitated a moment. "China has lived with cruelty all its existence."

"And Russia?" Chlöe asked.

Nikolai wiped his mustache with a napkin. "Let us say that I understand and am sympathetic to much in China. *You*, on the other hand, can understand little about either of our countries."

Assuredly not the cruelty, Chlöe had thought. Nor the dirt or poverty.

Her reliving of the dinner conversations was broken by the sound of shots. Chlöe sat bolt upright in bed. In the distance she heard shouting. More sharp, staccato bursts. Maybe it's firecrackers, she thought. Firecrackers reverberated at the oddest of hours in China.

Then she heard the hollow echoes of footsteps in the tiled hallway, muffled voices. The door to her room was thrown open. Silhouetted against the dim hall light was Ching-ling.

"Get dressed," she said, her voice imperious.

Chlöe's feet hit the cold floor. "What's wrong?" she asked.

"Ch'en's troops are marching on us." Chlöe remembered he was the warlord of Canton, the same one she'd beaten with her parasol. "Hurry. Come to my room." And she disappeared.

Chlöe grabbed the clothes she had thrown on a chair. Reaching Ching-ling's room, Chlöe saw her dressed in men's trousers and wished she had some. Ching-ling seemed to have grown at least a foot in height and stood ramrod straight. Her voice held no trace of fear.

Her husband was next to her and Chlöe heard her saying, "A woman will just impede you. It will be most inconvenient for you to have to worry about me."

He didn't seem to hear her. "We must leave immediately for the gunboat in the river," he said. "From there we can direct our men in resisting the rebels."

Madame Sun put a hand on her husband's arm. "Listen," she said. "I can't believe there can be much danger for me as a private person. Leave me behind. I will find my own way to the gunboat. But you are the salvation of China. You must escape. Take the guards and get out of here immediately. It is you they want. Not me."

He nodded his head. "All right. I will go. But I will leave all fifty of the bodyguard to protect you and the house."

"I will meet you at the gunboat," she said. He turned on his heel and left, nearly knocking Chlöe over. He said nothing to her, however.

Once he had gone, Chlöe saw Ching-ling twisting a handkerchief in her hands. She walked over to the window and opened it.

The Suns' house was halfway up a hill. Chlöe had thought one particular feature of it most strange. There was a walkway extending from the rooftop of their home across the quarter-mile-wide boulevard it faced. This walkway was a narrow bridge connecting the great house with the square gray stone building on the opposite side of the busy thoroughfare. In that building, surrounded by a courtyard and high walls, Dr. Sun had his offices. Thus, he did not have to confront either the crowds or the delays of busy traffic but could walk through the passageway to and from work.

From the open window, Chlöe could see the enemy firing downhill, and she could hear voices, faint from this distance, shouting, "Kill Sun. Kill Sun Yat-sen!" There was no returning gunfire, just rifles pointed silently into the night. On the ground below, as her eyes became accustomed to the darkness, Chlöe made out the crouched bodies of guards clasping rifles, bodies that did not move.

Ching-ling reached out and took Chlöe's hand. They stood there together, staring out into the now-silent darkness. All night long, sometimes with half an hour in between, rifle shots echoed into the night.

Shortly before dawn the door to Ching-ling's room burst open and Nikolai appeared. He held a pistol in his hand and his face was dark as storm clouds. "Where is the doctor?" he asked.

"He's gone," answered Ching-ling. "Hours ago. I haven't heard much gunfire, so I think perhaps he is safe."

"You've got to leave," the Russian said as he looked at Ching-ling, his glance barely grazing Chlöe. "I've come to take you away from here."

At that moment, as a red line against the dark sky presaged the light of day, fire from field guns burst from the enemy and cries from some of the bodyguard could be heard. Nikolai reached out and grabbed Chlöe in one arm and Ching-ling in the other, crashing them all to the floor. Shards of broken glass scattered over them as bullets raced along the windows.

Nikolai's arm was still thrown over Chlöe, forcing her to keep in her prone position.

"Why did you stay?" he whispered, his voice angry.

"Ching-ling convinced Dr. Sun that a woman would only hinder his escape."

"True," he muttered, "but damn her."

Louder, to Ching-ling this time, he said, "We've got to get out of here. You know as well as I what they'll do to you if they capture you."

Fear coursed down Chlöe's side, raising gooseflesh on her arm and along her left leg. She heard rifle fire and the rat-tat-tat of machine guns.

"Stay here," Nikolai ordered. "Let me reconnoiter and decide what is our best path." He crawled three or four paces before he stood, out of the range of gunfire.

In twenty minutes he returned, shoving a pistol at Madame Sun. "Here, I know you know how to shoot. Keep this." He looked at Chlöe but did not offer her a gun. "At least a third of our men are dead," he reported. "The rest are resisting with great determination. Our store of ammunition is running low and I want to keep that until the last minute."

"Yes," said Ching-ling, "there's no sense in remaining now." She looked to Nikolai for direction. Suddenly Chlöe realized that all night long Ching-ling had expected to die, and it had not mattered as long as Dr. Sun and the future of China escaped.

"The only hope for running for it is through the passageway, and their soldiers may be waiting at the end of that. But we'll have to chance it." Glancing at Chlöe, he asked Ching-ling, "Can you find her some pants?"

Ching-ling disappeared into the hallway, returning with loose-fitting, very wrinkled trousers and straw sandals, which she handed to Chlöe. "These might fit you," she said.

Nikolai said, "Ching-ling, I'm sorry. You can bring nothing with you." He closed the door, giving Chlöe the privacy to change. She heard their voices in the hallway.

"She'll just be in our way," he said.

"I know." Madame Sun sighed. "I know. But we must try to take her."

When Chlöe had changed her clothes, she followed Ching-ling and Nikolai up a narrow stairway to the rooftop, where the outdoor passageway loomed dark against the skyline. It was protected on both sides by solid rails, through which they could not even see. Nikolai—leading them—knelt, indicating that they should do the same. "Do not let even a hair of your head show," he whispered, beginning to crawl. But he was so tall that unless he had lain on the tiles and inched his way across, something of him inevitably showed. Before too long some of the enemy noticed motion on the bridge and began firing. Bullets whistled above them, but those that crashed into the rails protecting them were deflected and only their pounding was heard. Nikolai lay flat and began to inch along so that for a long time no sign of life was visible from the bridge. Gradually the gunfire ceased. Chlöe found herself breathing hard as she crawled along.

They heard shouting and rapid shots and someone cried out in pain, or was it death? Though it was not hot this early in the morning, Chlöe felt perspiration roll down her forehead, the salt stinging her eyes. She wondered if her knees were bloody from crawling along the hard tiles.

Once, she laughed, and Madame Sun twisted her head around to look at Chlöe, a question in her eyes. The idea of always having wanted a life different from that which Oneonta offered flitted through her mind, and she couldn't imagine anything more different than what she was experiencing. Just then Nikolai halted and Madame Sun butted into him while Chlöe slammed into Ching-ling. Without speaking, Nikolai pointed. Ahead of them, on the right, the rails had been smashed and there was no protection for perhaps six feet. They would be exposed to anyone below, anyone on the hill beyond, and anyone with guns.

The passageway was too narrow for Nikolai to turn around and talk to them. Chlöe could not hear what he was whispering to Ching-ling, but Ching-ling—in turn—twisted her head to tell Chlöe, "We shall have to make a run for it. They don't know how many of us there are. Nikolai will have to make a break for it, and if they see him, they'll concentrate on following him with gunfire, but they'll wait to see if someone follows. I am to wait fifteen minutes and then run. Then you will wait ten minutes."

She stretched out in the passageway, lying down, taking the weight off her knees, resting on her elbows, watching the hulk of Nikolai Zakarov slowly rise from its prone position and, crouching on the balls of his feet, sprint forward so that all Chlöe saw was a blur. She heard the sharp reports of guns, heard bullets whizzing, and saw the blot that Nikolai's racing body became. Ahead of them in the passage he kept running until, like a puppy, he abruptly stopped, lying down with his feet spread out behind him, not moving.

The gunfire spread out, randomly battering the wall along the way they had come, trying to penetrate the wall ahead, where the enemy knew someone had run, where Nikolai now lay.

Silence.

Ching-ling did not once turn around. When fifteen minutes were up, Chlöe saw her friend gather herself into a ball, hurtling out of hiding, rolling herself across the expanse where the side of the bridge had been demolished. Erratic, scattered gunfire.

The tiny figure of Madame Sun twirled around on the other side of the bridge, waving at Chlöe. Bullets began to shower against the walls of the passageway, machine-gun gunfire spattering above where Nikolai and Madame Sun now lay. Chlöe saw them, inch by inch, begin to move farther away, though they remained within sight of her. Sporadic shooting continued, and Chlöe knew she would have to make a dash for it. Then she saw Ching-ling crawling back toward her, saw her mouth moving, and strained to hear what she was saying. In a low voice, low enough for Chlöe to hear but not loud enough to sift to the ground, Ching-ling called, "Nikolai is going to move ahead and stand up. The enemy will then aim their fire at him. When you hear the gunfire, rush. They will be concentrating on him and not this empty space."

Before Chlöe could reply, Madame Sun crawled away, back toward Nikolai. In a moment she heard bullets whistling through the air, heard a barrage of gunfire aimed ahead of her. She hurled herself, trying to keep her knees bent so that once she reached the protected end, their shots could not hurt her. She wondered if Nikolai was dead. But Ching-ling, far ahead, was crawling rapidly. On hands and knees they inched across space to the back garden of the building where ordinarily Dr. Sun went to work.

As she jumped into Nikolai's waiting arms, Chlöe saw Madame Sun standing beneath a peach tree, wiping streaks of dirt from her face. Bombs sounded behind them. Nikolai planted her on the ground.

"Look at you!" Ching-ling cried to Nikolai. Blood had begun to seep through his jacket, staining the shoulder in an ever-widening circle. He looked down at it and rubbed his shoulder, wincing.

Another six inches and he'd have died trying to save me, thought Chlöe, wanting to reach out to touch him, wanting to take his jacket off and cleanse his wound even though she had no idea how to do it. But Ching-ling did. She led them down the stairs, to a Western-style bedroom, where she made him sit on the bed. Chlöe stood in the doorway as Madame Sun helped Nikolai take off his jacket, being careful not to let the already congealing blood stick to the fabric and rip the wound open even more.

"Ah," said Ching-ling, "it only grazed you. The bullet's not there, thank goodness. Chlöe, run downstairs and see if there's someone there to boil water. Bring some, and clean rags. I want to wash this wound before it becomes infected. See if there's some alcohol in the house too."

Chlöe took off, rushing down the stairs, having no idea where she was going or if there were servants in the building. But there was a dark kitchen in the rear, and a manservant poured boiled water into a thermos.

Chlöe stood by and watched Ching-ling cleanse the wound as a volley of machine-gun fire burst forth. The sound of breaking glass shattered the air. Someone screamed from below. Madame Sun, still kneeling next to Nikolai, ordered Chlöe, "Get down on the floor."

She continued bandaging Nikolai's wound, having stanched the flow of blood. They were in a small back room, facing a high wall where no bullets could enter. When Nikolai tried to rise from the bed, Ching-ling pressed a finger against his chest and commanded, "There's nothing you can do right now. And you've lost a bit of blood. Just stay right there."

The gunfire across the boulevard did not stop until four in the afternoon. Nikolai slept, and Ching-ling, grabbing Chlöe's arm, crept along the hallway to the back stairs. In the kitchen, now empty of servants except one who lay crumpled in a pool of blood, a hole in his left temple, Ching-ling, who didn't even stop to observe the dead man, said, "Tea and something to eat. We must not let our energy sag."

As they climbed up the stairs to the back bedroom, the house shook as though in an earthquake. The walls trembled, the heavens crashed in on them, white plaster sifted down from the ceiling, showering them. And the kitchen behind them collapsed under a fusillade of gunfire. Not once looking back, Ching-ling continued down the hall, never dropping the tray or spilling the tea she was carrying.

# CHAPTER 12

At twilight, as Nikolai awakened from his druglike sleep, the gunfire ceased and was replaced by the rumbling sound of thunder. With it came the chanting of hundreds of voices.

"They're battering down the gate," Ching-ling said. "Nikki, I want you to get Chlöe out of here. They want me, not either of you. Me and Dr. Sun.''

Nikolai nodded. "All right. But let's have none of that nonsense. We're all going together. Any men's clothes around here?'' he asked. "I mean, you're fine in those pants, but anything like topcoats, raincoats, that sort of thing, hats?''

Ching-ling jumped up and ran to another room, returning in a moment with a man's military cap on her head, her hair caught up under it. On top of her blue peasant outfit was a raincoat. Nikolai and Chlöe couldn't help laughing. They were both far too large for her.

Nikolai got up and walked out of the bedroom, down the hall and across it to the front of the building. He stood looking out, in that dim light, at the huge gates that quivered against the buttresses battering it from the other side. He rubbed his bearded chin and ran his fingers back and forth across his mustache. Turning to the women, he said, "When those gates break, there's going to be a rush of people running in to attack this place. They'll be searching for us and anyone else in the house. Whoever's in here won't stand a chance. Tell you what we'll do. We'll wait down there, right beside the gates, so close to the mob they won't even see us as they rush in. They won't be expecting us there. They'll rush blindly toward the house. We'll pretend we're part of the crowd, but we'll head in the opposite direction.''

He walked back to the bedroom and picked up his revolver which lay on the bed. His eyes met Ching-ling's, and she nodded her head.

Leading them out of the room and down the hallway, she moved like a graceful figurine, despite her ludicrous costume. At the doorway, Nikolai turned to Chlöe. "If we do become separated, get to Sha Mien Island, and the consul will take care of you. You're an American; you should be safe.''

Ching-ling was ahead of them, and Nikolai called, against the shouting and noise beyond the gates, "Get over there to the right so when they bash them down you won't get stomped.'' The high wooden gates swelled rhythmically and, with each push from beyond, they could hear the hinges creaking loose and wood splintering. A thousand voices were on the other side.

With a deafening roar the wide gates crashed down. Warriors with drawn bayonets rushed over the cracking doors. Chaos reigned. The disorganized mob shouted obscenities. Nikolai grabbed Ching-ling's hand, glanced around at Chlöe, and broke through the thinning throng. As the enemy troops rushed by, the trio picked their way through the savage masses, finding themselves eventually in a small lane, far from the marauders but not beyond their battle cries. Sporadic rifle fire filled the air, but now they were far enough away that it sounded like echoes.

Chlöe stumbled, seeing that what had broken her fall was a corpse. Its chest was caved in, the arms slashed, and its legs severed. Nikolai turned to look back, motioning to Ching-ling to wait.

From down an alley ran a group of soldiers, bayonets drawn. "Lie flat," Nikolai ordered, and motioned Ching-ling down. "Let them think we're dead, just other bodies." He threw an arm across Chlöe's back, and her face sank into the body beneath her. The soldiers ran on, shouting. Nikolai grabbed her arm, and she felt his arms under her, picking her up, forcing her to stand, jarring her into movement.

"Don't look at the bodies," she heard him say. "Just look straight ahead." He did not slow down for either of the women but kept up a fast pace until they had left the city, until they were out in the country and even he could not see the road, if there was one. He did, however, see the light from the farmhouse.

He didn't knock on the door but burst in, a big, dirty man with two bedraggled women, one a foreign devil. The elderly couple gasped and the woman's hand went to her mouth. The old man reached for a pitchfork and aimed it at Nikolai.

"We need help," said Ching-ling.

"Out," the man whined. "Out."

With that, Ching-ling fell on the floor in a dead faint.

The old woman ignored her husband and rushed forward, kneeling down at the same moment Chlöe did, next to Madame Sun. Part of Chlöe heard Nikolai explaining, in his elementary Chinese, that they meant no harm, that they were running from soldiers. The old man listened to Nikolai, his eyes skeptical as he lowered the pitchfork.

The old woman turned to him and rattled off something Chlöe did not understand. She did not know the Cantonese dialect.

The old man looked at his wife and trundled off to a dark corner of the room, where Chlöe heard him pouring water. He returned with a clay pot, which the old woman took, splashing the contents over Ching-ling's face.

Shaking her head much as a wet puppy would, Ching-ling

moaned slightly and forced her eyes open. When she saw Chlöe, her hand reached out and Chlöe grabbed it, trying to smile reassurance. Nikolai loomed over them, staring down with great concern.

"Oh, thank God," he said, which Chlöe thought funny coming from a Communist. He scrunched down beside them, reaching out for Ching-ling's wrist and feeling her pulse. "Are you all right?"

Ching-ling, holding on to Chlöe's hand, pulled herself to a sitting position. "I don't know what came over me," she said, her voice faint. "Of course I'm all right." She looked around and said, "We can't jeopardize these people, Nikki. We must get out of here. They could be shot if we're found here."

Still sitting on the hard-packed mud floor, Ching-ling turned to the old woman and asked, "Do you have any clothes I can buy? Old clothes? We need different clothes." From the pocket of her pants she pulled out a gold coin that glowed in the lamplight.

The old man reached for it and put it between his teeth. He made a sound as though of wonder.

They left a half hour later, after the old woman had boiled them some tea and exchanged clothes with Ching-ling, who wore a scarf over her head and carried a basket in which the old woman had put a few vegetables. The old man had given Chlöe a conical hat like the ones coolies wore.

The suction her bloody feet caused as they sloshed through the fields made great gasping sobs, and the mud gurgling through her toes felt warm and squishy. They were paralleling the river, heading south of the city. In the distance they could still hear gunfire. Three great booms, louder than any of the other noises, the sound of cannon.

"Ah." Ching-ling's arms reached straight up in the air in a gesture of exultation. "That means Dr. Sun has reached the gunboat and is safe."

She said something to Nikolai that Chlöe could not hear. They changed direction, heading back toward the city, still slightly south of it. Heading now toward the great river that had brought so many foreigners into China over the last century, the Pearl River, from whence Great Britain had gained its toehold—stranglehold, Ching-ling had called it—on China and started importing opium, introducing it to the Chinese in order to balance their own trade. The artery from Hong Kong to all of southern China. The river responsible for the subjugation of Cathay by foreign powers.

Behind them, to the east, a pink line began to trace itself across the horizon. They kept walking through the thick mud until Chlöe thought she could go no farther.

As they approached the city, Ching-ling brushed past Nikolai and began to lead. They entered the already busy streets and mingled, unnoticed, with the early-morning crowds. Finally, Ching-ling stopped in front of a small house and knocked on the door. There was no answer until Nikolai pounded, and then the door opened quickly.

Ching-ling murmured something and took the scarf from her head. The man stared at her blankly and then broke into a grin, gesturing that she should enter. Chlöe couldn't understand a word that was said.

The man, a foundry worker, ordered his wife to prepare breakfast for the hungry travelers. They had not slept in more than thirty hours. But Ching-ling refused to rest. The foundry worker disappeared for two hours. When he returned, they followed him, still in their disguises, down alleys that snaked in coils between mud flats and crumbling brick houses smelling of garbage. This was a part of the city that had not been affected by Ch'en's attack. Here the river was crowded with sampans and junks. An oceangoing steamer was pulled up to the wharf. Coolies, sweating in the late-morning sun, carried enormous packs on their bare backs, bending under their loads, traversing the gangplank. Shouting filled the air. Chlöe had to keep her eyes on Nikolai's huge shoulders and head towering above everyone else in order not to get lost in the crowd. Finally, the foundry worker stopped before a motor launch. He and Ching-ling spoke rapidly as she handed him some coins. Climbing into the launch, she gestured for Chlöe and Nikolai to follow. From the shadows came a man with a wide scar down his face, who looked as though he would as happily behead them as help. The two spoke together and, with nary a nod or smile, the scar-faced man climbed down into the boat and, with a twist of his hand, chugged the motor into life. He looked straight ahead, expertly gauging the distance between junks and sampans, zigzagging among them with apparent ease.

To the south of them Chlöe saw a large gunboat, with its name on the prow. *Yung Feng*, where Dr. Sun would be.

A rope ladder was lowered as they pulled alongside the ship. Ching-ling began to climb. Chlöe was still down the ladder when she heard Ching-ling's cry of, "Husband!" When hands reached out to help Chlöe onto the deck, she saw Ching-ling's arms around her husband, who stood there, smiling, his arms at his side. For just a second it seemed to Chlöe that he had been waiting for the real force of his life to come lend him direction.

They stayed on the gunboat for five days, until Chiang Kai-shek arrived from Shanghai in response to a telegram from Dr. Sun. Chlöe shared cramped quarters with Ching-ling and, since they had no clothing with them, they were forced to remain in the muddy peasant clothes in which they'd escaped the city. The food was terrible and Chlöe wondered if the little flakes of meat in the rice might be dog. She ate very little, existing almost entirely on oranges and peanuts.

As soon as Chiang arrived, Dr. Sun sent Ching-ling and Chlöe up north, with Nikolai to guard them. They went by steamer to Shanghai, and Chlöe was sick all five days they were at sea, seldom leaving her bunk. As soon as they arrived and Nikolai saw Ching-ling safely ensconced in her home on the Rue Molière, he caught the same steamer back to Canton.

Chlöe marveled that only two weeks had passed since Slade had left her in Canton.

# CHAPTER 13

Along with Chiang Kai-shek, Dr. Sun stayed on board the *Yung Feng* for a total of fifty-six days. At night Chiang slipped ashore with armed bodyguards to find food and, reportedly, live entertainment. Dr. Sun wrote to his wife that he and Chiang were both reading Sherlock Holmes stories.

Nikolai Zakarov, who worked in Canton itself, trying to hold together Dr. Sun's army, was disgusted. The Kuomintang soldiers seemed intent on having fun more than anything else. Ch'en's soldiers had burned the Suns' house and all their belongings.

When Chlöe heard the lengths to which Nikolai had been driven to defend all that Dr. Sun had tried to build up, she could not believe it was the same man she knew. Lou Sidney had told her the casualties in Chinese battles—and these were almost always pitched battles of Chinese against Chinese—were heavy and the result of bedlam and disorganization. There was no clear strategy, soldiers focusing more on seeking revenge on their adversaries than on winning battles. Lopping off heads, cutting out tongues, scalping live victims, were more interesting than concentrating on battle tactics. Any battle was played by prearranged, centuries-old rules.

Nikolai introduced modern tactics, well-oiled machines, and guns. The slaughter was so well organized and unexpected by the opposition that the enemy fell by the hundreds. With fewer than five hundred of the well-trained men from the Whampoa Academy, Nikolai fought off thousands.

Southern China was again safe for the republic and its dreams. Through Nikolai's triumph, the world learned that Dr. Sun had asked Russia for help. The State Department in the United States began to assemble a dossier on Dr. Sun and warned the President that he was a dangerous revolutionary in "secret conspiracy with the Bolsheviks." President Coolidge never admitted that he himself had turned a deaf ear to Dr. Sun's plea for help, a fact that would not be known for another sixty-some years. A decision that could have changed the world.

Instead, no one except the Russian, Zakarov, with Soviet-made weapons and Soviet-trained officers, came to Dr. Sun's aid.

Chlöe wrote to her parents, sketchily telling them of her experience, but she didn't give many details, knowing they would only worry about her. To Suzi and Cass, however, she wrote every detail, telling them not only all that happened, of how frightened she'd been, yet also the excitement she'd felt. It wasn't until writing to them that she realized a sense of adventure had predominated over fear. As the words flowed onto the paper and she shared herself with her good friends, she began to discover aspects of herself she had not been aware of. She ended the long letter able to say, "I'm surprised to realize how incredibly lucky I am. I bet no other American woman's had an adventure quite like mine. It makes me feel unique, a part of history, and here I am just twenty-two. It all seems fantastic, don't you think?" It made her feel close to Cass and Suzi, that she could share Ching-ling and Nikolai with them.

Slade, of course, had sent the story in but had never even mentioned her or any details of the escape except to write, "Madame Sun, disguised as a peasant, made a separate escape."

Ching-ling spent the time visiting not only with Chlöe, but with her mother, Mammy Soong, and her younger sister, Mei-ling, who lived together in a house that Mei-ling had urged her mother to buy two weeks after her father's funeral, a house that her father had refused her when he was alive, thinking it was unnecessarily ostentatious. And if Charlie Soong had thought it too ostentatious . . .

"My sister and I do not think at all alike," Ching-ling told Chlöe, who was visiting her for afternoon tea, "despite having been educated in America and being each other's only family for so many years. Mei-ling loves anything American and, indeed, is an American in thought. China depresses her after the United States. She became used to the luxury there and has no desire to live as Chinese do. I think my sister—my sisters—are very self-centered, selfish people. But I know them better than I know anyone else, and I love them even if I don't always like them."

Now that they were back in safety, Chlöe and Ching-ling managed to see each other every day, but it was Slade who was the center of Chlöe's life. He had been panicked, he told her, after thanking Nikolai profusely. "I'm in your debt, old man," he'd said to the big Russian.

He gathered Chlöe to him that first night home, holding her so tightly she could scarcely breathe. "God, I was so worried. Thank heavens you're safe."

He kissed her, and she felt herself alive with yearning at the softness of his mouth, at his tongue running across her lips, but—as usual—his lovemaking was over before it had really begun.

In the nights following her return he did not reach out to her again. Finally she curled next to him in their bed, feathering her fingers down his thighs, loving the feel of him, wanting him. When she did that, he turned to her, whispering, "Jesus Christ, what you do to me," and they met hurriedly before he turned over. Those nights when she lay waiting for him to reach out for her, forcing herself not to be the one to reach out, she longed for him to run a hand down her arm, across her breast, for his lips to search for hers in the darkness . . . and she waited. Until she heard the sound of his even breathing and knew he was asleep.

When he did make love to her nowadays, when he reached for her as though he were lit with hot desire, it was almost always after he'd been drinking—after they'd gone to the races, or to a gala at the Hotel Cathay, or after they'd been entertained at one of the consulates and she'd had her dance card filled before anyone else. That was when she saw him watching her from the sidelines before heading toward the bar. Those nights he reached for her. But always it left her yearning for more.

She found herself, even on land, seasick mornings. She waited until her suspicions were confirmed to tell Slade she was six weeks pregnant. She waited, filled with joyous anticipation, until an evening when they could be alone. She pictured the look in his eyes, the surprise and delight, the love.

"I've wonderful news," she said, walking over to the liquor cabinet, mixing him a drink, pouring mineral water for herself.

His eyebrows were knit together in anger as he stared at the newspaper in his hands.

Her heart stopped. "What's wrong?" she asked, offering him the drink.

"Wrong?" he asked. "Why do you ask that? What could be wrong?"

So filled was she with her own news, she ignored the thunderclouds in his eyes. She leaned over to put her arms around him, kissing his neck and whispering, "I'm pregnant."

The anger left his eyes. "Pregnant?" He reached out for her.

"It must have happened right before we went to Canton," she said, coming into his arms. "Isn't it wonderful?"

He reached for the newspaper he'd tossed on the sofa. "Well, that should fulfill you so you won't have to write any more of these flamboyant stories that Cass seems to have a penchant for printing!"

On the cover of the Sunday section of the *Chicago Times* was a photograph of Ching-ling and a blurb saying "American journalist Chlöe Cavanaugh's firsthand report . . ."

It was the long letter she'd sent Cass and Suzi. She reached for the paper with delight and began to read what she'd written. Seeing her words in print thrilled her.

"American journalist!" he snapped.

She didn't look up from the paper.

"I hope it's a boy," he said.

By the end of her second month of pregnancy, the queasiness disappeared except for an odd hour now and then. In fact, Chlöe felt bursting with energy after the lethargy of July.

Madame Sun now tutored Chlöe on the changes she advocated for her country. "So much about my country is backward and needs to be changed. Pretty soon, I'm afraid that China will populate itself off the face of the earth. Too many women have babies every year, so many of them girls they soon drown, of course. What it does to their bodies, their energies. You've seen Chinese women." Ching-ling's voice could never become sharp but it got an edge to it. "They become old long before their time. Peasant women give birth in the fields and go right on working. It is nothing to have twelve or thirteen children in ten years. Then the wife is discarded. The husband takes a concubine, someone younger, prettier. There is no hope for Chinese women until they have control over their own lives, over their fate. There is no hope for any country until its women are free."

Chlöe sighed. Thank goodness she had never known anything but freedom. She could do whatever she wanted. Suddenly she remembered Cass Monaghan saying, "Just because you're a woman, don't let the world tell you what to do. Do what *you* want."

"What about legalized abortion?" As she asked it, Chlöe had visions of back alleys, dirty fingernails, coat hangers searching for fetuses. She thought of all the unwanted babies, the ones sold into slavery at birth, the ones drowned at birth.

"Of course." Madame Sun arose and began pacing around the living room of her elegant Shanghai home. "If men had to have babies every year, if they could be raped, if they had to spend so much of their lives carrying babies around in their bellies or on their backs, you can certainly believe abortion would become legalized. It is the only way to save women. To permit them to have a choice in what to do with their own bodies, their own destinies."

Chlöe stared at her friend as she pulled on the handkerchief in her hands, her back to Chlöe, staring out the long, narrow window. "And the right to divorce. Now only men can choose to leave their wives. Women should also have that right. They can never"—she turned to face Chlöe—"I mean *never*, ever legally leave their husbands. If a woman runs away from her husband, it is perfectly accepted that she may be shot, that she should be imprisoned from there on in her husband's house, that any rights she may have had should be denied her. Oh, Chlöe, my dear"—Ching-ling walked swiftly across the room and reached out to touch Chlöe's shoulder—"women are chattel with no rights whatsoever in my country." Tears filled her eyes. "I do not think *any* country has treated women as my country has. . . . Footbinding and concubinage too. Barbaric."

Chlöe nodded. Barbaric, indeed.

Madame Sun looked despondent. "You don't even know what I'm talking about, do you? I mean, you do intellectually. You can agree all these practices are indeed evil. But you have no real understanding *here*, do you?" She placed her hand over her heart. "You don't understand, do you, that my whole life is dedicated to equality and democracy for all of us. When my husband brings China into the twentieth century, brings democracy to all of us, all four hundred fifty million Chinese. Then these things will change."

She sat down, as though exhausted, leaning over to take Chlöe's hand in her own. "I want you to understand. To see my country as I do. I want you to understand me and my husband and all of us who *have* to change our world. Come with me tomorrow morning."

"Come where?"

Madame Sun did not elucidate. "Wear comfortable shoes. We shall walk a great deal. You will never feel the same about China again."

In that she was right.

Chlöe thought she had seen China's worst sides. She thought she knew about its cruelty and its irreverence for human life. She thought she had seen its abysses of poverty.

But, as mists still swirled above the sluggish Hwang Pu's waters, as sunrise tinged the still, slate-gray sky, in the time of day when Shanghai was at its most quiet—though never silent—when the roosters crowed and donkeys brayed from all parts of the city, when the clip-clop of horses or the slapping of bare feet on cobblestones heralded the awakening of coolies who were bringing fruits and vegetables and meat into the city, when the streets were nearly empty of business, Ching-ling took Chlöe walking through the quarter where factories lined streets not far from the wharves.

They were big square old brick windowless buildings that smelled of decay. Ching-ling reached out and took hold of Chlöe's hand, leading her down an alley that ran behind the factories. Here they passed an open door, in front of which lay two small bodies, heat still shimmering above them in the morning air. "Don't say anything," Ching-ling whispered. "Just look, my dear. And then we'll talk."

Farther along in the alley, by the open door of the next factory, where even at this early hour Chlöe could hear looms thumping back and forth, was a lone body, that of a young girl who couldn't have been more than nine or ten, curled in the fetal position, her hands twisted between her drawn-up legs, her eyes open, staring, unblinking.

No bodies before the next building, but three by the door of the following one, and as Chlöe and Ching-ling stood, with Chlöe trying to decipher what this was all about, some part of her recognized that these were the bodies of dead children even though the hand of one of them jerked spasmodically. The slow padding of a horse against the cobblestones could be heard and, looking up, Chlöe saw it pulling a cart. Beside the wagon walked two coolies, one with a long pole, the other with a shovel. They scooped up the little bodies in front of the open factory doors.

Ching-ling squeezed Chlöe's hand tight.

"I've seen enough." Chlöe's voice sounded like a moan.

"No," said the Chinese woman, "you haven't. But I'll tell you about these as we follow this cart."

Pain shot through Chlöe's eyes. "The cart? It's a death wagon."

"Chlöe, these are unwanted children. Children who were sold either at birth or when very young, most of them girls, of course, but some little boys. Families sold them to get a few days' worth of food. Families who couldn't afford to feed them. Mothers and fathers who never think of them again once they are sold. Do you know what happens to them in these factories? They are tied to high stools so they can reach the looms. If they begin to fall over, they're poked awake. They weave all day long, twelve, fourteen hours. And are fed gruel maybe twice a day. They have little rugs under their looms, and that is where they sleep. They never leave the factory. They start work as young children and die there, Chlöe. The foremen pass through before dawn, to see which child has died, ready to throw its body out here, by the back doors, until the death wagon, as you call it, comes along every morning to collect the bodies."

Chlöe stopped, staring at her friend. Ching-ling did not let go of her hand. The whole time she talked she stared into Chlöe's eyes. Now she tugged at her arm and started walking again.

The cart ahead of them was wending its way through the alleys to the wharves, where effluvia floated in the thick, turgid water, greenish in the early dawn. Orange peels, and newspapers, and garbage of all kinds swam on the surface. While they watched, the man with the pole reached into the water and pulled forth a bloated form.

Chlöe held on tightly to Ching-ling's arm. It's not what I think, she told herself, but she knew it was.

"Those who died last night," Ching-ling said, her tone blank and even. "Or were killed and thrown in the river, dead, or who threw themselves into it. No trace of them left, perhaps none even in someone's heart. That smell? It's the smell of rot and decay."

Why was Ching-ling doing this to her? Chlöe wondered. Because she wanted to show her the truth? Or because she wanted Chlöe to understand her own dreams and ambitions for this land? "I am Chinese," said Ching-ling as though in answer to Chlöe's unstated question. "And I want China to become what I know it can. I want it to arise from its feudal system. I want life here to be something other than mere existence, mere sufferance from birth to death."

The sun now hit the water and reflected brightly from it. Anger coiled through Chlöe as she watched another body ladled onto the wagon. She felt herself disembodied, beginning to sink into the whirlpool whose dancing black circles beckoned her on.

Ching-ling asked, "Are you going to faint?"

"No." Chlöe was determined, pushing away the dizziness. "I'm *mad*."

"Let's have some tea," suggested Ching-ling, putting a hand through Chlöe's arm.

As they waited in the teahouse, Ching-ling said, "I suspected your sensibilities were keen. I do not believe people should escape all pain and horror in their lives. How can one become humble, empathetic, sympathetic without experience? How can one"—and now she smiled—"learn to love without some agony? And you are not even experiencing it, just witnessing it."

Chlöe reached out for the tea, surprised to find her hands steady. "What can *I* do?" she wanted to know.

"While we sit here I'm going to tell you more. Should this child of yours be a girl, you will love her profoundly. That I know. You will educate her and dream for her and spend many thousands of dollars on her before you are through. Her chances for happiness, insofar as you have anything to do with it, are very good. You will look at her, hopefully, with pride and even if it turns out that you are not proud of her, I suspect it will not dampen the love you will always feel. But let us say this girl child of yours were to be born to a Chinese family. One that cannot afford a dowry, one that must deny itself to feed her, or one that knows it will feed the girl child for twelve or fifteen years and, if she does marry, she will leave and they will never see her again, since she will now be in another family, under the domination of a mother-in-law. All that money and food will have been spent for naught. Better to sell the girl child immediately, before any money is lost on her. Sell her to a factory owner or to a brothel, so that by the time she is eight or nine or maybe as late as twelve she will bring the owner income.

His money spent on her will not be in vain. Perhaps her very first night as a prostitute, when she is still a virgin, he can regain all he has so far spent on the girl.

"And when she becomes too old to attract men, she will trail after the young prostitutes, bargaining for their services, seeing that they do not cheat on the brothel owner, tipping bellboys and elevator operators and coolies who bring business to her young women."

"Do her parents never wonder?" Chlöe asked, her heart pounding dully.

"I doubt it. They probably can't keep track of all the children they've had anyhow. It's called survival, Chlöe. Chinese survive. Very few of us do more than exist from day to day if we are lucky. Some of the more fortunate whores become concubines, taken from brothels and installed in a wealthy man's home, with honor and perhaps children just as the wife or wives have. She will be called 'auntie' and be as favored as the wife. Until the owner loses interest or she ages. Women are owned in China, Chlöe."

Chlöe thought that Madame Sun could never be owned. And she said so aloud.

"Ah." Ching-ling smiled. "I am owned. By my dreams for my country. I am not free. But you are right, I cannot be owned as Chinese women are. Neither can my sisters. Not that we can throw off the mantle that surrounds us, that still surrounds women everywhere, but we are as much the products of America as China. Even my father spent his youth growing up and being educated in America. We don't even think like Chinese. My sisters would like China to be like America. I just want it to be free to find out what it is, free from foreign domination, from any kind of domination. Free from warlords and from starvation and from floods and pestilence."

"You really believe, don't you, that what you do can help change the world?" Chlöe couldn't imagine anything she could do ever mattering *that* much.

There wasn't a moment's hesitation. "Of course. It's the premise on which my whole life is predicated."

"Do you think it can all happen in your lifetime?"

Madame Sun's eyes were on some far-distant horizon, Chlöe could see that. A fire burned in her eyes, a flame that lit her whole being. "Of course. That is what my life is about."

What, Chlöe wondered, was her own life about?

# CHAPTER 14

Now that she'd spent so much time with Ching-ling, Chlöe had a different attitude toward the Chinese. Madame Sun's homes, both the one that had been burned in Canton and the one here on the Rue Molière that she and Dr. Sun had owned for years, were as clean as Chlöe's mother's Oneonta kitchen. Ching-ling told her she had grown up outside Shanghai at the turn of the century, with Western plumbing, admittedly "the first in the country." But it was available, anyway. Chlöe saw the energy Madame Sun projected, the organization evident in all she undertook.

If Ching-ling was like this, there must be others. Chlöe suspected it was but a matter of education. She saw how hardworking the Chinese were. She had never seen people work harder at more physically grueling labor and even then they barely eked out a living. Certainly no one could call the Chinese lazy. And, in Shanghai at least, more of them knew bits of English or French or German than Westerners knew of their language. No, Chlöe no longer thought the Chinese hopeless. With people like Madame Sun at the helm, at last there was hope.

One morning, as Chlöe luxuriated in her bath, eyes closed, her hand hanging over the side of the tub, stroking the emerald dragon, she heard a knock on the door. An-wei, her maid, entered and announced, "Madame Sun is here."

Ching-ling, so early in the morning?

"I'll be there in a moment."

Slipping into her dressing gown, she glanced in the mirror. Her hair was a tangled web. She ran a brush through it, unsnarling strands that stuck together.

Ching-ling never came out this early in the day, not to call anyhow. Something might be seriously wrong. When Chlöe appeared in the living room, Ching-ling arose from the chair where she had seated herself. Chlöe never ceased to be amazed at how regal such a small person could look. Today she wore a peacock-blue Chinese dress of fine silk but her shoes were high-heeled American ones.

"I have come to say good-bye," she said in her sweet voice. "I could not bear to leave without bidding you farewell."

"Where are you going?" The two women stood facing each other, Chlöe a full four or five inches taller than the Chinese woman.

"Dr. Sun," Ching-ling never referred to her husband any other way, "has sent word that it is safe to return to Canton. I am leaving within the hour." She reached out to take Chlöe's hands.

"I'm sorry," said Chlöe, holding her Chinese friend's hands. She smiled self-consciously. "Not, I mean, about Canton. But about losing you."

"Yes." Ching-ling nodded. "I cannot begin to tell you what your friendship these past few months has meant to me. You are someone with whom I have been able to share parts of myself, someone to be open and honest with and to laugh with. You mean more to me than I can tell you."

"You do me great honor," said Chlöe. "I cherish your friendship and our experiences together. Even when we were in danger . . ."

"I can scarcely forgive myself that I put you in such a position." Ching-ling let go of Chlöe's hands, gazing into her eyes. "But it has formed a bond, and I recognize that. This is not the last time we shall meet. I wish you were able to return with me, to be there so I could talk with you each day. Of course, I shall be back in Shanghai to visit my family. I don't know that I shall have the temerity to invite you back to Canton." She laughed that musical laugh Chlöe had learned to love so well. "I shall write to you, as I hope you will me," she said.

"I promise," said Chlöe, wanting to put her arms around the slender woman but knowing this was a form of intimacy alien to Chinese. She knew also that her life would be less full with this exciting woman no longer an everyday part of it.

Ching-ling reached up and brushed her cheek against Chlöe's. "Farewell, my friend," she said, and sailed out of the room, leaving only a trace of the scent of jasmine behind her.

On those rare evenings when Chlöe and Slade dined at home, Lou Sidney often dropped by after dinner. He grilled Chlöe on her experiences with the Suns, saying that firsthand information would lend him insight into their characters.

Sometimes when Slade was out for the evening, Lou came anyhow. At those times he filled Chlöe in, more than Slade did, on events and the course he thought they were taking.

"I don't envision the end of the warlord system, but it's changing. For the first time, really, the disparate parts of China seem eager for unification. If the warlord up north and Dr. Sun can get together, they'd create a powerful combination. I'd think they could roll across the rest of China."

"With no bloodshed?" asked Chlöe, who had become inordinately fond of the knowledgeable Lou.

He smiled with that sardonic twist of his lips and, lighting his cigarette, picked up the scotch Chlöe always provided him. "No bloodshed? Chlöe, my dear, this is China, a country that seemingly respects human life not a'tall. A land that seems to take orgiastic pleasure in the most sadistic ways of extinguishing life. A land that scarcely blinks when three and a half million of its quarter of the world's population dies in one year from floods and famine. No bloodshed, you ask?"

"Do you really think China has no respect for human life?" The vision of her trip to the back alleys with Ching-ling floated into Chlöe's consciousness. "Don't mothers love their sons and people love their relatives and their husbands and wives . . . ?"

Lou held up his hand. "Love is a luxury of the middle class, my dear. And China has no middle class. Now, familial love, yes, they have families. But Chinese show that kind of love in a way totally different from the Western world."

Chlöe shook her head. "What about the love between a man and a woman?" Certainly that must be universal.

"I suspect the Orient is far more civilized about that than we are. I think we get it confused with our glands."

Chlöe laughed.

"I suspect they are more intelligent about relationships. They separate sexual desire and families. They have no expectations, really, when they enter marriage. Hell, they meet each other for the first time at the wedding. How could they be disappointed? I suppose a man hopes for an attractive bride and a woman hopes for a kind, diligent husband. But beyond that, they expect precious little. Peasants might even care more for a hardworking than a good-looking woman. I don't know."

Slade arrived and interrupted their talk. It was after nine.

"I'm discussing love with your wife," Lou said.

Slade leaned over and kissed Chlöe's cheek. He grinned at Lou, with whom he spent part of every day in their shared office. Lou had none of the fakeness and pretensions that Chlöe had come to associate with most of the people she saw.

"Don't stop because I'm here." Slade went over to the tray on the sideboard and poured himself a whiskey. Returning, he seated himself on the sofa beside Chlöe but looked over at Lou. "Well, have you decided it's here to stay?"

"We're talking of the nature of love," Chlöe said.

"And nature is what I say Western love is so often confused with," Lou said, his long face looking wistful.

Slade nodded. "I think women confuse them more than men. Women hope—expect, really—that whenever you bed them, something emotional happens."

Chlöe jerked her head to look at her husband. He returned her look, his gaze level.

"Romance," said Lou, "no matter how passionately it begins, cannot endure."

"Then isn't it replaced with a more abiding kind of love?" asked Chlöe, who recently had been wondering if her romantic feelings for Slade were diminishing. Not her love for him, but the romance with which she'd entered marriage.

"And there," said Lou, putting his glass on the table, "is where we started. What is love? On that questioning note, I shall leave."

As the months passed and Chlöe's pregnancy grew increasingly obvious, she found herself filled with a wonderful sense of well-being. She had already learned that once pregnancy began to show, the Western women of Shanghai stayed closeted as though they had some contagious disease. Their only contact with society took place in the afternoons, when solicitous friends came to call and tell the gossip of what was happening in the great outside world. Perhaps by not acknowledging the pregnancy publicly, one could ignore how one became pregnant. It was a society that Chlöe didn't understand, though she had been brought up with the same values, if not as formal.

Slade suggested she avoid the consulate dinners where company was mixed. She took to wearing jackets or loose-fitting blouses that hid her swelling belly, with which she had actually fallen in love. She had begun to feel life in it, a stitch here, a kick, she swore, there. And she would put her hand on her stomach, quickly trying to feel a little foot or an elbow, though neither had yet been discernible. She knew better, knew the baby was not yet large enough, but she would lie in bed at night and say to Slade, "Ooh. I felt it. Here," and she'd put his hand on her stomach, hoping he could feel it too, but he hadn't yet. A baby, a little human being, she marveled, was growing inside her. She would move into the circle of Slade's arm then and curl up to him, thinking that before too many months there would be visible proof of their love, a baby they created together.

When she talked like that he'd smile and his arm around her would tighten.

While Ann Leighton and Kitty Blake carried on with their teas and luncheons, while Slade preferred her to stay at home rather than waddle to dinners and balls, Chlöe's friendship with Daisy Maxwell deepened.

She clapped her hands with pleasure when Daisy suggested a picnic. "Just you and me. Let's rent a junk and take a lunch out on the river and have no men at all. Just us."

As the junk's sail waved gently in the soft breeze, Daisy admitted to envy at Chlöe's pregnancy, wanting to know how Chlöe felt, how she slept, wanted to put her hand on Chlöe's belly, and laughed with delight when she felt the baby move.

"Why don't you get married and have babies?" Chlöe asked.

A sadness flitted across Daisy's face before she answered. "The only man I've ever loved is the one man I can't have."

Chlöe wondered if that's why Daisy had left America, if that was why she stayed in Shanghai.

"There must be others you find attractive." Chlöe thought Daisy should be over the pain by now; she'd been in Shanghai five years. And if what Ann Leighton had said had any truth to it, Daisy found many men attractive.

Daisy's eyes took on a faraway look. "I'm an incurable romantic, my dear. A one-man woman. No other will do."

Chlöe thought of some man in Kansas City or San Francisco or Willow Point, wherever he might be, a man with a wife and children, happy. And of Daisy, thousands of miles away from home, in Oriental exile, sleeping with any man who came along because the boy back home had chosen another woman.

"But children, Daisy. Just marry someone you like and have children. You'll find more happiness than you have now."

"Why?" Daisy's eyes sparkled. "Do I seem sad to you, Chlöe?"

"No," Chlöe admitted, feeling the baby press against the hand she had laid on her belly, "you never seem sad, Daisy. It's just that—"

"Don't do that to me, Chlöe. Let me live my life as I see fit. Let me hunger for love I can never consummate and take my fun where I may. So, come on . . . let's eat."

The next day Chlöe said to Slade, "I think Daisy's happy but not content."

"Who is?" Slade murmured, looking up from his desk in the room next to their bedroom.

"I am," Chlöe said. "You mean you're not?"

Slade turned back to the yellow-lined pages on which he was writing and erasing so furiously. "I'm not pregnant."

"You think that's why I'm so content?" she asked, walking over and putting her arms around his neck. He stopped writing as she leaned down and put her cheek against his head. "Then you better keep me this way all the time. I love the feeling. It's as though all's right with the world."

He was staring at the work on his desk, impatiently tapping his pencil.

"Would you like me to get out of your hair?" she asked, leaning over and kissing his ear. "You're trying to get work done, aren't you? Well, serves you right for coming home in the middle of the day. You hardly ever do that, and now I see why. I'm bothering you."

He reached up for her hand and turned his face, pulling her to him and kissing her. He laughed. "You *are* a distraction. Yes, go get out of my hair. I'll be through here in about an hour. But then I've got to go back to the office and cable this to Cass."

"Cass," she said, walking over to the mirror and straightening her hair. "I'm so fond of that man. I wish Suzi and Grant would get married."

Slade shrugged his shoulders. He knew Chlöe was raising a rhetorical point and expected no answer. "Get out of here." He laughed.

"Okay." She smiled. "I'll go shopping. Serve you right. I'll spend all your money and buy some beautiful things for the baby."

Which she did.

She wandered in and out of shops, buying a hand-embroidered soft-flannel receiving quilt in one, a rattle that resembled a dragon in another, smiling to herself the whole time.

She felt as though she were the most fortunate person in the world. Living for these few years in this incomprehensible land among people she'd never have known at home. The stories she'd have to tell her children and their children! They'd stare at her in awe, with eyes wide, and ask, "Really, Grandmother? You lived in China? Daddy was born in China?"

"Tell us again about how you escaped bullets dressed as a peasant." And she'd smile and repeat it all to them, tell them how the food of China smelled and how many servants she'd had, and how she'd picnicked on a junk—surrounded by garbage in the Hwang Pu—with a crazy red-headed lady named Daisy.

On the way home, in the rickshaw, she held the little flannel quilt against her cheek and closed her eyes, trying to envision what this baby who was growing inside her would look like.

She was but dimly aware of the commotion at first, until she heard the shouts and the pounding of horses' hooves across the cobblestones, heard screams rend the air.

As she opened her eyes, the poles of the rickshaw thudded to the ground, jolting her so that she slid down them, too stunned to move. Her rickshaw boy was running in the distance, his back disappearing around a corner. Crowds rushed by as she heard gunshots. In her awkward pregnant shape she found herself unable to rise quickly enough. She heard someone crying but did not see the soldiers thundering down the avenue, now nearly emptied of people, shooting their guns into the air, careening straight ahead.

As she looked up, it seemed to her that beasts breathing fire hurtled out of nowhere, trampling everything before them. She heard the laughter of one soldier as he cried, "Foreign devil," heading straight for her.

She tried to stand, but her foot slipped and she damned the vanity of high heels. A shadow raced toward her, the rider screaming like a banshee. The horse's hooves pummeled her, and then it was gone, the screeches and shots of the soldiers fading.

Pain knifed itself through her. One hand went to her bleeding face, the other tried to grasp her belly, which she thought had been slit open, but her arm wouldn't move. From the elbow down it hung limply, swaying, no longer connected to the bone.

The searing pain carried her into its swirling maelstrom, whose circle grew smaller and smaller as it whirled her into its center. She took a deep breath as it pulled her into its dark vortex, crying out, trying to claw herself up, but found herself drowning in blackness.

# CHAPTER 15

Chlöe didn't talk to anyone during the five days she stayed in the American Baptist Hospital. She felt liquid being spooned through her lips and the pillows being plumped behind her, heard whispers and the starched rustle of uniforms. Slade's lips touched her cheek. She felt his hand on her forehead and heard him say, "There'll be others." But she couldn't see him. Couldn't see anything. Except gray. No colors, no figures, no shadows, just blank grayness.

She was dimly aware of a male voice saying at one point, "This will pass. She's comatose as a way of escaping what she doesn't want to recognize. It's a way of avoiding the truth. I suggest taking her home, where she's surrounded by familiar things, and within weeks she'll be back to normal. There's nothing to be done to hurry this along. Her mind just denies what's happened."

What happened? she wondered, staring into the gray mist. What do I deny?

Nothing roused Chlöe out of her depression. She just lay staring at the ceiling, not seeing anything.

When silhouettes did begin to play themselves against the gray background, the first she recognized were golden bars of light flooding into her bedroom. Then the last leaves of the willow danced outside the window as they gracefully plummeted to the ground in the winter wind.

Daisy was the first person she saw. Whenever she opened her eyes, there was Daisy, her hand resting lightly around Chlöe's, her eyes concerned, smiling into Chlöe's when she opened them. She had no idea where she was. It was Daisy who told her what had happened. Chlöe heard herself cry, and it sounded like a heart splintering.

The next morning Slade came into the room, looking trim and neat. "Hi, there, sweetheart," he said. His eyes had questions in them as he leaned down and kissed her forehead. "Well, you've been out of it. Glad to see my girl back with us again."

She patted the edge of the bed and he sat down beside her, his hand reaching for hers.

"How long—how long have I been like this?"

"Almost two weeks," Slade said, pulling her hand to his lips. "You had us mighty worried."

"Oh, darling," she whispered.

"Just get better quickly," he said. "The doctor says there's no reason we can't have another, that you can't get pregnant again in a few months. But don't worry about that. I just care that you're all right. There's all the time in the world for more children."

She looked at him and began to cry. "I love you," she said. "You're such a nice man."

"I love you too," he said, getting up. "I hope you know that. I've got to get going."

She lay in bed for another week, unable to think or talk of anything but the lost baby. Then one day Daisy said, "Today you are going to get up."

Chlöe shook her head. She never wanted to get up again.

But Daisy would not be dissuaded. "Yes, up. It's time to live again. Losing an unborn child is no reason to stop living."

Chlöe knew she was right.

And in the mail that day, by special courier, Chlöe received a letter that would take her not only out of herself but out of Shanghai, to parts of China she had never seen.

Madame Sun's brother, the financial wizard T. V. Soong, was bringing twentieth-century banking methods to the archaic feudal system, and a loan of ten million Russian dollars helped infuse money into the economy.

Provinces were still under the authority of warlords, broken down into smaller areas where local warlords extracted taxes from peasants and passed a portion of these onto the warlord ruling their larger provinces. Peasants were not interested in a unified China. They wanted no controls over them. A unified China was not on their list of priorities; that was left to the college students, the intellectuals. The peasants knew of nothing different from the lives they lived, and they were afraid of change. When villages tried to evade payment of taxes, warlords had been known to wipe those villages off the face of the earth. Payment of taxes meant protection from all other warlords, all invaders . . . and sometimes it meant help in times of famine. Change meant repercussions; the vast majority of the nearly half a billion Chinese people wanted life to continue as it was, because change usually meant something for the worse. The rest of the world, however, thought there was nothing worse than the way the Chinese existed . . . if it ever thought of China at all.

Oblivious to the immense storm clouds of change enveloping them, a large portion of the world's population was on the brink of profound change.

Madame Sun's letter to Chlöe advised her that they were planning to leave Canton for Peking on November 17 on board a Japanese steamer. En route, they would stop in Japan, where Dr. Sun was to deliver a speech. They planned to arrive in Tientsin, on the north China coast but a few hours' train ride from Peking, in early December. If all went well, Dr. Sun would become China's president.

She hoped she was making an offer that neither Chlöe nor Slade could refuse. She invited them to be the only foreign journalists to accompany the presidential train. Slade could report the trip and the inauguration to the world and she, Ching-ling, would have the pleasure of Chlöe's company. Between the lines it was implied that Chlöe might find the human factor in all this and report it to the world as well. Fortunately, Slade did not see the invisible words.

"Tell me you will come," Ching-ling urged.

Once Slade saw the message, he wasted no time cabling an acceptance. He also saw the trip as a turn of events that could pull Chlöe out of herself. She saw it that way too.

When they met Madame Sun's ship in Tientsin, Ching-ling, in a manner more American than Chinese, hugged Chlöe. "I have been looking forward to seeing you again." But worry clouded her eyes. "Dr. Sun is not well. He has complained about stomach pains. We must get him to the hotel immediately and I shall send for a doctor."

Coming down the gangplank with the man the newspapers were now calling "the Father of the Chinese Republic" was Nikolai. His hand was tucked under Dr. Sun's elbow, and it was evident that the doctor was indeed ill.

Dr. Sun was ensconced in the hotel and in bed, with Ching-ling hovering about him. Chlöe thought they might all catch pneumonia. It was twenty-eight degrees outside, and she thought it must be below freezing in their rooms as well. Even wrapped in her sable, she could see her breath in front of the mirror, under the single forty-watt bulb that dangled from the center of the ceiling. Shanghai was cold enough, but here in Tientsin the frigid dampness insinuated itself throughout her body. I spend more energy trying to keep warm than I do doing anything else, she thought.

Nikolai invited Chlöe and Slade to accompany him to a Russian tearoom. Tientsin was crowded with Russian expatriates, all of them refugees from the Bolsheviks. Nobility Nikolai had worked toward overthrowing, all of them representing the way of life that he dedicated himself to eradicating. He realized the irony of this. "Nevertheless, there I can enjoy the kind of tea, the dark bread, the borscht, the latkes that I can find no place else in China."

"I understand," Chlöe murmured, pulling her fur around her as they exited the hotel into the icy air. "Sometimes I yearn for apple pie or gingerbread cookies . . ."

". . . or a peanut butter and jelly sandwich." Slade laughed, slipping his hand through Chlöe's arm. Her hands remained planted in the deep pockets of her coat.

"There are many Russians in Tientsin. More than in Shanghai, even. Hundreds, maybe thousands of them."

The tearoom to which he took them was warm, smelling of damp wool and cabbage, beets and spiced tea. Each table had an ornate silver candelabrum in its center and the candles' flames danced in the darkness, throwing shadows onto the ceiling and the customers.

Nikolai insisted they try borscht, potato latkes, and the heavy, thick pumpernickel. His eyes shone as he said, "Ironic. But it brings back my youth. My miserable youth, yet here I find myself nostalgic about it." He smiled, the whiteness of his teeth dazzling against the dark beard and mustache.

The waiter appeared with glasses of strong orange-spiced tea, which Nikolai gulped down.

Steaming bowls of soup appeared. "Ah, borscht. The ubiquitous Russian beet mixed with whatever was left over. There was always cabbage. Borscht is peasant food, you know. Yet it has found its way into Chinese Russian tearooms." He burst into laughter. As he ladled a spoonful into his mouth, he said, "It's good. Better than my mother could make, but then, this isn't made out of leftover garbage."

Chlöe, who had been unable to imagine anyone yearning for beet soup, was pleasantly surprised. They ate without talking until Nikolai finished his borscht. He leaned his elbows on the table and talked more to her than to Slade. "In Russia there were nights of insurmountable beauty when the moon shone on the snow, the bare branches of trees like ghosts in the moonlight. Snowflakes as large as Cantonese oranges."

His eyes mesmerized her.

"I remember one night as though it were yesterday, yet it must have been when I was nine or ten, and I awoke in the dark—it was summer—to the strains of a balalaika. I have never heard more haunting music. It played for hours and I felt an incredible happiness, like none I have known since. It wailed into me with its sad music and perhaps has never left. I can will that sound into myself even now in the middle of a night."

His eyes had a faraway look.

"Do you miss Russia?" Chlöe asked.

Nikolai shook his head as though to clear it and return himself to the here and now. "Odd, isn't it? I never felt anything but hunger and discomfort any time I lived in my country. I had to fight to survive.

"Where I was really happy, if I've ever been, was in Detroit. Playing baseball of a Sunday afternoon. My in-laws and my sons with me at the lake. The men I worked with, drank beer with, the ones," he smiled, "who called me Nick."

He leaned forward, his elbows on the table, his eyes intense, looking directly at Slade, then Chlöe. "That's what I'm fighting for. So everyone may live that way."

"Why," Slade asked what Chlöe was thinking, "weren't you content to stay there in Detroit, with your wife and children and your happiness? Most immigrants are. That's their dream."

Nikolai nodded. He understood. "I have asked myself that many times. For many years. I do not think there is a simple answer. You—why are you not back in America in comfort?" He aimed the question at Slade.

"That's easy. Ego. Yearning for fame. Adventure."

Chlöe was warm enough to take her coat off now.

Nikolai ordered more tea. "Maybe my reasons are similar. The idea that I, one man, might help change the world. Adventure." Nikolai turned to her. "And you. What is a beautiful woman like you doing here?"

She smiled, and answered, "That's easy. I'm here for love."

Slade's hand squeezed hers under the table. Nikolai closed his eyes for a minute. "Is that," he asked after a minute, "what rules women's lives? Are you really so much less complex than we are?"

"You're saying we're simpler?" Chlöe shrugged, defensive. "I don't think we're lacking intellect . . ."

Nikolai's hand brushed through the air. "Forgive me if that's what I seemed to be implying. Intellect has nothing to do with how we live. I am asking if your motives are purer than ours. Is it love that dictates women's lives?" He sounded more as though he were wondering out loud than asking Chlöe for an answer.

"Yours involves love too."

Looking at her, he raised his eyebrows in question.

"Love of people, of humanity, of doing good. And Slade is involved in love too. Love of truth."

The three of them sat silently for a moment, then Nikolai smiled. "Chlöe, you are wonderful. You make us all sound so grand. As though we are such perfect, unselfish people doing all that the three of us do, all for love." His even, white teeth glittered beneath his bushy mustache.

Much later, after Slade and Nikolai had consumed several tall glasses of vodka, when Chlöe and Slade lay under heavy Chinese quilts, Slade reached out for her—the first time since her miscarriage—and she felt his lips upon her left breast. She closed her eyes and wondered if Nikolai's mustache scratched.

# CHAPTER 16

"I suspect it's an ulcer," the British doctor intoned, looking down at Dr. Sun. He prescribed medicine and bed rest for Dr. Sun.

Ching-ling would not leave her husband's side. She had no predilection for conversation—her only thought was her husband. He was too ill, too much in pain, to talk with Nikolai or any of his other advisers. Word was sent to Peking that they were delayed.

They remained in Tientsin for three frigid December weeks. There were paved streets in the foreign quarter, which—like Shanghai—had a large international settlement replete with solid Victorian buildings and homes, where grass grew, though now it was winter brown. There were Americans and British and Belgians and Russians and French, but Tientsin's largest foreign contingent was German.

In the international settlement there were gaslights on the streets, and foreign cars competed with horses and donkeys for the right of way. Tientsin had the largest American naval base in China and sailors fought for Tientsin duty. There was wide-open gambling, White Russian princesses in the brothels, and always a fight or two to let off steam. The American navy men loved north China duty.

Tientsin was already an industrial city, one of the few in the Orient. Its smokestacks spewed gray steam into the pewter sky and people coughed, little hard, hacking sounds, all winter long. The city was surrounded by oil tanks, for this was the headquarters of Standard Oil, whose oil filled the lamps of China.

A warlord ruled it but, for a fee, agreed to vow loyalty to a central government and a president to rule all of China. Dr. Sun, before his collapse, was supposed to meet him for a private talk and then the entourage would entrain to Peking, a journey of but a hundred miles.

Madame Sun left her husband's room only for a Christmas dinner, and then she was so distracted that it became the most dismal Christmas Chlöe ever spent.

Inevitably, they ended up talking politics. Slade liked to gently provoke Nikolai, not that the big Russian needed much prodding.

Slade asked, "What's democracy if not the voice of the common man? And how does the common man rise if not through incentive? Through capitalism?"

"Capitalism," answered Nikolai, "has nothing to do with true democracy. Capitalism is a further continuance of imperialism, where money and power are in the hands of the few."

"What do you want?" Chlöe asked, including Madame Sun in her nod. "Do you want to convince everyone that your concept of the world is the only real one?"

Nikolai paused, his fork in midair. He thought a moment. "Yes. I want to do that to everyone. Give them my vision of the world. I want to make the world one of brotherhood, where there is no starvation and no one is homeless, where those who work hard get their just rewards, where jobs and medicine are available for everyone, where—"

"You're an idealist," Slade commented. "Study history. Idealism never works. Idealists become tyrants, so sure are they that theirs is the only way."

Nikolai looked at Slade and smiled broadly. "I am an arrogant son of a bitch. Go on, tell me."

"You're a dreamer," said Slade, gulping the vodka to which Nikolai had introduced him.

"The world needs some idealists," said Chlöe.

"You think," Nikolai hunched his broad shoulders closer to Slade, "I dream the impossible, is that it?"

Slade nodded. "Worldwide brotherhood? Of course it's impossible."

Nikolai's eyes took on an intensity. "I want to change the world. I don't want men to work fourteen hours a day in mines or see men work hard and still have to look on while their families starve to death. I don't want to see children frozen in the streets or women begging. I don't want to see newborn babies in trash cans."

He was blinking rapidly. A vein in his neck throbbed. "In Russia, the people had no rights. Not many steps removed from the Middle Ages, unless you were rich and noble. Or just rich. The rich lived opulent lives—furs, luxuries, decadence."

Chlöe stopped stroking her fur coat.

"Therefore, I and all who believe as fervently as I do are dangerous to society. I am a threat. I know that. I upset the status quo. I am considered subversive. Not just in my country, but in yours too."

"Wasn't it hard," asked Chlöe, "to think of returning to Russia and a difficult life after your years in America?"

He looked at her in that strange, indecipherable way of his. "I admit, if this will assuage your chauvinism, that my years in America were the most comfortable of my life. But they never seduced me. I've always known I am a part of the winds of change, that the twentieth century is mine, and that I am a cog in the wheel of worldwide revolution."

"You *are* arrogant." Chlöe laughed. She had always found people insufferable who considered themselves absolutely right. Yet, instead, she was mesmerized by Nikolai. She could tell Slade was too. How wonderful to thoroughly believe in something. He and Madame Sun. To be part of something you believed truly great and noble. She envied them.

"Haven't the atrocities committed by the Communists in overthrowing the czarists bothered you?" Slade asked. Chlöe remembered the grisly murders of Nicholas and Alexandra and their family. She remembered reading of the beheadings, the massacres, the mutilation of any members of the nobility, the so-called White Russians, in one of whose tearooms they now sat.

Though Nikolai looked at Slade, it was as if his mind were searching into himself. Finally he said, "I know." His voice was

dull. "Two wrongs do not make a right. But you must try to understand that for all of history, Russian peasants have been treated as
not quite human. They have for eternity been forced to live a subhuman existence. Like the Chinese. Once the beasts were aroused,
once they understood that only the nobility was keeping them from
living like human beings, their fury knew no bounds. They struck—
and will strike—in retaliation for all their hundreds and thousands
of years of subjugation, for their ancestors, for freedom for all mankind."

Chlöe, who had been sipping tea and listening, asked, "Do you
think they really thought those things?"

Nikolai shook his head. "But it was there within them. They
needed to obliterate it, to kill all that total domination meant to
them, to make an instinctive strike for freedom."

"You can accept this—this vengeance?" Chlöe asked.

"Yes," he said. "I condone it. It is time. There is no other
way."

Ching-ling reached out and put a hand on Chlöe's arm. "As
you are traveling through this land, look around you. See how so
much of the world lives, then you may begin to understand."

Chlöe was looking at Nikolai. "But what have you to do with
China? You could be helping Russians who live this subhuman existence you describe."

Nikolai looked at Ching-ling. She smiled at him, her tired face
filled with affection.

"Perhaps I can help answer that," she said, her voice soft. "Chinese students saw in the Russian revolt a chance for ourselves. If
Russia could overthrow centuries of domination, so could we."

Ching-ling paused, and Nikolai took over. "In July 1922, just
two and a half years ago, a small group of men gathered in Shanghai." He paused to laugh.

Ching-ling smiled. "Yes, in a pretty pink building, a girls' school
on Joyful Undertaking Street. Does that not sound propitious?"

"There they formed the First Congress of the Chinese Communist Party." Nikolai laced his fingers together. Chlöe leaned back
so that her neck rubbed the soft fur on the back of her chair.

"A tentative beginning," said Madame Sun. "It alarmed the
Shanghai gangsters, the 'Green Gang' of Big-eared Tu." Nikolai
nodded, ordering another vodka. Slade signaled another for himself
too. "Dr. Sun had asked the Western powers for help in forming
the Kuomintang. None would help."

"Except Russia." Nikolai grinned.

Ching-ling smiled. "So Nikolai was sent."

"Nationalism is not yet rampant in China," Nikolai admitted. "I predict it will be. We want a country imbued with the ideals I share with Dr. and Madame Sun. An army and a country free of dependence on any warlord."

"Now," Ching-ling's voice was almost a whisper, "we are heading to Dr. Sun's lifelong dream. He will head a new government, one that will personify the ideals of freedom."

"Of communism," murmured Nikolai. "They are one and the same."

Slade and Chlöe exchanged looks.

Ching-ling pushed back her chair and rose. "I do not want to interrupt this Christmas party. Please, it is not far back to the hotel. I want to walk. I want to return to Dr. Sun. Do not bother yourselves. I shall see you later."

When she had gone and Nikolai ordered more tea for Chlöe, Slade said, "Do you really think Dr. Sun will be a great president?"

"The best president would be Ching-ling," Nikolai said seriously. "That is the human being with iron will and vision. She is a born leader. She is a person of absolute integrity, the conscience of China. But I do not negate Dr. Sun. For the past twenty-some years his name has come to represent independence. The world has found him sometimes eccentric, usually ineffectual, and what Lenin thought of as naïve. Yet he is spokesman for this country.

"The world does not want China to change. It does not want its markets upset; it does not want China to raise itself and take hold of its own future, or even its present. When the people—the common man—break forth, the rich are slain and the balance of power is upset."

Chlöe looked at this man, this giant Russian who spoke so intensely. "And you? Would you slay for your dream?"

Nikolai's eyes met hers. "I have," he said. "And, if necessary, I shall again. I believe. And everything else is secondary to that."

Dr. Sun's health was the leading story in all Chinese-language newspapers. The Western papers carried no notice of it at all. The British doctor was unable to diagnose his illness. On the last day of the year 1924, a special train rushed Dr. Sun and his entourage to Peking. Chlöe and Slade rode that train in a compartment by themselves.

The trip was only a hundred miles. Chlöe wondered why they'd spent three and a half weeks in Tientsin when they could have sped to a hospital in a matter of hours. Low clouds hemming in the gray winter day made her feel claustrophobic. Looking out the window, she found the landscape barren and unattractive.

"What are those, do you think?" she asked Slade, indicating the pyramidal structures that dotted the countryside.

"Graves, I'd imagine," he answered.

They were the only distinguishing feature of the flat land, with occasional walled towns, the bricks of the walls and the huts made from mud of the same color as the earth. It was utterly dreary. Fields, walls, houses all the same monochromatic gray or tan. There were few trees, a cluster or a single one standing random sentinel.

Chlöe fell asleep while Slade stared out the window. Half an hour later he poked her. "Wake up," he said. "You'll want to see."

Sparsely timbered but magnificently rugged mountains were silhouetted against the northwest skyline. Now, in and around the villages were stands of trees, pines, and firs rising dark blue-green. Little Mongolian ponies pulled carts. Men walked behind their burros. Outside one small village were a dozen camels, their humps rising like hillocks against the horizon.

The train swung around a horseshoe curve and corner towers of the immense solid walls of Peking came into view. Massive pagodas adorned the tops of the city's gates. At the train station a crowd of nearly one hundred thousand jammed the station. Dr. Sun, the father of the revolution, looked up from his stretcher and tried to smile.

Dr. Sun was taken to the Peking Hotel. There he was put to bed, and a waiting doctor administered an injection that lessened his pain, permitting him to sleep uninterrupted through the night. Ching-ling, obviously anguished and looking as though she had not slept for nights, pressed Chlöe's hand.

"Whenever I invite you to be my guest, something happens, doesn't it? Come by tomorrow, and I shall try to tear myself away from my husband for a bit. I'm sorry I have ignored you."

Chlöe didn't mind. It was the most time she'd spent with Slade since their honeymoon. Chlöe and Slade rode the slowly chugging elevator to the top floor.

It was not until the next morning that Chlöe began to see beauty again. She awoke at dawn and lay listening to roosters crowing.

Mist shrouded the still-sleeping city. In the early-morning light

she gazed upon the darkened Forbidden City as from a mountaintop.
Though mist swirled below her, she discerned shapes as it began to
dissolve. Shining roofs began to emerge like goldfishes swimming in
a pool. The pointed roofs seemed disembodied, floating in limbo,
their edges curling upward. They swam in the mist, a whole shoal
of yellow fishes, hidden again as the fog enveloped and drowned
them.

Wrapping her coat around her, she returned to the room, where
a maid brought a steaming carafe of tea and two covered cups. Slade,
with only one eye open, said, "For God's sake, don't they take
marriage into account? They just open the door and walk in to leave
tea. What if we'd been doing something that required privacy?"

Chlöe smiled at him and dropped her fur coat on a chair. "Like
this?" she suggested, walking toward him as she stripped her nightgown off and threw it into the air.

Slade opened the other eye. "Stop," he said.

She did.

"Just let me look at you a minute. My God, you *are* the most
beautiful of women." She could hear the smile in his voice. "Yeah,
like this." He opened his arms so that she walked into them, laying
herself on top of him, loving the feel of his body against hers.

"Go lock the door," he suggested as their lips met.

"No," she said. "I don't want to leave you." She flicked her
tongue in his ear.

"Oh, who the hell cares about privacy?" he asked, laughter in
his voice.

Ten minutes later they did not hear the slight knock on the
door, so it was in this intimate way that Ching-ling found them.
She seemed to take no notice.

She stood in the doorway, oblivious as they tried to slow themselves down, tried to stop in the midst of what could not easily be
stopped, and they heard her say, "He has cancer. He is dying,"
before disappearing.

# CHAPTER 17

How would I feel, Chlöe wondered, had I just learned that Slade
was dying? If I knew I had him only months, or weeks, longer? If I

knew that whatever short time he had left in this world would be spent in pain?

She could not imagine. Wanting to empathize with her friend, but never having experienced anything like the tragedy facing Ching-ling, she could only offer empty words. Her recent loss of the unborn baby, she realized, could not equal losing someone who had been alive and beloved, who had been a part of the fabric of one's life. Dr. Sun's death, Chlöe realized, would be not only the loss of the most important person in Ching-ling's world, but of a whole way of living. He was the core around which she had dedicated her life.

He was, as far as Chlöe could tell, China's only real hope. And yet, Slade had said, "Once in power, I really doubt his ability to get things done. He's lived in a dream world all these years. He thinks everything will be easy to achieve."

Chlöe turned and walked back into the hotel room, clutching her fur coat around her. Slade had just finished dressing.

"Nikolai called. They're moving Dr. Sun to the Peking Union Medical College and are going to operate. Nikolai's waiting for us in the lobby. Let's all get some breakfast first." He put an arm around Chlöe and kissed her cheek.

Snow was falling, and all sounds were muted. None of the three talked as they walked through the nearly silent city after the hotel breakfast. Camels from Mongolia wandered the icy streets, their bells jangling, drivers shouting at them. Burros laden with chopped wood jostled with coolies, who ran with cotton-soled shoes along the frozen streets. Icicles hung from the curved roofs, and Chlöe saw her breath float into the frigid air.

The hospital at the medical college was a splendid new building, a surprise in this city of antiquity. "Funded by the Rockefeller Foundation," Slade explained, smiling at Nikolai. "Shows you what capitalism can do."

Nikolai gazed at the building appreciatively. "Perhaps if capitalism always worked so, I would be an advocate of your kind of democracy," he admitted. "I don't know of any hospitals this splendid looking in Russia."

They sat with Ching-ling all morning. Eventually others joined them. Ching-ling embraced one of them, a man Chlöe had not met before who appeared to be Ching-ling's age or perhaps a bit older. She was too distraught to make introductions, which Nikolai did for her.

"This is Sun Fo, Dr. Sun's son," he said, introducing them to the young man.

Chlöe stared at him. It had not dawned on her that the doctor had children older than Ching-ling. Not for the first time, she wondered how Ching-ling could possibly have made love with her husband, so much older than she. Had she suffered it? Had they even made love? Perhaps it was a platonic marriage. But Chlöe knew better. She had so often seen the look in Ching-ling's eyes when she gazed at her husband. Chlöe knew her ardor for Slade was no match for Ching-ling's feelings for Dr. Sun.

Shortly after noon, Dr. Taylor, an American medical missionary renowned in Peking for his skill, appeared. He took Ching-ling's hands in his and, looking directly at her, said, "Advanced cancer of the liver. It's inoperable." She flinched, and he continued. "It's but a matter of time. Weeks . . ."

As the days passed into weeks, as January gave way to February with no abatement of the icy winds blowing across the steppes, Slade said to Chlöe, "I can't stay here forever, waiting for the good doctor to die."

Waiting was more exhausting than working hard, Chlöe thought.

"The vultures are getting on my nerves," Slade said after Chlöe had told him that at this point she could not leave Ching-ling. "I'm not suggesting you leave. I should get back to Shanghai and see what's going on with the rest of the country. All of Peking is on hold waiting for the doctor to die. I suggest you stay here, keep Ching-ling company. Anything that happens you can wire to me."

"What if this continues for months?" Chlöe asked, wondering how long she could bear to be away from Slade.

He reached down to tousle her hair. "Darling, it's not going to be months. When he dies I'll come back up for the funeral. But for the interim, be my eyes and ears, huh?"

He trusts me, Chlöe thought. He thinks I'm capable of knowing what's important and what's not. Warmth spread over her, and she reached up to grasp his hand, pulling it to her lips.

"Your man in Peking?" She smiled.

"Yeah." He leaned over and kissed her forehead. "Not that anyone who's ever seen you would you confuse you with a man."

———

Dr. Sun was moved to the elaborate home belonging to the diplomat Wellington Koo. It was here that the remnant of life left to him was spent. Madame Sun seldom left his side.

When she did tear herself from the sickroom, it was to dine with Chlöe and Nikolai, or to take morning walks in the frigid atmosphere, marching as fast as possible, inhaling deeply, as though to fortify herself with cleansing air. Often Chlöe accompanied her.

"You know, of course," Ching-ling's voice was muffled against her black wool scarf, "this means the unification of China will not yet take place."

That's what Nikolai said too. There was no other single person for whom the country would rally. For more than thirty years Dr. Sun had symbolized a dream. An unselfish, idealistic dream of China for the Chinese, with no hint of corruption, no robbing of the people for his own profit. No other single person in the whole vast land could replace him.

"It's not," Nikolai said to Chlöe when they were alone, "that Dr. Sun is a strong leader. I'm not even sure he knows how to lead. But he is a symbol. Your country's symbol is your flag and perhaps the Declaration of Independence. Or maybe the Constitution. When America was founded, perhaps it was George Washington. For the Chinese only Dr. Sun Yat-sen stands as a symbol."

"What will happen?" asked Chlöe, sipping tea. She thought she spent most of her time in Peking drinking tea.

Nikolai shrugged his shoulders, hunched over, clasping his two enormous hands together in front of his face. He stared at them. "Your guess is as good as mine. I suppose there are those who will fight to be his successor. But they will be after individual power, not the dream."

Chlöe looked at him, at the glum expression on his face, heard the depression in his voice.

"Chiang Kai-shek. He's probably the one. He'll certainly try. There are others too. But you know, Chiang's got the only organized army in China behind him. He's been leader of the Whampoa Academy, after all. And he did spend a couple of months in Moscow. However, I've gotten so I don't quite trust him."

"You mean his dream and yours may diverge?" Chlöe couldn't help needling Nikolai.

"It's no laughing matter, Chlöe." Nikolai's voice was gruff. "China for the Chinese, or China for Chiang Kai-shek."

"Well, Chiang may be thinking, 'China for the Chinese, or China for the Communists.' " Chlöe scalded her throat on the tea.

"He's hooked up with those cutthroats in Shanghai. Big-eared Tu and his Green Gang, who don't care about the Chinese people at all. They grip Shanghai in a stranglehold. No one can do business there without their say-so. They'd love to be the men behind the scenes of the rest of the country too. Smuggle dope, control prostitution, sell whiskey, arrange disappearances, supervise banking—you name it. They'll choose a puppet to finance and find ways to control that person and thus China."

Chlöe couldn't envision a group like that running the country. Any country. Certainly such a thing wasn't possible.

"Too bad Ching-ling is a woman," Nikolai muttered.

"There's a precedent," Chlöe reminded him. "After all, the dowager empress headed the Empire for many years."

Nikolai reached over and took Chlöe's hand in his big paw. "My dear, she ruled by reason of inheritance. No woman can be elected to office. You must know that."

Chlöe remembered Cass's saying, You can be anything you want, except president. "In China, you mean?"

"Anyplace, I mean. And it's one of the reasons I'm a Communist. I believe in equality for all humankind, not just mankind." He turned her hand over and stared at her palm. "Just because you have a smaller hand does not mean you have a smaller brain. Or less will. Or vision."

"Will Russia ever have a woman president?" Chlöe was aware of Nikolai's hand around hers.

"I hope so," he said, his black eyes piercing hers. "It's what we're about. I imagine," his smile touched only his lips, "we'll beat you to it. We'll have women in our government councils before you do. I hope we all do before the century's out."

Chlöe smiled. "You're giving us plenty of time. Another seventy-five years."

"Historically, a moment. Come on." He pushed back his chair and got up. "It's late."

At 9:30 on Thursday morning, March 12, 1925, Dr. Sun Yat-sen, Father of the Chinese Republic, died. Chlöe and Nikolai were with Ching-ling when it happened. So were her sister Ai-ling, and brother-in-law H.H., and Dr. Sun's son, Sun Fo. T.V. had also arrived.

At the end Nikolai heard Dr. Sun say, "If only the Russians

continue to help . . ." as he closed his eyes. H.H. swore he'd said "Don't make trouble for the Christians." Chiang Kai-shek, far south in Canton, later averred that the last words Dr. Sun whispered were "Chiang Kai-shek."

Only the Russian embassy lowered its flag. A week later there was a small Christian funeral attended by the family, Chlöe, Slade, and Nikolai. Two days later there was a public funeral, after which Dr. Sun's body lay in state for two weeks while half a million people came to pay their respects.

Looking so frail that Chlöe wondered if she could last the day, Ching-ling leaned on her stepson's arm. "He wanted to be buried in Nanking, on the Purple Mountain, near the first Ming emperor," said Ching-ling, her voice breaking.

H.H. took her other arm. "And so he shall be," he assured his sister-in-law, "as soon as a mausoleum befitting him can be built. For now he shall rest here, in the Western Hills."

"He is lying in a strange place," complained Ching-ling. "He never felt at home in Peking. He hardly knew this place."

H.H. patted her hand.

The family tried to talk Ching-ling into returning to Shanghai. Dr. Sun had left her his only possessions, the house on the Rue Molière there and all his books. There was nothing else. But Ching-ling would have none of Shanghai or comfort from her family.

She reached up and put a hand on Nikolai's arm. "No," she said, her voice determined. "I shall return to Canton to continue the fight. I don't have a minute to lose. His dream *shall* come true. I swear to God it will."

"Swear to God," repeated Slade, who had arrived for the funeral. Standing behind Chlöe, he whispered as though to himself, "And what will God have wrought? I fear to know. I fear now that all hell shall break loose."

# PART II

## 1925–1928

# CHAPTER 18

"For heaven's sake, Chlöe!" Ann Leighton shook her head and, with obvious irritation, stared down at the cards on the table in front of her. "You went to four spades with that hand? Where's your mind?"

Not in the marble-floored oval room of the American consulate, that was for sure. Chlöe didn't even have the courtesy to look embarrassed. She wanted out, not only of the bridge party, but out of the building. She wanted to be somewhere where she could pat her belly, tell herself life was once again growing there. Wanted to keep her hand there, against her skin, and let the new being within feel the love she already felt for it. Spring was the right time either to give birth, she thought, or to be newly pregnant. The baby was due almost exactly nine months after Dr. Sun's death.

Slade was as pleased as she was. It was just six months since the miscarriage, perfect timing, the doctor said. Chlöe refused to ride in a rickshaw. She insisted on walking everyplace, even at night, even to the other side of the city. In those cases Slade tried to arrange for a taxi. Never again a rickshaw while pregnant, she vowed. And never again hibernating simply because her belly was swollen with child.

Despite the happiness of pregnancy, she felt different about her life since returning from Peking. Playing bridge afternoons drove her mad. Whenever she tried to make conversation about China, blank stares faced her. Someone said, "Don't tell me you're becoming a Chink lover?"

She had smiled, albeit stiffly, and responded, "Yes, I think I am."

The only sound was the clinking of saucers against cups that were set down. Then conversation resumed as though Chlöe had not said anything.

That morning as she and Slade were breakfasting, she had said, "I really don't understand it. You'd think that by having slanted

eyes and yellow skin they're retarded. The Americans and British
all talk of the inscrutable ways of the Chinese, yet the Chinese I
know are more open about things that matter than any of these silly
women who flutter around in organdy at garden parties and arrange
musicales and desserts. I'm sick of these damn never-ending parties.
At least when I'm with Lou or Daisy we talk of . . . I don't know
. . . metaphysical things, I guess. Questions that have no answers."

Slade smiled at her with amusement as he cracked open his soft-
boiled egg. "Like what? Seems to me Lou always has answers."

Chlöe sipped the oolong tea, her elbows resting on the table.
A single azalea swam in a shallow bowl. She had gathered it from
the garden before breakfast, while the dew still clung to it. "Oh, all
the whys. Why are there wars? Why do people want power? Why
are some people so sure they're right they can't let anyone else think
differently? Why do some people enjoy inflicting pain? Why is there
always some degree of tension between men and women? Why—"

Slade's hand reached out and circled Chlöe's wrist. "Hey, halt
there. Have I missed something?"

She looked at him and then smiled. "Oh, you mean about men
and women? It just seems in male-female—I mean romantic not platonic—relationships there's a tightness that keeps it exciting. Keeps
us on our toes. Like when I know it's time for you to come home
from work, some sort of excitement begins in me, low in my belly
at first, and then spreads upward until I actually feel it in my chest,
and then it works its way into my head. When you're late I feel
deflated. When you don't get home until after I'm asleep, all the
excitement dissipates and I feel depressed. Now, what do you call
that except tension?"

Slade tilted his head to the side. "I didn't know you felt that
way."

Chlöe sighed. "I do. So why am I married to a man who keeps
such irregular hours and end up spending so many evenings alone?"

"Seems to me we go out most evenings." Slade stood up, wiping
his mouth with the grass-linen napkin. He leaned over to brush his
lips across Chlöe's cheek. "I promise not to be late tonight. How's
that?"

"You can't be," she said, holding on to his hand. "There's the
dinner for the new French ambassador."

"Damn, I forgot."

"You could always come home early and I'll have a drink ready
for you and we can sit and you can tell me all about your day,"

suggested Chlöe, kissing his hand as he grinned. He began to walk toward the door, then turned around.

"How about David?" he asked. Every day he tried out a new name, but so far Chlöe rejected them all.

"Too common," she said.

Many of the evenings when Slade was gone, Chlöe wrote. Long letters to her family and to Cass and Suzi. She bought a notebook and began to write her impressions of China and the Chinese in it. When she was writing, nothing else existed. She relived the incident of which she wrote. Never was she an outsider merely observing, but a full participant who not only saw but felt.

If a servant entered the room to light the lamps, she looked up, surprised. She had been in another place and another time. Sometimes it was as though she heard voices and she simply wrote down what she overheard.

One day in the street she had seen a young woman trying to sell her child and she wrote of the woman that night, trying to put herself inside the young mother in order to understand how a woman would feel when she saw her baby replaced by a few coins.

When Slade came home at midnight and she heard his footsteps on the tile floor, she would slip her notebook into the drawer, but nothing could call her mind back to the here and now. Fortunately Slade was always tired and never seemed to notice.

She was fully aware that when she wrote details of her life to Cass that he might publish them. She took particular care with those letters, sometimes copying them three and four times. She knew Slade was irritated when he saw her letters in print, when he sensed her entering his domain. Yet she refused to stop sharing herself with Cass and Suzi, and she did receive immense pleasure upon seeing her words in print.

Slade had never mentioned the series of articles Cass had printed under her byline, headlined "A Wife's Vigil." They concentrated on Ching-ling rather than on Dr. Sun's death.

Two afternoons a week she still continued her lessons with Mr. Yang. Though her Chinese had long been adequate for communication, she found the language endlessly fascinating. She had progressed to writing, enjoying spending hours with a brush, trying to perfect her characters, sitting back and studying the ideographs she formed, comparing them with ones from the books Mr. Yang had lent her.

His continual history lessons intrigued her the most and made her question. On Tuesday and Thursday afternoons he would carry her to another world, philosophical as well as historical. Afterward she would spend hours thinking about what she had learned.

"Do you realize," he'd asked, "that over a fifth of the world's population is Chinese?" He went on. "We had a magnificent civilization when Europe was in the darkness of the Middle Ages. Marco Polo found us the richest, most enlightened, and most advanced of civilizations." Mr. Yang sighed, placing his teacup on the saucer. "Unlike your Christian theology, we believe man was created *before* either heaven or earth. Man is the master. And what is important about man is his ability to reason: the life of the mind."

But so many Chinese aren't capable of that, Chlöe thought. There are so many uneducated.

Later, she discussed this with Lou, who said, "I like to think of myself as a logical, rational being, a man of the mind. But the Chinese carry it so far that their rationality makes them passive."

"And patient," Chlöe suggested.

"True, but it can become a vice. Their tendency to pacifism, which is a serious political problem in these times, is an example. An ancient Chinese adage says that when a man fights, it means the fool has lost his ability to reason. To become strong and unified, however, China is going to have to permit passion to replace rationality."

Chlöe was surprised to hear Lou talk of passion.

"Yet the Chinese endure against impossible odds. Each year famine and flood together kill three million Chinese."

Chlöe held up her hand. "Lou, that's not possible. At home, if any town in America is flooded and even a dozen people are lost it's front-page news across the country. And I never hear of anything like that here."

"Sure," he said, lighting his cigarette. Chlöe thought, Someday I'm going to have the guts to ask him to desist. But not yet. "That's because it's news there. Here, each year when the Yellow and Yangtze rivers flood, wiping out villages for hundreds of miles, it's not news. It's seasonal. Chlöe, in this last year twenty-nine thousand bodies were picked off the streets of Shanghai alone. Dead of hunger. The majority, of course, were female infants left by their parents to starve. Those years when famine ravages the north and people die walking south to forage for food wherever it may be, no one takes notice. Three million people a year do die from famine and floods, my dear. But the Chinese endure. They endure despite either bad or next to no government, they endure despite pestilence, corruption, taxation beyond normal human endurance, physical labor unparalleled anyplace else in the world. Jesus Christ, at least four hundred million of them labor like domestic animals do in America!"

Chlöe touched her belly. She couldn't imagine this unborn child of hers starving to death.

Lou continued. "You and I, Chlöe, would probably perish to have to live in the unbelievable poverty, filth, and physical discomfort that Chinese accept with stoicism. Accept and multiply."

"How can they go on?" It was a rhetorical question.

Lou didn't even attempt an answer.

Chlöe sighed. "China's like a ripe melon waiting to be exploited by whoever can unite it, isn't it?"

Lou's eyes narrowed. "You've got it to a T."

From time to time Chlöe received letters from Ching-ling. This time she wrote that she was outraged at Chiang Kai-shek, who sent a traditional Chinese intermediary to propose to her, suggesting an alliance between them would solidify Dr. Sun's dreams. "I remember," she wrote, "Kai-shek's discussing with my husband, when he was alive, the viability of marrying my sister Mei-ling. He thought an alliance with the Soongs would further his career, and Mei-ling, after all, is nearly thirty and unmarried. I am offended that Kai-shek would even think my support could be bought. I don't trust that man. He loves China not nearly so well as himself. I don't place confidence in him, and I think Nikki finally agrees. Besides, Kai-shek already has a wife as well as several concubines. That's common knowledge."

Yet, Chlöe thought as she put the letter down, Dr. Sun also had a wife when Ching-ling married him. That had apparently not deterred her. Chlöe had only met Chiang once, forming no personal opinion other than that his eyes shone with fire yet seemed hidden at the same time. She admired his having stayed nearly two months on the gunboat with Dr. Sun when they lay outside Canton in the Pearl River that time.

Since the baby was due near Christmastime, Slade felt perfectly at ease about leaving for Canton to investigate what was happening to the revolutionary forces, if indeed there were any, in late November.

"I'll be back in ten days," he assured Chlöe. "I've just got to see what or if anything's happening down there."

As it turned out, he was still gone more than three weeks later when Chlöe—who had felt sluggish for days—went to bed early one evening. She read longer than usual, feeling restless and irritated that Slade was not there. He knew the baby was due any day. After she'd read the same page three times, she tossed the book on the floor and turned out the light. She lay there, staring into the darkness, her hands on her swollen belly, and felt dampness between her legs. Her water had broken. Then an ache, too dull to be a pain. She lay there and grinned. She was about to have the baby. Where was Slade? He should be with her. But she could not waste time in anger, for she was about to give birth and her whole being responded to the idea.

She knew she had better get to the hospital. But she refused to go by rickshaw, and besides, she doubted that any would be available at this hour of the night, at least not in this section of the city, where so few Westerners lived. She sat up and shivered as her feet touched the cold floor. She would send her maid, An-wei, to fetch Lou. He would get her to the hospital. He wouldn't mind that it was after midnight.

While she waited for An-wei to return with Lou, she packed a few clothes and the book she'd been reading as well as a baby quilt and the clothes she had bought just for this child's homecoming. They were lying in a bassinet in a corner of the room, in the cradle she had stared at for so many weeks now, singing silently to the yet-unborn creature. The on-again off-again pains excited rather than frightened her. Suddenly a searing terrible pain—as though a grapefruit had been inserted in her rectum—clutched her. Was this normal? No one had warned her about that kind of feeling. The pressure increased until she had to stand, but she could do nothing to alleviate the discomfort. God, it hurt! She balled her fists until her knuckles were white, until her nails dug into the palms of her hands and she had to concentrate on that pain rather than whatever was pushing down on her. Ahh, that was better; the pressure lessened.

It was three-quarters of an hour before Lou arrived. "I've a taxi," he said, breathless. "Are you all right?"

Chlöe nodded. The pains came rapidly, the rectal pressure expanding from grapefruit to watermelon proportions. It was so sharp she couldn't talk.

Panic lit Lou's eyes.

The nurse at the American Baptist Hospital seemed in no rush, sighing and saying, "Dr. Adams won't be thrilled to be awakened at this hour," as though Chlöe had misbehaved.

Daisy rushed in, breathless and disheveled. The nurses let her ride up to the second floor in the elevator with Chlöe and stay as a nurse wrapped Chlöe in a rough, shapeless white muslin shirt that barely covered her.

"You'll have to leave," Chlöe heard the nurse say, but Chlöe reached out to touch her friend's hand. "Please let her stay."

The nurse shook her head. "My, no. That's against the rules." The nurse looked unsympathetic when Chlöe arched her back and moaned. Chlöe suspected the woman had never had a child, that she was a missionary nurse because she was more interested in serving God than in comforting humanity. Then thoughts of anything other than her pain—of the baby who was struggling to enter the world, of the little human being she and Slade had created—fled her mind.

"Oh, God," she screamed, feeling the pain rip through her, searing along her arms and legs and through her head as well as her belly. The nurse came back, making little tsk-tsk sounds, and took Chlöe by the ankles, holding her legs together.

"Let's not let this baby enter the world before the doctor gets here," said the nurse, her glasses glinting in the glare of the overhead light. Chlöe kicked her, freeing a leg. Damn her, she thought as she worked to control a scream.

"Oh, come, come," said the nurse, acting as though Chlöe were a naughty child. "No temper tantrums."

Just then the doctor arrived, sleep and a smile both in his eyes. "Why do babies always arrive at night?" he asked no one in particular. "Well, Mrs. Cavanaugh, I hear you're just about ready. This is pretty quick for a first baby. You haven't been here even an hour. Let's take a look."

He jackknifed Chlöe's legs and stuck something inside her. She couldn't tell whether it was an instrument or his fingers. She couldn't feel it. She saw him nod his head. "Ah, there it is. Miss Gray, wheel her into the delivery room and we'll need ether."

"No," Chlöe cried out. "I don't want to be unconscious. I want to be with my baby when it comes into the world. Please!" Another pain made her wince and the world was black. Even when the doctor's voice answered, she couldn't see him.

"Mrs. Cavanaugh, don't be sentimental. You don't want to go through that. It'll exhaust you."

Shouldn't it? she thought. Shouldn't I be exhausted from creating life? "I can stand any pain if I know it'll soon be over. I *want* to feel it," she said. "I don't want to miss a minute of it."

The nurse slid her onto a cart and wheeled her down the hall. The doctor followed, donning rubber gloves once they entered the delivery room. A different nurse stood waiting, in a green uniform and rubber gloves also. She was younger and was smiling at Chlöe.

Miss Gray said, "She doesn't want ether."

The young nurse, whose blond hair was pinned away from her face, continued to smile. "I'd want to see it too," she said in a soft voice, and Chlöe felt relief at the young woman's sympathetic touch.

Someone screamed. Chlöe realized it was she as the doctor said, "Damn fool, no anesthesia," before he bent over and all she could see between her jackknifed legs was the top of his balding head. "Push," he said, and she strained so hard she thought she might burst.

"Easy," he said, "don't bust a gut. You don't want to tear."

The young nurse stood beside him, alternating her gaze between Chlöe's eyes, when she smiled reassuringly, and between her legs.

"Again," he said. "Not so hard, but push again."

The pain between her legs was gigantic, and she cried, "Ether."

"Too late," she heard the doctor declare. "One more push. My God, I've never seen a white woman have a baby so easily. Here it is, by God, not even forceps," he said as the pain crushed into her. Then suddenly the pressure lessened and she heard voices murmuring. In a minute the young blond nurse held the red baby up by its heels, gently patting its back until it let out a gurgly cry, while the doctor again said, "Push. Let's get rid of this placenta. Come on."

Chlöe was tired. More so even than that night she and Chingling and Nikolai struggled over the fields outside Canton. All she could see was the bright overhead light. She couldn't hear anything except a buzzing, a soft electric sound. She closed her eyes.

After what seemed like hours, though it couldn't have been more than a few minutes because she was still in the delivery room, the young nurse's soft voice said, "Here, would you like to hold him a minute?"

Him? She hadn't even wondered. She opened her eyes but was too tired to raise her arms. She looked at her son, wrapped in a swaddling quilt already, his red face blotchy, his head pointed, looking for all the world like a chipmunk. She began to laugh, and the nurse placed him in the cradle of Chlöe's arm. Mustering all her energy, Chlöe raised her head and nuzzled the soft fuzz of his damp little head on her chin.

I've created a human being. My path to immortality, she thought. Now part of me shall live forever. Through my son. The child I have borne. And she slept.

The next day Slade returned from Canton. By then she had already named the baby Damien Cassius Cavanaugh.

Slade rolled his eyes heavenward but nevertheless grinned and said, "My son."

My son, thought Chlöe.

# CHAPTER 19

For the first three months Chlöe refused to hire a baby nurse. She wanted to do everything for Damien herself, dragging around tired but happy. Slade was irritated at her for keeping the cradle in their bedroom.

"Certainly in the middle of the night someone else can care for him!" he said, his voice as tired as Chlöe felt.

"But no one else can nurse him," Chlöe said.

"In China people hire wet nurses," he said, "so parents can get their sleep."

But Chlöe would hear none of it. She refused to resume their social life because she could not take Damien with her. He was a good excuse. At first the women of the Western community dropped in to coo over the baby, to bring little gifts and to share child-rearing tales with Chlöe, but when she made no move to attend afternoon bridge or the garden parties that began again in the spring, or even to come to consulate dinners, the invitations dwindled.

Slade objected. "Chlöe, it's not just you. I have to be careful how we treat these people. What they feed me keeps my job here going."

Chlöe shook her head, though her eyes were on their sleeping son. "Nonsense. They need you far more than you need them. You're going to hear everything that happens whether they individually feed you or not. Nothing much happens in the consulates here, anyhow. They don't create the news."

Slade nodded in agreement. "Nevertheless, our relationships with the other Americans here, with the government officials—"

Chlöe interrupted him, raising her eyes to meet his. "You function very well with them. I don't really think I'm necessary. Look at Lou. He goes to all social functions without a woman. I'd rather stay with Damien. He won't be a baby long."

Slade laughed at that. "My God, honey, he'll need to be taken care of for years."

But Chlöe would not let anyone else take care of him.

Slade walked over to the cupboard and poured himself a whiskey, straight. Then he walked back to Chlöe, leaned down, and kissed her ear. "I should stay home with you and Damien tonight, but I can't. Do you know what's happening in Canton?"

Chlöe shook her head, not quite ready to shift so quickly from one topic to another.

"The Kuomintang, from the secret reports I've gotten, are ready to march north. Just what that means I'm not sure. Whether they've begun or are going to shortly I've no idea. But this movement is going to be big."

"Does it involve Ching-ling?"

Slade nodded. "And Nikolai, though I've a gut-level feeling that by the time they get north, Chiang will have the upper hand. After all, he's trained all those Whampoa cadets, whose loyalty he's gained. A well-disciplined army can work wonders over ideals."

"Are they all coming together?" Chlöe had trouble imagining Ching-ling marching north for hundreds of miles, yet she knew her friend had an iron will.

"I've no idea. Just rumors so far. I need to check them out."

His hand squeezed her shoulder.

She spent the evening on the verandah, in the comfort of their creaking rocker, watching the twinkling lights from boats on the river, hearing voices in the dark as sampans swept by unseen in the night.

She wondered if she'd feel this kind of happiness back in Oneonta if Slade worked there. But even if she were back there, her brothers and sisters were grown up now and gone from home.

Unable now to imagine her life without Damien, Chlöe pitied her parents. What was left for her mother now that all the children were gone? Did she read three books instead of one a week? Did her mother now sit through two showings of Rudolph Valentino movies? Funny, Chlöe had never really thought of her parents individually. They'd always been a single entity. Now she wondered what her mother must think about. She'd always just pictured her as "Mother," whose life was lived solely to take care of the children. And now that there were no children, what kind of life did her mother have? Was she just passing time?

Could she dare to ask her that in a letter? Her mother wrote twice a month. Daddy wrote about twice a year. They told her what each of her brothers and sisters was doing, what was happening with neighbors or people she might know at the church, about the street-cars in Oneonta, and how Doc had added a new soda fountain at the pharmacy. But they never said anything about themselves. Never mentioned how they felt about something, or what they thought. She wondered if her mother ever thought of things that had nothing at all to do with Daddy or with the family. If she ever looked at the stars and wanted to fly to them, or if she . . . she what?

Finally, unable to imagine her parents without their children, she went up to the nursery and sat next to Damien, who either felt her presence or was actually hungry, for he awoke and she nursed him, feeling the pull at her breast like the ocean must feel the pull of the moon.

She awoke when she heard Slade, reaching out for him when he lay down next to her. But he turned on his side, his back to her. And she fell back asleep.

In the morning, as he toweled himself dry after his bath, she lay watching him, with Damien still cuddled in her arm after nursing him.

"Ching-ling and Nikolai are on their way to Wuhan," he said. "The Kuomintang's split in two. Chiang is coming up here, to Shanghai."

"Where's Wuhan?" she wondered aloud, listening to Damien coo.

"Up the Yangtze several hundred miles," he said as he sat down beside her and reached over for Damien. He held him expertly, as though he were used to children, and smiled into his son's eyes. The boy gurgled bubbles at him. Slade kissed the boy and then laid him back down in the circle of Chlöe's arm.

"A son, Chlöe. You've given me the son I've always wanted."

Then he shifted topics. "It'll take months and months for them to get to Wuhan. The railroad doesn't even go all the way. I imagine there'll be battles along the way."

"Battles? Whatever for?"

"My dear, the Kuomintang intends to be the ruling party of this land. Whether by popular acclaim or by submission. Though I empathize with their goals, I cannot condone the means I suspect they'll use."

"But Ching-ling won't participate in battles," she said vehemently.

"Darling, you *are* naïve." Slade stood up and went over to the wardrobe, fishing a shirt and trousers from their hangers. "Do you think ideals really can be achieved easily? I suspect there will be much bloodshed before it's all over."

At breakfast he said, "I imagine in the next few months I'll be popping off to see what's happening with Chiang's troops and to see Ching-ling and Nikolai, so I can get a feel for what's going on.

"You know none of the Europeans or Americans wants change. We'll be thrown out, no doubt about it. We're part of the problem over here. But I was talking more of Big-eared Tu and his Green Gang."

Chlöe laughed. "Big-eared Tu. Isn't that an awful name?"

"He's an awful man. He and his mobsters own Shanghai. They control all the prostitution, gambling, white slavery, and protection. Every business in this city pays protection to them. All important favors are granted through Big-eared Tu. He holds the balance of lives in his hand. If he wanted me, or you, or anyone, dead, there'd be no trace of us forever after. He likes the status quo. It's made him a millionaire many times over. He likes the power, the phenomenal control. He doesn't want to give that up. He owns this part of China."

"How come so few people have heard of him?" she asked, spooning her soft-boiled egg onto her toast.

"He likes to stay in the background."

"Have you ever seen him?"

Slade smiled. "Oh, yes. I've even had an interview with him."

Why hadn't he told her such things before? What else happened in his life he didn't share with her?

"You've never written about it."

He shook his head, gulping down his too-hot coffee. "I'd like to continue living. He now and then feeds me things he wants the world to know."

"You don't like him, I can tell."

"Like him? Chlöe, Big-eared Tu and that brilliant, though I think evil, crippled friend of his, Chang Ching-chang, have such a stranglehold on Shanghai and other large parts of China that I sometimes give up any hope for the future."

"Are you afraid of them?" Chlöe held her spoon in midair. Slade had never talked of these things to her.

"Afraid of them?" Slade looked at her. "Honey, they scare the shit out of me."

# CHAPTER 20

Revolutionary fervor swept through China's cities. The countryside heard little about it, except when actually confronted by soldiers. However, China—as usual—had no organization to anything it did. Every now and then one heard of workers' strikes at the factories in Wuhan or Canton. Gunfire was heard sporadically in Shanghai, but nothing much ever came from any of these rebellious threats. Life went on as always.

Certainly, Chlöe thought, now that they had been in China almost three years, Slade might consider returning to America, asking Cass for another assignment. But Slade told her he was just now getting his finger on the real pulse of this country, moving beyond the superficial impressions of China, so impenetrable and overwhelming to many Westerners.

Then, in June, Chlöe received a letter from Ching-ling—postmarked Wuhan. It arrived at noon, on one of those rare days when Slade was home for lunch. Chlöe opened it as Slade ate. She read aloud,

My dear friend,
    You have not heard from me for such a long time because I have been everywhere, yet nowhere near anyplace where I could mail a letter. I was not even sure we would be alive at the end of our journey. But rejoice. Obviously we are.

*We left Canton five months ago, and it has taken us all that time to travel just six hundred miles to Wuhan.*

*Now that I am safe in Wuhan and life once again has some semblance of order, I so often wish you were with me. I am in sore need of a woman friend. Nikolai is as good a friend as one can have, but he is not a woman with a woman's sympathies and understanding, at least not on the level that I share with you.*

*I am exhausted from the long trip and from the heat and humidity of a Yangtze River valley summer. I think were I refreshed for a few weeks I could give more energy to the important job I must do, so I have decided to permit myself a vacation if you and Damien (I long to see your son) will come with me to Lu-shan, a village high in the mountains between Shanghai and Wuhan.*

*I promise that if you come to visit I shall tell you all about our hair-raising trip. Doesn't that intrigue you? Perhaps it could be made into a movie, but no one would believe it. It is safe in Lu-shan, my dear, so your son will be in no jeopardy and it is away from the pestilences that a China summer so often brings.*

*Now that my life is a bit calmer than it's been these past months, I yearn for your company, and I want to see that precious son of yours.*

*Your devoted friend,*
*Ching-ling*

After she finished the letter, Chlöe laid it on the table as Slade grinned and said, "Lou's just come back from Wuhan, you know. He thinks I ought to go take a look. I could go upriver with you as far as," he looked at the letter again, "Chiuchang."

Slade went on talking. "Wuhan's got the most organized workers of any city. It's where the revolution started in 1911, you know. Wanna go?" he asked. "You and Damien. It'll give us at least a few days together on the boat." He was looking at her.

"That sounds nice," Chlöe said. "Ever since Damien's birth we never seem to do things together anymore." Why? she wondered. What did having a child do to estrange couples? She thought it was supposed to bind them closer together. Maybe that's what happened to women, they became mothers and found it so fulfilling that all sense of adventure fled. All desire for anything other than protecting and caring for one's baby ceased to exist. Nothing else seemed important compared to this little human being who had come from her own body.

The idea of getting away from malaria and typhoid and all else that a summer in Shanghai threatened appealed to Chlöe. Showing off Damien to Ching-ling . . . She thought perhaps she did need a change. The idea of cool mountain air . . . She couldn't tell Slade that she knew Ching-ling's invitation included a story no one else in the world could have.

"It does sound lovely," she said, running a finger down his arm.

He smiled, getting up from the table, and said, "I'll make arrangements this afternoon and send a cable to Ching-ling."

Slade booked their passage on one of the clean little British river steamers that plied the Yangtze. The river was crowded with dozens of oceangoing vessels, its hundreds of junks and sampans, the small, crowded boats that were home to thousands of Chinese, crafts that never sailed, that were caught between other tiny rotting boats where babies were tied to masts with thongs so they could not fall overboard, where some families spent their entire cramped lives.

She was not prepared for the immensity of the Yangtze delta. The lower region of the Yangtze was a labyrinth of waterways, lakes mostly, plus the man-made canals. The Grand Canal led all the way to Peking, an engineering feat achieved centuries before. Along the banks were dikes, which usually lost the battle to floods.

Mulberry trees lined the banks of the river. Stone bridges, looking from a distance like humpbacked whales, linked picturesque villages. Little skiffs loaded with vegetables and rice were paddled downriver toward Shanghai. As with all waterways in China, effluvia floated by, garbage and refuse that smelled like a cesspool. It was so thick with scum, one could not see below the water's surface. At the edge of the river, women washed clothes, beating them against rocks while their children played in the water. Chlöe did not wonder that so many of them died before the age of five.

Madame Sun was waiting for her at Chiuchang. After much joyous fussing by Ching-ling, Chlöe and Damien left Slade on the steamer, climbing into a rickshaw to follow Ching-ling through the village streets to a resthouse. There they dined early on bean curd and noodles with hot sauce before they retired to their room. Ching-ling told Chlöe they would have to arise at dawn so the bearers could be back from the mountain before dark.

They slept on inch-thick cotton bedrolls laid on benches. Chlöe slept little, for she was unused to wooden beds. Every time she turned, her hip hit the hard boards, and when she did arise, before dawn, her back ached arthritically.

They breakfasted on rice and boiled eggs, both of which Damien enjoyed, and then climbed into rattan sedan chairs. They were open and uncurtained, unlike those preferred by ladies in the city to prevent the outside world from staring in. These allowed passengers to enjoy the scenery. In less than two hours they came to the foothills of the mountains towering in front of them. Here they stopped at another resthouse, partaking of tea and little cakes.

They changed bearers, and Chlöe learned that the people of the flatland could not climb mountains with the agility of the mountain men. This time the sedan chairs were of bamboo, with posts suspended across the carriers' shoulders.

As they began their ascent, Chlöe felt a first hint of the magic to come. Through emerald-green tufts of grass, with water so clear that every stone was visible, a stream tumbled out of the mountains. The little houses were constructed of rocks instead of the dung-colored brick mud of the plains. Chestnuts, oaks, and pines replaced bamboo, and the narrow path wound between giant boulders as the trackers rose higher.

Leaning out of the chair, she gazed down into gorges where the waterfalls created pools, pools that became rivers. The twisting trail zigzagged so abruptly that as the front bearers turned a curve, her chair swung out crazily over the escarpments, dangling dangerously into thin air. Chlöe held Damien tightly.

But there was never a misstep, a break in rhythm, or a stumble as the sedan bearers kept up their astonishing pace.

Suddenly, as though crossing over some invisible line, the air turned sharply cool. Loud cries of joy filled the air, for the sweating bearers welcomed the cool air upon their hot bodies. Leaving the valley's heat behind infused them with new life and energy. At last they reached the mountain summit. The bearers ran through a stone village so picturesque that Chlöe amused herself with the thought that she had entered a fairyland. Tall trees arched over the neatly laid out narrow streets, creating a canopy. Later Ching-ling told her that only ten years before, Chinese were forbidden from the village proper. Now there was a Russian settlement and rich Chinese built enormous summer houses. The Chinese also bought houses that the whites had built twenty and thirty years before. At the turn of the century this had been a most popular resort for missionaries, the foreigners who had made China their home but feared malaria that summer and its mosquitoes brought, who sought to escape the fall scourge of cholera, brought on by flies. White people who preferred to stay in China despite the seasons of pestilence rather than take the long passage home, but who worried about their children—these were the people who at the turn of the century discovered the haven of Lu-shan.

In the morning after breakfast, when Chlöe put Damien down for a nap, she and Ching-ling took a walk, climbing among the ferns and lilies up the hill behind their house.

It was wonderful to be with Ching-ling again. Part of Chlöe hoped Ching-ling would not tell her about the trip north from Canton to Wuhan. She thought it would be lovely to be just two women friends on vacation, picking flowers, with no problems, no thoughts of the greater world, no intrusions of reality.

But she knew Ching-ling better than to expect that. Her friend thought of little else than China and her important role in the future of it.

"One of the purposes of our trip from Canton to Wuhan was to spread the word," Ching-ling began. "There are hundreds of millions of Chinese who don't even know that the dowager empress is dead, or that there is life beyond their villages. Or that there is hope. They are living as Chinese have lived for thousands of years. The most a Chinese peasant can dream is that his harvest may enable him, sometime in his lifetime, to buy a larger plot of ground, and when he gets old or," she smiled grimly, "when he perceives his wife as getting old, he can afford a concubine. Those are their highest dreams. Their daily life focuses on whether or not there is enough to eat, whether a man can afford tobacco for his pipe. And for women, of course, there are no dreams. They work in the fields with their husbands, they have their babies in the fields, and are back at work within the hour. If they live with their mothers-in-law, they have no life of their own, and probably their husbands do not even speak to them in front of other family members.

"How to pay the taxes so their land will not be taken from them—land on which their fathers and grandfathers and generations of fathers before them raised food—is their primary concern. When they go to the villages or towns to sell their rice or to buy some luxury with an extra coin from a good harvest, they stand in awe in front of stores, looking at goods they can never even hope to own. They see rickshaws owned by the rich, clothing of silk, granaries piled high, jewels, lamps . . . but none of these things are for them.

"They are the victims of the warlord's soldiers who—if the farmer cannot pay his taxes—can be beaten, thrown off the land, have the women of his family raped. That means dishonor to the man of the family. He will probably never touch the woman again. She has brought shame to the family. Can you imagine this, Chlöe? I have known these things all my life, but I have not really seen them. I am, after all, one of the privileged."

Ching-ling arose from the settee on the porch overlooking the woods, cool in the shade. It probably never got hot up here, Chlöe thought, they were so high up, nearly a mile. It was so refreshing after late June in Shanghai and the humidity of the Yangtze. "Come, let me show you my favorite spot and I shall go on. I have things inside me that I must share, things that horrify yet exhilarate me at the same time. Damien will be safe now that he's napping. But even if he wakens, my maid will take good care of him. She's been with me for over eight years, and I'd trust her with my life."

They walked, hand in hand, down a lane lined with little stone houses, past the village itself to a promontory where the view literally took Chlöe's breath. In the clear mountain air they could see for hundreds of miles. In the distance they could even see the brown ribbon of the Yangtze winding through the green fields. Every inch of tillable land was graced by rice paddies, cultivated up to the top of each hill.

Chlöe walked closer to the edge, an exhilarating feeling. A strong wind could whip her off the promontory. But there was not even a breeze. I like it, she thought. I like being on the edge.

She walked back to the pine trees, where Ching-ling had seated herself and Ching-ling said, "Here, sit down. I love sitting in pine needles. Just smell them."

Ching-ling began to talk. "One purpose of our trek to Wuhan was to awaken the peasants, to let them know revolution is alive in the land and to show them they needn't put up with all the degradation they've gone through for centuries. Another reason was to see whether we had to fight the warlords in each district or if they'd join us."

She paused.

Chlöe looked at her. "And?" she urged.

Ching-ling's eyes met Chlöe's. Pain was reflected there. Finally she said, "I remember reading Shakespeare in college—I forget which play it was—but I remember having to memorize something about the sound and the fury." She paused and her eyes glistened. Chlöe thought for a moment that her friend was going to cry.

"That's what it was, Chlöe. Sound and fury. I don't know why I'm not insane from all I witnessed, all I partook in. Once they've begun to awaken and understand that they do not have to live like subhumans, that there is hope, that the common people can have something to say about their own destinies, there's no limit to their rage. They ran around burning the houses of the landlords, the ones who had taxed them and taken their lands, who had bought their daughters. They raped the landlords' daughters and their wives. . . .

"They dismembered the landlords, they hanged them, they disemboweled and beheaded them. . . ."

"Garroted?" Chlöe heard herself exclaim, remembering how horrified she'd been to learn of such a sadistic practice.

Ching-ling stopped talking for a minute, thinking. "No. No garroting. I guess because all this violence was spontaneous—garroting takes time and intention. This was a passionate uprising, a collective instinctive reflex."

Chlöe wondered if Ching-ling wasn't perhaps making excuses for what she had witnessed.

"I have always known that compared to your American culture, we Chinese are cruel. But I had no idea to what extent my people would go. Chlöe, it froze my heart. But it made me realize that my people cannot much longer go on as they have. We must free ourselves. When I saw peasants forcing a man to watch as they impaled his daughter on a bamboo reed whose end had been cut to a sharp point, as I listened to her screams and heard them laughing, I knew then that such had been done to their own wives and daughters. These actions were retribution. An eye for an eye, goes the saying. Chlöe, it was ghastly."

Chlöe thought she might be ill. Her mind was locked on a bamboo bayonet being pushed up her own vagina and the thought nearly doubled her over with pain. "Oh, my God."

Ching-ling continued. "Man's inhumanity to man. Isn't that the story of civilization, of the world from its beginning? If I absorbed my history lessons well, that really is a thumbnail sketch of the story of our world. Men enjoy hurting others. They get pleasure from it. I want to help eradicate that. If all people have full bellies, if they have some leisure so that all life is not work work work, if they are not penalized for being poor and uneducated, if they have time to learn, if they have hope for the future—then, and only then, will cruelty be abolished."

Did Ching-ling really believe that? Did she have such faith in human nature that she really believed what she was saying?

"I saw men beat other men to death with shovels, I saw them smash heads wide open with axes, I saw them cut arms off and leave the victims writhing on the ground. I saw them indiscriminately kill all the women dressed in silks and furs."

There was silence.

Ching-ling looked at her friend, her eyes softening, and said, "I didn't try to stop them, Chlöe. I did nothing to urge them on . . . but I did nothing to halt them either. Sometimes I felt the thrill of it all, felt the fervor of revolution. Then I didn't mind the bloodshed. Perhaps I've realized ever since Dr. Sun's death that it would require violence. A sleeping giant is awakening."

Chlöe let go of her friend's hand and asked, "How can you advocate something that requires such violence?" Her voice was filled with censure. "How can you willingly add to what you call man's inhumanity to man? Oh, Ching-ling!"

"I think," Ching-ling spoke slowly, trying to find the right words, "that when you believe in something as strongly as I believe in democracy for China, for helping it into the twentieth century, to eradicating the wrongs of a thousand years or more, then you are willing to do anything to achieve your goal. You tell yourself the end justifies the means. And you believe it. Chlöe, I would kill. I myself would kill someone who stood in the way of my dream. Someone who stood between the Chinese people and liberation."

Chlöe shivered. "I couldn't kill. No matter what, I couldn't kill."

"We all can kill if something matters enough."

Chlöe didn't debate the point, but she knew she couldn't. She couldn't even imagine voluntarily hurting someone. She was sure she must have hurt a few people in the course of her lifetime, but certainly it had not been done maliciously or with forethought. She had always championed the underdog, rescued the runts of the litter, turned bullies away from hurting the smallest or the oddest in class. She couldn't imagine someone getting pleasure from hurting another. No, she could not do any of that. It made her sick to hear about it.

"Aren't there other ways?" she asked her friend. "Does it have to be violence?"

"You have never been one of the underprivileged. One of those who had no hope, who were ground under the heels of the wealthy and greedy, living your life in fear and meekness. When the halter is taken away, when you yourself feel some sense of power, vengeance seems just. What would you advocate? Talking?"

Chlöe nodded dumbly.

"I had hoped you would not be judgmental," Ching-ling said. "I hoped you would listen and, even if you couldn't understand, you would not be angry with me. Or with my cause. I hoped you would let me get this out, say these things aloud and not feel guilty."

"I am not against your cause," Chlöe's voice was but a whisper, "but I am against these methods."

"They are not mine," said Ching-ling. "They are the common man rising up, the cry of subjugation, the howling from the wilderness, the shrieks of those who see light for the first time, the very first time since time itself began. They are instinctive reactions to all the wrongs that have been wrought in the name of greed and power."

Then she burst into tears and, leaning over, buried herself in Chlöe's breast.

Chlöe's arms enfolded her, and she held the sobbing woman who would become known as the conscience of China.

# CHAPTER 21

Their remaining days on the mountain at Lu-shan were tranquil. Ching-ling sang to Damien and held him as often as Chlöe did. Her eyes softened when he was in her arms, and gradually the tension left her body, Chlöe could tell.

"We're going to grow fat, being so lazy and eating so much." Ching-ling laughed. "Isn't it wonderful!"

"It is," Chlöe agreed. "We'll get quite spoiled and not want to do anything when we leave here."

"I can't bear to think of leaving. This is so lovely. Yet the thought of returning invigorates me. But, my dear," Ching-ling reached out and placed her hand over Chlöe's, "you don't know how much these two weeks have meant to me. I am refreshed. I shall be going back to Nikolai, who has had no rest. I don't know how he does it. We are most fortunate to have such a dedicated person guiding us. I wonder what we would do without him."

"Do you trust him? I mean, after all, he is a Russian. Is he trying to infiltrate your group and take China for Russia?"

Ching-ling said, "I trust Nikolai with my life. I trusted him with my husband's life, which is even more. Nikolai is selfless. He lusts after no power, but a dream."

"Have you thought of remarriage? Of Nikolai, perhaps."

Ching-ling shook her head. "Never. I will never let another man enter my life. Nothing must deter me from my goal. No other man could ever measure up to Dr. Sun. Besides"—she smiled that sweet smile of hers—"no Chinese woman of good reputation would marry again. Here a widow is revered, Chlöe, and I have my part to play in this drama that is unfolding in my country. I do not have room in my heart for two masters. Nor could I bear to ruin a friendship like the one Nikolai and I have. He is a true friend. We are tied by a common goal, but there is no fire between us. America showed me I must have fire with a man in order to share my life with him. Perhaps that view of men has ruined any hope for happiness I could find with another after Dr. Sun. Dr. Sun, you see, supplied me with everything, mainly with a reason for living."

Chlöe wondered how that old, ineffective man—at least that's what he'd been like when she'd known him—could inspire such dedication in her beloved friend.

"Besides," Ching-ling smiled, "Nikolai has no time in his life for a woman. Sometimes I think he would be a good monk. All his fire and passion go into dreams."

After a minute she said, "It may not be safe for Damien in China, Chlöe. Perhaps you should take him home."

"Why?" She opened her blouse so she could nurse him, listening to him gurgle contentedly.

"There will be civil war. Peasants against the upper classes. I am afraid it may turn out to be Chiang against the rest of us. I do not trust him as much as Nikolai does. He's on his way to Shanghai, you know, but his armies have not yet reached there. He is eradicating whole villages, I hear, and blaming us. When we each left Canton, it was understood that he and his armies would march directly north and take Shanghai. We would come northwest and take

Wuhan. On the way we would educate the people as to our goals and recruit them to our cause.

"*We* have succeeded. Any bloodletting has been due to the peasants. Wuhan, being the most industrialized city in the nation, is ripe for unionizing, for our brand of thinking. It welcomed us literally with open arms. It is a city alive, filled with unbelievable excitement and hope. But Chiang has destroyed villages, killing multitudes of peasants."

Chlöe asked, "Why would he kill the peasants . . . the backbone of the nation? What reason can he possibly have?"

"A show of might, perhaps. He is blaming the Communists for the mayhem. I suspect he is out to destroy us too, but Nikolai says we must not jump to conclusions. He does not believe Chiang shares our dream. He wants China to leap into world prominence, that is true, but he would like to be at the helm. He lusts for power, and I suspect will annihilate anyone who does not agree with him. He frightens me."

"And your people. Have they not just annihilated those who don't agree with them?"

Ching-ling nodded. "It is more that they have murdered those who have done them wrong. Retribution. Justice, even."

Chlöe cared what happened to China mainly because her close friends were involved, because they were lit with inner fires. She now understood how missionaries gave up comfort and home to devote their lives in wildernesses to causes they so completely believed in.

The steamer heading upriver to Wuhan appeared before the one that would take Chlöe down to Shanghai, and Chlöe felt an ache as she watched her friend's ship pull away from the dock.

It was only after she had turned away from the river and started back to the inn that she realized she was being followed. A woman wrapped in filthy rags waddled behind her, not more than a dozen steps away. When Chlöe turned a corner, the woman followed. Finally Chlöe stopped abruptly and turned around to confront the woman. Better to face the beggar than to give in to the prickly sensation of fear that was creeping across her neck.

"I have no money with me," she said.

The obviously pregnant woman nodded dumbly, just staring at Chlöe and Damien.

"Leave me alone. I can't give you anything." Chlöe turned on her heel and continued walking, trying to push aside her fear. The woman did not look dangerous, but Chlöe was disquieted. She did not like having her footsteps dogged.

She went into the inn, hoping the woman would not follow. At least she felt safe there. In the morning, however, when she opened her door, the woman was asleep on the stone stoop. As soon as the door opened, she jumped up—not easy to do in her cumbersome state.

Chlöe thought it would be better to get rid of her and searched through her purse for several coins. Handing them to the woman, she left to find breakfast. But the woman followed her and Damien. What more does she want? Chlöe wondered, irritation having replaced fear. In the tearoom she ordered tea and noodles.

The woman stood outside by the door, her dark eyes glued to Damien. Oh, God, thought Chlöe, is she going to try to kidnap him? She held him ever tighter. He was covered with prickly heat and, though fussy, was not bawling as he had endlessly the previous day.

"Take some noodles and tea to that woman sitting by the doorway," Chlöe instructed the waiter. The young man made a sound of disapproval deep in his throat, but when Chlöe held out coins, he did as she told him. The woman reached up and practically inhaled the noodles, clutching the cup of tea as though it were salvation.

She continued to sit and stare at Chlöe until Chlöe arose and left the restaurant. Then she whispered, "Su-lin."

It's her name, Chlöe realized, turning around to look back at the woman huddled in the doorway.

She did not look around again until she returned to the inn. Then, when she saw the woman nowhere in sight, Chlöe felt infinite relief.

Sedan bearers took her and her luggage to the ship. Despite her two idyllic weeks with Ching-ling, Chlöe felt a surge of excitement to be returning to Shanghai and to Slade.

Several British and American men were on board, missionaries or businessmen heading to the city or homeward bound after their tours of duty. They sat around the dining table at night telling China stories, and none was ever flattering to the Chinese.

"I'm going home to a decent woman," one said. "Like you, ma'am." He nodded.

Chlöe wondered what being a decent woman meant. She guessed it meant being white.

She had left Damien asleep, so she rushed back to her cabin after dinner. Sitting on one of the beds, smiling with delight as she held Damien, was the pregnant woman she had last seen at the inn. Chlöe noted she had bottomless eyes.

The woman looked up and grinned, revealing a hole where three teeth should have been.

"I new nurse," she said. "My name Su-lin."

Her accent was north Chinese. "Get out," said Chlöe, furious at this intrusion.

"I good nurse. Very good nurse. I have baby soon. They can play together."

Chlöe wanted nothing to do with this slovenly woman who trailed her.

"Get out," she repeated. "I don't need a nurse. Give me my son."

Su-lin held Damien out to Chlöe.

"How did you get on this ship?" Chlöe demanded, wondering how she was going to get rid of this creature. She certainly wasn't what that man meant by a decent woman.

"These coins you gave me yesterday." The toothless grin flashed. "Bought ticket."

Oh, God, what would she ever do in Shanghai? She wouldn't find a job, not looking like she did. She was a woman of uncertain age—a beggar, a wretched, dirty woman with tangled hair.

"Have you ever been to Shanghai?" Chlöe was amazed to find herself even conversing with the woman.

The woman shook her head. "No, but it will be no worse than places I have been. I'm good nurse."

No one would let the woman around their children, Chlöe reflected.

"Get out," Chlöe said again. "I don't need you." Certainly she was not going to take responsibility for this woman's having followed her.

She pulled Damien close to her that night, thinking of what Su-lin might do to him. Would she steal him?

In the morning Su-lin was again asleep outside her door.

Does she think she's protecting me? Chlöe wondered, and was surprised to find herself bringing the woman back rice cakes and tea. The woman gulped them down hungrily.

"When did you eat last?" asked Chlöe, refusing to invite the woman into her cabin.

"Yesterday morning, when you sent tea to me."

"Before that?"

The woman shrugged, indicating she didn't recall. "Long time," she said.

"You're going to have a baby," Chlöe said.

The toothless grin flashed again and Su-lin patted her belly. "This time no one take it away from me."

Chlöe looked at her. "Why would anyone take it from you?"

"Others taken from me. Owners of whorehouse sold them. I never even saw them. Two boys, three girls. All sold. This time no one take from me. I keep."

Chlöe's hand involuntarily clasped her chest. This woman had had five children ripped from her, sold even before she saw them?

Before she knew what she was doing, Chlöe said, "Come into my room, come take a bath. I'll send for more food. When is this baby due?"

Su-lin looked vacant.

"Don't you know when you slept with its father?" Obviously there was no husband.

"Sleep every night, every day with many men," said Su-lin. "I ran away over two moons ago, and have been traveling ever since. I knew I could stop when I saw you."

Oh, God, thought Chlöe. I don't want this responsibility.

Want it or not, when she arrived back in Shanghai, Su-lin was with her. And within another two months Su-lin gave birth to a frail yellow baby whom Chlöe didn't give a chance of lasting, considering his mother's lack of nutrition. Su-lin called her son Han, and proved not only to be an excellent mother but a very good nurse for Damien.

# CHAPTER 22

Big-eared Tu and his Green Gang struck.

They ransomed Shanghai, forcing the city's leading businessmen to loan Chiang Kai-shek three million dollars. In exchange, Chiang promised to protect them from the Communists. There was nothing business leaders feared more than the masses rising, nothing they dreaded more than labor unions and strikes and the accompanying hikes in salaries. They paid.

At four o'clock in the morning a bugle blasted from Chiang's headquarters. Chiang sat on his gunboat in the harbor. Homes of known Communists were blasted, labor union offices were bombed, the staccato bursts of machine guns exploded private homes, and anyone unfortunate enough to be out on the streets at such an hour might be shot. The soldiers had orders to shoot anyone not wearing a white armband. Only the soldiers wore the identifying white stripes.

It took nine hours for the gunfire to stop. Thousands of citizens died.

Later it took eighteen trucks to collect the corpses.

The wives and daughters of the dead were sold to brothels and to factories. Chiang's armies raised a good deal of money in this manner.

Shanghai stood quiet, stunned into silence and inaction. The European and American community, of course, had stayed in the Bund, behind their heavy doors and drawn drapes.

From Wuhan, Ching-ling sent a proclamation disowning Chiang Kai-shek and his actions, expelling him from the Kuomintang. An order for Chiang's arrest was issued by the party.

In Shanghai they laughed. The military power of China was in Shanghai, not in Wuhan, in the hands of Big-eared Tu and the Green Gang, masquerading under the banner of Chiang Kai-shek.

Chiang issued his own proclamation, discouraging students from extremism. His own son wrote: "My father has become my enemy. He has died as a revolutionary. He has betrayed the revolution. Down with the traitor!"

Anyone who disagreed with the policies of the Green Gang was publicly burned, garroted, beheaded, impaled on bamboo poles, or disappeared. Before executing many of them, the army troops were permitted, amid much laughter and joking, to disembowel the wives and daughters of these recalcitrant men. They forced the husbands and fathers to watch as they wound the intestines around the naked dead women. Then they buried the men alive.

In the Bund, in the consulates and the banks and the foreign concessions, after two days, business went on as usual. Slade assured Chlöe they were safe. Chiang did not want to alienate the West. "He'll woo us," Slade said. In his quest for power, Chiang needed the foreigners. Westerners sighed and shook their heads. A few of the younger wives begged their husbands to ask the State Department for transfers.

Dinner parties and Saturday evening dances began again. Chlöe thought of going home.

"We've been here over three years," she said to Slade. "I want to go someplace where it's not so dangerous, where our children can grow up without my fearing so for their lives. I want Damien to have a normal upbringing."

"My God." Slade laughed. "He's not even a year old. We'll be back in the U.S. by the time he's ready for school. You're asking me to leave this country now? Absolutely not. This is where news is. This whole country's changing right before our very eyes."

Yes, but it wasn't changing as she thought it should. What happened in Shanghai frightened and angered her. She knew that what was published in Cass's paper and in the London and New York papers was overshadowed by the articles Henry Luce was publishing in his new magazine. Henry Luce, born in China of American missionary parents, was in love with China and his weekly *Time* reflected this passion. He was convinced China was becoming a Christian country, and to this end he supported Chiang Kai-shek with his considerable energies. *Time* was more readable than the factual accounts carried near the back of the first section of the world's newspapers.

When Su-lin was not caring for her Han, she made herself useful. Damien was never alone. If Chlöe was not overseeing him, Su-lin was. Chlöe had only to look as though she wanted something, and Su-lin would rush for it.

"She nurses you as much as she does that kid of hers." Slade laughed. "You know, she probably thinks she owes you her life. You'll end up being responsible for her. You'll probably never get rid of her." A few minutes later he said, "I think I'll go up to Manchuria and Shantung. The Japs are infiltrating those provinces and I want to see what's going on."

"How long will you be gone this time?" Chlöe asked. It seemed to her he was gone half the year.

Slade shrugged. "I dunno. Three, four weeks. I want to take a good look around. Hey, don't look like that! You and Damien'll be okay. The heat of the summer's past. Cholera and typhoid have taken their toll for this year. You can go to any parties without me."

"I don't even like to go to those things anymore."

"I know." He sighed. "All you seem interested in is being a mother."

"What's wrong with that?" she asked defensively.

Slade shook his head. "Well, the rest of the world hasn't stopped, you know. The only other Westerners you even seem to like are Lou and Daisy."

"Have you noticed we see more and more of them as a couple?" Chlöe said.

"Women are proverbial matchmakers, aren't you? Yeah, but they're never together anyplace but here."

"Do you think," asked Chlöe, "that Lou's seen those stars above her bed?"

Slade raised his eyebrows and cocked his head. "And if he has?"

Her eyes opened wide. "Nothing, I suppose. But I wonder why they don't get married."

Slade said nothing.

"I mean, do you think they go to bed?"

"I don't think it's any of our business. But if they do, that's no reason they have to get married."

To most Americans in 1926, it *was* a reason to get married. Chlöe had never questioned it. "Do you think they're in love?" she pursued.

"For Christ's sake, just because the four of us have a good time together doesn't mean they have to want to spend their lives together."

She looked at her husband. "You know, I can't even imagine going to bed with someone other than you. And if you listen to what they say about Daisy, she's done it with lots of men."

"Daisy isn't you. I'd hope you wouldn't think of going to bed with another man."

She walked over to him and put her arms around his waist, looking up into his eyes. "Do you ever think of other women—in that way?"

Slade leaned over to kiss her. "Shall I prove it's you I want to go to bed with," he whispered, taking her hand.

Twenty-five minutes later he was fast asleep. Chlöe lay staring into the darkness, her nerve ends alive with yearning, wondering why he stopped so quickly, why he moaned so soon, why he stopped when she wanted—needed—to go on. When she silently cried for release. She remembered the few occasions he had taken the time to . . . to let her *feel*, to reach the peaks she had only sensed were there. She wondered why she couldn't talk to him about it. Why she couldn't say, "Slade, slow down. Wait for me." Or even, "Touch me here. Right here, where it drives me wild." Or, "Don't stop," when his lips brushed her breasts. But he always did stop. Far too soon.

In the morning he left for the north.

Slade had been gone ten days when Damien developed a slight fever. Chlöe met Daisy for lunch and, as usual when with her friend, spent the afternoon laughing. Su-lin greeted Chlöe at three in the afternoon with the news that she didn't think Damien was well. He seemed a bit hot, and had awakened from his nap slightly cranky. Chlöe reached for him. He wasn't *that* hot, she thought, wondering if she should send for the doctor.

There were only three Western doctors in Shanghai then, two at the American Baptist Hospital and the naval doctor, who attended to civilians only in times of emergency, like summer cholera and malaria. The surgeon at the hospital never made house calls, but once in a while the other doctor did, if he had time.

It was seven before she decided she should ask him to come. When the doctor arrived, it was eight. He examined Damien and took his temperature.

"Hardly anything," he said. "Just a low-grade infection. Not much of a fever. Just enough to make him fussy." Chlöe could tell he was irritated to have been called. But she felt vast relief. "Here, give him some of these tablets, and he'll probably be fine by morning. I'd say nothing to worry about."

But she was worried enough that she slept in the bed beside his crib.

At three he awoke crying. She turned on the light beside her bed, reaching over to gather him in her arms. He smelled terrible.

His diapers and sheets were covered with diarrhea. His hands had twisted into the mess and he'd rubbed his eyes. Oh, God, she thought, gagging at the smell.

She sponged him off, tossing the messy sheets into a pile. Holding him in one arm, she searched for other sheets, wondering where An-wei kept them. Damien cried the entire time.

She kept reminding herself what the doctor had told her. A low-grade infection. Nothing to worry about. The heat of the summer had passed. There were no diseases rampaging the city.

She sat up the rest of the night, rocking him, changing his diapers every few minutes for an hour, and then every half hour. He dozed on her shoulder. Toward dawn, she too fell asleep, her son in her arms.

She awakened with his vomiting on her nightgown.

By midmorning there were no clean diapers left. Chlöe sent for the doctor again. When he sent word that he could not come until evening, until he left the hospital, she called her rickshaw boy and, with Damien crying in her arms, had the boy run all the way to the hospital.

"Flu's going around," he said. "Mrs. Cavanaugh, it's nothing to worry about. Babies get diarrhea all the time, especially here in China. He has no fever today. It'll just have to run its course. All new mothers fret when their babies get ill. Believe me, it's no cause for alarm. Just keep bathing him, keeping him clean, and feed him purified water. Don't let him get dehydrated. That's where the problem is. Dehydration."

Su-lin brought in a Chinese doctor in the afternoon, a thin man with long, dirty fingernails, a scraggly white beard, and beady eyes. Chlöe couldn't take him seriously. He prescribed chicken soup and weak tea. She ignored the other folk remedies he prescribed, but Su-lin cooked up chicken broth and they spooned it into the fussy baby's mouth. Damien vomited it up.

By evening Chlöe thought the baby looked sunken-eyed. She walked around, staring down at him, looking at him from every angle, wondering if it was her imagination or if the skin around his eyes really had sunk. She told herself she was nuts. It couldn't be. He wasn't crying much now, but lay listless. The skin around his mouth wrinkled.

She fell asleep when Damien dozed but awoke with a start when he murmured. She changed his diapers again, grateful that Su-lin had cut up rag substitutes. She spent half the night changing his sheets and diapers, washing him off. Toward three she slept.

In the morning Damien didn't awaken. For a moment Chlöe's heart stopped. But she saw him breathing. She leaned over and his eyes fluttered awake, but he didn't look at her though she was right in front of him.

Dear God, she thought, his eyes aren't focusing. He was burning with fever. His skin tented up—she pulled it gently from his arm and it stayed puffed up in the air. There was no elasticity at all. Dehydration, she thought in panic. There's no water. She picked him up, but he just lay there, not reacting at all, his eyes open but unfocused. Dear God in heaven!

"Su-lin," she called, "tell the rickshaw boy to fetch the doctor. Tell him it's an emergency." Looking at her son, she was overwhelmed by a sense of helplessness, more frightened than she'd ever been in her life.

Damien regurgitated every ounce of water she siphoned into him. It slobbered in little streams out of the corner of his mouth. He was burning up. His breathing became labored, and so did hers. Trying to fight down the panic and fear that surged through her, she prayed. Dear God, if you're there, please, please save my son!

And she told herself again, Lots of little babies get sick. The doctor said it's a low-grade infection. He also said don't let him get dehydrated. But Damien kept down no water, and the diarrhea never ceased. His breathing came in labored spurts, sounding as though he were gasping for life itself, she thought, her stomach in a knot.

And then she told herself, Don't be so dramatic. You're just making it worse.

He lay in the crib with no clothes on, for he soiled whatever she put on him. She stared at him as he gasped for breath. He resembled a skeleton as the skin between his ribs sucked in.

While she waited for the doctor she wept with her powerlessness. Damien's arms and legs jerked as he fought for breath, and she reached out to take him in her arms, clasping him to her. He wheezed, inhaling a great gulp of air. Then he let go of it, and lay limp.

His little chest rose and fell ever so slightly. He opened his eyes, but she knew he didn't see her. He gulped again, his arms and legs jerking spasmodically. He did that again . . . and again . . . and again. Until he gasped, and this time his arms and legs didn't spasm. He lay limp in her arms.

Her own breath came in ragged convulsions.

Holding the baby, she walked over to the rocking chair and sat down, rocking gently, singing to him. His cheeks grew whiter and his lips took on a bluish tinge. She reached for his hand, raising it to her lips, and saw that his fingers were the blue of his lips.

She raised him to her mouth, put her lips on his, and knew before she did it that she would feel no breath. His chest no longer heaved. And she screamed, a wailing, keening cry that brought Su-lin and An-wei and Gao Hu.

She could not stop sobbing. He wasn't dead. He couldn't be. Just yesterday morning he had been so full of life, trying to walk across the garden by himself. He couldn't be gone. She knew he couldn't be dead; at the same time she couldn't stop bawling, giant gasping sobs that had no end.

The doctor never arrived until nine o'clock, eight hours after Damien died in his mother's arms.

Chlöe had not let go of him in all that time. She hugged him to her chest and carried him around as she wailed. Her weeping stopped after an hour, and then she made no sound at all. She seemed not to hear what anyone said, even when Daisy came at Su-lin's call.

Daisy, her own eyes red-rimmed, said, "Chlöe, oh, dear dear Chlöe . . ."

Chlöe heard her not at all.

Daisy sent for Lou.

But Lou could comfort only Daisy, for Chlöe neither saw nor heard them. When she was at the point of collapse, she sank onto the bed, her arms still wrapped around Damien, and slept with the dead baby in her arms.

The doctor, when he finally arrived, tried to take the baby from the sleeping woman. Chlöe awoke with fury.

"A low-grade infection!" she screamed, wrapping Damien tighter in her arms. "Get out of here." Her hollow eyes followed him as he left the room, saying to Daisy, "Get that baby from her."

But no one could.

In the morning, when Chlöe awoke, Daisy forced tea down her, but Chlöe held on to Damien, saying, "Tell Su-lin to bring his porridge here. I'll feed him."

She walked around the house and out into the garden, clutching her dead, naked son.

It was not until late in the morning that Daisy grabbed her wrist and said, "Chlöe. Damien's dead."

Chlöe stared at her for moments before she sank onto the grass and began to cry, rocking back and forth with Damien still in her arms.

Then, as Daisy stood nearby, Chlöe and Su-lin, who would not leave Chlöe, bathed his cold body. Daisy found clean clothes and they dressed him in his little white linen suit. During the whole process Chlöe never talked or cried again. She let Daisy tell her what to do.

"Where do you want him buried?" Daisy asked.

At this Chlöe did focus her eyes on her friend, saying, "I don't know. Maybe here, by the pampas grass."

"I don't think they'll let you," said Daisy.

Lou made arrangements to bury Damien in the Protestant cemetery.

There was no way to get hold of Slade.

After the funeral Chlöe sat in the rocking chair for two days, staring into nothingness, singing to herself. Singing lullabies.

# CHAPTER 23

The Blue Express was the first modern train that China had ever seen, speeding from Shanghai by way of Nanking to Peking.

Slade, along with Lou and Daisy, stood on the station platform as Chlöe disappeared into the crushing crowds. For a few minutes she wondered if she might be trampled to death. It was the first time since Damien's death three months before that she'd cared about living. She was going to travel all the way north to Peking alone. Added to this was the pride she felt that Slade trusted her, that he was relying on her.

Having been borne along by the weight of the crowds and hustled down the long stairway, she stared at the long train. Two coal tenders were behind the black locomotive, which hissed steam into the dark, cavernous station. Chlöe trotted beside it, though most of the people hurtled into the nearest wooden carriages, already overflowing with peasants. They leaned out the windows and crammed onto the hard wooden church-pew seats. Many were forced to stand in the aisles.

She was looking for one of the first-class coaches, which would be of steel rather than wood. In the distance she could see the caboose, to whose railing peasants were already clinging. Wondering if they could hold on for all the hours of the trip, she shivered, feeling guiltily fortunate.

The first-class carriages were composed entirely of compartments. Chlöe noted there were very few Chinese. Most were Europeans, all of whom seemed to know English and were shouting it Chinese style—at the top of their voices.

She pushed through to the next coach and discovered she was the last person in her compartment. The other five were already there. A United States Army major was the only one standing, his back to her, storing suitcases in racks overhead.

There were two young women animatedly talking together and, across from them, another young woman staring straight ahead. Seated near the door, next to the two young women, was a man whom Chlöe guessed to be about forty, a pencil-thin mustache looking as though it had been painted above his almost equally thin lips.

"I say," he said with a decidedly British accent, and reached for her bag. Handing it to the major, he stood while Chlöe seated herself and then he introduced himself. "Donald McArthur," he said with a slight bow from the waist.

"I'm Mrs. Cavanaugh," she said, and smiled around the compartment. "Chlöe Cavanaugh."

The young blonde by the window gave a bright smile. "Nancy Lloyd," she said. "And this is my friend Amy Lowell."

The major turned around and Chlöe could see he was quite nice looking. She guessed him to be in his early thirties, and he stood erect, as though he represented the whole United States armed forces. "Major Hughes," he said, "at your service. Allan Hughes." He sat down next to the young lady who had not spoken.

Nancy explained. "She's my maid, Imogene. She doesn't speak English at all. She's French."

Imagine that, thought Chlöe. Having a French maid and bringing her along from America.

Major Hughes said, "Japan's far cleaner and more efficient than China." He began to titillate the girls with tales of white slavery and kidnapping and how Chinese enjoyed torturing prisoners. "There are bandits up in Shantung province, you know. We'll be passing through it."

Chlöe tried not to show her amusement. He was so obviously trying to impress the young women. "There are roving bands of them," he told the wide-eyed girls across from him.

"Oh, goodness," said Miss Lloyd. "Are we in danger?"

"Hardly," he answered as though he were sure of his answers. "They loot towns and villages and kidnap the inhabitants for ransom, but they leave foreigners alone."

"They bloody well better," said Mr. McArthur.

Chlöe closed her eyes. When she did so, in her mind's eye Damien sat in front of her, smiling, his hand clasped around her finger.

With a thunderous jerk the train pulled out of the station. I'm glad I have something new to look forward to, she thought, something I've never done before, nothing I can compare to anything old in my life. But she couldn't open her eyes. For if she did, she might lose Damien.

With the *clickclickclick* of the iron wheels on the tracks, the train journey began.

Maybe when she returned to Shanghai, when she and Slade had time to talk, she could ask him again when he was thinking of returning home. She wanted desperately to return to places that were clean and safe. Where her children wouldn't die.

Mr. McArthur interrupted her thoughts, asking why she was going to Peking.

"I'm going to cover a story up there for the *Chicago Times*," she answered, feeling a surge of pride.

They all looked at her then. Chlöe imagined they didn't believe her. A woman reporter? She felt quite important.

"How d'ya do that without being able to speak Chinese?" asked Mr. McArthur.

Chlöe looked at him, cocking her head sideways. "Do you speak it?"

"A bit." He nodded.

She launched into a discussion of the differences between Shanghai and Peking in her perfect Mandarin, while his mouth hung open in amazement. Imogene turned to look at her for the first time. Then she began to giggle.

"How did you ever learn that?" asked Nancy. "I didn't think Americans could really speak it."

Chlöe was the first of the group to retire. Imogene had the bunk above hers and though Imogene had not said a word all day, Chlöe volunteered to walk to the sleeping car with her and help her into the upper bunk. The murmur of the *clickety clickety clickety* sound of the train along the tracks lulled Chlöe to sleep, to thankful dreamlessness.

She had no idea what time it was when the brakes ground to a screeching halt and she was nearly tumbled into the aisle. She pulled the curtains aside to look out the window. All she could see at first was the moon, silvery against the blackness. Then she heard gunshots. As her eyes became accustomed to the darkness, as loud voices reverberated within the compartment, people screamed. A vanguard of riders steered their horses down the embankment, rifles shooting randomly into the air.

At that moment Imogene hurled herself into Chlöe's berth,

gasping little sobs. Chlöe reached for the young woman's hand while trying to find her own clothes.

Pandemonium had broken loose. People yelled, trying to scramble into their clothes, running aimlessly along the corridor. The door to the compartment opened, and Chlöe heard shouting. "Stop! Halt! Come as you are, leave the train at once."

She looked down at herself, at the silken nightgown, and grabbed for her robe, silken also but covering her more, fashioned in the style of the Chinese dresses she had taken to wearing around the house. She had carefully put her clothes at the bottom of the bed, but as she began to reach for them, the curtains of her berth ripped open. A Chinese face grinned at her. Its owner grabbed her arm and said, "Do not linger. Come as you are."

As he said that, a Belgian businessman who had been in the next compartment threw a teapot at him. What he was doing with a teapot in his bed Chlöe couldn't imagine. But the Chinese turned quickly, cocked his rifle, and shot the man in the hand.

There was silence. No one moved. The wounded man moaned, and a woman screamed. Moving toward the Belgians, the Chinese cocked his rifle again and said, "Someone who speaks Chinese, tell everyone to get out of this car or I shoot again!"

Chlöe translated. No one hesitated. No one turned to grab their precious belongings, or slippers, or clothes that would decently cover them. Outside, other men with guns were waiting, lining the passengers up against the embankment. Chlöe looked at her watch. It was just after two. She shivered in the chill air. Along the embankment, soldiers stood guard over all the passengers in the sleeping cars. The peasants in the wooden cars, the ones who had been packed like sardines, remained on the train.

From the baggage car and from the first-class cars soldiers emerged with suitcases, with bags, with everything they could lay their hands on. They shouted and grinned. Chlöe envied the women who'd had the presence of mind to toss coats over their nightgowns. She hoped the bandits would take all the things, all the valuables and whatever else they wanted, and leave, let them get back on the train instead of standing out in the cold, humiliated and scared.

A few women started to cry, and confusion reigned. Imogene reached out for Chlöe's hand.

A man whose face Chlöe could not see rode down the line. His big horse was between them and the train, heading toward the locomotive. He raised his left arm and gave a shout that Chlöe could not understand. As the whistle cried into the night and steam hissed into the air, Chlöe watched as the train chugged slowly, inch by inch at first, picking up speed as it disappeared into the night. The peasants, still crowded into the wooden cars, leaned out the windows, shouting no one could understand what.

Oh, dear God in heaven, she thought, trying to get her bearings. In the distance were the craggy, unyielding Shantung Mountains.

The shadowed man on the big horse gave a shrill cry and, as though by signal, the bandits divided themselves along either side of the line of prisoners, prodding them to walk. Imogene began to cry. Chlöe reached out to touch the Frenchwoman, but the bandit beside her prodded her with his rifle. Two bandits were at the side of each prisoner, precluding any thought of escape. Chlöe figured there must be close to two hundred kidnapped passengers. She couldn't understand why she wasn't more frightened.

Damned mad was more like it. The rocky terrain tore through her slippers, and she suspected her feet were already bloody. The full moon made it possible to see that nothing but fields and mountains lay ahead of them. Imogene was right on her heels, tripping constantly. Except for a sob now and then, the single line of passengers was silent.

The major warned us, Chlöe thought, beginning to breathe heavily as the flat land turned to hills. And I thought he was trying to frighten and impress the girls. I didn't believe him. As Imogene fell against her, Chlöe turned to help the young woman, taking her hand.

They walked and walked up into the mountains, their feet cut to ribbons. Chlöe heard a voice spit forth "Outrageous." She agreed. It was. But she was too tired to try to talk. They all kept stumbling now. Her side began to ache. Certainly it would be dawn soon. Why that brought her hope she didn't know. They must be getting to someplace. They couldn't be kept walking for days. Or could they?

A jagged ribbon of red presaged dawn. Never stopping walking, she turned to look back down the mountain. For half a mile the passengers and their captors were spread out on the narrow mountain path. Beyond them—for farther than the eye could see—there was a disorganized straggling line of bandits carrying all the loot from the train. Several had mattresses across their shoulders, ones they must have torn from the berths. From the looks of them, they hadn't missed a single suitcase in the baggage car.

She had to laugh, for one of the bandits had discovered a brassiere, which he had tied around his waist and filled with trinkets.

The sun splintered shards of bright color into the pale sky, and the clouds hanging above the horizon turned pink, then purple, fading—as the group continued up the mountain—into shades of rose and lavender, until the clouds dissipated, leaving the sky a bright azure. Chlöe thought it all quite beautiful. The saw-toothed mountain range was to the east, while behind them were the plains that stretched into infinity. Certainly before long, help would arrive. The bandits couldn't get away with this kidnapping of two hundred foreigners. Who could be so foolish as to abduct so many foreigners, people whose governments would pursue their safety? That was what consulates were for, she told herself.

The day turned hot. They had been marching and climbing for eight hours, Chlöe saw by her watch. The trail narrowed, a mere dirty path between rocks that became boulders. The summit appeared above her. And Imogene fell. The sweating bandit to her left picked the Frenchwoman up and carried her on his back, with hardly a grunt.

As she reached the peak of the mountain, Chlöe saw a fort looming in front of them. The train passengers ahead of her had already been herded into a large stone-walled courtyard and collapsed, eliciting moans, feet bleeding. Some of the women were crying. In a far corner was a water trough, whether for horses or people no one asked. They drank it dry, huddling on the ground, exhausted, in pain.

Chlöe looked around. They all would have been terribly embarrassed to be caught in such states of dishabille in any other circumstances. Her silk nightgown and robe were muddied.

"Here," said Major Hughes, talking to Imogene, who lay in a heap. He pulled off his pajama top and began to rip it, wrapping the shreds of cotton around Imogene's bleeding feet. His own feet were bloody too, but he went around offering his makeshift bandages to the women nearby.

Nancy and Amy hobbled over to Chlöe, slumping to the hard ground beside Imogene. Neither of the young women complained, though fright and exhaustion were evident in their eyes.

Amy, her voice quivering, asked, "Do you think they'll rape us?"

For a while Chlöe had wondered the same thing, but now she said, "I doubt it. If that's what they wanted, they'd have done it already. They're out for something bigger, I wager."

"Like what?" asked Nancy.

Major Hughes, returning from his ministrations and now devoid of any clothing except his pajama bottoms, answered from behind her. "Ransom. They'll barter us for money."

Chlöe turned to look at him. He stood there, sweat streaked across his dusty chest. He scrunched down, studying Imogene, who lay flat on her back, hardly blinking. "Are you all right?" he asked. She just stared at him.

"I gave her some water," Chlöe said.

"The water up this high in the mountains ought to be all right, but be careful of drinking it any other place," he warned. "We could all die of cholera or dysentery."

They sat tending their wounds for the rest of the afternoon. Small groups of bandits disappeared; others huddled in the shadows of the wall, where it was cooler. Late in the afternoon there was a tumult at the wide entrance gates, and men on horseback rode in, carrying large baskets and earthenware jugs. The bandits handed a raw egg to each of the prisoners, most of whom stood staring blankly at the eggs.

A rotund British colonel climbed up on a ledge and motioned for attention. "Permit me . . ." he cried. It was the first time anyone had made any effort to speak to the group as a whole. ". . . to show you how to eat a raw egg."

Laughter. Did the bandits really mean this to be their meal for the day? "Here, this is how to do it. Chip, carefully, ever so small a hole in your egg and then"—he held his head back—"in this fashion suck out the contents, trying not to lose a precious drop." He demonstrated.

"Oh, goodness," said Amy, making a face of disgust.

Chlöe thought it tasted awful. She noticed several people spitting, throwing their eggs away. A raw egg, the first thing they'd been offered to eat all day.

As clouds gathered and darkness descended, they were quiet. Thunder rumbled and, in the distance, they could see lightning playing against the mountaintops. Chlöe wondered if they were going to be kept outdoors in the courtyard if it rained. As night drew closer she began to feel chilly in nothing more than her nightgown and robe. She wondered how the men who had followed Major Hughes' example—tearing their pajama tops to shreds in order to bandage twisted ankles and bleeding feet—would fare. Though the day had been hot, she knew the night would be cold this high in the mountains. The night before they had spent marching, and the exercise had warmed them. But tonight?

One of the bandits climbed on the ledge to announce that the time of rest was over and they would make ready to march. Protests went up from the group. They were not only frightened, they were debilitated from the long march of the previous night, these people who were used to very little exercise. Like artillery, thunder echoed in loud staccato bursts. No moon to light their way tonight.

One of the bandits came over to Imogene and lifted her up, carrying her across the compound and sitting her on a donkey. Not wanting to be separated, Chlöe, along with Nancy and Amy, followed. She looked around for Major Hughes, feeling safer when he was near. He waved, calling, "Don't worry. I'll keep an eye on you."

"It's amazing, isn't it," said Amy, "that there isn't more pandemonium? I'm scared to death and yet none of us is hysterical or anything of the sort."

Chlöe nodded. She'd been trying all day to analyze why they were all acting rather calmly in the face of such an extraordinary incident. Incident? That's really hardly the word for it, is it? she thought, wondering if Slade knew yet about the kidnapping. Actually, she thought, if I get out of this, he'll think it's a great story. Cass will love it too. Slade's even encouraging this one. . . .

As they marched, at gunpoint, through the gate at the other end of the courtyard, starting the downward journey on the opposite side of the mountain, rain began to pelt them. Within minutes it was a deluge pummeling their backs and chests. The narrow path, strewn already with rocks and stones, became slippery. Chlöe, falling, reached out into the empty air only to slide in the soggy dirt, clammy mud sluicing over her. The rain poured down so hard that she could hardly see for the rivulets running down her face. The mud sucked at her bloody feet; they hurt so much she thought she couldn't walk any farther. She wanted to cry, but she'd be damned if she'd give in to it. She heard one of the women sniffling, crying, "I can't go on." She felt that way too.

Nancy and Amy, directly behind her, made no sounds. Walking at such a pace, high in the mountains, made talk difficult. Chlöe's heart thumped so loudly, she feared it might burst. The rain settled into a gentleness, no longer pelting them, but it was cold and they were drenched. We'll die of pneumonia before anything else, she thought. She wondered how Slade would take the death of a son and a wife in one year.

The bandits held guns on them, but she imagined if they had been going to shoot, they would have done so already rather than sloshing through the rain with close to two hundred prisoners.

It was still dark when they came to a valley and Chlöe heard the rushing of a stream. A light shone ahead. Dogs barked. The sound gave comfort to Chlöe. People who had dogs couldn't be all bad. Except, she reminded herself, Chinese kept dogs not as pets but as they did pigs and chickens, for eating.

Even in the dark she could see a mud wall ahead of them, the line of people before her disappearing through it. As she walked through the heavy wooden door, the smell warmed her. The odor of the stable reminded her of the comforting smell of manure and straw and horseflesh that her grandfather's farm had always held for her. The floors were dry and there was a roof.

An oil lantern hung from an overhead beam, and as soon as each prisoner entered and realized they were indoors, that they were protected from the weather, they fell into the straw. Despite their wet clothes, they were sound asleep within minutes.

The sun was high in the sky when they were awakened by the sound of a gong reverberating. Bandits walked among them, handing out mugs of tea. When one handed Chlöe her mug, she asked, "Is there no food?" He stared at her without replying.

The British colonel who had demonstrated how to suck a raw egg had taken over the leadership role and tried asking when they would be fed. The Chinese looked at him. Chlöe thought the colonel had probably served in China for years and still didn't know the language. She turned to the bandit near her and repeated the colonel's question.

"*Mei-yao.*" The young man shrugged his shoulders.

"There isn't any," Chlöe called.

The young bandit tapped Chlöe on the shoulder and patted his own stomach, murmuring that they had no food either. Chlöe translated.

Sometime after midnight of the fifth night of marching, they started to descend. They slid and fell down the mountain path, but at least it was no longer raining. Not, she thought, that they could have gotten much dirtier. The hems of her nightgown and robe were already tattered, but the prisoners had given up any thought as to how they looked.

It was still dark when Chlöe heard a torrent of water cascading over rocks. Here they halted, squatting and sitting beside the path, waiting for they knew not what. Chlöe wished she could squat on her heels in that position the Chinese maintained for hours. She had tried, but her balance was precarious and she always toppled over. Perhaps their leg muscles were different, she thought.

Major Hughes sat beside her. "I've an idea," he said, "that this is it. Our destination."

"What makes you think so?" Chlöe asked, looking around, able to see only dim shapes in the hour before dawn.

"Fresh water. I think there's a village up ahead. This section of the country is noted for caves. This place is easily defended, for it's in a valley surrounded by mountains, I suspect."

Chlöe looked around and asked, "How can you tell?" She couldn't see much of anything.

"Though I haven't been here before, I've studied the terrain," he answered. "Maybe at last we'll be fed decently."

"What do you think they're going to do with us?" She hadn't faced what was going to happen to them after they stopped marching. It had seemed as if they were destined to walk forever.

"If we're fortunate, they'll just keep us until we're ransomed."

"Looking like we do," she smiled, "I doubt anyone would want to pay money for us."

He laughed, and she thought him a very nice person. Earlier, on the train, he had seemed rather arrogant, but he had lost that patina of superiority and had spent his time trying to alleviate the pain of the women around him.

Probably fewer than a quarter of the prisoners were women, and all of the women, except for six of them—herself, Nancy, Amy, Imogene, and two middle-aged missionaries—were with men. Women did not travel alone through China. Or much of anywhere else, she guessed.

When dawn came, it proved the major was correct. They were on the outskirts of a small village whose dwellings were no more than huts. But there were scrawny cattle here, pigs, chickens, and a few dogs. They were offered their first substantial meal, a soup laden with vegetables and a small portion of stringy meat. Chlöe was surprised she couldn't eat more than she did.

A sharp, dissonant, ear-splitting whistle blew.

Into the center of the crowd walked a lean, erect man. His face looked as though it had been chiseled out of stone, its high cheekbones pronounced, the eyes widely spaced, the nose straight. He was tall, as northern Chinese so often were, taller than the Chinese men Chlöe had seen in Shanghai. Unlike the soldiers with whom they'd been traveling, his khaki uniform fit him well. He wore hand-crafted leather boots. He was a man, Chlöe thought, used to expensive clothes. He walked with assurance, if not arrogance. Perhaps he wasn't Chinese after all. There was a joke in Shanghai that if you saw an Oriental with clothes that fit, he must be Japanese.

He stood, hands on his hips, and began to talk. He did not shout or try to make himself heard above the multitude, but within thirty seconds the crowd hushed as his voice carried to the outer edges of the circle.

"I am sorry for the inconvenience you have been caused."

Silence.

"It is, of course, nothing to the inconvenience foreigners have caused my people over the years."

Silence.

Then he looked over the crowd, and impatience flooded his face. "Is there anyone here who understands me?"

Chlöe and a few others raised their hands. His eyes stopped at her. She was the only woman who spoke his language. He reached out his right arm, at a right angle to his body, and beckoned her with his fingers. "Come," he said. "You. Translate."

He did not speak again until she'd threaded her way through the multitude and stood in front of him. He had studied her as she'd approached him and now did not look directly at her.

"You will receive one meal a day. You are free to walk around in this valley. If you try to escape, however, you will be shot. This is your only warning."

The bandit chief's voice was clear and he enunciated slowly. His bearing showed that he took for granted that whatever he said would be listened to. Chlöe had never seen a Chinese man like him before. His eyes were cold, like looking down the barrel of a gun.

"Is there anyone here who can write in Chinese?"

Chlöe and one other raised their hands. Now the bandit chief's intelligent eyes reflected amusement. He's thinking "a woman!" she could tell. Wouldn't you know. A woman! She loved the idea that this thought frustrated him. But his smile was more like laughter and in a quiet voice he asked, "What is your name?"

"I am Mrs. Slade Cavanaugh," she answered.

"Where is your husband?"

"He is in Nanking."

"And he permitted you to take a train alone?"

She nodded.

"You will write the letters for me. Find out the nationalities that are represented here. We will send letters to every consulate. I will send for you later."

Then he raised his head to look out at the crowd. His voice like molten steel, he announced, "If, within two weeks, there are no ransom payments, each day one of you will be killed."

Oh, my God!

"One person each day will die," he repeated. "And *you* will vote to decide who."

# CHAPTER 24

Snow Leopard was what his men called him.

At dusk, after the women had been assigned one enormous cave and the men three others, he sent for Chlöe. The kidnapped group was given another meal of soup, this one with turnips and noodles in it as well as shreds of unidentifiable meat.

The British colonel, whose name was Colonel Higgins but whom Chlöe and Nancy and Amy secretly called Colonel Blimp, laughed derisively. "By the time any letters are delivered, our armies will have rescued us. Mark my word."

"I find this all rather refreshing," Nancy giggled, staring out of the cave into the valley that was filled with the smoke from dozens of charcoal braziers heating the villagers' evening meals. "I don't have to pretend to be such a lady in these circumstances." She looked down at her clothes and then at Amy and Chlöe. "We all look like whores," she tittered. "Maybe even worse. We might as well be naked."

"Oh, Nancy." Amy looked shocked. "What do you know about such women?"

Chlöe thought Nancy had a point. She had days before abandoned any feeling of modesty. One needn't use much imagination
to see through most of the nightgowns the women wore. A few
didn't even have the luck to have brought robes. She wished they
had quilts for the chilly nights. None had touched brush or comb
to her hair since they'd been kidnapped. Most of them looked wilder
than their captors. It was a marvel none of them were ill.

Now, though, when Snow Leopard sent for her, Chlöe wished
her robe did not cling to her, wished that her nightgown were not
so silken, so fragile.

Allan Hughes stood outside the women's cave. He said, "I'll
come along with you."

The tent was so dark that at first Chlöe could not see. But in
the center, behind a Western-style desk of teakwood, sat Snow Leopard under a swaying oil lamp. He looked at her as she approached,
walking across the large tent toward him.

"So," he said, his elbows on the desk and his fingers making a
pyramid in front of his chin.

Chlöe stood looking at him while he stared at her. She felt only
mildly frightened. He was a powerful-looking man, and his eyes glittered like coals, hard anthracite.

"My country has had women rulers," he said unexpectedly.

"Then you are ahead of my country," she said finally. It dawned
on her that this was his way of dealing with a foreign woman. "We
have not yet had women leaders." And probably won't in my lifetime, she thought. But you must deal with me, now, bandit. You
must cope with a woman. She wondered if he ever had before.

He clapped his hands and immediately a young Chinese woman
entered, carrying two bowls of tea. She carried them to a low table.
Gesturing for Chlöe to sit on the large bearskin rug in the center of
the tent, he himself remained seated at his desk.

"Come," he said, motioning with his long, slender hand. "We
shall behave in a civilized manner and have tea."

She didn't know how to sit gracefully on the ground in her
muddy and tattered garments. The young Chinese woman bent over,
handing Snow Leopard a bowl of the tea. Then she did the same
for Chlöe. He waved the young woman away. She exited, walking
backward.

Is she a servant or a concubine? wondered Chlöe. She'd never
seen a concubine before. At least not that she knew of. How many

did he have, this man of power? She looked at him. He was looking down at his desk.

Without looking up he sipped his tea and asked, "How many countries are represented among you?"

"Nine," she answered.

"So many." He was delighted. "We shall write them all in Chinese. They will be forced to translate. This is *my* country, and it shall be in *my* language. I shall send riders to Shanghai tonight."

"Two weeks isn't enough time to get answers, to get the money you want," Chlöe said, catching the tablet he tossed at her. "It will take several days for word to even reach them. You cannot kill someone within two weeks. You must be fair."

A frown creased his forehead as he raised a hand to silence her. "Do you not think that I know how far distances are? You are in *my* country," he said. His voice reflected resentment. "You are in no position to try to tell me what to do. You are *my* prisoner."

Chlöe licked the end of the pencil and said, "What do you wish me to say?" He intimidated her, she had to admit. All their lives were his. He was powerful looking despite his slenderness. One look into his eyes told her he was devoid of compassion.

"Write this," he said, his voice even. He dictated the letter to her. "Copy it nine times."

When she started to copy it, he interrupted. "Change *shot* to *beheaded*. That seems more immediate to you foreigners. Tell them we shall behead one person a day beginning in fifteen days if there are no moneys." He wanted two hundred thousand American dollars.

"You won't get it!"

Snow Leopard looked at her for a long time, but she did not lower her glance. "I have heard it told that foreign white women are not like ours. But I never met one before. Do they all talk before permission is granted? Or is that your own peculiar characteristic?"

"Women in my country," Chlöe said, "have equality. We do not wait for permission from men—for anything." I'm lying, she thought. But that's how it's supposed to be. I won't let him know otherwise. I won't let him see I'm scared. Not now, not of him this very minute.

"Ah." It sounded like a sigh. "That is what I, too, want for my country." He leaned down on his elbow again and seemed to be contemplating the thought as Chlöe arose and went to his desk, where a brush and ink jar sat. She seated herself and began to translate the letter he had dictated into Chinese, having to copy it nine times, for each of the consulates. He was silent, staring at her as she wrote the first four letters. Then he arose and paced around the tent, his hands clutched behind his back. When she finished he was seated cross-legged on a settee across from her, hands resting on his knees, staring at her with anticipation.

"Why are you traveling alone?" he asked abruptly. "Chinese women do not travel alone."

"I am going to Peking, to get information for my husband. American women travel all over the world, often alone." She wondered if this was true.

"You should be home. With children. China is not safe for a woman."

Chlöe permitted herself a little laugh. "It doesn't seem safe for anyone, man or woman, with people like you kidnapping trains."

His steely eyes studied her. "My men have had no pay for many months," he finally said. "They have families to support. People to feed. I have people to protect."

"You protect people by endangering others?"

"I protect many towns in this province. From other warlords who would kill and rape." Ah, so she had met her first warlord! "I protect my towns. However, they have not had money to pay me this spring. The floods . . . But they have paid me loyally over the years. I shall not abandon them for something that is not their fault. The Yellow River wreaked havoc. All of my people need to eat."

All of my people.

"Do you know one million people died from the flood this year? One million people washed away. Others are starving because there is no food." He was quiet for a minute and then resumed. "Tell your Americans that if ransom is not paid, all these people will die."

Chlöe continued writing with the brush and ink.

"After the first few die, perhaps they will see we are serious. They will pay attention then and send money."

Chlöe looked up from her writing. "Do you think this is the way to get foreign powers to respect China?"

"China?" He laughed. "Until China rears up and takes its place among the nations of the world, none of them will respect us. For over a hundred years the foreign powers have taken advantage of us. Don't talk to me of respect!"

He waited until she put aside the sheet of paper she had been filling up and reached for another page. Then he waved his hand in the air. "Wait. Put your brush down for a moment."

She did so. The light from the swinging lantern hanging above them flickered shadows on his golden face, chiseled like stone.

"Now tell me," he said, "do you think starvation and disease are inescapable? In your country dams hold back flood waters. But here nothing holds back the Yellow River in spring. It is fed by melting snows in Tibet and rushes thousands of miles, gathering water from streams along the way. Nothing can control that."

"Oh, yes," Chlöe said. "Dams could be constructed and water can be used efficiently. In my country people no longer die of cholera or typhoid or the plague. If I had stayed in my country, " her eyes clouded, "my son would still be alive. Yours is a dirty country, that's why there's so much disease and death."

He looked at her and then studied his fingernails. "I have heard that Americans are peculiar about sanitation."

She was amazed to find herself relaxing. "It's true. The hardest thing I've had to get accustomed to in your country is lack of cleanliness. And the smells of China."

"Ah, yes." Snow Leopard smiled, waving his long, slender hand. "In spring, the flowers—"

"No, no, I mean the stench. The awful smell of China. It smells dirty. It smells unwashed. It breeds flies and mosquitoes . . . and they breed malaria and all the other diseases."

"Why have not the foreign powers helped in that way? They introduced opium to my people. They have never done good here. They have been evil."

Chlöe had no answer for that. But she said, "Your country is not organized. It has no way to do all the things that need doing. People in Shantung don't want to help the people in Yennan or Kiangsi. You are interested only in what is right around you."

"I have traveled," he said. "I care deeply about my country."

His voice had the quality of a small boy's boasting.

"Can you read?" Chlöe asked.

He coughed. "I am a graduate of the Shantung Military Institute. I read many things."

"Then you should study history."

"I read history. I know that yesterday has to do with today and tomorrow." His voice hardened. "I do not want to be like the past. I want my people to go forward."

"What people do you mean?" she asked, amazed to realize that she was enjoying herself enormously. "The people in these mountains, in this province you protect?"

He shook his head. "Not only the people in these villages. I mean all the peoples of China. My people."

"Do you protect them from the Japanese?" she asked. They had infiltrated Shantung these last seven years.

"I kill any Japanese I ever see," he proclaimed.

He was silent, so she finished the last two letters, then put the brush down and stretched her cramped fingers. He called out a name and a soldier ran in, bending over in an attitude of subservience.

"The letters," he told her, "will be in Shanghai in two days' time, two days of hard riding."

Chlöe stood. "It is cold and damp in the caves and we have very few clothes. Are there quilts someplace?"

He did not rise. "No, I regret this. There are not quilts for my men either."

As she turned to leave, her back toward him, he said, "Your hair is not like other foreigners. It is very Chinese." His voice was very low.

I haven't combed it in a week, she thought. It's a tangled mess.

"Like silk," he said.

# CHAPTER 25

She dreamed that night of his hand twisting through her hair, drawing it to his lips and saying, "Like silk."

But when he looked at her his eyes were sad. For a long time he didn't say anything, staring at her, into her, while his lips caressed the strand of hair. Then his hand reached out and the back of it brushed her cheek, with tenderness.

"It pains me to do what must be done." His voice was hoarse.

She watched him, wondering what must be done. And then she knew. Tears began to gather in her eyes and one ran down her cheek.

"Would you prefer to be shot or guillotined?"

She was surprised he knew the word guillotined. He pronounced it with a French accent.

"I do not like the thought of killing you, you of all people," he said. "You of all women."

And he kissed her hair again. Like silk.

She wondered what his lips would feel like, if they would taste of death . . . wondered what death tasted like.

His hand moved to her torn silk robe and slipped it off her shoulder, his finger tracing the strap of her nightgown, running across her breast. She felt a pulse beating in her throat, wondering if he could hear her heart. He leaned over and kissed her breast, and she heard him sigh.

A bugle blew.

He raised his head and looked into her soul, reaching for her hand. "Come," he said as he replaced her robe. "It is time." He arose, his hand leading her. As he opened the door she saw the sunrise, the pale sky rimmed with red against the jagged mountains.

The prisoners settled into domesticity. Where the river pooled and eddied, they rinsed their clothes and bathed, though they lacked soap with which to wash. Leaving the water, they shivered until the sun warmed and dried them. They made themselves steaming cups of tea over the charcoal braziers in front of the caves and sat in the sun and told each other stories about themselves and reassured one another that they would be rescued soon, probably with great fanfare.

They counted the days off. Six. Five, four, three, two. And then there was one. No one could understand why there had been no word from any of the consulates. Certainly among them they could raise two hundred thousand dollars. That was a thousand dollars for each of the prisoners. Surely they would be rescued.

It was Sunday. The missionaries conducted church services in the morning. No one mentioned that this was the final day. No one said anything about it.

Chlöe kept looking for Snow Leopard. She had not seen him for three and a half days. Perhaps he had ridden out of the camp on some path other than the one they'd come in on. There might be another way out of the valley. Yet something within her knew he was in his tent. That he had stayed there, holed up. She had seen a young Chinese woman enter, but she left early yesterday morning.

Certainly he would not kill any of them. It was an idle threat. Yet, once made, might he not have to do it to save face? Major Hughes and some of the men wondered aloud about that early in the morning. What would they do if Snow Leopard was serious? Draw straws?

"The women are out of it," said Allan Hughes.

"Certainly," blubbered Colonel Higgins.

Was there a fairer way to decide? Did it mean that tonight one of them would be dead? Gone forever? Killed in a valley in the mountains of China? Murdered because none of the governments had acted?

For a moment Chlöe found herself far angrier at America and the other countries for not having paid the ransom than at Snow Leopard for kidnapping them.

They tried to act as though it was no different from any other day, but at noon Snow Leopard walked down the village street, kicking up dust at his heels. Approaching them, he was silent. A hush came over the crowd. People stood watching him, not wanting to believe his threat.

He stood still, his level gaze encompassing the crowd. "It is the day," he said as though announcing something they did not know. "There has been no word from any of your countries. One of you will die tonight."

Some man whose name Chlöe had forgotten stepped forward. "For what purpose? The consulates won't know of it. It won't spur them to rush money here."

Snow Leopard shrugged. "Before two hundred of you die they will know of it. At midnight one of you will give your life. Determine in some fashion which of you it is to be. *You* choose."

There was no sound except the roar of the river beyond them. He turned on his heel and began to walk back to his tent. Chlöe broke from the crowd and ran after him, crying, "You're a barbarian. The world's right. Chinese are nothing more than barbarians, uncivilized barbarians."

At the first word out of her mouth, he stopped. Not turning around, he stood with his back to her. Then he did turn, slowly, grinning. "I knew it must be you! Barbarian, you say? You act like this and think *you* are civilized? No Chinese woman would behave so."

"I am not a Chinese woman. And I am glad I'm not. I would be ashamed to have the men in my country be so barbaric." She now felt anger at this man, fury at the position he was putting them in.

He walked over to her and lowered his voice. His eyes glittered. "Do you wish to sacrifice yourself?"

Oh, God. She had not thought he would choose her to be the first victim. He had said it was up to them.

He cocked his head to the side. "You wish to play hero? Or you prefer being a martyr? Do you really want to save these people? Well, you can play for time until the consulates send money. I will give you an alternative, if that is what you wish." His grin was wicked. "I will show you I am not a barbarian. I will show you there are other ways than death."

No one could hear him except Chlöe, his voice was so low. "Spare them death, if you will. Come to my tent at nine tonight. Tell them that. Tell them you will save them. That by your bedding with me they will live." He laughed a silent laugh. "I have never bedded a white woman."

Her face went pale, and her mouth was so dry she could not speak. I can't, she thought. "I won't," she spat out.

"Do you prefer to watch them die one by one? Is that preferable to bedding with me?" He grabbed her wrist and held it tightly.

"You're hurting me," she whispered.

"No," he said. "You are hurting yourself. One of them will die at midnight should you choose not to come to my tent at nine. Make a choice. You have all day. Keep in mind that if you say no, they need not know that you could have spared one of them. Only you and I shall know that."

She wrested her wrist from his grasp.

He gave her a long look and then, turning abruptly, marched away.

"What did he say?" Allan Hughes came forward. Chlöe didn't answer. She stared straight ahead, seeing nothing. Then she walked through the trees to the river, sparkling in the bright sunlight, its foam bursting into the air where it cascaded over rocks.

I'll be a murderer, won't I? she asked herself. If I refuse, I shall be responsible for someone's death.

No one followed her. They stood wondering how to determine who would die tonight. Chlöe heard none of it. She heard only the river's roar, felt only the icy splinters of water that splattered against her now and then. I will kill someone just as much as he will, won't I? The responsibility of it was too awesome to comprehend.

They could never forgive her should she refuse. But he said they needn't know. However, she would know. Was her body more important than the life of one of her comrades?

Damn him, she thought.

She turned to the people she now had the power to save and saw Allan Hughes walking toward her. She glanced up at him, sitting as she was by the river's edge, her arms hugging her bent knees. He sat down on the grass beside her, plucking a blade and twisting it between his fingers. The bright sun blinded her.

"You look weary. Do you have so much of the weight of our world on your shoulders?"

Her fingers wound together so tightly she hurt herself. She was surprised to hear herself sigh so loudly. "Oh, Allan, he gave me a choice. I can save everyone. Or at least someone. Tonight."

Allan was silent, staring at her. She didn't have to explain; he understood immediately. "Oh, my dear. I am so sorry." He reached out to take her hand. "Though I must admit," he smiled at her, "that were I in such a position, I would spare lives if I could have you."

Surprised, she looked at him.

"I don't really have a choice, do I?" she asked finally.

"Given the person I understand that you are, no." His voice was quiet as he let go of her hand.

"You tell them," she said. "I can't. If I go to his tent at nine, no one will die . . . tonight, anyway."

But Allan made no move.

They sat silently for several minutes, she staring at the river, he gazing at her. At last he asked, "How will you feel afterward? About yourself, I mean?"

"You surprise me, Allan. You're really much nicer than you seemed when we got on the train. I didn't know army men thought about such things."

"I don't, ordinarily." He crushed the blade of grass in his fingers. "But this is not an ordinary situation."

"I probably shall feel quite proud that I've saved someone."

"At the expense of yourself, that is. I mean, some of these people," he nodded toward the passengers, "will consider you immoral, you know."

She cocked her head to the side, and asked, "Really? Do you think so? It won't matter to them that I might be saving their lives?"

"Logic has little to do with people's feelings," he said. "You'll be a scarlet woman. A heroine, of course. But scarlet nonetheless.

It's the Brits, mainly, who'll feel that way. Funny, or ironic, but I'll bet the missionaries are the ones who'll be most compassionate; they'll consider what you're going to do heroic."

"Actually," Chlöe said, "it doesn't really matter what anyone else thinks."

Allan put a hand on her shoulder. "That's how it should be. It's you who have to live with yourself."

"Allan, you are either destined to become a great general or be a total failure in the army." Chlöe tried to smile, and this time she reached out and took his hand. "You're not like others."

"Nor are you, my dear, which I'm sure is why Snow Leopard singled you out." Then he asked, "Have you thought how your husband will react to this?"

Slade? "He'd think I'm doing the right thing. Allan, can one possibly compare my going to Snow Leopard with a person's life?"

"What if no help comes tomorrow? Or the next day? Or for six months?"

"Perhaps he won't like me," she said. "But what difference is two hundred times over one, once I've done it?" She thought to herself, Will that make me a concubine? "Tell them, Allan. Tell them while I sit here."

Ten minutes later Nancy ran over to her, her eyes shining. "Oh, Chlöe, you lucky duck. How romantic! How exciting! Seduced by a Chinese warlord, and such a handsome one too. How I envy you! It's straight out of a novel, isn't it? Doesn't it just give you gooseflesh all over? And when we get home you'll be a heroine. Oh, Chlöe, it's all too too exciting!"

Chlöe stared at her.

Nancy bubbled on. "Tell him if he wants someone tomorrow night, I'll volunteer. It'll make such a wonderful story to tell at home. And he's so good-looking. Like right out of the movies."

Wonderful story! A night with a Chinese warlord. This wasn't the story she had come after.

The rest of the group was divided. Allan was right. Most of the Englishmen objected, claiming they would rather die for a woman's honor. But the rest of them, including the British women, breathed a sigh of relief. One by one, during the afternoon, they approached Chlöe, thanking her, telling her she was admirable. A heroine.

A heroine because a two-bit Chinese warlord had never bedded a white woman before.

Shortly before supper several of the women whom she knew

least approached her. They thought, they said, that what she was going to do was an act of loving compassion, but they were disturbed about what would happen after just one night if no consulates were heard from tomorrow, or the next day. They did not want Snow Leopard to send for each of the women and force himself on all of them.

Chlöe already sensed that this was not Snow Leopard's aim. He was finding a way to humiliate her, show her that women in China were subject to men. Yet he had said, "Your hair is like silk." Perhaps desire mingled with his other feelings. She suspected he did not desire all the women. But she did not say anything as she listened to the women.

"If he likes you," one of the women said, "he may send for you each night . . . or send for another woman."

Chlöe looked at them, studying the five faces. "You're suggesting I try to please him, is that it?"

One of the younger women stared at the ground, embarrassed.

"Yes," answered Mrs. Logan, who seemed to be the ringleader. "We humbly beseech you. As long as you are going to him anyway, for one night . . ."

And so they helped bathe Chlöe and dried her hair and pulled it back into swirls, piling it on her head. They pinched her cheeks and one of them donated earrings that she had been wearing when kidnapped.

It was dark by nine, and the five women surrounded Chlöe like moths around a flame. She had taken off her ragged nightgown and wore only her robe.

Allan Hughes broke into the circle and reached out an arm, offering to take Chlöe's hand. She felt like a vestal virgin being sent to slaughter. The camp was quiet. Everyone was staring at her. She thought she might throw up. She had been unable to eat her supper. One of the women leaned forward and twisted a tendril of her hair.

Chlöe dared not look at the crowd of people, but—with her back erect—she began to walk toward the village, down the street that would lead her to Snow Leopard's tent. As she did so, the crowd roared, a loud, indecipherable sound, and Chlöe *did* feel like the heroine of a novel, going to give her body to save a life.

They did not see a tear run down her cheek. She didn't even know why. She was not afraid. She was angry that a man had such power over her. Over all of them. But she knew she must not show it. She must please him, please him in whatever way she possibly could.

And she wondered if a Chinese made love in the same way an American did.

# CHAPTER 26

He sat behind his desk, wearing his uniform with the collar unbuttoned. Hands resting on the desk, he looked not only official but also at ease. His eyes traveled the length of her tattered robe.

Instead of fright, Chlöe was surprised to experience a thrill. She thought she'd heard somewhere that Chinese did not kiss. What would he do first?

"I notice you affect Chinese dress," he said, and clapped his hands.

A servant bowed into the room. Snow Leopard barked an order so quickly and abruptly that Chlöe did not catch it. Then, still sitting at his desk, his legs sprawled underneath it, he said, "I am sorry to have inconvenienced you so that your clothes have become muddy and torn. I can rectify that for you, but not for the others."

The servant returned. Folded neatly over his arms was lustrous silk, a dark, regal purple. Snow Leopard reached for it, and its folds fell open, shimmering in the lamplight. An elegant dress, not tattered or dirty.

"It belongs to one of my wives," he said, throwing it across his desk at her. She caught it.

The smooth, soft fabric licked her hands.

"It is yours now." His eyes had not left her.

"Wives? You have wives?"

He nodded, as if it was of no consequence. "Of course. Four."

Four wives!

She held the dress in her arms.

"I will leave you for a few moments so that you may change your clothing," he said. "I have something I must attend to. When I return we shall have supper." He stood beside his desk, and asked, "You'd like that, wouldn't you? Pheasant . . ."

"Yes," she said, so hungry she could taste the bird. "I'd like that very much." Perhaps he was better at wooing a woman than an American!

He laughed.

No mirror being in the room, she could not study her reflection, but she knew that the imperial color matched her eyes perfectly. He had chosen this color for her, just for her. Its silkiness caressed her body.

"Stand right where you are. Don't move."

A harsh voice spat the words into the tent.

She heard movement behind her.

"Now turn."

Chlöe did so slowly, and for the first time that evening she experienced fear. A man her height, anger blazing from his dark eyes, held a pistol aimed at her heart.

Involuntarily, her hands flew to her chest.

"Hands at your sides," said the soldier. From the insignia on his shoulders, she could tell he was an officer. He came over to her, walking behind her, the length of his body fitting against hers, the gun jammed into her ribs.

"One move, one sound . . ." He didn't need to finish the sentence.

They stood that way, Chlöe trying not to shake, for what seemed an eternity.

Finally the man spoke. "You're the prize, huh? The one he gets while we're out there waiting. Waiting for foreign devils to come marching down on us, so *he* can fuck a white woman! How the hell is that going to impress your consulates? Send us money or we'll sleep with your women! What a threat! Certainly no government cares what happens to women! He should have let us kill a man tonight. Behead him in front of the others. Or garrote him, that would be better. Watch him die inch by quarter inch right in front of their eyes. That'd put fear into them. They'd begin to be scared of a Chinese then. But no, he's got to have you!"

Chlöe could not control her shivering. "What are you going to do?" she asked.

The man made a harsh sound that she took for a laugh. "Take over the reins. Get rid of him, what do you think? Then we'll kill one of you. *And*, if I want you or any other woman, or any of the officers want a white woman, we can have them. We'll kill someone else tomorrow night. . . ."

As his voice grated on her, she thought she heard footsteps, faintly at first, until her captor stopped talking, hearing them also.

"Not one move," he whispered, holding her in front of him, the pistol held under her right breast, aimed directly at the doorway.

The curtain billowed before Snow Leopard's hand parted it. In that second, when her captor's attention centered on the doorway, Chlöe jerked from the man's embrace, jarring his arm, upsetting his balance. His finger, on the trigger, sent a bullet soaring through the tent top just as she turned around, scissoring her leg into the air between his legs, kicking him in the groin. Letting out an anguished cry, like that of a wounded wild animal, he clutched himself, falling backward.

Snow Leopard was on him in an instant.

The dazed man, bent over, moaned, hatred in his pained eyes.

"What? What have you done?" exclaimed Snow Leopard, glancing at Chlöe.

She shook so convulsively she couldn't answer, her teeth chattering.

Snow Leopard reached out an arm, grabbing her wrist. "Stop that! What happened!"

"He was g-g-going to k-k-kill you," she said, her voice barely audible.

Snow Leopard stood up, staring down at the man crumpled on the floor, bawling, in the fetal position.

"Who is he?" asked Chlöe, trying to gain control of herself.

"Wang is one of my top officers," he responded, his voice emotionless. "A trusted lieutenant." He looked down at the man on the tent floor. "Is this true?"

Hatred flew from Wang's eyes. He straightened his legs, trying to stand up. "You are no leader," he shouted. "You are weak. Women. Opium. You care more for your own pleasures than for the money we need. Yes, it's true."

"Why didn't you talk to me about it?" Snow Leopard's voice was even.

"Ha," snorted the man. "You often think resolution can be made by reasoning. Too much thinking renders one impotent."

"What's going to happen to him?" Chlöe asked. Certainly he wasn't going to let the man go. He'd jail him or something, wouldn't he?

"Would you have killed me?" Snow Leopard asked Wang.

"I would now too." Wang stared defiantly.

Snow Leopard stared into him, and shaking his head, he said, "Go."

The man looked startled but tried to pull himself erect, and began to walk from the room. When Snow Leopard's bullet tore through him he did not even try to look back before he fell.

Within seconds a young man ran into the room. "Lao. Help me with Wang. Let us get him out of here," Snow Leopard barked.

The young man gave Snow Leopard a perplexed look and then stared at Chlöe before grabbing Wang's legs while Snow Leopard took his shoulders. They disappeared through the tent opening, leaving Chlöe alone.

"Dear God," she said aloud. She sat down at Snow Leopard's desk and put her head in her hands, hoping she wasn't going to cry.

Snow Leopard was back in less than five minutes. Following him was a young woman, her back bent subserviently as she carried a tray. As though nothing had happened, Snow Leopard turned to Chlöe. "Have you ever drunk our wine?"

"No." She shook her head. She wanted to be horrified but couldn't help smiling to herself. *He wants to show me he is not a barbarian. In such an incongruous situation, he is saving face.*

He sat down on the bearskin rug and gestured that she should do the same. It was not easy with such a tight dress. "I have tasted French wines," he said, and she realized he was trying to demonstrate a degree of sophistication. "Our wines cannot compare with those of Europe, I must admit, but I have some that is quite nice. Rice wine."

On the tray the young woman set on a low table were a slender carafe and two amazingly thin porcelain wineglasses. Snow Leopard said, "You pour."

The young woman withdrew. They were alone.

Chlöe, leaning forward, poured the wine, watching the golden liquid shine against the background of the flickering fire. It was strange, she thought, that she felt no fear. No hate. She did not think he was going to hurt her. She did not think he was a sadist. He had shot Wang quickly. And at odd moments he seemed like a little boy trying to show off.

"You have not eaten well in these weeks, I know," he said, clapping his hands. Three young women filed into the tent bearing large platters of steaming food. On one was a heavenly smelling roast pheasant, so tender that the meat was breaking away from the bones. There were green and orange vegetables on a bed of rice. Thousand-year-old eggs, tiny prawns wrapped in transparent rice flour, and mushrooms, larger than any she had ever seen, bathed in a white sauce.

He was staring at her, amusement now reflected in his eyes, and he smiled, raising his wineglass in a toast. "Honored guest," he murmured.

With what had recently transpired, it was all Chlöe could do not to laugh. He had to prove he was as civilized as anyone she might know. And, in some way she could not define, she appreciated his gesture. The shocking thought that most of the evening might be fun occurred to her.

Certainly the food smelled wonderful. She could tell it had been prepared with care. He had known she would come, of course.

"I am hungry," he said, reaching over to grab a prawn. "I usually eat much earlier."

She wanted to seem ladylike; she wanted to pretend she had no hunger. But instead she dived in, practically shoveling the wonderful food into her mouth.

"Tell me," he said, "are all foreign women like you?"

"No more than all Chinese men are like you."

He smiled at her, showing very white, even teeth. "I shall tell you about women in China," he said. "Women in China are here to serve men."

Chlöe nodded. "I know that. It makes me very sad."

He jerked his head at that. "Sad? I do not understand."

"Women in America, and in Europe, in all civilized countries," she accentuated *civilized,* "are human beings to be taken into consideration. We are allowed to vote and have a say in how we run our country. We can even run for office."

He laughed at that. "And tell men what to think?"

"No, that's not how it is. We don't tell each other how to think. We think for ourselves."

Snow Leopard looked at her with curiosity. "I think you believe what you are saying. Well, we do not have such a thing in China. No one votes. How can we vote when most of us have no education, no knowledge? It is impossible."

Chlöe nodded. "I know. But perhaps someday you will. Voting is a sign of freedom for people. It lets people decide for themselves how their country will be run."

"The Celestial Kingdom has been living with its way for thousands of more years than you have been in existence."

"I do not think so," countered Chlöe. "I think you have been existing, not living. I think in China one is doomed from birth to a lifetime of poverty, of subservience, to no choice in how to live."

"I have chosen," he said. "I am a warlord. I am important."

"You're educated. You were obviously born to money. You are one of the few." By now Chlöe had stopped eating, fuller of food than she'd been in weeks. She sipped the tea, fragrant with chrysanthemums.

I saved this man's life, she thought, looking at the finely chiseled face, shadows dancing on his golden skin as the lantern swung overhead. I saw him shoot a man. And now I am going to be seduced. He was not going to be a barbarian and just take her. It dawned on her that as unsophisticated as she thought Snow Leopard was, he had latched on to a secret more men should learn. That by drawing her into conversation, by acting as though he were interested in what she had to say, by building up some kind of relationship—whatever it was—he was wooing the woman. And she was surprised to find herself responding to his gestures.

"You would not be permitted to act like you do were you a Chinese woman."

Chlöe shrugged. "Madame Sun Yat-sen does." Perhaps he had no idea of whom she was talking.

"Yes," he said. "And she was educated in your country."

Ah, he was somewhat informed.

She nodded. "And once people experience the freedom of my country, it is difficult to ever become a vassal again."

"Your women," he shifted his position, crossing his legs, and Chlöe thought that even in a long gown he seemed very masculine, "what purpose do they serve if not to serve men?"

"We raise families, for one thing."

"So do Chinese women," he said.

"But in America it is a joint effort. The woman has as much to say about the children as the man. I admit, they live where the man's job is, the woman does the cooking and sewing and cleaning—"

"So?" he interrupted. "It sounds like my country."

"No, we do not also work in the fields." But she realized that farm women did. That women who lived on Iowa farms and on

Montana ranches probably worked beside their husbands. But she did not correct herself. "We are not men's servants. We talk when we want. Women even have jobs sometimes."

"So do Chinese women," he said. "Sometimes they work in stores, and sometimes hawk vegetables, and sometimes in brothels. . . ."

"Yes, but in America women who work are paid. They have money of their own to spend. Sometimes women even live alone."

He looked at her as though he had trouble understanding anyone living alone. "Because they want to?"

Chlöe nodded. "Often. Sometimes because they cannot find husbands. Sometimes because they are widows."

"You." He looked at her, his eyes grazing her breasts. "You have lived alone?"

"No," she admitted. "I lived in my father's house and then my husband's." She could not imagine living alone, couldn't even begin to envision a life without Slade. Without a man. "But there is a difference. I have no mother-in-law to rule me. I am the mistress in my own home. My husband is allowed to show affection to me. We are friends as well."

He guffawed. "Friends? A man and a woman?"

"As well as lovers."

"Love. Such a strange concept. You think love exists between a husband and wife?"

"Don't you?" Why else marriage? she wondered.

"In China we marry women we have never seen before. They bring us children, cook our food, help us . . . but love?"

"You save your love for concubines, then?"

She had never had such a conversation.

He smiled. "Concubines fill a need. A physical need. But love? It is true that sometimes we are consumed with desire. But desire is not love. Tell me, how do you define this word—love?"

Chlöe thought for a minute. "It is the strongest feeling in the world. There are many kinds of love. I love my family—my parents and brothers and sisters. I love my friends. I love my country. But the kind of love I'm talking about is the overriding love of a man and a woman. The feeling that one is not quite whole if the other person is not there. The feeling that I would do anything for my husband, and he for me. The feeling that we share an intimacy such as we could with no one else. The feeling of trust . . . of being willing to dare anything for love. I would give my life for my husband if it would save him. And I know he would do the same for me."

Snow Leopard snorted. "What nonsense! Give one's life for a woman!"

"There are things for which you are willing to give your life," she said, "or you wouldn't be in the business of being a warlord. You are willing to endanger yourself in battles. You did not assume this position, or fight for it or however you got it, just for money. Power, maybe. But you seem to also have love for your land and your people."

"That is different. It has nothing to do with love."

"Not love of country?"

He bit his lip, thinking. "I might have to die to protect my villages, my province. But that is for honor. Honor is worth dying for."

"The concept of honor is worth giving your life for but people aren't? You are willing to die to save face but not for love?"

He thought for a while. "Perhaps I do love some people, since you are permitting a broad use of the word. I thought I loved Wang. And, using your interpretation, I love some ideas. But not a woman, certainly. I can find many women to do the work of cooking or cleaning or even meeting my physical needs. For the latter, I prefer a woman who does not talk. I like pretty women. Young women who are willing to do whatever I ask. But after an hour or two I no longer care about them. I want them gone. Women are— dispensable."

Chlöe wondered if many men felt that way.

"Do you never talk with women?" she asked.

"I am talking with one now," he reminded her, and got up to pace around the room.

"But women of your own, Chinese women?"

He did not look at her. "And what should I talk about with them?"

"I don't know. Ideas. Whatever it is you think about. Whatever you feel. Whatever fills your soul."

He raised his eyebrows and was quiet for several minutes. "I cannot imagine confiding to a woman what I think about. A woman would never understand."

"What do you feel for women, then?"

He did not look at her. "What do I feel?" he repeated to himself. "Women are human beings, of course. But here to serve men. They need not be educated. They have feelings, of course, but they are here to do man's bidding, and men know that. So do women. They are trophies in war. We do not kill women in war, in attacks."

"Is that how you feel when you are making love to them?" She couldn't imagine she'd said such a daring thing.

"Make love to them? Ah, I see. That is what you call it? Love has nothing to do with it. Women are there to relieve our physical needs."

"Then why are you offering to save a life to have me?" she asked. "You can have any woman you want. Why do you want me instead of some other, someone who may enjoy you?"

His eyes narrowed. "How do you know you would not enjoy me?"

"Because you obviously do not care about giving pleasure to a woman. You do not consider her desires . . . her—"

"Her desires?" He laughed. "Please a woman?" Then he looked at her for a long time, during which she met his gaze levelly. She'd be damned if he thought he could intimidate her.

Then, his face devoid of expression, he said, "You saved my life tonight. Had you not been here, I would be dead instead of him."

"You killed him awfully quickly."

"Chinese justice is swift."

Yes, she'd heard that before.

"If I don't lay a finger on you, will you promise not to repeat a thing that has happened here? I do not want the rest of my men to know about Wang. They will realize he has disappeared, of course. If there was a junta, they will get the message. If he acted alone, it does not matter. You must come to me every night, but you must not tell anyone that I have not bedded you. You must pretend to all those people out there," his arm gestured widely, "that we have spent the night together in bed."

She clenched her teeth so her mouth would not drop open.

He continued, his eyes lowering to gaze at the outlines of her body. Then he smiled. "I do not mind your feet. Big feet are all right. I think binding of women's feet is barbaric."

She wanted to interrupt him and ask if he thought women were as nothing, why should it bother him whether or not their feet were bound, but she didn't. He seemed to sense her question, for he said, "I do think that women are human beings, and I am against pain, unnecessary pain. I am against crippling so that they cannot work.

I find it disgusting to see women hobble around, scarcely able to move. So, you see I am humane. But also, I am telling you so that you know it is not your large feet that repel me."

Repel? He finds me repulsive? Chlöe's initial relief at his statement was mingled with rejection.

"Your skin is too white. Your breasts are too large. You are not made delicately like Chinese women. You are too tall. Almost as tall as many men. I have no desire for you."

It took Chlöe a minute to assimilate this. She would not have to sleep with him, and for this she breathed more easily.

He continued. "I am no barbarian. I do not take a white woman who does not want me. I have no real desire for a woman who finds me offensive. I am aware of your qualities of nobility . . . that you came to me to save the lives of your compatriots. I admire that.

"And besides, now that I owe my life to you, I would like to hear what the outside world is like. Why did you save me when you knew what I intended to do with you?"

"It seemed like the lesser of two evils." She permitted herself a smile.

He thought about that. "Swear on everything you hold sacred that you will never tell anyone that I have not violated you."

He looked at her as though waiting for an answer.

"You don't want to lose face, is that it?"

He studied his fingernails and then looked over at her. "Whatever my reasons are, are you willing to meet them? I mean you will never, for any reason, tell people that we did not fuck." She cringed at the slang term. "I mean even after you are rescued—for, of course, you will be, ransom will be paid eventually—you will tell no one that I did not . . ."

She crossed her hands in her lap and looked at him. "I thank you and promise on all I hold sacred never to tell anyone. The world will think we made love. I promise that. Again, I thank you."

His gaze explored the ceiling. "I need no thanks. It is a small enough gesture for saving my life."

They were silent, then he stood and walked to the far side of the room, where he reached for something and held it out for Chlöe to see.

"This was in the booty my men took from the train. It looks to be a game of some kind. Is it?"

"Yes, it's cribbage," she said.

"Teach me to play it," he said. "I am tired of so much talk in one night."

He sat down opposite her, placing the cribbage board between them, looking at her as though awaiting directions.

"Would you really have killed these men one by one?" she asked.

He shrugged. "It would have depended on my mood. Come, teach me to play."

Relief swept through Chlöe, but at the same time she thought it might be fun to teach a Chinese man how to kiss.

# CHAPTER 27

The second night he asked her how her fellow captives treated her now that she had come to him.

She considered for a moment and said, "Most of them feel sorry for me. I think what they try to do is comfort me. A few treat me like . . . oh, I don't know. Some thank me and others must think I'm enjoying being with you and act as though I'm immoral."

"But you are saving their lives." Then he hesitated. "It is true, is it not, you are enjoying being with me?"

"It's true." She smiled. "Much to my surprise. I am enjoying my time with you. I do not think we shall ever understand each other, being from such different cultures. But yes, I enjoy you."

"We may not," he arose and paced around the room, as was his habit, "understand each other, but we can learn of other ways than our own. These people . . . the ones who think you are doing wrong even though it means they may live, they cannot understand ways other than their own?"

She nodded. "I guess not. A few of them must think death is preferable to sleeping with someone other than one's husband."

He thought about that for a moment. "You have not told them the truth?"

"Of course not. You said that is our secret."

He laughed. "Give me the name of one of them."

"Mrs. Wilkins. She's a sour-faced woman anyhow, and I imagine she thinks anything that is not decreed by her God is wrong."

After another lavish meal, he asked Chlöe what America was like. He was surprised to hear that the vast majority of children went to school and did not have to work, amazed to hear of home milk deliveries, that many people owned cars, and that trains crisscrossed the country. He was astonished to learn of the leisure that Americans had, of picnics and vacations, that women safely walked the streets alone, and about moving pictures. And about kissing. Disbelieving of people whose skin was black, about skating on ice, and of women wearing dresses so short that their legs showed. And of petting dogs. He made a face when Chlöe said, "My dog slept on my bed with me when I was a little girl."

He found it difficult to believe that people could drink water right out of a tap, or that grass grew around houses or of lawn mowers and the fact that villages did not need men and guns to protect them.

When morning came, he said to her, "Tell them that perhaps you will not come back to me tonight."

She gave him a puzzled look. But he said, "Mrs. Wilkins will criticize you no longer. I shall take care of that."

"Don't hurt her," Chlöe begged.

There was amusement in his eyes as he said, "I am, after all, not a barbarian.

"However, in reality, if there is no word from any of the consulates today, I shall expect you at nine tonight," he said. "Tonight it is time to talk politics."

To Allan Hughes, the only one in whom she confided anything, she said, "He is not like we think he is. He has cruel streaks in what seems to be a normal Chinese manner, but he was a gentleman with me. It has not been . . . unpleasant. He asks many questions about America. Though he is a man I can never understand, a man who would disgust me were he in America, I do not dislike Snow Leopard."

"Isn't that like complimenting a rapist?" Allan asked.

She had better be careful. "That is the least part of the evening," she said. "We talk mostly."

Late that afternoon one of the soldiers, a sword hanging awkwardly at his side, marched down the street and into the circle in front of the caves. He began to shout, not waiting for a translator, rushed through his speech, and, turning on his heel, marched away.

One of the men who understood the language paled, and turned to the rest of them.

"He has announced that since Mrs. Cavanaugh has refused to come again to his tent, one of the victims will be shot at midnight. He has decreed it to be Mr. Wilkins." Stunned into silence, the crowd looked at her. Why had she not told them?

A wail keened through the air before Mrs. Wilkins crumpled to the ground. For a minute Chlöe was as surprised as the rest of them. And then she understood. Snow Leopard was teaching a lesson, for her sake.

For her sake.

It was all she could do not to smile. He was doing her a favor.

Nancy and Amy came running to her. "Oh, Chlöe, you said no?" cried Nancy. "Did you tell him I'd come? You can't let Mr. Wilkins die."

Harold Wilkins, a nondescript man who worked for Standard Oil, and his wife had spent all their years in China trying to convert the heathens, even though they were not missionaries. Chlöe suspected the wife believed the worst of everybody.

Her fellow prisoners crowded around her. A few of the women patted her hand, saying they understood, when suddenly Mrs. Wilkins burst in front of her, throwing herself onto the ground at Chlöe's feet, grabbing the hem of her gown, begging, entreating her to return to Snow Leopard. He laughed when she told him about it later.

In the evening he paced around the tent, alternately sitting in the chair, his legs crossed, smoking a cigarette, and staring intensely at her. Sometimes he would lie on the fur rug, his hands under his head, questioning, listening.

She asked him, "Have you killed many people?"

"Of course," he answered as though it were of no importance.

"How many?" She wondered if he was really evil, for so often he sounded like an inquisitive boy, trying to absorb so many new facts. She equated evil with murder. Yet Snow Leopard did not seem evil to her.

He shook his head. "I don't know. Hundreds. Maybe more."

"Why have you killed?"

"For the normal, usual reasons."

"I can't think of any normal reasons. Unless people are outlaws, bad men, they don't kill in my country."

"I hear America is a violent country. But tonight, let us talk of my country." And he asked her questions of Chiang Kai-shek and of Sun Yat-sen, who had been dead now for nearly two years. She told him of Ching-ling and Nikolai and what they were trying to achieve. She talked of the futility of hoping to unite China. He asked of the Japanese, whom he did not trust, who had been granted this province of China by the League of Nations. He felt it was not up to an outside government to give away land that belonged to the Celestial Kingdom.

Their discourse was broken by the sound of gunfire and shouting in the distance. Snow Leopard leapt from the rug where he had been lounging, his body taut. In long strides he was across the room and out of the tent, his muffled voice calling out something she could not hear.

Snow Leopard strode back into the tent, not looking at her. He walked to the chair where his gun belt lay. Strapping it around his waist and over his shoulder, he picked up his rifle. He jammed his feet into boots. Then he looked over at her.

"You are about to be rescued," he said. "I gambled and lost. I could not imagine they would rather risk the death of a few than pay the money. Perhaps face is as important to your country as to mine."

"Where are you going?"

"To a place where my men will be safe. Where as few will die as necessary. One of my men is already dead at the top of the mountain. That was the first gunfire you heard. Your armies are coming down the mountain on horseback. They cannot see, for there is no moon. So it will be slow for them. I am going where we shall not meet again."

He walked over to her.

"If I had found some other way to solve our problems, we would not have had these last three nights," he said, his eyes meeting hers. "For that I am not sorry."

"I don't approve of you, you know that," she said. "But I have also enjoyed these nights. I have seen into the Chinese mind, or at least one Chinese man's mind, as I never have before."

In the background there was yelling, the stamping of running feet, horses' neighing.

Amazed, she found herself sorry to see him leave.

He put his hand up and touched her cheek for a second. Then he reached down and took her hand, turning it over so that hers lay in the palm of his, and he looked at it before enclosing it with his large fist. He smiled at her.

"You are the first woman who has seemed to me to be a—human

being." He shook his head as though to rid himself of what he had said. "I mean, like a man. I mean, worthy."

He reached down and grabbed his jacket and was gone, disappearing into the night, into the tumult she heard outside.

Chlöe sat down. Let them find her here, in Snow Leopard's tent. Where a man had questioned her and listened to her answers. Where a man had granted her the power over life and death. Where, ironically, for the first time in her life she had felt really important. And all this had been bestowed on her by a man who had had only one use for women.

# CHAPTER 28

It took them two and a half days on horseback to return to where railroad cars awaited them. A bedraggled-looking group, their nightclothes tattered and dirty, they laughed and joked all the way. Now that they were safe, and having been treated halfway decently, they told the British and American forces who had rescued them the tales they would tell their children and grandchildren and anyone who would listen for years to come.

By the time they arrived back in Shanghai—two hundred half-dressed, unkempt Westerners pouring off the train—they found themselves heroes. Chlöe in particular.

Lou was one of the first people she saw.

"Where's Slade?" she asked, hugging him.

"Milling around here someplace," Lou said, taking his raincoat off and pulling it across Chlöe's shoulders. "We've all been crazy with worry about you."

Chlöe strained to search for Slade among the hundreds crowding the station.

"You're a legend already," Lou said.

Chlöe raised her eyebrows and turned to face him.

"The woman who's sacrificed herself to save her comrades."

"Oh." She dismissed that with a shrug, her eyes again scanning the crowd. His words made her feel fraudulent.

At last she saw Slade weaving through the crowd, waving, calling out to her, something she couldn't hear.

Lou saw the expression on her face and turned to look. "He didn't even know you'd been kidnapped for more than a week," Lou told her. "He went up to Nanking right after you left, you know, and didn't hear a word about it. When he did, he wanted to go charging up there himself or send planes searching for you."

Of course. So like Slade, who, in a minute, was beside her, his arms around her, murmuring into her hair, "Darling!"

The crush of the crowds became unbearable.

"Let's get out of here," he said, taking her hand.

"I'll stay here," Lou volunteered, "to talk with others."

"And I'll take home with me the one who can tell us the story of all stories," Slade said. "Come on. Here." He pulled Lou's coat from her shoulders and held out the sleeves, indicating Chlöe should put the coat on. She slid her arms into the sleeves of the too-big coat, and Slade wrapped it around her. "Come on, before everyone sees you looking like this."

Everyone looks like this, she thought, her hand in his, following him. He's ashamed of me, of how I'm dressed—or undressed. He doesn't want people to see me. She looked down at herself, realizing that she never would have dreamed of appearing in public like this. Would never have consented to have company in her own home while dressed like this. She wore the purple satin gown Snow Leopard had given her, but it was wrinkled and mud-spattered, though not nearly so much as the clothes of the others, who'd had no change at all.

Slade held her hand tight as the coolie trotted through the streets. Chlöe wanted to feel his warmth, have him hold her, but he did not put his arm around her in public.

"My God," he said, "when I returned from Nanking and Wuhan to hear you'd been kidnapped, I was wild with worry. Did they kill the bastards?"

Chlöe shook her head. "No, they escaped."

"When we get home, after a bath and decent food, you can tell me all about it. America's in a rage that the Chinese have let this happen. Chiang says it was Communists who did it."

"The leader wasn't a Communist at all. He hardly knows what communism is. When we talked about it, he said such an idea could never work."

"When you talked about it? What the hell was it, an ideological sparring match?"

She smiled. "Sort of."

He let go of her hand and stared at her.

"It's not like it seemed," she whispered. "I'll tell you all about it." Of course she had promised never to tell anyone. But she had to tell Slade. He wasn't anyone. He was a part of her. She had to tell him the truth.

Daisy was waiting at the house, so Chlöe could not talk with Slade privately. Her friend hugged her and tears filled her eyes. "I was so afraid for you," she said as she ordered a bath for Chlöe.

When Chlöe finally emerged from the tub, she fell into bed and slept until evening. By the time she awoke, Slade and Daisy were gone. The house was dark, the servants padding around quietly in their cotton-soled shoes. Chlöe sat up. She had not meant to fall asleep. She wanted to see Daisy, talk with Slade, feel his arms around her, feel the comfort and security he represented. Feel at home.

An-wei came running in, bowing as she always did when she entered a room. She greeted Chlöe enthusiastically, welcoming her home, saying she was proud to be the servant of such a heroine. Mr. Cavanaugh would be home by eight. Could she do anything for the madame?

"Yes," Chlöe said, "I would like a glass of orange juice."

She sauntered into the living room, feeling in limbo. Home, and yet alone. On the table were a huge bowl of chrysanthemums and a note from Slade. "I'll be home for dinner. I didn't want to disturb you. Oh, God, I'm glad you're home! I love you."

But when he came, accompanying him were Lou and Daisy. He and Lou had spent the afternoon interviewing the others who had been kidnapped. Lou came tonight not just as a friend invited to dinner but as someone who wanted her story. Slade said only he and Lou would get her exclusive story, that he had refused requests from other reporters. There was an advantage to being married to the heroine of such a drama.

Chlöe said, "I'm no heroine," and felt trapped and upset by them. She wanted to tell them the truth, tell them that she had ended up enjoying herself, that she had sacrificed nothing. She would tell Slade later. Tell him the truth. But he could not publish that. That would be just between them.

She said, "Let's eat first, please. Let me look at your faces. I'm so happy to see them again. Let me hear what's been happening here while I've been gone. Let's wait to relive my experiences until after we've dined."

"Of course, darling," said Slade, pouring a whiskey and soda for himself and Lou. "You haven't eaten a decent meal the whole time, from all reports."

But after dinner they wanted to hear every detail. Lou asked if she minded if he took notes. He looked over at Slade when Chlöe told about Snow Leopard's proposal that if she came to him he would spare lives. For every night that she came, men would live. She even told, with a straight face, that on the third night she had refused to return, since she knew that was the story they must already have heard, but that she had been forced to return by pity for Mr. Wilkins's wife. She wondered how she could tell such a bald-faced lie without laughing. But she did.

She told them what Snow Leopard was like and why he kidnapped them. "I think perhaps it's the first time he's spent talking with an American. With a woman, at that," Chlöe ventured.

"So," said Slade, "he did not just 'use' you? Did he talk to you before or after?"

"Before or after?" she asked, nonplussed for a minute. "Oh, he talked to me all night long."

What must Slade be thinking? He must, in his mind's eye, see her being made love to by this man she was describing, wondering if she enjoyed it, if she just lay there. Wondering if he'd forced her, if she'd been in misery every moment.

"Chlöe," said Lou, his voice quiet and level. "Did he hurt you? Was he cruel? I don't want to hear any intimate details, but the world will want to know something. You're already the main topic of conversation in the city."

Chlöe looked at Slade and could see pain in his eyes. His wife had been raped, or seduced. She could read it in his eyes. Go away, she wanted to cry to her friends. Let me be with my husband and tell him—tell him the truth. But all three of them stared at her expectantly, awaiting the answer.

What could she say? What should she tell them?

"No," she said slowly, "he was not cruel to me. I do not think he understood an American woman."

"He wanted to humiliate you, didn't he?" Slade asked, his voice absolutely even.

Chlöe looked over at him. "No, not at all. I don't think he had ever really talked with a woman before. He wanted to know of our ways, about the rest of China, what's happening in the world."

She saw they thought she was evading the issue. Oh, God, must she keep the promise now that they were all safe? Couldn't she tell them the truth? Yet something inside her said Snow Leopard had kept his part of the bargain, and so must she.

Three pairs of eyes were staring at her, waiting for something to tell the world about this heroine, this woman who saved lives by sacrificing herself. She knew that women like Nancy and Amy considered her deeds the height of romance. Snow Leopard was an enigmatic Oriental who desired the beautiful young American woman.

She would feed that. He would like that. "He had never had a Western woman, and he has no respect for women. He uses them for his own needs and that's all. But he is not cruel. Just quick. It was all over with very quickly. So quickly I hardly knew what had happened."

"A typical Chinese man," muttered Daisy again.

"A small price," Chlöe said, wanting to justify her actions to her friends, "to pay for men's lives."

Slade walked over and put an arm around her. "I'm very proud of you, darling." He leaned down and kissed her cheek. She felt a tremor in his hands upon her shoulders.

"I have to have a picture of you, Chlöe," said Lou. "I'll come around with a camera tomorrow. You understand, old man?" he asked Slade.

Slade nodded. "Of course. Even I'll have to."

After Lou and Daisy left, Slade poured himself a drink. He raised his glass in the air and nodded his head, toasting her. "Married to a genuine heroine, I am." His mouth smiled but his eyes did not. "I don't know many women who would have done what you did, my dear."

"Oh, Slade." Chlöe went over to him, putting her arms around his waist as he sipped his drink before placing it on the table and encircling her with his arms. "It really wasn't like that at all, but you mustn't print the truth. I made a promise."

He arched his eyebrows, waiting.

"He didn't touch me. We just talked. He fed me wonderful food and we talked all night for three nights. He made me promise not to tell anyone he hadn't touched me. If I would promise, he would spare not only lives, but me. I saved him, you see." She told him about Wang.

Slade took his arms from around her and stared at her.

"It's true, I swear it is," she said, putting her head against his shoulder, her arms around him tightening. "But no one can know it. He kept his promise and I must keep mine."

Slade reached for his drink. He was silent for so long that Chlöe finally looked up at him, and the look in his eyes made her draw away from him.

"It's true," she said again. "He didn't touch me." That wasn't quite true, for she remembered his hand against her cheek.

"Do you really expect me to believe that?" His laugh had a ragged quality to it.

"Oh, Slade," she cried, anguished that he might have doubt. "I've never lied to you. Have we ever lied to each other?"

He turned from her and walked across the room, then turned to her and said, "Let's go to bed. It's been a long day."

"No." She ran to him. "Slade darling, believe me. Please. He said he had no desire for a woman whom he knew would be repulsed by him. And he did not find me attractive. He told me so. He had no desire for a foreign woman like me."

"Sure." Yeah, sure.

"Slade." Her voice was anguished. "It's true. We talked. We talked of the things I told you and Lou we talked of. He didn't want a woman who would find him disgusting."

Slade turned to her. "Was he disgusting? You seemed really rather fond of him as you talked of him."

"He's a most fascinating person." Chlöe reached out to grab Slade's arm, but he moved ahead of her, into the bedroom. "I was never afraid of him. But, Slade, he didn't even want me. You must believe that."

Slade ripped off his tie and threw it on the bureau. "Chlöe, I can't imagine any man in the world not desiring you. And maybe what you are saying is true. Give me time to assimilate that. But you were willing, weren't you? You were willing to have this man touch you, to feel his hands on you, to have him inside you. You were willing to do that?"

"Of course," she said. "I had a choice. To do that or to watch someone die."

He walked over to her and put his hands on her arms. "And, darling, for that I admire you. It is the stuff of which heroines are made. I admire your willingness to sacrifice yourself. I admire your nobility of spirit. Understand that I admire you, Chlöe. I'm proud of you."

"Then why can't you believe me?"

"I'll try," he said, throwing his shirt on a chair and sitting on the edge of the bed to take off his shoes. "Give me some time. I'll try. I'm glad you're not asking me to tell that story to the world, because they'd never believe you. You're already a heroine, albeit a scarlet one, in Shanghai society. You'll be feted and touted as a savior, a heroine, someone to be admired. At the same time, it will be a two-edged sword. You have soiled yourself in their eyes, Chlöe."

"Oh, God," she cried, walking over and kneeling beside him. "Would they rather I had let their men die?"

His hands played with her hair, twisting a tendril gently. "No, and the conscious, intelligent parts of them will champion you. But intellect has nothing to do with how we live our lives. Men will look at you differently, and women will silently wonder how it is to make love with a Chinese. And you will never again be the same to them."

She stared up at him, now through tears. "You mean this is to be my reward?"

Slade got up and went over to the bureau, opening a drawer and finding his pajamas. He stood with his back to her and undressed, stepping into his nightclothes. He was silent.

She stood up and undressed, puzzled and not understanding. He turned to look at her, naked in the dim light, and laughed, a not pleasant sound. "Do you really expect me or anyone to believe this man who had never had a white woman before didn't desire you?"

"Oh, try to understand. You don't find Chinese women beautiful, do you? Well, a Chinese didn't find my kind of looks attractive. Slade." She felt tired. Defeated. "Please believe me. He never touched me. He really didn't."

Her nightgown slid over her head as Slade crawled into bed. "All right." He sighed. "I shall try. But know this. You needn't lie to me. I admire your self-sacrifice and nobility. I'm proud of you."

She curled next to him, kissing his neck, and he turned on his side to kiss her, his lips touching hers with tenderness. "I'm glad you're home. That's what matters." His lips touched hers as his hands reached under her nightgown. "And I love you."

She gave herself up to his lovemaking, to the feel of his body against hers, to the frenzy within Slade. They threw off the covers and their nightclothes and clung to each other, kissed each other with a wildness, but Slade could do nothing.

"I'm sorry, darling," he whispered. "Give me more time. Let me believe that some other man has not done this to you."

And he turned on his side, his back to her.

# CHAPTER 29

In the spring, Ching-ling arrived in Shanghai from Wuhan.

Chlöe had been able to focus only on the fact that Slade had not touched her since her kidnapping. In public he got in the habit of draping an arm around her shoulder, but when they were alone, he didn't come near her. He came to bed every night long after she was asleep. Sometimes he didn't come home until after midnight. She knew he didn't want to come to bed when she was awake. He'd feel he ought to make love to her and somehow he couldn't.

The situation wasn't helped by Cass's cable. "In your own words, Chlöe, the first-hand details. The world's eager to hear your story. Brave girl!"

Slade made a sound that she took for laughter. "This time it's warranted," he said. "Write of the barbarian who kidnaps the glamorous American. Not quite a vestal virgin, but . . . The world will lap it up."

Damn him! He had a habit of making her feel she'd done something wrong. She knew he didn't believe that Snow Leopard had not touched her. Maybe it didn't matter; the idea that the world thought she'd sacrificed her body was enough for him.

The story was picked up by every wire service and circulated the globe. Chlöe Cavanaugh and Snow Leopard.

She, Slade, and Lou often dined together, and there was no lack of laughter and lively discussion, but Slade never came near her when they were alone.

A few weeks after the "incident of the Blue Express," as it had come to be called, the fuss about Chlöe died down, but Slade had been right. Men looked at her differently now, in a way she couldn't define even to herself. At first the consular wives had made a great to-do over her, but Chlöe was thankful when that period was over. What she didn't know was that the Western women of Shanghai told every newcomer the story of Chlöe's scarlet heroics.

Chlöe wanted desperately to confide in Ching-ling, and was sorely tempted despite her promise to Snow Leopard, but Ching-ling was too involved with matters of national import for Chlöe to take her time for such a small personal problem. Madame Sun did, however, invite Chlöe and Slade to dine at her mother's.

Chlöe had met Mammy Soong years earlier, shortly after she

and Ching-ling made their escape from Canton, and Mammy Soong was gracious to Chlöe, as though meeting an old friend. Nearing sixty, Mammy was still a dynamo. Standing less than five feet tall, she looked like none of her beautiful daughters. While not homely, she was plain, but her face spoke of character. While they waited for T.V. and Mei-ling, she played the piano for them. It was an instrument not usually found in Chinese homes.

She smiled when Slade complimented her on her playing. "It was thought that my piano playing and big feet would make me unmarriageable," she said. "Instead, they brought me the most interesting husband and exceptional children in the whole country." Unlike all her children, she did not speak English.

Ching-ling smiled fondly at her mother. "Mammy has never been like the other women of our country. Perhaps that explains all of us children."

Mammy shook her head. "Nothing explains you, my little cabbage. You are not like anyone else." She smiled fondly across the room at her middle daughter, who sat, hands folded on her lap, looking as though she must have been descended from a line of beautiful women. Then Mammy turned to Slade and said, "I am proud of all my children. I think perhaps because of them, China will never be like it was. I see them as forces for the future."

"And the present too, I'd say," murmured Chlöe.

Just then the dramatic Mei-ling swept in. More beautiful than her photographs but not so much as her older sister, Mei-ling had no tendency toward shyness as did Ching-ling. Ching-ling sat quietly, looking delicate and thoughtful. She always looked remote, but Chlöe thought it was her way of protecting herself. When she was with Ching-ling, the Chinese woman often let down many of her defenses, but even here at home Ching-ling appeared to be on the outside looking in. Mei-ling, on the other hand, enjoyed—in fact, demanded—being the center of attention. There was about her a haughtiness, as though she were used to being treated as royalty. She laughed prettily but was tightly wound. Slade used the word *imperious* to describe her. Chlöe couldn't decide whether she liked Mei-ling. She did not feel at ease with her, though Ching-ling's sister was bright and made easy social conversation.

She seemed far more American than Chinese. Ching-ling told Chlöe that when Mei-ling first returned from a dozen years in America, after her graduation from Wellesley, she refused to wear Chinese clothes and preferred to speak English. China appalled her with its dirtiness, its crowds, its lack of sophistication, its poverty, its lack of sanitation.

Mei-ling alone in the family wore American makeup. She knew she was beautiful and it freed her to use her considerable charm on everyone she met, winning them with her savoir faire and her ready wit.

Ching-ling dwelled on a different plane from her sister, seeming to carry tragedy within her, as though she were burdened with the problems of the world. In fact, Slade had once commented that he thought Ching-ling's look of perpetual melancholy was what created the transcendent beauty of her face.

Ching-ling told Chlöe that Mei-ling turned down all the men who'd proposed over the years and was thirty years old now. And single. Something that Chinese women never were.

"I'd rather be a spinster than married to just another wealthy Chinese," Mei-ling said.

The Soong sisters had been ruined for typical Chinese marriages. They had been educated in America, they had big feet, they had minds of their own, and they were wealthy beyond needing husbands to support and care for them.

"I'm not interested in money," Mei-ling was fond of saying. Having it all her life, she took it for granted.

Just then, their brother T.V., who *was* interested in money, entered the room. T.V.'s perpetual smile was rigid, looking as though he was expected to smile rather than really meaning it. Yet, in reality he was a genial man, although he seldom seemed to pay attention to the conversations around him. It appeared as if his mind were someplace more important, and it probably was: on balance sheets, in places that solved China's finances, on matters of more influence than idle conversation and social amenities.

He looked more like Ai-ling, the eldest, than either of his other sisters, with a round face on which were perched spectacles that enhanced his sober mien. He had been heard to say that the masses of Chinese people frightened him.

Despite this, Ching-ling told Chlöe that of all her siblings she felt closest to T.V. He had been at Harvard when she was in America, and they spent vacations together with his many American friends. He had perhaps the quickest mind of all the Soongs, including his father, Charlie. Chlöe overheard him talking with Slade.

"No, no," T.V. said, a faint bead of perspiration on his upper lip, "you must understand. I *like* working with figures. I enjoy ledger sheets. I enjoy problem solving."

He was busy at this young age trying to solve the financial chaos of the Celestial Kingdom. Having spent several years as Dr. Sun's adviser, he now worked closely with Chiang Kai-shek. Unlike Mei-ling, who was at home in conservative politics, or Ching-ling, who had long ago moved to the far left, T.V. was caught between the two ideologies.

He was torn, too, between his sisters. The love he held for Ching-ling, his gentle sister with romantic ideals for the future of China, was obvious. Yet he succumbed to the right in China's politics because it represented the order and the efficiency he had striven for ever since exposure to them in the United States. If he could fulfill one wish for China, it would be to make it efficient. Both Mei-ling and Ching-ling relied on his judgment and advice.

The maid announced dinner. They proceeded into the formal dining room, Mei-ling chatting on about the house when Slade commented on its loveliness. "I begged Papa to buy it," she said, "but he thought it was too ostentatious."

Chlöe knew that two weeks after her father's death, Mei-ling talked her mother into moving into it and, together, they'd lived there since Charlie's death eight years before.

"Mammy and I are having an argument," Mei-ling announced. Chlöe was surprised she would bring it up in front of guests, when it was obvious she wanted her brother's and sister's opinions.

"Big feet or no," she smiled mischievously, "Chiang Kai-shek has asked for my hand."

Chlöe noticed Mammy Soong's lips tighten, though she said nothing.

Ching-ling's head jerked up, but instead of responding to Mei-ling she glanced over at Chlöe, who knew that Chiang had proposed to Ching-ling last year. Not only that, he already had two wives. And, Lou had mentioned, many other women. Ching-ling nodded her head so imperceptibly, Chlöe guessed she was the only one who noticed.

T.V. said, "Well, he's fabulously rich by now."

Chlöe wondered how. He had been nothing more than commandant of Whampoa Military Academy a year and a half before. Certainly Ching-ling and Nikolai, dedicated to the same cause, were not fabulously rich. Where had Chiang's money come from?

Mei-ling tossed her head. "His money doesn't interest me. I would not be bored with Kai-shek," she said, calling him by the familiar name.

"You *are* easily bored," said T.V. "And you are right. Life with Chiang would not be boring. He is on the edge of power, power greater than any we know."

Darkness shadowed Ching-ling's eyes, but she remained silent.

"Tell me." Mei-ling turned her dazzling smile on Slade. "You are a journalist. You know what America thinks and have your fingers on the pulse of China. What do you think of Chiang Kai-shek? Is he going to be the next ruler of China?"

Slade glanced down at his plate before replying. He knew how Ching-ling felt. He knew what she was fighting for. He had several times met Chiang, whom he did not trust. Chlöe knew all this was going through his mind.

"I can't predict the future," he said finally, raising his eyes to look across the table at Mei-ling. "I have no crystal ball. He does seem to be gaining strength all the time. But I am suspicious of his ties to the Green Gang."

"Oh, that." Mei-ling waved her hand as though to dismiss the thought. "I can break him of those ties. He no longer needs them."

"That he has allowed himself to be used by them at all is a worry," Slade went on. "They do not care about China, but about themselves. Without their considerable aid, Chiang Kai-shek would not be where he is today."

The flash left Mei-ling's eyes, and she said, "I think you are wrong. The future of China—"

Slade interrupted. "What about the massacres?"

Mei-ling's expression was petulant. "He's only trying to get rid of the Communists," she answered. "The excesses I'm sure are due to the fervor and enthusiasm of the common soldiers."

Chlöe was surprised when Ching-ling made no retort. Certainly Mei-ling knew she was aligned with the Communists.

"I can do nothing by myself." It was as though Mei-ling were thinking aloud. "I am a woman. But as Madame Chiang Kai-shek I can take charge of my destiny, and that of millions of people. Perhaps of China."

The same dream yet so different. Two sisters with the same intimations of glory. One for herself, one for her country.

T.V. asked, "You say you and Mammy disagree? Mammy, what is your objection?"

Mei-ling, unlike Ching-ling, would never disobey her family.

"No daughter of mine will ever marry a man who is not a Christian." Mammy pronounced it as though there would be no quibbling or debate.

Chlöe saw Ching-ling almost visibly breathe a sigh of relief.

The next day Ching-ling called on Chlöe. Putting her small hands out to hold Chlöe's, she said, "My dear, you are so obviously unhappy. Have you not recovered from Damien's death? Not that anyone can ever recover from the loss of a child."

Chlöe shook her head. "No, I am sure I shall always carry that within me."

"You can have others." Ching-ling let go of Chlöe and went to seat herself in the chair by the window.

Chlöe wanted desperately to confide in her friend, but now that the invitation stood there, she was unable to. If she said that Slade hadn't touched her in months, that she hadn't felt his hand on her breast or the touch of his kiss, she would be betraying Slade, wouldn't she? Besides, what could Ching-ling do to help?

"Nothing seems to matter anymore," she answered, and that much was true. She had lost Damien and now felt she had lost Slade too.

"Is it China?" her friend asked, gazing across the room at her.

Chlöe shook her head. "Oh, I don't know. If we'd never come, life would have been so different. I'd have my children." And my husband too. "Sometimes it seems too much for me to bear. I don't know any way out. But out of what, I'm not sure."

Ching-ling rose from her chair and walked in that graceful way of hers over to Chlöe. "Come back to Wuhan with me," she suggested. "Perhaps a change of pace will benefit you. You have gone from being heroic back to a life of tea parties and idle chatter. I suspect this Snow Leopard has influenced you too. Rape is not something one gets over easily, I'm sure."

"He didn't rape me," Chlöe said.

Now Ching-ling turned to face her friend. "It amounts to the same, doesn't it? He really gave you no choice. Surrender or be responsible for someone's death. He violated you, Chlöe, and you are not used to the ways of Chinese men. He used you, of course, as most Chinese men use women, as nothing more than a vessel. You feel a loss of dignity, and an invasion of yourself, I should imagine."

No, Chlöe wanted to cry. He gave me dignity. He gave me importance. But all she did say was "It wasn't like that at all."

"I suspect you just haven't let yourself face it. That's why you carry this great sadness around with you. Doesn't Slade try to reassure you?"

"Reassure me about what?" Chlöe asked.

"That you are important in other ways that . . . than the way this Snow Leopard used you? Chlöe, no American woman can go through such an ordeal and not come out scarred. China is used to it. I have been in villages where battles have occurred and men have spied women hiding, and together three or four soldiers will grab the woman, let down their pants and use her, one after another, leaving a frightened, whimpering woman. It means nothing to soldiers. I suspect the woman has been scared of dying, but she expects little more than that in life. China is different."

But he didn't do that to me, Chlöe wanted to defend him.

"Come to Wuhan with me," Ching-ling said again. "Nikolai and I will put you to work and take your mind off yourself. It will be a change of scenery and pace. And I sorely need a friend. Not that Nikolai isn't a good friend, but he is not a woman."

Slade, always eager to have information from the left wing of the Kuomintang, made no objections about Chlöe's proposed visit.

When she and Ching-ling boarded the ship, Chlöe had no hint that she would find in Wuhan what she had never found before.

# CHAPTER 30

After Shanghai and Peking, Wuhan was the third most important city in China. Directly astride China's greatest river, it was halfway between Shanghai to the east and Chungking to the west. Foreign vessels that plied the Yangtze headquartered at Wuhan. The U.S. Navy kept a warship patrolling the river in waters here.

It was not only the Yangtze that made Wuhan so important. The city was also midway between Peking and Canton. Halfway between east and west, halfway between north and south. By 1927 it was sprawling, dirty, more industrialized than any other Chinese city. Because of its heavy industrialization, it was ripe for rebellion.

Its dismal working conditions readied the workers to respond to the dreams of people like Nikolai Zakarov and Madame Sun.

The last time Chlöe had chugged up the Yangtze had been with Damien in her arms, to meet Ching-ling and spend those idyllic weeks up in the mountains of Lu-shan. She tried not to think of that, yet found her arms still aching for her lost son. If I live to be a hundred, she thought, I shall miss him. Think of him. Yearn for him.

From beside her, leaning on the railing, Ching-ling pointed to the city as they approached. "Wuhan used to be three separate cities," she said. "But it spread out and is formed into one now, with a central government. There on the north is what used to be called Hankow." Chlöe saw great gray pillars of smoke belching from tall brick columns. "The ironworks," Ching-ling explained. "There are arsenals here that manufacture guns."

Chlöe nodded. She knew gunpowder had been invented in China.

"Cigarette factories."

It seemed to Chlöe that almost all Chinese men smoked cigarettes. Never the women. Even coolies had cigarettes dangling from their mouths. On trains smoke enveloped her and the smell made her nearly as nauseated as the ubiquitous odor of urine.

Ching-ling continued. "The laborers sing now at the goat-processing plants, and the tallow and leather factories, in the factories where matches are made, in those that make glass. There are metallurgy plants and flour mills, noodle factories, packing plants. Wuhan is quite modern compared to the rest of China's industrial areas. Look, over there you see sprinklers on a roof, to retard fire."

Indeed, the mood of Wuhan was much gayer, more vital, than that of either Shanghai or Peking. The eyes of the workers sparkled with hope: their gait reflected an energy lacking in the other parts of China Chlöe had seen.

"Here," said Ching-ling as they walked down the gangplank toward the waiting rickshaws, "Nikolai shows them the way to freedom. What's wonderful about him is that he has no desire to control. He wants to advise. He wants *us* to show people the possibilities in life. He wants to show, not tell, them what to do. He knows it takes time."

Despite Ching-ling's earlier protestations, Chlöe thought her friend must be in love with the Russian. That night, when he came to dinner, she could understand any attraction Nikolai might hold for Ching-ling.

Chlöe had always liked him. She'd always found him attractive, and he made her laugh. At the same time, she respected his total devotion to a cause he found the most important in the world. But she had forgotten how imposing his physical presence was. Surrounded by his bushy beard and thick mustache, his teeth flashed white when he dazzled her with his smile, reaching out his big hands to take hers.

"Chlöe, how wonderful to see you. It has been far too long." His eyes met hers with affection. Infectious energy radiated from him. "The time has agreed with you, though."

Ching-ling embarrassed her by saying, "It has, hasn't it? She gets more beautiful all the time even though she looks so sad."

Chlöe hadn't realized that her inner feelings were so obvious. Maybe they weren't to others.

Ching-ling and Nikolai looked as though they belonged on the stage. The Chinese woman's loveliness, her erect regal stance that commanded attention whenever she entered any room, was enhanced by a peacock-blue silk dress of the simple Chinese design that Chlöe so loved. The black mandarin collar accentuated the depth of Ching-ling's eyes, sparkling in the lamplight like live coals. Without even thinking Chlöe said, "I want to wear a dress like that." She hadn't worn Chinese clothing since the incident of the Blue Express.

"Nothing could be simpler," said her friend. "Tomorrow we'll go to the tailor's. I've a feeling there will be nothing to fit someone of your height in any of the shops." Chlöe did not consider herself *that* tall at five six, but she was half a head taller than nearly all Chinese women.

"We shall all soon be Oriental," Nikolai, who was himself wearing the blue peasant trousers so universal in China, said with a laugh. "Though I, too, had to have mine specially made." His shirt, however, was loose and flowing in the Russian style, caught around his waist with a colorful belt. He looked like a Tartar, Chlöe thought, aware again of the Oriental cast to his features. Just the slight slant of his eyes was what did it, she thought, yet his eyes were not those of the Orient. They were large and searching, they were never indecipherable. Nikolai wore his passions in public, and Chlöe had heard that was a Russian trait.

Slade had once commented on this characteristic. "Haven't you ever read Dostoevski? *The Brothers Karamazov?* God, I couldn't get through it for all their emotionalizing. Russians *feel*, and don't mind admitting it." He said it as though he were criticizing them. Chlöe, however, found it a charming characteristic. She wished Americans showed their emotions more. Men, anyhow. She didn't think the men she knew *ever* showed what they really felt, deep inside. Sometimes Lou did, but not in public. Only when they were alone together, though she imagined anyone who met him was aware of his sensitivity.

But Slade and her father and other American and British men—and now that she thought of it, German and French and Belgian—hid any emotion, except perhaps anger, that they might feel. She wondered sometimes if they hid it or just didn't feel the things she felt. Men seemed to consider a display of emotion a sign of weakness. She never could understand that. And, as she looked at Nikolai again, chewing on a chicken leg in much the same fashion as the Chinese did, she thought it was a part of him she most liked.

"We could use your help," Nikolai said. "You write Chinese. We need help with our newspaper."

Chlöe laughed. "I can't imagine helping a revolutionary newspaper."

Nikolai, who had finished eating, wiped his hands on a napkin and said, his eyes lit with an inner fire, "One of our immediate goals is education. How can people achieve if they cannot read? Our presses run off leaflets by the thousands yet I know the people cannot read. We have classes every night all over the city. It is the key to freedom. An uninformed people is an enslaved people. Perhaps you can help with a class."

"Teach my people to read, Chlöe." Ching-ling's breathless voice sounded like a rallying cry.

Teach? Chlöe smiled. "I left home so I wouldn't have to be a teacher."

Nikolai gazed at her. "Why? I can't imagine a more noble profession."

Chlöe shrugged her shoulders. "So I wouldn't have to put in time in such a dull job. So my life could be more interesting than being imprisoned in a classroom."

Nikolai's voice was incredulous. "A chance to influence the thoughts of everyone you encounter? A chance to change the world? An opportunity to provide people with the tools of freedom?" His voice cracked.

Chlöe had never seen education this way.

Nikolai pounded his fist on the table, rattling the glassware. "There is no preordained fate. We must show the people that they can be the masters of their own lives."

"Oh, Nikolai." Chlöe found herself excited. It had been a long time since she'd participated in the give and take of a conversation like this. "You can't believe that completely."

"But I do," he said.

"And so do I," murmured Ching-ling.

"Do you believe your fate was to stay at home and become a teacher?" he asked. "You took charge of your own life and made other things happen, did you not?"

Chlöe nodded her head in agreement. "Only to come halfway around the world and find I may be tossed into the role of teacher after all."

"We needn't argue about that. I believe we are creatures of free will. Whatever the reasons, you are here and can help us if you choose to."

Chlöe laughed a silvery, happy laugh. "If I choose to? I doubt that you and Ching-ling will allow me any choice."

"Good, then it is settled." Nikolai clapped his hands. "Ching-ling will bring you down to the warehouse tomorrow and you can help us with the paper. Tomorrow night there are a dozen people just waiting for another teacher. We shall start a new class."

Chlöe felt herself being drawn into something she wasn't altogether sure she was ready for but that she had no wish to avoid. Her friends made her feel important, as though she had something to give. They needed her. After so many months of feeling abandoned by Slade, everything in her reacted positively to her friends' invitations. Even physically, she felt a surge of life; deep within her belly a knot began to unwind.

# CHAPTER 31

For the first time in the four years that Chlöe had lived in China she was thrown totally into Chinese life. The only other Westerner with whom she had any contact was Nikolai. Surrounded by Chinese, she began to dress exclusively in Chinese gowns, and even began to think in Chinese. The European life she'd lived in Shanghai faded.

She became accustomed to thin cotton mattresses on hard boards, experienced a ten-hour workday, learned how to set up the presses that rolled off the words written for the Chinese workers.

Spending all her days at the warehouse on Han Chun Road, she was surrounded by men who wore red stars on the collars of their shirts or on their pockets, who—grinningly—gave each other the clenched-fist salute that had become their trademark. Nikolai sat in a cavernous room on the second floor receiving callers all day long, pacing, waving his arms as he talked, shaking hands. Chlöe watched him, observing the boundless energy, his flamboyant yet unselfconscious gestures. He wasn't even aware of the picture he created, she mused.

For the first time that Chlöe had ever seen, women were active in the politics of this country. A majority of the young women bobbed their hair as a symbol of liberation, not only for China but for women. In the warehouse—which was the political center not only of Wuhan, but of the cause—they handled the same jobs as the men. A charged energy was visible. Their faces were not the stoic faces of the rest of China. They were bright with excitement, their eyes dancing. Dedicated to a cause much larger than themselves, they found freedom and meaning for their lives.

All day Chlöe copied tracts about the possibilities inherent in this mammoth land. She oversaw running the presses that spat out thousands of leaflets. Her eyes, too, took on a light that had long been missing. The fever of dedication seeped into her, and she often forgot to stop to eat.

Ching-ling was everywhere. But it was not until evening that either Ching-ling or Nikolai took time from their tasks for dining or for conversation. At six o'clock work stopped, and both her friends began to relax. Fulfillment shone in their eyes, those dark eyes that surrounded her life now.

After work, the three of them walked, arm in arm, to a restaurant and drank cheap Chinese wine. Ching-ling and Nikolai introduced Chlöe to new dishes, and not until she tried them did they tell her what she was eating. They laughed at the look on Chlöe's face when they told her she'd just eaten sliced goose fried in its own blood. They showed her how to dip pieces of the fowl into a white vinegar and garlic sauce. There was shark's fin prepared with crab-meat in chicken stock. Hot thinly sliced strips of lamb, snake, eel, and carp, and sauces such as Chlöe had never even heard of.

Three nights a week, at seven-thirty, Chlöe accompanied Nikolai to a dwelling where twelve men and women crowded themselves into the small dirt-floored room lit only by an overhead kerosene lantern. Here she taught them how to read their own language. Nikolai left her there for two hours, returning to walk her back to Ching-ling's little house. He did not like the idea of her walking the streets alone at night.

By the end of a month Chlöe began to wonder what was happening to her. She was changing, she could tell. It was not so much politically, for she was still convinced that Ching-ling and Nikolai were living in dream worlds.

Part of the novel feeling was her dozen students. She looked at them, their fingers tracing the Chinese characters and trying to translate the pictures into words. When someone's eyes lit up with understanding, she felt . . . she couldn't even begin to describe to herself what it was she felt. Some awesome power. She was helping people to expand horizons that had been closed to them all their lives. She gave them the tools for living and for growing. Whatever this indefinable thing was, she half expected to find herself taller. One day she said aloud to herself, "I like me," and smiled at the wondrous feeling.

She hardly thought of Slade.

When Nikolai walked her and Ching-ling home after dinner, home to the little house that Ching-ling had rented—the house with just four small rooms, which was nevertheless exquisite in its appointments—and Ching-ling would go to bed, exhausted from the day's activities, Chlöe and Nikolai found themselves arguing late into the night. Their arguments were always good-natured, even when Nikolai would pound a fist on the table and stare into her with those black eyes of his and say, "Chlöe, you can't possibly think that!"

She would respond just as heatedly, "Nikolai, you're a dreamer. Communism stands no more chance of working than Christianity. Both premises are based on the inherent good of mankind. On the willingness of all of us to share equally, based on the idea that people are not selfish, and won't pile up possessions beyond what are needed. That we are our brother's keepers. Nikolai, study history! *You* can't believe that ideas like these are viable!"

And he would stare at her, sighing, "Ah, Chlöe, I feel sorry for you that you have so little faith in human nature."

"And you," she replied, "have so little knowledge of human nature."

One night when she had been in Wuhan five weeks, Chlöe and her friends were dining in one of their favorite restaurants, but Ching-ling left early to keep an appointment. Chlöe and Nikolai were silent for a while, and then he leaned across the table, his big paw of a hand reaching out to cover hers. He said, "It's not just Damien, is it?"

Chlöe was surprised. "What isn't?"

"You haven't even mentioned Slade in all this time. I imagine you write to him."

Yes, she had. But just twice. And received only one letter from him.

"If I were forced to be apart from someone I loved, I would not find it easy. Look at Ching-ling. Whenever she was apart from Dr. Sun, all she could think of was being with him again."

The silence hung in the air.

"It's none of my business, is it?" the Russian asked.

Chlöe smiled wistfully. "Nikolai, you surprise me. I didn't know you ever thought of individuals. I thought you were unaware of anything other than your cause."

He took his hand away and leaned back in his chair. "You do me a disservice. I have studied the pain in people's eyes as long as I've been alive. I used to think it all came from not having enough to eat, from not being treated with human dignity. And," he waved his hand in the air, "do not get me wrong. I still think that is a great majority of what is wrong with the world. But I have learned there are other kinds of pain. Ones that have to do with the human heart, no matter how full a belly or how important a person."

Chlöe stared at him. Had he felt that? Pain in his heart for someone? She remembered he'd been married . . . still was, for all she knew—to a woman he would probably never see again. And he had sons he would never know.

He stood up. "Come on. Let's walk," he suggested. "The weather on a night like this shouldn't be wasted." They walked out into the early summer air, and for once China did not smell fetid. "You didn't come just to help us, did you?" he said, his voice low. "You came to get away."

Chlöe didn't know what to say. She had been longing to confide in Ching-ling, yet had not permitted herself an opportunity. She had not expected interest from this quarter.

"Go on, tell me it's none of my damn business," he said, stopping and putting his hands on her arms. "It's not, I realize that. But I've strong shoulders, Chlöe. You would not be the first person to dampen them with tears."

She looked at him through the darkness and said, "It's so odd, Nikolai. I never think of you as—"

"As a person?" he interjected. "I am just an automaton dedicated to a cause, with no personal life, no insights, no desires except the cause? Not as a man?"

Chlöe felt herself blushing with embarrassment and was glad it was dark. "I guess so." Her voice was a whisper.

He laughed. "That's all right. It's rather accurate. But let's not talk of me right now. And if you'd rather not talk about that haunted look in your eyes, we needn't. I thought perhaps you needed . . ."

"It's not that," Chlöe said. "I don't know what to say. It's true, something isn't right about my marriage. It's been that way ever since I was kidnapped." She wanted so much to tell him the truth about Snow Leopard. "Oh, Nikolai, ever since . . . ever since that time." She found herself crying. Nikolai stopped and turned toward her, wrapping his arms around her and holding her against his chest. He let her cry, and she wept with the months and months of frustration and sense of failure boiling up within her. While still gasping for breath, between tears, she said, "He hasn't come near me. Not once has he even kissed me or put his arms around me."

Oh, God, she felt like a traitor to Slade. Their marriage was a private affair. She heard Nikolai's intake of breath.

"I often feel like we're not married anymore. Like he doesn't love me. Like I could be his sister." She stopped as he pulled out a large dark handkerchief, handing it to her.

He didn't say anything for a long time, but took her hand and continued walking. After a while he asked, "You are happy being here, then?"

"Can't you tell?" It felt nice to have his hand wrapped around hers, showing he cared. "I feel needed . . . useful . . . wanted, things I haven't felt in almost a year. Not since Damien . . ."

It felt good just to say even this much aloud.

Wuhan, while not as sophisticated as Shanghai by any means, did have a few bars which were frequented by sailors and other

Westerners. And into one of these Nikolai pulled Chlöe. There was little light and smoke curled around the room like a snake. But there were tables behind curtains, which lent an air of privacy.

Nikolai ordered Chinese beer for himself and oolong tea for Chlöe.

They sat with their hands on the table in front of them. He stared at her so long that at last she smiled. I don't feel self-conscious with him, she thought. I never have. Before she realized it, she was confiding things she hadn't even been aware she'd thought.

"It's funny," she said, talking more to herself than to him. "I was brought up to think I wouldn't be quite whole unless I had a man. You know, it's like women have no meaning unless we see ourselves reflected in a man's eyes. Unless we feel desired by a man. We feel that when we marry, one other person is going to meet all our needs, our needs for everything. And it's not true. No one person can meet everything we need."

"I learned that long ago," Nikolai murmured as he sipped his beer from the bottle.

"I think maybe I'm just growing up," Chlöe said, amazed at her own thoughts. "I've always had good friends. Not just Ching-ling. But Dorothy, Suzi, Daisy." Names that meant nothing to Nikolai. He continued to stare at her, into her.

"No men?" he asked. "I have found friends of both sexes. If you do not open yourself to friendships with men, you are eliminating half the human race. You mustn't leave men out of friendships just because they're men."

Men? As friends? She nodded her head. "Of course. Lou. He's a journalist in Shanghai. He's a good friend. One of the few I think I have in Shanghai."

Nikolai said nothing.

Chlöe thought aloud. "And Cass. Cass Monaghan. He's Slade's boss. I guess I haven't thought of him as a friend because he's the father of a friend. But he's a friend too. Perhaps the best friend Slade and I have. He taught me a lot about life before I got married. And I think," she smiled, "I should also include you."

Nikolai leaned his big bulk back and tilted his chair, his eyes serious, never leaving hers. "How are you defining friends as different from lovers, husbands?"

She had to think about that. While she was contemplating the question, Nikolai asked, "You do not think it possible for husbands to be friends?"

"Oh, yes," she said hurriedly. "But I always thought it was romance, marriage, a relationship with a man that was all important. But right now I think maybe platonic friendship is as important."

"Perhaps," Nikolai suggested, "because we do not demand that friends supply us with all that we hope lovers will?"

She had not thought of this before.

"From friends we do not ask as much, perhaps. We do not have the great, all-encompassing expectations from them that we do from wives or husbands."

"Maybe Slade and I should have had more time to develop a friendship before getting married."

"I think," Nikolai now stared into his beer, holding it up to what light there was in the room, "that people tend to marry more for glandular attraction than because they have anything in common."

She turned pleading eyes to Nikolai. "Tell me, why would—would another man's having had me make Slade stop desiring me?"

"You expect me to have one answer for all men?" he asked, his voice gentle. "I don't know. I think it has something to do with ego. Some men want to think they are the only ones to have *had* you, to own you. It is a matter of possession."

"All men want virgins for wives. Do you think that's why?"

Nikolai looked across the table at her. "All men do not require that a woman be a virgin for marriage. There are tribes in Africa where one must prove the woman is capable of conceiving before a man will consider marrying her. It is mainly your Christian countries, Chlöe, that do this to women. A woman, in your country, is both someone to put on a pedestal and someone who represents sin. Many men, I believe, dislike women for arousing sin—evil—in them. There is no logic to one's thinking. I don't know why Slade avoids you. It is careless and unkind, when you needed reassurance. I would never have done that. I would have let you know that I thought you were heroic."

She looked across the table as he continued. "And I do. I think what you did was wonderful. If you were my wife, I would love you even more for your incredible bravery."

His eyes met hers and held them. She leaned forward as though being pulled toward him, but caught herself. She asked, "What about your wife? Why did you marry her?"

He ordered another beer and then cocked his head to the side. "I was in a foreign country. I was lonely. I was twenty-one years old and yearned for a woman. Perhaps not just any woman, but a woman I could talk with as well as make love with. Someone who believes as I do and with whom I could find a partner. In youth we are romantics. But, actually, though I told myself at the time that she was all these things, I think I badly wanted to go to bed with someone. That is the history of marriage the world over, I suspect."

"You were not friends?"

He nodded his head. "I was always aware of her mainly as a woman rather than a person."

"Isn't that what it's all about?" Chlöe asked.

"I don't think so. I will not negate sexual magnetism. It is a big and important part of marriage, of love. But marriage should be based on much more than that, and too seldom do we do that. I prefer to find friendship and then, if it comes, let it grow into affection, into sexual attraction. . . ."

"Is that how it is with you and Ching-ling?" Chlöe blurted out.

Nikolai stared at her, and then he laughed, a loud, raucous sound.

"Chlöe, what Ching-ling and I have is far too important to ever be tinged with sexual attraction, with romantic emotionalism. First of all, she will never consider remarriage. She is loyal to the ideals of Dr. Sun and dedicates her life to that. She will allow nothing to interfere with that goal. She is someone I love profoundly, the dearest friend a human being could have. I admire her, I respect her, sometimes I am in awe of her. She is closer to me than a sister. But Ching-ling and I are not in love. Is that what you thought? I must tell you, much as I feel for her, I have never desired her as a woman."

"What is love anyway?" Chlöe asked, spreading her fingers out on the table and studying them. "You love Ching-ling. You love communism. I love my friends. I love potato chips, and trees, and the lake in Cooperstown, and the Monaghan summer home in northern Michigan." What, she wondered, did Nikolai love? What places that she had never heard of? "I love the idea of freedom and democracy, and I still love my dead children, even the one that was never born, and Slade. . . ."

Nikolai studied her. "Love? I do not know the answer. I have never felt it for a woman the way I have seen other men do. I love Russia and the idea of equality for all mankind as some men love women. I lust for that. I have not had time to give to love. And," he laughed, "I have lived my adult life in foreign countries, with whose women I have little in common."

Chlöe sighed.

"But know," he said, reaching over to put his hand around her wrist, "that had you given yourself to that warlord and you were my woman, I would be incredibly proud of you. I would want you more than ever for the inner being that you are."

"Thank you, Nikolai," she said, and was surprised to feel a tear coursing down her cheek.

"Do you still love your husband?" Nikolai asked.

*Had* her love for Slade dissolved? She felt abandoned, that she knew. Did she need to feel loved in order to love? God, what a mystery life was. "I don't know," she answered. "But I'm not ready to return to Shanghai yet."

He put his arm around her shoulders as they walked back to Ching-ling's house.

# CHAPTER 32

The night air was still muggy from the day's heat. It reminded her of home, Oneonta. Summer nights there she used to awaken with her pillow soaked from perspiration. Her hair clung to her neck. She had been warned that Wuhan summers could be unbearable. Half a world away they said the same thing about the weather as they'd said in New York, "It's not so much the heat as the humidity." Humidity always enervated her. She thought Shanghai summers were hot, but Wuhan surpassed even those.

At 9:15 she began to glance at her watch every few minutes. Not that she wanted her class to be over, but she knew Nikolai would soon be there, as he always had been these last two months. When she heard the door open and saw his enormous frame fill the doorway, her heart beat faster. Excitement rose in her chest, her belly tightened. His dark eyes stared at her across the dimly lit room. He ran his fingers through his great bushy beard and didn't smile.

She'd just left him two hours before, yet it seemed an eternity. Nights, after he'd left, when she lay on the hard, narrow bed with moonlight streaming into her room, past the high wall in the court-yard, she tried to concentrate on Slade. She tried to call his image up in her mind, but all she could see were the dark, bright eyes of

Nikolai. She fought to hold on to the things she had shared over the years with Slade, but they kept sliding away. What she thought of were the weeks of talk in which she and Nikolai had engaged . . . their exchanges, the parts of themselves they'd shared.

She closed her eyes and forced herself to think of Slade's slim, hard body, and of the tenderness of his kisses . . . the kisses she hadn't felt in so long. She tried to remember his touch, but it escaped her. Instead, in her imagination it was Nikolai's large hand that reached out for her, Nikolai's bushy beard that grazed her breast, his great body that slid between the sheets and covered her, his kisses that rained on her. She opened her eyes and, to her surprise, she had thrown off the sheet in the humid night, lying naked as the moonlight danced across her pale body.

Her hands moved to her breasts as she wondered if Nikolai's beard tickled, if he thought of her in his arms. She sighed with yearning. She was twenty-five years old and a married woman, yet no man had touched her in almost a year.

She realized she wanted him, wanted him to make love to her, with her. Wanted his body next to hers, in her, over her. Wanted to feel those big bearlike hands upon her, wanted his sensuous lips on hers. She wanted him to want her. She wanted to know he was thinking of her right then, that he was yearning for her, that he couldn't sleep with the desire that surged through him.

She balled her hands into fists and beat them against the hard pillow under her head.

That was the night before.

Now here he was, standing in the doorway of her classroom, and she thought, Oh, God. Her gaze locked on him. What am I letting myself do? Yet she was allowing it to happen, even helping it. I don't want to fight it, she told herself. I want . . .

As she walked through the room, he smiled, reaching to take her hand, leading her into the night, muggy and stifling no less than the daytime was. But his hand was dry and he did not let go of hers.

"It's too hot to sleep," he said. "Would you like to walk down by East Lake? There are nice paths there." The full moon shone directly on them; it was nearly as bright as day.

When they did arrive at the lake, Nikolai led her to the line of rowboats tied up for the night, saying, "Let us sit here, shall we?" He stepped into one of the boats, rocking it on the placid water.

They sat on bench seats facing each other, not talking for a while, though Nikolai kept her hand wrapped in his. The sounds of Wuhan faded, and the groves of bamboo looked like lace silhouetted against the moon.

Then Nikolai laughed and held her hand tighter. "Do you remember, it was just a few weeks ago, I told you I did not have time for love?"

"Yes." Her voice was low, and she waited for him to continue.

"I thought, perhaps, that time—that commodity of which I never seem to have enough—always precluded my getting involved with a woman. I thought that since I'm thirty-three years old and had never felt the wild schoolboylike passion within me that I was safe, and that there would never be temptations to lure me from my goal. I have been, I admit," he waved her hand along with his own, "single-minded. I would not let my wife, or even my sons, interfere with what I thought—and still think—is my mission in life."

He raised her hand and studied her fingers in the moonlight. "But then there is you. And there is no way to explain, is there, why suddenly one person enters your life and begins to take it over? Why every shadow becomes that person? Why, all day long, instead of concentrating on the jobs at hand, one finds oneself yearning for the sight of what is now the most important thing in the world. Do you know that today I looked for you all day, just glimpsing you once? All day, everyone who came into my office, everyone I passed in the hall . . . not one of them was you. When I did see you, for just a moment, I looked around to see if everyone near me could hear my heart."

Chlöe pulled his hand that still held hers and turned it over, kissing his palm while he looked at her from his seat.

"I wonder," he said, his voice gentle in the night, "if loving you will ruin our friendship. If you are going to say to me, No, Nikolai. I am married. I do not return your feeling." He let go of her hand and turned his face away from her. "I want you, Chlöe. I want you as I have never wanted another woman. You are inside me, in my bones, in my marrow, my blood. You pulsate within me. Each day the feeling becomes stronger, so overpowering that I can't sleep. I try to keep away from you during the day. I spend so much mental energy trying to keep away that I can't concentrate on my work." He laughed. "I have a disease. I can't shake it. A fever. So help me, I've tried not to give in to this feeling. I like Slade. I don't want to confuse *your* life. I don't want to create a dilemma for you. But you have taken over my life, my waking and dreaming times."

His words wound themselves around her and she thought, I love him. She said, "I love you too."

He stood up, and water poured over the side of the little boat. He jumped out onto the dock and reached to lift Chlöe out. "Come," he said, walking toward the trees, where it was dark. He turned, taking her into his arms, enveloping her. She looked up into the face she now could not see, feeling his breath as his lips touched hers, an urgency in him that she surrendered to, surprised at the softness of his lips, of his tongue against hers, of his murmuring in her ear, "My love. My beautiful, beloved love." He kissed her with such ferocity that she stopped thinking, kissing him back, loving the feel of his mouth against hers, his body so close to her. She melted against him while the world ceased to exist. Only his body and his hands and his mouth existed . . . and her own body came to life for the first time in so long.

He held her as though he would never let her go. "Do you know what I first thought about you?" He kissed her ear. "I thought you were far too beautiful to have any intellect. I thought, Here's another American woman who's been cradled in luxury and will be the perfect example of what we are fighting against."

"Oh, Nikolai," murmured Chlöe. "I was never rich. Empty-headed maybe."

"I know. I know," he murmured into her hair. She could tell by his tone of voice that he was smiling. He put a finger under her chin. "But I liked you, Chlöe. You began to talk, and I discovered you were curious and receptive and intelligent, and your smile captivated me."

He leaned down and touched her lips again, gently, softly. She thought, No one's ever kissed me the way Nikolai does. She felt his kisses in the core of her being, in the center of her stomach, in the middle of her brain. For a moment he had to hold her, so dizzy did his kisses make her.

"I haven't kissed a woman in so many years," he said. "I don't remember it ever being like this." His hungry mouth met hers again. "And what did you think of me that first day we met in Madame Sun's living room in Canton?"

She laughed, trying to remember. "I thought you probably would be an ogre. I'd never met a Communist. I didn't know anything about them except that my father thought they were all evil. I thought you were the biggest man I'd ever seen."

With his arms still encircling her, he said, "It's late. I'll take you home. Though I don't want to."

Their arms wound around each other, they were silent all the way back to Ching-ling's. At her door he said, "I love you. I don't know what we're going to do about all this. Live each day as it comes, I guess. I don't know what's going to happen—with all this chaos that Chiang has created—tomorrow. Or the next day. All I know is I shall love you then. And every day forever after. And hope you will be by my side, wherever we are. But I cannot face thinking of that now. It is enough to love."

She stood on tiptoe, but even then he had to lean over so she could put her arms around his neck and kiss him. As his tongue touched hers, she thought, I want to go to bed with him. I want to make love. I want to give myself to him. I want us to be one, even if but for a little while.

Ching-ling was still up when Chlöe entered the house. The Chinese woman was seated at her desk, writing. She looked up when she heard Chlöe.

"I was beginning to worry about you," said Ching-ling. "You never stay out this late."

"It's so hot, Nikolai and I took a walk up to East Lake."

Ching-ling gave Chlöe a long look, and then she said, "So, the inevitable has happened, eh?"

"Inevitable?"

"Oh, my dear, it has only been a matter of time."

Chlöe stared at her friend. Ching-ling got up and walked over to her and put a hand on Chlöe's arm. "Dr. Sun was married, too, when I met him. We cannot help these things."

"I don't know," Chlöe admitted, "that I believe that. But I don't want it to stop, whatever it is."

Thank God it was Ching-ling and not her mother who intuited what was happening, a friend who did not stand in judgment.

"I have always thought Slade was not good enough for you."

Chlöe's head jerked. "What do you mean, not good enough?"

"He is not a big enough man for you, Chlöe. I know, he is a big important American journalist. And certainly I need him to help tell the world of our cause. But as a man he is stationary. Whereas *you* grow all the time. You will one day be too big for Slade. Perhaps that is part of his trouble now. You have broken out of your role as wife and become heroic. Maybe it has nothing to do with this Snow

Leopard's semen within you. Perhaps it is that Slade feels less like a man, and he cannot cope with that."

Chlöe's mouth fell open with astonishment. She sat down in the nearest chair.

"You will see, my dear. You are fated for great things, and not all men can handle that. They sense it but don't understand it in a woman. I am that way." Yes, Chlöe knew that Ching-ling was. But certainly not she herself.

She'd always looked up to Slade, feeling she'd just been along for the ride. She was his wife, his woman. That was her role in life. She wasn't destined for great things.

But she did not want to think of Slade now. She had come from Nikolai's arms and wanted to go to bed and lie there, remembering his kisses. She wanted to lie awake, filled with yearning for him. She did not want to think of any part of her relationship with Slade tonight. She wanted to relive tonight's moments, when Nikolai kissed her in a way that touched her more than Slade, or any of the boys of her youth, ever had.

Ching-ling called over her shoulder, "You and Nikolai. It is destiny."

# CHAPTER 33

"I don't believe it!" said Nikolai.

Ching-ling sank into a chair. "So Chiang is correct after all," she said, her voice dulled.

The palm of Nikolai's hand hit his forehead as though trying to clear away the words on the sheet of paper in front of him.

Chlöe wanted to say, I told you so. All along I've told you these Russians of yours, these Communists, are not reliable. She'd told him he lived in a world of dreams, that in the ten years since the Russian Revolution millions of dissidents had been murdered or incarcerated in dungeons—or sent off to exile in the Siberian wilderness. Nikolai's answer was always "But once we are in charge and begin to get things done, and people see how different life is, they will agree with us. There will be no need for repression. I am here," she knew he meant here, in life, "to fight repression."

Nikolai *had* been disturbed about the fact that *who* ruled the Communist Party, and therefore all of the Soviets, seemed to take precedence over anything else in Russia. Lenin had been his hero, but now it was a fight between Trotsky and Stalin. Lenin had sent Nikolai to China not only to help the Chinese people but to proselytize and convert another nation to communism. Now he was gone.

After Lenin, Trotsky assured him that Russia had no interest in acquiring China—its land or its peoples. Only in that the Chinese join them in their example to the world, the example of what was possible for the common man.

Now the balance of power in the Kremlin was in jeopardy. Josef Stalin was wresting the leadership into his hands, and his alone. He sent a message to Nikolai to the effect that he was tired of waiting— tired of hearing about the internal strife rampant throughout China, tired of hearing more about Chiang Kai-shek than about communism, and that he feared for the future of the Party.

"Therefore," his message said, "I order you to arm twenty thousand Party members, create a new fifty-thousand-man worker-peasant army, purge the unreliable from your Party, and confiscate land."

"Purge the unreliable?" That could have only one interpretation. Death to any non-Communists.

For over a year Chiang had publicly predicted Russia secretly planned a takeover. The Communists, he pronounced, were not interested in China for the Chinese, but China for the Russians. He did not begin this kind of talk until after Nikolai and Ching-ling and the more radical elements from Canton began their northwest march to Wuhan. Then, when he and his Whampoa Military Academy army began to wind themselves up the east coast toward Shanghai, Chiang had begun to separate himself from the left wing of the Kuomintang. That was more than a year ago.

"This isn't why Lenin sent me here." Nikolai looked up from his desk. "This hasn't been my purpose. No matter whose orders, I shall not do it!"

"It puts you in an untenable position, doesn't it?" Ching-ling raised her inexpressibly sad gaze to meet his. "We'll receive no more help unless you follow these orders, yet there's no way for you to do so."

Nikolai nodded. "You're right, of course. We'll get no more guns to fight off Chiang and his bandits. Our troops are now on their way to Peking to beat Chiang to the capital."

"You have effectively been double-crossed, haven't you?" Chlöe finally asked. "First of all, by Chiang Kai-shek, and now by Russia."

Nikolai nodded. "When he hears that our troops are trying to beat them to Peking, he'll simply send others to crush us, particularly once he hears of this message from Stalin. He'll announce to the world he was right, and the world will be on his side. Gunboats up and down the river from all the foreign nations will come to his aid."

"Oh, Nikolai, what are we going to do?" Ching-ling's voice could hardly be heard.

Nikolai was quiet for a few moments. All that could be heard was the ticking of the clock. Chlöe realized she might as well not have been there in the cavernous warehouse office. Whatever she might say would be irrelevant. She felt pain for her two friends as she watched a vein pulse in Nikolai's temple. His hands, folded on the desk in front of him, were clenched.

"Stalin's running scared," he guessed. "He would leave us alone to develop communism by popularity were he not afraid of Chiang's power and the demise of communism here. He's seen us as allies, a huge communistic continent. But now he must feel he has to resort to power. Squash those who don't believe as we do!"

Chlöe couldn't help herself. "Don't you feel that way too? Wouldn't you do anything for your cause?"

He looked over at her, his eyes reflecting his inner agony. "If there is no other way, yes. I helped do that in Russia. I would do it again. But there is another way here. I know—I know it in every fiber of my being . . . Oh, God, I don't know what I believe at this moment."

At dinner Nikolai couldn't eat. Ching-ling just played with her food, but then she always ate sparingly. Chlöe was ashamed to clean her plate. Finally, Nikolai said, "I'm not very good company. If you'll excuse me, I think I'll go back to my room."

Chlöe's heart ached. She had seen Ching-ling depressed and saddened before, but never Nikolai. She'd thought he wouldn't know what the word *defeat* meant.

When he stood and started to leave, he turned around and said to Ching-ling, "It's not communism, our brotherhood, you know. Stalin's afraid. He's trying to consolidate his power in Russia and perhaps he sees China as one way to do it. He doesn't really know what goes on here."

Already he was making excuses.

It wasn't until after Ching-ling went to bed and Chlöe sat writing a letter to her parents that she realized she wanted to go to Nikolai, to comfort him. He might have wanted to be alone, but he'd been alone four hours. She couldn't stand the thought of his suffering all by himself.

Though she knew where he lived, she had never been to his lodgings. She walked through the dark streets, not nervous to be alone in the convoluted alleys. China had long since ceased to frighten her.

Nikolai's room faced the street. Chlöe knocked several times before he answered. She could tell from his eyes that he had not been asleep, and he was still dressed in the clothes he had worn all day.

"Chlöe?" His voice registered surprise. "It's after eleven. You shouldn't be out on the streets."

"I had to come, Nikolai." They stood there awkwardly, until she said, "Aren't you going to invite me in?"

"Of course." He stood aside and gestured her into his room. A lantern burned on a bedside table, its flickering light casting shadows against the wall. A narrow bed stood in one corner. A table and three chairs filled the center of the room. In another corner was a trunk. That's all there was.

Closing the door, he did not follow her. He stood unmoving. "No one has ever come to comfort me before," he said. "That's why you're here, isn't it?"

She turned to face him. "Of course. I'm here because you're in pain and I love you. If I can't share your pain, I want to be with you while you go through it. I don't want you to be alone."

He came over and gathered her in his arms. "Sweet Chlöe. My darling." He did not kiss her, just held her pressed against his chest. She heard the pounding of his heart. Then he walked over and sat on the edge of the bed. "I can't talk. I have nothing to say tonight. I am not good company." He looked at her. "Nevertheless I am glad you came. It is something new to me. Someone coming because she cares about me." He reached out a hand, but she did not come to him.

Instead, she stood near the table at the center of the room and began to take off her clothes. She did it slowly, hearing his intake of breath as she started. Knowing that he had wanted her for a long time, knowing that he was staring at her with desire, knowing that she had yearned for him. And for a long time desire had been kindling within her. Before he even touched her, she felt herself coming alive, her body tingling. Even though she knew he was in despair, she could not help smiling over at him, still sitting on the edge of that narrow bed. She kicked off her shoes and threw her clothing with abandon around the room.

"Jesus," he whispered as she slowly walked toward him. Stopping in front of him, she reached out to pull him to her, to bury his head in her breasts, to feel his lips against her, hear his moans as his arms encircled her, crushing her into him. His mouth encircled her left breast and she felt fire ignite within her, felt desire course throughout her body, felt a power she had never felt with Slade, an urgency deeper than she had ever experienced.

She began to undo his shirt, pulling it off him and seeing his great hairy chest, so unlike Slade's slim, hairless one. She pulled him, and he stood up, loosening his pants and sliding out of them as she pushed him back onto the bed. His long form lay the length of it. He could not, would not, let go of her. She stretched herself on top of him, loving the feel of him against her. The meeting of their bodies should have lit up the room, but there was only the dim glare of the lantern. Leaning down, she traced her tongue along his lips.

He whispered, "My Chlöe!" His hands moved, then, to cup her breasts and he looked at them, murmuring over and over, "So beautiful, so beautiful." His mouth covered hers, his tongue flicking back and forth until she spread her legs wide against him, feeling his hardness between her legs.

"Don't rush," he whispered. "I have waited too long for this." She felt his hand trail down her back, feathering across her buttocks, pulling her hard against him as he raised his lips to hers and kissed her, a long, slow, kiss. Then he looked into her eyes and moved, turning her over onto her back, leaning over to kiss her stomach, and she thought, his beard isn't scratchy at all.

Running his hands down her legs, he rained kisses on the insides of her thighs. She jackknifed her legs, raising herself to him as he pressed against her, surprisingly light for someone so big. Their bodies—as if entities of their own—moved in rhythm against each other. His mouth met hers as they undulated in a choreography so wild that the hard, narrow bed shook. Chlöe spread her legs around him, clasping him to her, whispering, "Nikolai, I want you. Now. Please!"

He entered her, plunging deep within her, so that she thought he must have become her. He clutched her to him and their deep breathing came in unison. The world was about to explode as they moved faster, faster in tandem, until she knew this must be how fireworks felt when they burst into the night sky in all their jewellike splinters of fire.

It did not subside. It kept coming and coming as Nikolai moved faster and deeper until he cried aloud, but even then they could not stop the momentum.

After they were spent they clung to each other. They lay there for a long time, unmoving. Literally one. And she said, "It has never been this way before."

He moved from her, lying on his back, sighing heavily, putting one hand under his head and looking up at the ceiling, the other hand around her.

She turned on her side and feathered her fingers along his furry chest, leaning over to kiss it. His hand touched the back of her head, keeping it on his chest, close to him. His arm lay across her shoulders and she thought, There has never been a more beautiful moment.

Finally he said, "Until these last few days, I have never once doubted that I've known what is the most important thing in the world. But now," he raised her head from his chest and met her eyes, "you are the most important thing in the world. In my world. I have never known what love meant before. But now you make everything else bearable."

# CHAPTER 34

"It's nice to see you so happy," Ching-ling commented when she and Chlöe were alone.

"I should feel guilty," Chlöe said, "but I feel more alive than I've felt in years."

Even when we're apart I can taste him, she thought, smiling to herself. Smell him. I can feel his hands on me. In her mind she could look into his eyes, so deep that she felt herself drowning within him. She felt his lips upon hers, his arms wrapped around her, his body next to hers, and his words of love in her ear.

A young man arrived in Chlöe's print shop with a message from Nikolai. "Come to my office immediately."

When she opened the closed door, unusual in itself, standing in the enormous room were Nikolai and Ching-ling, T.V., and Slade. Slade and T.V. glanced at her, but their eyes were on the other two, who were staring at Chlöe.

Nikolai said, "T.V. brings a message that Chiang has put a price on my head."

Dear God in heaven, thought Chlöe, her eyes riveted on Nikolai's.

T.V. coughed. "You must leave the country. And you, dear sister," Ching-ling had always been T.V.'s favorite, "should leave too. At least for a while. I fear for your life."

Ching-ling stood erect, her small frame regal. "I divorce our cause from Chiang Kai-shek. I shall publicly announce that I consider him a traitor and a usurper of Dr. Sun's ideals."

"That," said T.V., "is why I fear for your life."

She turned fiery eyes on him. "I shall not keep quiet. I shall spend the rest of my life dedicated not only to Dr. Sun's ideals but to the eradication of Chiang Kai-shek. Any revolution that excludes peasants and workers is false."

She reached out to take Nikolai's hand as both of them stood facing the others. "Today Chinese peasants are worse off than ever. Chiang will not fight to overthrow imperialism. He will continue to enslave the Chinese peasants and workers for his own benefit." Her voice rose. "Revolution in China is inevitable. I am not in despair for the revolution. I am in despair over the length of time it will take to accomplish it now that Chiang has strayed so far from our original path."

Slade walked over to Chlöe.

Nikolai's shoulders slumped. "China is now in the hands of right-wing militant fascists."

T.V. nodded. "We must get you two out of here. That is why we have come."

"What do you suggest?" Ching-ling asked, her voice plaintive. "That I return to America?"

"No." It was almost a bark from Nikolai.

Slade turned to face Nikolai as Chlöe's chest tightened. She couldn't help looking at Nikolai rather than at Slade. Slade was so neat, so clean, so removed from all that had happened to her these past months. He did not look as though he were anything but a foreigner, someone who did not belong here.

She knew Nikolai on a deeper level than she'd ever known her husband. Husband. She looked at him, wondering if there was a deeper level to him.

"Do not go to the imperial powers who back Chiang," Nikolai was saying to Ching-ling. "That is just adding to the impossible situation. Come with me. A public visit to Moscow would dramatically demonstrate your separation from that fascist traitor."

Ching-ling glanced over at her brother, who imperceptibly nodded his head.

"You've got to leave immediately," Slade said, his voice urgent. "In fact, you've got to go into hiding even sooner. As soon as you leave this building, in fact."

"What do you propose?" Nikolai asked, his voice emotionless. "Leaving for Russia tonight?"

Slade nodded.

"You must both leave," T.V. reiterated.

Ching-ling gasped a little sob. "Leave China? Must I?"

T.V. nodded. "Until it is safe for you to return."

In a barely audible voice Ching-ling whispered, "You mean as long as Chiang is in power?"

Like a broken record, T.V. repeated, "Until it is safe."

"I have an idea." Slade left Chlöe's side and walked to the desk behind which Nikolai stood. "I suggest that you and Ching-ling not travel through China together. So that one of you can be assured of escape."

T.V. said, "I can get you," he nodded at his sister, "down the Yangtze, disguised."

"From there we can get you on a ship in Shanghai," Slade said to her, his enthusiasm consuming him. "It will then be easy to get you to Vladivostok." He looked at her. "There we can get the Trans-Siberian Railroad into Mongolia and get you to Ulan Bator, where you can get a plane for Moscow."

Ching-ling's eyes were steel.

"I shall come with you as far as Ulan Bator, where you'll be safe," he said.

Nikolai looked at Slade, his black eyes narrowing. "This is not an act of altruism, is it? It's accompanying Dr. Sun's widow to exile for a story available to no one else." There was no bitterness in his voice.

"You're right, of course," Slade acknowledged, flashing him a smile. "A story that the world will devour. And Chlöe," he turned to her, "can go overland with you so that story will be mine too. Stalin's man in China and how he escaped the clutches of Chiang Kai-shek."

"I am not Stalin's man," Nikolai said.

What Chlöe heard was *Chlöe can go with you.* Her eyes darted to Ching-ling's.

"You can't be disguised." Slade grinned. "You're bigger than any Chinese could ever be. You stand out everyplace. But you can get the train north to its terminus in Sian."

Chlöe had no idea where that was.

"From there I can get you a car or even a convoy and you can head north into Mongolia." T.V. was thinking aloud. "At Ulan Bator we can arrange for a Russian plane to be waiting. You'll be safe there. You'll probably be safe the entire trip. You'll be ahead of any messages offering rewards for you—dead or alive."

Nikolai's smile did not touch his eyes. "Dead or alive? Hmm."

Now Slade turned to Chlöe. "Would you mind dreadfully? If you accompany him, you can report it all to me and we'll have that exclusive story, too."

Why, she wondered, wasn't he going with Nikolai and she with Ching-ling? Slade answered her thought. "The trip with Ching-ling will be more dangerous because it involves returning to Shanghai. We must disguise her and help her through the city. I don't want you to get near Shanghai with her. You'll be safer, even if not as comfortable, going by train and car northward."

You don't know what you're doing, Chlöe thought. You should not let Nikolai and me be free to roam this continent together, out under the stars in the steppes. She knew that Ulan Bator was thousands of miles north, beyond the Gobi Desert. She knew they would spend weeks traversing wild country, locked together in their own wildness.

"Slade never even asked me how I felt about such a journey."

"Perhaps he knows you so well that he doesn't have to," Ching-ling ventured.

"Perhaps he cares more about his stories than he does me."

Ching-ling made no response as she indicated to her maid what should be packed. Then she said, "How do you feel about parting from Nikolai?"

Chlöe had not allowed herself time to think of that. Now tears welled in her eyes. "I feel I'm losing my two dearest friends."

Ching-ling walked over and, standing on tiptoe, put her arms around Chlöe. "These times do not allow for personal relationships. I shall sorely miss you too. I shall miss China. But I shall not stop working toward my goal."

Which is hopeless, thought Chlöe.

"Sit down," said Ching-ling. "Let us have a last cup of tea together, and listen to what I have to say."

Chlöe sat, waiting until the maid brought tea. Then Ching-ling came to sit in the chair across from Chlöe. "My dear, you do not see how important you are, either to yourself or the world."

Chlöe's head shot up. "Important?"

Ching-ling nodded. "I think you are important to my country too. I am leaving, but you will be staying. I hope you will be here when I return."

"When will that be?" Chlöe found herself shaking and put her hands around the cup to warm herself, even though the summer heat was stifling.

Ching-ling smiled and said, "Not as long as T.V. thinks. I cannot live in exile. My life is dedicated to a free China, where the peasants and workers have control over their own lives."

"What have I to do with that?"

Ching-ling reached out and put her hand on Chlöe's arm. "I am not asking you to adopt my cause as yours. I am telling you to act as your heart tells you to. I am telling you to listen to yourself and not just Slade. When you acted on your own, you rose to heroism. You saved lives and grew in stature, no matter that you submitted yourself to a man to do so. For that Slade denigrated you. Don't let that happen again. You cannot control how others think of you, but you can act in ways that you know are right for you."

"Are you telling me something about Nikolai and me?"

Ching-ling shook her head. "No. I am trying to tell you something about you. I am saying you can be a complete person without relying on a man. Though I miss Dr. Sun every day of my life, I am growing. I do not have to rely on others to see myself. I know what my path through life is to be. And I will not let any man or any outside force deter me. I do not suggest that you be so dedicated, especially when you have no cause. But I tell you to garner inside yourself the strength I see within you."

Chlöe was bewildered. "I'm not sure what you mean."

"I am talking about truth. Inner truth. No matter what anyone else thinks about you or tries to influence you, I am talking about that which Shakespeare said better than I can. 'Above all, to thine own self be true.' I forget the rest but something about if you're true to yourself then you cannot be false to anyone else. That's what I'm telling you. Permit yourself the freedom of thought, and consequently action, to be your own self, Chlöe. Dare to dream great dreams. Dare to think of yourself as something other than a man's wife. Do not let that be your limitation."

Suddenly Chlöe remembered an early morning in the mist of Lake Michigan and Cass telling her much the same thing. "But you were so devoted to Dr. Sun that you were just his wife when he was alive."

Ching-ling laughed her beautiful bell-like laugh. "Don't underestimate me. I was much more than that. I was his partner. I worked for *our* dream. And I continue to dedicate my life to that. I know what China calls me. The Chinese Joan of Arc. I know the stories that abound . . . that I have led armies in battle, that sort of thing. Rubbish, all, but I am a rallying point for our cause. I cannot fight physical battles, of course. But I shall fight *for* China with every breath I have should I live to be eighty. Or one hundred." She knelt next to Chlöe and said, "Don't ever let Slade make you feel inferior again. It should never have mattered to him that Snow Leopard had you. He is doing the same thing to you now, in a different way. Go with Nikolai, he says, not knowing whether a trip through the mountains and deserts is dangerous. Go for *my* story. Go as *my* dutiful wife.

"My dear, if you want to go, go, but not for those reasons. Go for your soul."

She walked over to the packed trunk and called for her maid. "Move this out to the litter," she said. Then she turned to Chlöe and reached up to kiss her cheek. "I shall see you again, my dear friend. This is just another event that binds us together."

"Are you afraid?" Chlöe grasped her friend's hands.

"I have never let fear stop me from doing anything," replied Ching-ling. "Of course I am afraid. However, I am as angry as I am frightened. But I am not defeated. Nor do I believe China is. The journey will take longer than I'd hoped. I'd expected freedom to come in 1923 and here it is 1927. Who knows, now, when it will come? But come to this sleeping giant it must. And it shall come from within, from the people themselves."

She gave Chlöe's hand a squeeze and, turning on her heel, sailed from the room.

# CHAPTER 35

T.V. had assured Nikolai he would see that a whole car of the train was at their disposal. Nikolai and Chlöe, along with five other Russians and three Chinese, occupied it all. As the train wound north through the provinces of Hupeh and Honan, they saw the death and destruction, the silent browned countryside. Bark had been stripped from trees, which were bare of leaves. A fine dust blew over the earth that Chiang's armies had ruined.

Beside the railroad tracks, bodies lay scattered in contorted positions, covered with flies and picked at by buzzards whose giant black wings flapped noisily.

The smell of death wafted through their car, yet with closed windows the heat was unbearable, so they suffered the odor of genocide.

Chlöe and Nikolai had not had a moment alone since leaving Wuhan. They all slept stretched out on the hard wooden seats of the rail car. There was never any privacy, and Nikolai spent most of his days staring morosely out the window as the hot breeze riffled through his mass of hair. Over and over he kept repeating, "We have failed."

In vain Chlöe tried to reassure him. But it was true.

Nikolai saw his dreams vanquished, in China at least. "And not," he kept repeating, "just by Chiang, but by my own people. By Stalin, who does not understand. He thinks any revolution is only through the masses of factory workers in the cities. He does not know *this* land. Here it will be only through the peasants that China can change."

Chlöe thought it best to remain silent, to leave him to his despair, so she rose from the seat beside him and went to sit three rows behind him, staring alternately out the window at the monotonous landscape and at the back of Nikolai's head. His unruly hair was so long it hid his neck, and he kept running his right hand through the tangled mane as though at times he wanted to pull it out.

The whole five days they spent in the train she might as well not have been there. Nikolai was too wrapped up in his sense of failure, in the end of the dream.

Would he now be a small frog in a big pond? He would no longer be *the* Russian, *the* Communist leading others to equality. His whole way of life, as well as his dream, was gone. How to go on? And why? His raison d'être had been ripped away. What was left? he must be wondering.

She saw what was left. A man of enormous energy and vision who must now turn his attention someplace other than China. A man among men, a giant really. But she knew that was not what he was seeing as he stared endlessly out at the decimated brown land through which the train rumbled so slowly.

Finally they arrived at Ling Pao, the end of the rail line. Chlöe could sense T.V.'s hand in their arrangements, for only T.V., of all the Chinese she knew, operated with efficiency. Waiting for them at the station were two large Dodges, one a luxury sedan. There were also two motorcycles and a truck. Once the luggage and extra cans of gasoline were packed into the truck, the motorcycles led the convoy out of the hot, dusty city, along the road to Sian.

Nikolai did not really communicate with Chlöe until they left the train, until two of the Russians took over the truck and the other three jumped into the second Dodge, leaving the biggest car for Nikolai and Chlöe and their Chinese driver. Then—when all the vehicles pulled out of Ling Pao and headed west toward Sian—and only then did Nikolai turn to Chlöe and take her hand in his, searching her eyes.

She leaned over and kissed him, his bushy beard soft against her chin.

"Am I to lose China and you at the same time?" he whispered against her ear. "If I urged you, would you come with me?"

She hadn't thought of that. She had thought of losing Nikolai, had thought Nikolai felt he had already lost himself.

"To Russia, with you, you mean?"

He nodded, and she saw that his eyes were filled with pain.

Moscow? Cold, gray Russia? A nation in as much turmoil as China? It would be self-banishment. No. She didn't even want to contemplate it. She couldn't. She didn't share Nikolai's dream. It was not what drove her. But then, nothing drove her, did it? Did nothing matter except moments of love, except what she found with this huge Russian holding her hand so tightly? It was not enough to give up everything for, was it? Or was it?

When she didn't answer, he put an arm around her shoulders and said, "Would that we had more time. Would that what we have found together had time to blossom, to flower, to become a part of our lives forever."

She looked up at him and said, "Perhaps there is never enough time, Nikolai, for anything that we truly want."

He nodded. "The world always intrudes, does it not? Things over which we have no control decide our destiny after all."

We are not the masters of our fate, Chlöe silently agreed, and I am certainly not the master of my soul. "You know, don't you," her voice was so low he had to bend to hear her, "that my heart and soul are yours? But I cannot leave with you."

He was silent for several moments as the car bumped over potholes. He leaned his head against the back of the seat and said, "I know." Then he smiled and sat up straight. "I have felt sorry for myself too many days. I'm sure I shall again. Even more so, for soon I shall lose you too. Let us milk these days, perhaps these weeks, we have together so that we shall never forget them. Let us find whatever happiness this brief time allows us, now that we are going beyond the world's reach. Shall we do that?"

"Oh, yes," she said, her head on his shoulder as he pulled her close to him. The car swayed, and they both laughed. Yes, let this be love like dreams are made of, she said to herself. Let it be something we can keep within our hearts forever.

All the way to Sian, though, they were kept apart in the inns in which they stayed. Chlöe had never been this far off the beaten track in the interior of China and was aghast at the lack of facilities the inns offered.

"I'd rather sleep out under the stars," she said, screwing up her face at the third inn they'd pulled up to.

"Americans *are* spoiled." Nikolai shook his head. "Come, walk with me before dinner. Look out there at those mountains and forget your dirt. Come, let me look into your eyes and kiss you, let us find someplace where no one is around."

"I doubt there is such a place in China." Chlöe sighed. But they found one out in the desert, out in a field of melons, behind a huge tree that stood like a sentinel, alone, guarding the fruit on the vines. There he kissed her as though there were no tomorrow.

Sian—the last community of any size they would see for weeks. The ancient capital of China, dating back to prerecorded history. People had inhabited this space of land since time immemorial.

"Imagine," Chlöe said, looking around, "a city as old as earliest civilization." Coming from a country that thought two hundred years ancient history, she could scarcely comprehend a city thousands of years old that had been the capital of twelve dynasties.

"Do you know," Nikolai told her, "that once the coolies who worked on the mausoleums here finished their jobs they were slaughtered and buried in the tombs?"

Violence in China, unless she saw it firsthand—as in the countryside they'd just passed through—no longer surprised Chlöe. "Why?"

"So they could not tell what treasures were buried in the tombs."

Sian was just at its birth as a great industrial center, and smoke rising from its factories obliterated the hills to the south.

Sian was also where their trek across the northern deserts began. When they made camp each night, dragging two large canvas tents from the truck, two of the Russians set up an old Maxim machine gun on the highest hillock and took turns standing guard all night. Farmers gathered in the distance to watch the white men they'd never seen before.

Chlöe thought the land through which they journeyed was straight out of nightmares. Perhaps, she thought, we've traveled to a different planet. As far as the eye could see, the land was filled with frightening, fantastic, strange shapes. There were rows after rows of dunes that resembled scoops of ice cream straight out of her father's soda fountain. There were bluffs that resembled fantastic castles. There were surrealistic hollows that made Chlöe think of a hand with long, slender fingers that must have been slammed into the sands by an angry God. The desert was not just sand dunes, she discovered, but rocks—mile after mile of rocks.

They came to Yenan, the northernmost city, after which there were no roads for more than eight hundred miles. Nikolai told her, "Genghis Khan and his Mongols swept through here on their way to conquer China." It was still the headquarters for hundreds of nomads who roamed through the northern mountains and deserts with their goats and sheep, searching for water and green pastures.

It was surrounded by rock-ribbed, striated hills. The walls surrounding the city were higher than those that encircled other Chinese cities. They crawled up the hills, becoming part of them, stopping where the hills ended.

"This could be a perfect headquarters," Nikolai observed. "The hilltops could be fortified, and the road south could be watched. No one could attack without being seen. Machine guns could be placed up there. . . ."

"This city is cut off from everyplace. No soldiers are ever going to come up here, not just to capture this small city."

Nikolai looked at her. "Chlöe, there is no place in China that will be free from the war that is going to overtake this nation."

She was silent. Let him think that, let him think that the work he has done here will be of value, that China really is going to change. But she knew Chiang would never send his armies to this remote spot. Yenan would never be important.

By the time they reached the Great Wall, they'd traveled more than eight hundred miles in three and a half weeks. Seven hundred miles lay ahead of them, all across the steppes of the great Gobi Desert of Mongolia.

# *CHAPTER 36*

The sun streaked through the tattered curtains as a raven cawed into the silent air. Nikolai feathered his hand across her breast, tracing desire with his tongue. The fire within started anew.

Chlöe could tell from the slant of the sun's rays on the walls that they had slept the afternoon away. She closed her eyes, wanting Nikolai to never stop. She wanted to feel his hands upon her, his lips against hers, wanted to lie like this forever, naked in the afternoon sunlight. She had no other thought than love, than Nikolai . . . no thoughts at all, really, giving herself up to sensations, to the moment.

His exploring fingers pressed her thighs open and he kissed the soft flesh on the insides of her legs, whispering words in Russian she did not understand, but she knew they were words of love. Her body came alive, the sparks he lit blazing. She opened her eyes to see him smiling at her.

He brushed his beard across her breasts and laughed, his teeth gleaming against his black mustache, his eyes filled with tenderness. He rolled her over onto him, pulling her down so that she stretched herself against him, smiling as she moved slowly upon him, regulating a rhythm back and forth. He reached for her hands and, pulling them to his mouth, kissed the palms as she swayed against him, holding him tight within her.

"Stay there," he said, his arms encircling her, forcing her to lie against him as his mouth met hers. As he rose to her, she pushed against him, pushed back and forth until she heard him cry and felt herself on the edge, shivering, a great spasm overcoming her so she didn't move, but froze, moaning.

She sighed, falling against him.

They lay still then, not moving until she rolled off him and onto her back, lying in silence, holding hands, eyes closed, breathing in unison. The raven cawed again.

She heard the gravelly sound of wagons rolling across the stone courtyard and oxen lowing, heard the cry of men urging the beasts on as the sun turned gold against the dirty curtains. Chlöe turned on her side, tossing one leg over Nikolai's, her head on his shoulder, and smiled up at him. It was all as though in a dream, hazy, not quite within reach, and she saw the surprise in his eyes, saw him mouth "Chlöe," but it was Slade's voice she heard.

She sat upright, swinging her legs over the side of the bed, clasping her arms across her breasts.

The sweet voice of Ching-ling drifted up from the courtyard and, naked, Chlöe dashed to the window. Next to the Dodge was a wagon piled high with hay, with suitcases and boxes and with Ching-ling, who jumped from the cart into Slade's arms. With them were her maid and a young Chinese man.

"Oh, God." Chlöe turned to face Nikolai, whose face froze. He bent over and picked up his clothes, donning them as she stood silhouetted against the curtains.

"Get dressed," he said, his voice curt. "For heaven's sake, get dressed."

Chlöe stared around, looking for her clothes, flung all around the room in what had been joyful abandon three hours before. Swiftly, she began to dress.

Nikolai said, "I'll go down. You needn't hurry. Better comb

your hair." He started for the door, but turned and looked at her. Walking back to her, reaching out to hug her to him, he said, "If only there were more time. Oh, my love." He leaned down and kissed her. Then he turned and left the room, slamming the door behind him.

I wish I'd known it was the last time, Chlöe thought, kneeling on the floor to look for her other shoe. I wish it could have been slow and languid and I'd have consciously remembered each moment, each touch, each sensation.

Yet another part of her knew each of Nikolai's touches, each kiss that was burned into her forever.

As she reached under the bed for the shoe, the door opened and Slade stood there, hands on hips, laughing, his eyes filled with excitement. In three steps he was across the room, reaching down to pull her up off the floor and into his arms, swinging her around. "Isn't this the damnedest adventure of all time?" he asked, planting a kiss on her lips.

It was the first time he had kissed her in more than fourteen months.

He didn't wait for an answer, but grabbed the hand that wasn't holding the shoe and propelled her out the door, dragging her down the stairs. With one shoe on and one shoe off she hobbled, led by Slade, into the courtyard, where Ching-ling was giving her maid instructions about the luggage. There seemed to be half a ton of it.

Ching-ling's face was drawn and tired. Her eyes held the sadness of the world within them. She looked frailer than she ever had, though her shoulders were still erect and she held herself in that way she had of suggesting one born to royalty. Holding out her hands to Chlöe, she stretched up to kiss her cheek. "I'm so glad to find you safe. We worried about you the whole time."

"Let's talk over food," Slade exclaimed. "We're starving."

"Let me wash up first," protested Ching-ling.

"There's no water in the inn," said Chlöe. "Come with me. Up this alley are washbasins. And for other things, well, up that alley over there." Up that narrow dark alley, turning a corner, were six stinking holes in the ground.

"When did you get here?" she heard Slade asking Nikolai as the two women walked off by themselves.

"Are you all right?" Ching-ling reached out to put a hand on Chlöe's arm.

"Are you?"

"No, of course not. Physically, yes—perhaps a little bit the worse for wear. But inside I feel dead. I fear all is lost."

"Perhaps Chiang will be overthrown."

They arrived at a low hut and turned in. Large round wooden tubs of water stood on high tables. Ching-ling reached for a small metal bowl, dented and dull, and scooped water from one of the larger vats. She splashed it on her face, bending over so Chlöe could not see her. There was no soap in sight. Her muffled voice said, "My sister is going to marry a murderer, an oppressor, a man who cares only about using China for his own ends and not about the Chinese people. My sister is going to be the First Lady of China."

As you once were, for such a brief time, thought Chlöe, reaching out for a towel that had been used by who knew how many and handing it to her friend. "I have heard it said," she ventured, "that of the Soong daughters, one loves money, the other loves power, and the third loves China."

This forced a small smile to Ching-ling's face. She nodded her head. "Yes, I, too, have heard that. Though Mei-ling is extravagant, it is not money she is after. She's always had enough money. Ai-ling is the one who thinks money is power and sees to piling up earthly goods. I wouldn't be surprised if she and that sweet husband of hers aren't about the richest people in the whole country by now. I don't know why, but she's the one pushing Mei-ling into this marriage. Mammy approved only after Chiang said he'd divorce his two wives and convert to Christianity. Of course he didn't volunteer to give up his concubines, but Mammy probably doesn't know about them.

"Mei-ling says that she loves China and that by marrying Chiang she can improve the living conditions of the peasants. We shall see."

Ching-ling started to dry her face with the towel but noticed its foulness and shook her head. She placed the towel on the table and said, "We *are* hungry. We haven't eaten anything decent in three days."

"I doubt you'll find anything decent at this inn," Chlöe said. "But it's edible."

"Mongolia," uttered Ching-ling, wonder in her voice as they began to walk back to the courtyard. "I am in Mongolia. I am on my way to Moscow and who knows how long I shall be banished from my country."

"Certainly when Mei-ling marries Chiang you can return, can't you?" asked Chlöe. "He won't kill his own sister-in-law?"

Ching-ling shrugged. "Who knows what the future will bring?" Before they emerged into the sunlight, now slanting its rays upward as the sun began to sink behind the mountains, she asked, "What about you, dear friend? You and Nikolai?"

"It's the end, isn't it?" A jagged pain seared across Chlöe's chest.

"How can love like that have an end?" asked Ching-ling. "My devotion to Dr. Sun will never end."

"Ah, but you were tied by the same dream. Nikolai and I aren't. That may make the difference. I can't leave and go with you."

A sad smile spread across Ching-ling's face. "I guess I was fantasizing, hoping that you might choose to come with us. All along this trip I've told myself there was the chance you might make that choice, that Nikolai and I together would lure you."

Chlöe stopped and turned to look down at Ching-ling. "My dear, my dear dear friend. I do love you, Ching-ling. And I love Nikolai more than I've ever loved Slade. Maybe partly because I so admire him, even though I don't share his vision. But I'm not even tempted to come with you. It's not even a consideration. You must understand that. I am an American, and somehow that influences my decisions. I am also married, perhaps not faithfully so, certainly not happily so this last year, but I am married. I may not have kept all my vows, but I cannot leave this marriage lightly."

Ching-ling reached over and put her small hands around Chlöe's. She shook her head and then they walked to meet Nikolai and Slade, who appeared in high good humor.

"Let's eat," Slade said, throwing his arms around Ching-ling's and Chlöe's shoulders, heading toward the inn.

Even though she hadn't eaten a regular meal in three days, Ching-ling barely picked at her food. Slade did most of the talking, gesturing with his chopsticks as he described their journey, his eyes as excited as his voice.

"You should've seen her." He gesticulated, pointing at Ching-ling. "She dressed as a peasant, and I couldn't tell her from the rest of them on the ship down the Yangtze."

Chlöe remembered another time, back in Canton, when Ching-ling masqueraded as a peasant for another escape.

"T.V. and I didn't even look for her, didn't pay her any attention in case we were being observed, but no one was even aware of us. Once we arrived in Shanghai, she insisted on stopping at her home on the Rue Molière and picking up things she needed if she was leaving the country. I was sure someone would see her sneak in, but they didn't."

"That's because," interrupted Ching-ling, "we waited until morning and I pretended to be the egg lady. Then I stayed in the house three days sorting out my affairs. No one even came to the door."

"Of course, T.V. was afraid she'd be discovered and held prisoner in her own home while Chiang used her name to purify his indiscriminate slaughter across China. Or, if she spoke against him, T.V. was not even sure her relationship with Mei-ling would keep her from being murdered." Slade was stuffing noodles with bits of fried pork into his mouth as he talked.

"T.V. arranged for a Russian freighter to take us to Vladivostok. I was on board by late afternoon, waiting for her, and I can tell you, I was nervous. I was sure she'd been discovered. My nerves were on edge by nightfall, and I stood at the railing for hours, until midnight, sick with worry."

"Well, we couldn't even leave before dark," Ching-ling intervened. "My brother had arranged for two men to pick me up, and we were all dressed as beggars. We wound through the streets and in and out of alleys in case someone was following us. When we arrived at the waterfront, the two men took me to the smallest sampan I ever saw. They turned me over to the owner, who rowed me through the garbage-strewn Hwang Pu, between warships from a score of countries, the countries who think they own Shanghai, if not China. That little boat swayed, so unsteady I was sure we would fall overboard, but we drifted silently in the dark shadows between these enormous ships, beside creaking junks, for three hours before I could be smuggled aboard the freighter."

Just telling this seemed to have exhausted her.

"And then," Slade picked up the story, "we had to stop in Japan and when word got out that Madame Sun was aboard, American journalists descended on us, but I wouldn't let her talk to them. I didn't even let them take her picture." He smiled smugly. "We got off with their barely getting a glance at her. When we disembarked at Vladivostok we had to wait three days for the train."

Chlöe and Nikolai were looking at him, but he seemed to have finished.

"Well?" Chlöe finally asked.

Slade looked up from his plate and said, "Well? Well, smooth sailing from there on. Hot train, with dusty wind blowing. Awful food, all of it gray. We got off at Ulan-Ude so we could come down here and meet you. That was slow and pretty bad."

"I'm sorry we have to go over that route again," chimed in Ching-ling.

"We don't," said Nikolai. "A Soviet aircraft will take us to the Trans-Siberian Railroad at Verkhneudinsk. It's already here, await-ing your arrival."

Chlöe looked up, startled. Nikolai had not told her that. When had he arranged for that? His eyes met hers.

"So?" Slade put down his chopsticks. "This is the end of the line, then?"

The three of them stared at him. "The end of the line." Ni-kolai's voice was soft. "I guess it is. For now, anyway."

Slade leaned forward, elbows on the table. "I want you both to know that it's been wonderful knowing you, not just for your stories either. I admire you both more than I can tell you. I don't envy you, however. I'm glad to be going back to China instead of heading into Russia."

Wouldn't they all like to be going back, Chlöe thought.

"I'm very tired," said Ching-ling. "Do you mind if I retire?" She looked at Nikolai. "Do we fly off tomorrow?"

He nodded. "As soon as you're ready. They've just been waiting for you."

She put a hand on his shoulder. "Thank goodness I have you, Nikki." As she left the dining room her shoulders sagged ever so slightly.

"That is some woman," marveled Slade.

"So is your wife," Nikolai said, his eyes meeting Chlöe's. "You have every reason to be proud of her. She never caved in in the face of danger; she never complained about discomfort. She is a rare woman indeed."

Slade cocked an eyebrow and looked at Chlöe. "She is that, isn't she? And I imagine hearing your story will be something. So," he turned to Nikolai, "there was danger and discomfort, huh? Fine, it'll make for good reading." He stood up and reached his hand out to Chlöe. "Come, sweetheart mine, I, too, am tired. Let's go to our room."

Chlöe's heart stopped for just a few seconds, but it stopped nevertheless. She knew it had. She did not let her eyes meet Nikolai's. She stood, and though she had slept the afternoon away, she said, "Yes, I'm sure I'll be asleep the minute my head touches the pillow."

Slade followed her up the stairs and down the hall. As soon as he closed the door, she felt his hand on her arm. "Do you know," he pulled her close to him and she could feel his warmth along her back, "your hair is awry, you look disheveled, your skin is peeling from the sun on the Gobi, yet you have never looked more appealing." He kissed her neck. And she thought, Oh, God, you choose now to touch me again, now to try to make amends for more than a year of not coming near me.

His arms encircled her.

Damn, she thought. I'm just not up to this. So, when they were in bed she just lay there, unmoving, unflinching, letting Slade make love to her for the first time in fourteen months. She couldn't respond as his eager kisses rained upon her. But he didn't seem to notice. Or if so, he paid no heed. When he was finished, he said, "You're one gutsy lady, aren't you? I don't know of another woman who would have dared to brave danger like you have. Isn't it exciting? Do you know we're the only Americans, the only people in the whole world who will have this for the history books?" He rolled over on his side and before he fell asleep, said, "God, this is good."

Chlöe lay staring up at the ceiling, seeing nothing in the dark. She wanted a bath. Badly.

# CHAPTER 37

In the morning they sat over breakfast, making desultory conversation, trying to draw these last minutes out.

My best friend and my lover, going away perhaps forever. Chlöe wondered if her heart would break right then, right there at this table in the courtyard where they had long ago finished the hard, dry rolls, the sweet ripe melon, and the strong, bitter tea. She wondered if it would make a sound, a popping or a sound like thunder. If she would be the only person to hear it or if everyone would look at her and wonder what had happened. Did hearts make audible sounds when they broke? Underneath the table she rubbed her foot along Nikolai's leg. His eyes met hers for just a moment while Slade reached out and grasped her hand.

"You'll be heroes in America," Slade said to Ching-ling and Nikolai as though that would make up for all they were being forced to abandon.

Finally, Nikolai said, "if we're to reach our destination by afternoon, we must leave."

There was no airport in Ulan Bator, but outside the town in a level field sat a Soviet plane, more cumbersome than any Chlöe had ever seen.

Ching-ling reached up and kissed Chlöe, squeezing her hand and saying, "We shall meet again, my dear. My heart goes with you." Then she turned to Slade, raising her graceful hand to take his. "Thank you for playing Sir Galahad. I have enjoyed your company. You were brave to do something that could have been very dangerous for you."

Slade nodded. "It's been fun. But that doesn't mean I can't imagine the pain you feel. I shall do all I can to help the world to understand."

"I know that," said Ching-ling.

Nikolai, turning to Slade, put his arms around him. "Thank you for your help and . . . your wife's. I hope your story helps." Then he turned to Chlöe, hesitating but a moment before gathering her in his arms, saying, "You are the best of traveling companions. And a rare friend." Then he let her go.

Chlöe couldn't control the tears welling up in her eyes. She began to cry as she leaned over to kiss Ching-ling's cheeks and to grasp Nikolai's hand. She didn't care if Slade was looking, she brought Nikolai's hand to her lips and kissed it lightly. "You, too," tears spilled down her cheeks, "are a rare friend. It's been an unforgettable trip."

With that, Nikolai jumped up on the wing, pushing Ching-ling into the plane ahead of him and, turning, waved at Slade and Chlöe, who was drying her tears with the back of her hand. Oh, my love, she cried silently. Farewell, my love . . .

Slade squeezed her hand and smiled. "Come on, we better get going too. I want to hear all about your trip and write it down. It'll be fun traveling across the desert until we get to the train."

"You think that only because you haven't been doing it for weeks." She resented his presence. It was all such fun to him. He wasn't suffering from a broken heart.

"That's true," he said. "But I bet you've never lain out under the stars and made love. And that's what we're going to do every night. Jesus, something about excitement, about being on the edge of danger makes me horny. God, I could take you here, right now, it's so exciting. Come on, let's go back to the hotel and make love before we start off. Jesus, I don't know if I can wait that long."

Why, she wondered, did he choose now to be the Slade of old, to want her, to be unable to keep his hands off her? Yet, when they did make love, she again could not move. She remembered her mother saying, "Honey, you don't have to do anything. You just have to lie there." And now she understood. When the man didn't tap anything within you, you just suffered the lovemaking. It never dawned on her to say, "Not now, Slade. Not now." Or to talk about all that time when he had not touched her at all.

He made love to her all four nights they were on the train, and most of the early mornings. But all Chlöe could think of was that he lacked Nikolai's passion . . . and the tenderness. Nor did he taste like Nikolai, or feel like him, or have his touch—the touch that awakened fires of overwhelming love. He lay on top of her and she thought, This is just a man. This isn't a moral giant. This isn't a man who thinks I'm the most wonderful person in the world. This isn't a man who's ever been guided by a dream larger than himself, or a man dedicated to a vision, a man who thinks the most important thing he can do is help free the peoples of the world. A man who truly believes in brotherhood. Slade is not the man Nikolai is. And she lay there, under him, unmoving, which seemed to excite him even more.

When they returned to Shanghai, he expected her to be content with the life she'd known before. "Let's throw a party. You've been gone four months."

But Chlöe didn't want to throw a party. For a few weeks she just wanted to sit in the garden and watch the river life, read books, and feel the touch of autumn in the air. The chrysanthemums were in bloom and gave off their bittersweet odor that she so loved. She picked one and held it in her hand as she sat in the wooden swing on the porch and rocked gently back and forth. It was here one day that she thought, I'm pregnant.

Slade was overjoyed. "I don't know that there's anything I want more than a son. Immortality." Chlöe wondered why a daughter couldn't give him the same immortality.

But as the months passed and winter came to Shanghai, she couldn't find excitement within herself over this expected child. I won't let myself be disappointed again, she said to herself. I won't hope and have something happen. She now thought that this was compounded with the worry . . . what if it looked like Nikolai?

What if it did? Wouldn't that give her something of Nikolai to hold on to forever?

But she knew a part of her life would end if the child looked like Nikolai. Just as a part of her had died when Nikolai flew out of her life.

In November Slade and Chlöe were invited to the wedding of Generalissimo Chiang Kai-shek and Miss Soong Mei-ling. Mammy Soong had been won over when Chiang publicly, in the traditional way of Chinese husbands, proclaimed that his previous wives were no longer married to him. Big-eared Tu had conveniently arranged for Chiang's latest wife—an intelligent young woman very obviously with child—to attend Columbia University. He gave her a modest fortune to live on with the proviso she spend the rest of her life in the United States. Chiang claimed that his first wife was no longer Mrs. Chiang Kai-shek, and that before he had never married for love, as he was now doing. Chlöe wondered, Love for what?

The romance delighted the country itself and America. Americans forgave him all the atrocities that it had ignored anyway, and said to one another, smiling, "He's converting to Christianity." The pagan Orient was being Westernized. Chiang and his American-raised wife could do no wrong in the American press.

The ceremony was held on December 1 at the Majestic Hotel, which was crowded with thirteen hundred guests, of which Chlöe and Slade were two. They were accompanied by Lou and Daisy, whom Chlöe thought looked wan lately.

Guests were frisked at the door by what Slade called "Green Gang thugs." From the gaily decorated ballroom hung an enormous photo of Dr. Sun, who appeared to approve of the nuptials.

Chiang Kai-shek and his best man, Mei-ling's brother-in-law H. H. Kung, wore formal European attire, striped pants and tails. Guests climbed on chairs, trying to see above the whirring newsreel cameras as Mei-ling and her entourage entered to the strains of Mendelssohn. Mei-ling's bridesmaids, dressed in peach gowns imported from America, followed Ai-ling's two youngest children, who were dressed in black velvet knickers and jackets with frilly satin collars and cuffs.

Mei-ling herself was enveloped in a gossamer gown of silver and white, caught on one side with a corsage of orange blossoms. She was hidden by a veil of Chantilly lace that fell down her back. A long train of filmy white embroidered with silver trailed behind her. She rested her arm on that of her brother T.V. The other hand held pink carnations tied with white and silver ribbons.

When she reached the altar, she and Chiang turned, posing under the portrait of Dr. Sun. They bowed together as though promising to dedicate their lives to Dr. Sun's ideals, while the world's newsreel cameras whirred noisily.

Yes, thought Chlöe, every paper in the Western world will carry this on the front page, while Ching-ling is shivering in Moscow. The stories of Ching-ling's and Nikolai's escapes had been carried on the front page only by Cass. Other papers, if they had used them at all, buried them somewhere where few Americans saw or read them. And they seemed to have affected no one at all anywhere.

When they arrived home, Slade said to Chlöe, "Don't wait up for me. I've got to cable all this in detail tonight so it'll make the front page in Chicago tomorrow."

The story of the wedding not only made the headlines of the *Chicago Times* but was at the top of page one of the *New York Times*, the *Times* of London, the *San Francisco Chronicle*, and every other paper of every other city of the Western world.

In this year of 1928, Chiang Kai-shek focused his rage against the Communists, which he perceived as the only enemy standing between him and his goal. By brute force he let loose upon China a vehemence unequaled in a country that had no equal in violence. Chlöe heard stories that sickened her.

One afternoon Slade brought Lou home with him, half carrying him out of the rickshaw, laying him down on the sofa, and saying, "Find some brandy."

He started to tell Chlöe what happened, but Lou interrupted. "No," his voice was weak, "let me tell it."

Slade gave him a quizzical look and then poured brandy for himself, too, sitting across from Lou. Chlöe took the other chair.

Lou leaned up on one elbow shaking his head after swallowing a large belt of the brandy, and said, "We were coming down the street and heard a commotion. Over a hundred suspected Reds were digging a large shallow cavity. We stood and watched, afraid of what we were about to see, yet glued to the spot. Then the men, and about four or five women too, were lined up, while young soldiers—no more than young boys grinning at the sport that was entertaining them—bound each of the prisoner's hands and feet, then forced them to lie in the shallow grave they had dug for themselves." He stopped and laid his head back on a pillow, quiet for a few minutes, his face pale and drawn. Slade poured them both another slug of brandy.

Lou continued, his voice faint, as though the telling of it might exorcise it from his system. "With those damned unwieldy rifles the Chinese get hold of from who knows where, those soldiers systematically shot the group, laughing at their screams. Not even finishing everyone off, but covering the bodies—many still alive—with dirt while some still shook with spasms."

Chlöe shivered as gooseflesh ran down her back.

"I vomited," Lou admitted, "and I'm not ashamed of it. Anyone whose skin doesn't crawl at such inhumanity isn't worth being human."

Chlöe dreamed of the scene that night and one she had heard two days before, of soldiers having sport with young women Communists, jamming rifles up their vaginas and pulling the triggers. And laughing. Laughing.

For the first time in years, bubonic plague struck. Cholera came early, with the flies, and carried off thousands of people. Typhoid, polio, and smallpox were also rampant. Chlöe made doubly sure all their water was boiled. The British doctor assured them they were safe from smallpox if they'd been vaccinated already, which Slade and Chlöe both had been, but advised strongly that those who had not been vaccinated do so immediately. Summer meant sickness in 1928 as it had not for years.

Chlöe was, if not content, willing to sit around on her verandah and stare into space, waiting for the imminent birth of what Slade hoped was his path to immortality. She decided she hated China. Certainly she was not going to raise a child here.

She wanted to get out of this country that had robbed her of so much during these years. "I want to leave China," she said aloud, and began to cry.

She awoke in the morning coughing, thinking, I cried too much last night. All morning her throat became sorer and dizziness overcame her until she could scarcely move across the room.

"What's wrong?" asked Slade, looking up from his desk. "Your time come?"

She reached out a hand and sank to the bed. "I don't know." Her voice was but a whisper. "It's not supposed to be for another month. But I do feel strange."

"I'll send for the doctor," said Slade, immediately fetching one of the boys, telling him to run for the doctor.

But the doctor sent word that he couldn't come, so rampant was the city with disease that he wasn't able to leave the hospital. Slade's eyes hardened, and Chlöe wondered if it was panic she saw reflected there. She could hardly raise her head from the pillow, dampened with her perspiration.

"I'll go see if I can't get the naval doctor," Slade said before running from the house. When he returned, hours later, it was with no doctor.

"No one can come," he said, his tie askew and his collar unbuttoned. His face was flushed from the heat and his exertions. By the time he arrived, Chlöe was aflame with fever, though Su-lin sat beside her and laid cold cloths on her head.

Slade couldn't sit still. "For Christ's sake, not a goddamned doctor can come. Arbuckle even said not to bother to bring you to the hospital. There's no room, and besides, everyone there is contagious with something or other. Goddamn climate."

Chlöe whispered and Slade leaned over to hear her. "Please. Let's leave this country." She had spent the day vomiting, alternating between chills and fever.

Slade held her as she leaned over, heaving into a bowl. The fever drained her of strength; at the same time, severe abdominal cramps caused her to clutch herself into the fetal position, crying with the sheer agony of sickness.

It was twilight when Dr. Arbuckle did arrive. "Sorry, Slade. It's a miracle I got here at all. It doesn't look good," he murmured, lifting the damp sheets to examine Chlöe. She felt his hands touching her, heard whispers, felt Slade sit on the bed and cradle her against him.

"Is it typhus?" she heard him ask the doctor, though his voice sounded a million miles away.

Perhaps the doctor nodded, for she heard no answer.

She didn't know how much later she heard Dr. Arbuckle's voice floating over the room, bouncing off the wall.

"Oh, Jesus," Slade's voice said.

Chlöe tried to open her eyes, but that required more energy than she could muster.

"The baby. Can't you take it? It's nearly due."

There was a pause, and for a second Chlöe thought they had moved away from her, but then she felt the doctor's hand on her wrist, feeling her pulse, and his voice said, "I can save her or the baby, Slade. I can't save them both. Which is it to be?"

# PART III
## 1928–1935

# CHAPTER 38

During her long recovery, Slade was solicitous. Only when she was beginning to regain her strength did he tell her Dr. Arbuckle said she could never have children again. It was Daisy who told her it had been a son. Slade never mentioned it.

Slade stayed home evenings, as he had stayed with her all during her illness and recovery, most of which Chlöe couldn't remember. He sat in a chair near the bed and told her what was happening in Shanghai and in the rest of China. Sometimes he talked even when she drifted in and out of consciousness.

He told her that Japanese troops had entered Jinan, but she had no idea where Jinan was. North someplace. Chiang's armies did not resist them, as he was more intent on eradicating what he saw as the supreme threat, Communists. He was too busy sending his armies to the western provinces, trying to subjugate these provinces to the Kuomintang, to pay attention to a foreign invasion.

Slade read her a letter from Ching-ling, saying she was disillusioned with Moscow and was going on to Berlin. Everything in Russia, she wrote, was predicated on fear, and certainly that was no way to live. She didn't see Soviet peasants as any better off than the Chinese peasants. Communism had not yet accomplished what it set out to do. The present rulers were no better than the czars, she thought, more interested in their own power than their own people.

"I want to go home," she said over and over. "Back to America."

She just wanted out. Out of this damnable country that had robbed her of so much. Better that she should have married some boy in Oneonta and lived the repetitive, placid life she imagined her parents led. She'd have had children and summer picnics with deviled eggs and potato salad, dill pickles and lemonade. And gone swimming up in Cooperstown, in crystal clear Otsego Lake. She'd have taught her children to ice-skate on her uncle's pond, and put her arms around them, kissing them good night, smelling their soft, childish cleanliness. Her lips ached with yearning to kiss her children who would never be.

Finally, one night in the early fall Slade said, "I have just the thing to get you out of this depression. Look, hon, it's all right. So we don't have children. There are lots of other things in this world."

"Would you like a divorce?" her flat voice asked. "So you could have children with someone else?"

He looked at her sharply and his voice had a knife edge to it as he answered, "What I'd like is for you to go on living. Let's have an adventure."

"I want to go home."

"I can't leave here. I don't want to. We could have lost three kids at home. You could have been hit by a car instead of a rickshaw. Damien could have caught polio or diphtheria. You could have caught any number of diseases instead of typhus. It's not just this country. It's fate. Now, what I have in mind . . ."

She looked at him as he talked and thought they didn't really know each other. Perhaps they never had. Certainly laughing and holding hands and kissing each other for a week in Chicago was no way to get to know someone. And that was, after all, all she'd known of him before casting her lot with him. She wondered if she loved him. She hadn't felt close to him in years. She'd resented him ever since he'd reacted to the Blue Express incident as he had. Now she resented the fact that he wasn't Nikolai. That he wasn't as depressed and defeated as she was about this last baby. The last baby ever. Now he'd have no immortality.

She closed her eyes and his words kept pouring forth. She couldn't help listening.

". . . the two biggest threats, as I see it, aside from the Japs, are the Communists and—"

"I thought Chiang had gotten rid of them when he put a price on Nikolai's head. He's slaughtered every left-leaning person around."

Slade smiled. It was the first energy Chlöe had put into any conversation. "They're in hiding. Up in the hills of Hunan. There's a young rebel up there, leading a group of them, militarizing them. And I'd like to get an interview. Mao something. Mao Tse-tung I think it is. No one's exactly sure where he is, but I'd like us to go searching for him. He's some young guy in his early thirties, my age. Can you imagine? Someone my age trying to fight a whole country?"

"Us? You want *us* to go?" Chlöe sat upright and opened her eyes.

"Well, don't you think it might be just what the doctor ordered? Not just an American journalist going back into the hinterland, but his wife too. Look what you've done already. That story the first year we were here when Ching-ling and Nick and you had to crawl out of the Suns' house in Canton." He couldn't bring himself to mention the Blue Express. "You worked with Ching-ling and Nick in Wuhan. Then that escape across the Gobi. God, Chlöe, I'm helping to make you famous whether you know it or not."

She turned on her side and put her hands under her cheek, resting on the pillow.

He nodded, his eyes shining. "Then, up north somewhere, some warlord, a General Lu-tang, is raising Cain with the Japs. He seems to be the only one fighting them. He's not a Communist, but from what I hear he's furious that Chiang ignores the Japs encroaching on Chinese soil. So he's anti-Chiang, anti-communistic, pro-China in a land where warlords are usually only pro their own little pieces of land. These seem to me to be two adversaries that Chiang would like to locate and behead. Or probably garrote. C'mon, you want to come? They'll be great interviews."

"If you can find them," Chlöe said, realizing she was throwing cold water onto his enthusiasm. At the same time, she felt stirrings of excitement, the first she'd felt since Ulan Bator, really. For a year.

"Don't ask where I got it." Slade grinned, one foot on the running board of the giant Stutz Bearcat. It was the longest car Chlöe had ever seen. "It's obviously seen better days, but it's in good running condition, so I'm told. It'll be like going camping."

But it wasn't. They stopped nights in dirty little Chinese inns, in some of which there were no individual rooms but where they had to sleep on the floor with a dozen or so others, all of them men.

The scenery here, going into the country of rice paddies and peanut fields, the land where hills were terraced with tea plants, was so different from any she'd seen before. So unlike the parched arid area north of the Great Wall, unlike the route to Peking, or to Sian. They headed southwest, through primitive villages where white people had never been seen, villages that were the same as they had been a thousand years ago, with water wheels pulled by children and

women when there were no beasts of burden about. The farther they
went, the hillier it became, with pines scenting the air and clouds
hovering over the tops of the hills that became mountains. Auto-
mobiles or trucks had come before them, they could see, for they'd
left deep tire marks. But finally they had to leave their car and
shoulder their supplies in knapsacks. Chlöe wore rugged shoes and
a pair of Su-lin's peasant coolie pants held at the waist with the
largest safety pin she could find. She found herself laughing for the
first time in over a year. Slade reached out and grabbed her hand,
smiling.

They'd been told Mao's ragtag army was camped at the top of
a mountain. Along the way they passed men in tatters, heating food
over small fires. "I wonder if those are their arms," Slade mused,
looking at shovels and picks by their sides. "If so, I think this army
is no threat to Chiang."

They did look a motley group, each one they passed, little bands
of men who looked suspiciously at them but made no moves toward
them. They were all near emaciation. Yet grinning. Their sunken
eyes lit with fervor.

In late afternoon Chlöe and Slade reached the summit, sweating
even in the chill October air. Here a red flag flapped in the breeze.
On it a black hammer and sickle stood out against a white star.

A tall young man, taller than any but northern Chinese,
emerged from the temple, which was but one of several ancient
stone dwellings on the mountaintop. He looked at them with raised
eyebrows, saying nothing, waiting for Slade to do the talking.

Slade introduced himself and Chlöe, explaining that they hoped
for an interview with Mao. They would like to carry his side of the
story to the outside world. The young man turned and left, reenter-
ing the temple. Slade put down his pack and helped Chlöe with
hers. She was tired and wanted a drink of water. She brushed her
hair out of her eyes.

In ten minutes the young man returned, saying, "Follow me."

The temple smelled of mildew, dampness, and antiquity. They
walked through its large halls toward the back, where, in a cell-like,
monastic room, they came upon a slim young man sitting at a desk.
He wore the Chinese peasant clothes of rumpled blue, though his
were cleaner than most. He stamped out a cigarette, held in tobacco-
stained fingers, and when he smiled at them, Chlöe could see his
teeth were discolored from smoking. He looked like an intellectual

masquerading as a peasant. Unlike most Orientals, he looked directly at them.

Indicating two wooden chairs while he remained seated, he asked, "So? You want to tell our story to the world, huh?"

Slade said, yes, he would like to do that.

Mao nodded for a minute and then said, "I do not care about the world. I would like other Chinese to know about us, to know what it is that we fight for and fight against, what we want for our country and our peoples. The great majority can't read, so we must instruct them in other ways. Let them see what we practice, inflame them by letting them know that their lot need not always be as it has been, that if we unite . . ." He lit a cigarette, holding the crumpled package out to Slade. "Ah, an American who does not smoke."

Chlöe wondered if he found it unusual for a woman to be up there. As though reading her mind, he turned to her and said, "We have a number of women here. In our society women are the equal of men. All human beings are equal." His voice held pride.

"In our country too," offered Slade, and Chlöe looked at him, wondering if he believed his own words. Were Mao's words as empty as Slade's? Or did they both believe what they were saying?

Chlöe studied the man Slade had said was a revolutionary leader. He certainly didn't match any picture she had mentally painted. His skin was soft, like a woman's, and he parted his hair in the middle. A prominent, and Chlöe thought quite ugly, mole jutted out under his lower lip.

"Russian communism is wrong for China," she heard Mao say. "There it is the factory workers who led the people. Here it must be the peasants." That's what Nikolai had said.

He leaned back, lighting one cigarette from another. "My countrymen will rise into a flood so powerful that the Yellow River will be as nothing. Someday we will harness the Yellow and the Yangtze, but we shall never harness the people. They shall find freedom. They will never die of hunger again. We shall show them what can be done through strength."

"And how will you do this?" Slade asked.

"We shall be so fierce that no power on earth can stop us. We shall wash across the land and shake off imperialism and the habits that keep us subjects."

"What habits?" Slade asked.

The young Chinese looked at him as though he were a slightly retarded child. "Like opium. It will be illegal." He leaned forward, resting his elbow on the table in front of him. "Do you know what we do now, for opium users? Death. When the peasants join us, we warn them." He smiled. "It is my powers of persuasion that permit even bandit chieftains and their gangs to join us. They must first forswear the use of opium. Break that habit and energy will seep into their bodies."

Slade started to say something, but was interrupted by the entrance of a tall, scholarly-looking man who announced that dinner was served. They would be honored to have Slade and Chlöe be their guests, though the meal was humble. Of course they were welcome to stay overnight too.

Chlöe had said nothing, nor had Mao aimed any conversation her way, despite his assertion that women were equal in his communist society.

They stayed on the mountain with Mao and his ragtag army for four days. The young Chinese revolutionary read them poetry he had written, and told them that he believed the Chinese people, once they were awakened to conditions in the country, would not need a leader. The people could govern themselves.

This time Chlöe asked a question. "Isn't that anarchy?"

Mao's eyes met hers. "There will be no need for leaders when everyone shares and shares equally. There will be no evil, no corruption, no selfishness. But first we must awaken the populace."

"What," asked Slade, "about the Japanese?"

"They must be banished, as must the Americans, the English, the Germans, the French, the Belgians . . ."

"But, unlike the Japs, the Europeans are not battering your east coast and taking over your land."

"They might just as well have, all these past hundred years," Mao said calmly. "We shall overthrow all foreigners, all imperialists. China for the Chinese."

"Do you think the Japanese will come farther than Shantung province?" asked Chlöe. Slade gave her a surprised look.

Mao turned to her. "Who can tell? I do not trust any foreigners. They all think China is a piece of pie that can be divided up among themselves. They care nothing for the Chinese people. But if Japan pursues the path it seems to have started, then they must be repulsed before China can unite. Chiang is blind. He thinks his enemy is us. It is really foreigners."

"But if you win," Chlöe pursued, "you will run China and Chiang will be out of power. So you are his enemy too."

Mao nodded. "But we are not the enemy of China. We are against all who wish to subjugate the Chinese people. Chiang does not care about China or the Chinese. That is the difference."

"How do you know yours is the right way?" Slade interjected. "Perhaps Chiang is not against the people, as you seem to think."

Chlöe exclaimed, "Slade, you don't even believe that!"

Anger shot from her husband's eyes, and then he relaxed, smiling ingenuously at Mao. "True. But I thought I could play devil's advocate. I don't know that either of these factions cares about the Chinese people. Perhaps they care more for their ideas than for people."

"We do not kill peasants as we go along. We try to convert them. If that is not possible, we shall pass through quickly and hope before too long to set up schools where they can learn and be converted that way."

"You sound very like a dear friend of mine," said Chlöe. "Madame Sun Yat-sen."

Mao's eyes danced for the first time. "I have not had the pleasure of meeting her, but certainly she is a giant among my countrymen. Her husband and her father worked hard to help overthrow the Manchus, and she works for the future of our country. Someday I hope our paths will cross."

The next morning Slade and Chlöe walked down the mountain, hoping the Stutz Bearcat was still there. It was.

As Slade chugged the engine into life, Chlöe asked, "Well, what do you think of him?"

After consulting his compass, Slade drove through the rutted fields. He didn't answer her question for a long time. Finally he said, "I often had to force myself not to laugh at him. He's naïve, childish, and a dreamer. He and his little army are like gnats—bothersome perhaps, but no threat to anyone. They'll never amount to anything. They won't either help or hinder the peasants. They're like a toy army, and Mao writes poetry and philosophizes rather than plans strategy."

Chlöe draped her arm along the top of the seat back. "He scares me," she said.

Slade looked over at her and laughed. "Scares? I thought he was anything but powerful."

"Didn't you see the look in his eyes?" she asked. "He may be what you call a dreamer, but his eyes reflect the fanaticism of an idealist. He won't stop until he gets his way."

"What about Ching-ling? And Nick? They're idealists, dreamers. Yet they don't scare you?"

"This Mao has something else. I think he would kill the peasants to get his way."

"Chlöe, you're imagining things. That was a gentle, slightly demented man who wants doors put back on huts, for God's sake!"

"Nevertheless," Chlöe murmured, "there's something about him I don't like."

"You don't like Chiang either."

"I don't think either of these men will be good leaders for China," she said, setting her lips in defiance.

Slade laughed. "But then, why should Chiang or Mao be different? No one in all its history has ever cared about ruling China for the Chinese. Maybe this General Lu-tang will prove to be different."

# CHAPTER 39

They had headed back into mountains that had no roads, stopping nights in resthouses along the trails. "Tell me something about this General Lu-tang," Chlöe said, lying on her stomach, hoping the pain would diminish. It had been years since she'd ridden a horse. She suspected Slade was as uncomfortable but he wouldn't admit it.

"I don't know much about him myself," Slade said in answer to her question about the warlord they were braving a thousand miles to find. "He's not typical, obviously. He senses the larger picture rather than worrying only about his own little piece of land. A Robin Hood type, from all one hears. He doesn't seem to amass riches for himself, if one is to believe what is rumored. He fights any enemies, other warlords, or Japs who encroach on lands he has sworn to defend.

"He is not feared by the people in his district, although he is noted for swift and cruel punishments . . . not toward people he protects, but his enemies. He has made more raids against the Japs than anyone, saying if he can fight them off up there in the far east, maybe he can save the rest of China, as though he owes allegiance to a *country*. He must be one of the few Chinese who senses anything larger than self. Him and Mao, if you're to believe them. As you know, that's rare in a Chinaman. Most Chinese can't even comprehend a whole country."

"It's a sleeping giant, isn't it?" Chlöe closed her eyes, her hands still spread out under her chin. "I mean, can you imagine what'll happen when all these people do get around to realizing they're the biggest country in the world, at least in terms of population? Can you imagine what influence they can wield when they gain knowledge of the outside world?"

"You've been listening to Ching-ling and Nick." Slade lowered himself onto a chair but sat more on his hip than his derrière. "China's not going to awaken in our lifetime. How can it? It needs radios, telephones, communication, schools. Chiang is not going to allow that. It's not only that he doesn't want to spend tax money, but he doesn't want them educated." Slade tugged at his ear, perplexed.

"He doesn't want all these millions of peasants knowing what's going on in China, does he?" asked Chlöe, enjoying the interchange with her husband.

Slade nodded in agreement. "He wants to maintain the status quo. My God, they're close to slaves now. These people have next to nothing to say about their own lives. Fields are eaten by locusts, droughts envelop the land, floods sweep everything in front of them to the sea. Pestilence, disease. God, Chlöe, is there any other country in the world that has so goddamn much bad luck?"

"Floods can be controlled by dams, and—"

"Yeah, well, what's going to stop drought? How are modern farming methods going to be introduced? How are nearly half a billion people going to get enough education and knowledge to learn how to feed themselves? Shit, they don't even know who the Japanese are, much less that they're encroaching on land they've never seen or heard of. Why should they fight for China, a concept they can't even understand?"

Chlöe gazed over at him. "Why do you like it here so much, then? You make it all sound hopeless. Yet you won't leave."

He grinned and shrugged his shoulders. " 'Cause there's a chance I'm wrong. I *want* to be wrong. I want to see these peasants awaken, rear back, and say, 'Dammit, this land belongs to *us*. Not the Japs. Not the British. Not the Americans or the French or the Germans . . .' "

"Well, the Germans aren't here anymore." She rolled over and stood up. She wished she had some antiseptic to rub on her saddle sores. Or to sit in. Something cool and soothing. "A lot of the Chinese in Shanghai and Peking are aware—"

"Sure. Ones who are where the action and the talk are. But do you realize how many of the people here are isolated and doing things the exact same way their ancestors did a thousand years ago?" His voice reflected irritated impatience.

"So, tell me about this general." She stood up and went over to the porcelain pitcher of hot water and poured a cupful.

"He's *aware*. Actually, sometimes the local warlords *are* more knowledgeable, seeing the winds of change as harbingers of the future. They have to know *whether* to fight and *whom*, and whether their positions are precarious. Many of the warlords are giving allegiance to Chiang, not because they want to, but because they know the Green Gang has tentacles that can reach out and eradicate them. The Green Gang pulls Chiang's strings like a puppet, make no bones about it. They don't give a g.d. about China. They love money and power. Period. Maybe in reverse order. And they run China. They get anything. I mean *anything*, they want."

"You're not answering my question, really." She sipped the tepid tea and walked over to the narrow slot that pretended to be a window. It was too dark to see anything anyhow.

He laughed. "I guess I'm not, am I? Maybe that's why we're going to see him. No one seems to know. He's not a bandit exactly. He's a warlord but something else besides. He seems to have some education. He's cruel to enemies yet compassionate to the people he's vowed to protect, if the stories I've heard are true. He's angry at what's happening with Chiang and the Japs, yet he can't abide Communists. I don't know what he wants. Maybe just to get the Japs out of China. My information says he's highly critical of Chiang and the Green Gang, yet that's only thirdhand. All I know is he sounds exciting, as if he's someone trying to defy the two forces at loggerheads in China, who sees Japan as the big enemy and resents Chiang for not facing that. God, Chlöe, I don't know. That's what we're going to find out."

In the meantime, she was having fun for the first time in a long time. She was seeing China from its back roads, from camels, from its non-roads, from horses and on foot, from trucks and cars, and from narrow paths that wound through mountains. She liked camping out under the stars far better than when they found these smelly inns. They always found trackers who were willing, for a fee, to lead them on to the next village. They'd been wending their way through the northeast wilderness heading for somewhere near Jinan, which the Japanese had already taken. General Lu-tang was somewhere up there fighting them. She hoped with more than shovels and picks.

They followed the guide who had been with them for three days, far longer than any of the other guides, who had simply taken them from one village to the next. Of course, they had passed through no villages the last two and a half days. This guide was young, probably in his mid-teens, tall like the north Chinese. He seldom talked, but he was friendly and smiled when they asked questions. His black eyes shone with intelligence and he walked these narrow, well-trodden paths without having to look down to see if a stone or root was in the way. His feet touched the dirt path as though he knew every inch of it.

When Slade asked him about this, the young man nodded and said, "I have spent my life in these mountains."

Chlöe thought him quite beautiful, but she wished he would answer rather than smile at their questions. He was very adept at answering their questions in such a way that they briefly thought they had answers but soon realized he had quite completely avoided providing any. He always knew where to find water just when Chlöe thought she might expire from thirst. When she awoke the fourth morning they'd been traversing these mountains with him, he was gone.

For a few moments she thought he'd simply gone off to attend to his ablutions. But she lay, watching the sun rise beyond the jagged peaks to the east, throwing gold and pink fingers into the sky. There was no sound, not of birds, not of wind, not the rustling of animals . . . nothing. She sat bolt upright. The horses were gone too. She leaned over and poked Slade awake. "The guide's gone," she said, trying not to let panic creep into her voice. "And so are the horses."

In one fluid motion Slade was out of his bedroll, running toward where they had hobbled the horses last night. He stopped when there was no sign of them. Turning around, he surveyed the landscape. Hill after hill after hill in every direction. Chlöe could tell by the sharp way he turned his head that he was bewildered too.

Where had they come from last night? She knew they'd

been coming from the southwest all along, and the sun indicated where east was. But where were they going? All these days multitudes of paths spread out from the one on which they traveled, like lines in one's hands. Chlöe had wondered how the boy knew which dirt path to follow. Sometimes three or four branched off within yards of each other. They were bound to get lost, left on their own.

"Dammit," said Slade, stooping to pick up his trousers and sticking first one leg in and then the other. In the middle of the path was a flagon of water and two small hard biscuits. It was as though the guide had completed one last thoughtful act before stealing the horses and disappearing, before dooming them to oblivion. They'd never find their way out of these mountains. And he'd known that.

But Slade had a different idea. "He'll be back," he prophesied.

"What makes you so sure?" Chlöe asked, hugging her arms around herself in the chill morning air, stamping her feet to get circulation going.

"I'm not sure, but it's a gut-level feeling. He's gone on to tell someone about us. He's probably one of the general's men. He'll give a report about us. And the general will decide whether to see us or let us get lost or send us back—or on a wild-goose chase. I think he wants us to wait right here and he took the horses so we *wouldn't* get lost, so we wouldn't try riding away and get on wrong trails. We can't get nearly as far on foot. I'm all for waiting here and letting him find us easily. Hey, come here. While we're waiting we could neck a little. You look slightly tousled but very seductive at sunrise on a mountaintop in China."

He reached out an arm and she walked over to him. As she took his hand he pulled her down to kiss her. "You haven't complained once this whole trip. Either to see Mao or to see this other guy. May I take this time to tell you I appreciate you, dear wife." As he kissed her again, his hand reached inside her blouse, touching her breast. He looked into her eyes and began to undo the buttons of her blouse, leaning over to kiss her neck, running his tongue down her breast, gently biting her nipple. She sighed, letting herself forget her fright, responding to Slade's pressure, to his hands, to his lips.

"C'mon," he whispered, "there's no one around. Let's make love on a mountaintop where only the sun can see us." He tugged at the pants he had so recently donned and kicked them off, tearing at his shirt, and he lay on the pine needles, lay naked as the rising sun goldened him, and smiled at Chlöe, "C'mon, hon. Get rid of them." He pulled at the Chinese peasant pants she was wearing.

Nervously, Chlöe looked around. "Someone could be watching," she said.

"Well, then, let's give 'em a thrill," he said, reaching over and stroking her leg. "Take that brassiere off, woman. It's in my way."

Chlöe thought, Danger does this to him, but she reached her arms behind her to unfasten the garment. This was the Slade she'd married, the one she'd missed these last years.

"God almighty," Slade said, staring at her as though he'd never seen her before. "You've got it all over Chinese women, Chlöe. You have the most beautiful breasts in the world."

"And how many Chinese women have you seen without clothes on?" She laughed, leaning over to kiss him. It had been so long since they had made love spontaneously, since she had felt her body responding to Slade. As his hands stroked her, she gave herself up to the intense pleasure of the moment, feeling the pressure within her mount. She felt the tingling anticipation that he was evoking in her body, the intense pleasure as he entered her, heard him moan as he came, and knew that in moments she would too, whispering to him, "Don't stop, please don't stop," but just as the pleasure became almost unbearable, just as she knew that she was on the verge, that in a moment . . . they heard the hard pounding of horses' hooves and Slade slid from her, reaching out for his pants, his eyes dazed but his actions quick.

He reached over and threw her trousers to her and said, "Hurry!"

She scurried into her clothes, her nerves raw with interrupted desire.

It was the guide, reining their two horses behind him. He was no longer dressed in his peasant clothes, but in a uniform. Like all Chinese uniforms, it was baggy and ill-fitting, but it bespoke importance and some organization. His even white teeth shone in the sunlight as he smiled. He stayed on his horse but threw the reins of the other two to Slade and bowed his head slightly.

"My father will see you," he said.

Slade turned to Chlöe with a grin. "Your father?" he said.

The young man nodded. "General Lu-tang."

Slade rolled up their sleeping bags and slung them over their horses, then he helped hoist Chlöe onto her horse.

The young man turned his horse around and said, "Follow me," as he began to ride quickly down the steep path.

They traveled in silence along the rocky paths for an hour, coming down from the mountains into a fertile valley. Perhaps a hundred tents were in neat rows, their flaps open, an uncharacteristic neatness evident everyplace. In the nearby stream half a dozen women were washing clothes, pounding them on rocks, in the time-honored way of attacking dirt. Men sat around cleaning guns, exchanging stories, smoking, laughing. They looked at the newcomers with curiosity, waving to the young man.

He looked neither to the left nor the right, but rode straight on toward the farthest tent.

"Wow," Slade said just loud enough for Chlöe to hear. "A Gatling gun. He must've captured it in battle. And other machine guns. God, they've a well-stocked arsenal here. All these men seem to have rifles of their own. Unheard of in China. Wonder if they really have ammunition for them all."

Chlöe was thinking, I've dreamed this before. Or it's déjà vu. Then she saw why she felt this way and stifled a gasp, her hand jerking to her cheek and her mouth opening.

Emerging from his tent, standing with his legs spread apart and his hands on his hips, lord of all he surveyed, was the man she knew as Snow Leopard. He was looking not at her but at Slade.

The young man stopped and Slade jumped down from his horse, walking up to the general with his hand outstretched. Chlöe heard him introduce himself. The general glanced at Slade's outstretched hand before reaching out his own. Then Slade said, "And this, General, is my wife."

The general now looked up at Chlöe, still astride her horse, and she noted the surprise in his eyes before he began to smile.

Without realizing it, she shook her head. Oh, God, Slade had never believed her. His interview would be ruined if he knew this was Snow Leopard.

Sitting erect in the saddle, still holding the reins of her horse, Chlöe acknowledged the introduction with a nod. "General Lutang, I am honored," she said.

He hesitated a moment and she noticed an invisible veil fall in front of his face.

"A pleasure," Snow Leopard said with blank eyes.

# CHAPTER 40

"What do I want?" The general gave an ironic laugh and waved the chicken leg in his left hand. "Freedom."

"Freedom?" Slade asked. "Define that."

The Chinese turned so that he could look at Chlöe without seeming to, but she met his eyes before they flickered to the waving tent top above them. A wind had sprung up and she could hear it howling down from the mountains.

"Freedom from . . . starvation. In other words, the ability to grow enough food so that people do not die. It also means taxes that do not starve people to death—"

"But," Slade interrupted, "isn't that how you make your living? You tax the people. The mandarin taxes you. The government taxes the mandarin."

Chlöe could not keep her eyes off him. He seemed to have grown since she'd last seen him. His clothes fit better, he had a patina of sophistication he had lacked before.

The general nodded in response to Slade's question. "I know, I know." They were dining on the floor, on thick carpets at a low table, and the general raised one knee, resting his elbow on it, the chicken leg still clutched in his fingers. "I do not have solutions to much. You asked me what I wanted. I am telling what I want, not how to go about getting it. I want China united. I had never known it is so big. I have spent," he turned to look at Chlöe, "almost two years traveling throughout it."

She leaned forward. "Where have you traveled, General?"

He leaned toward her, and Slade might just as well not have been in the room. "Everyplace. I have been in every province. In every large city. I have traveled both the Yangtze and Yellow rivers into the interior. I have been to Kunming and Tali, deep in the southwest, in Yunnan. I have been to the Laotian border, and the Tibetan one. I traveled to Chengdu in order to see the fertile Szechwan province, the breadbasket of China. I wanted to see what this China looked like. I wanted to hear my countrymen speak. I wanted to . . ." He smiled at her, though his eyes danced with what she thought was mockery. "I wanted to be *civilized*, to educate myself, and to see if there was some way I could help the people of my country."

Slade, with no sense that he was the third person, asked, "And what did you learn?"

The general turned his head sharply, as though he had forgotten Slade was present.

"I learned how little I knew. It was a humbling experience. I saw things in cities I had not known existed. I realized how many of us have been ignorant. We do not know what goes on beyond our own horizons. We do not know that dams can be built to control flooding. I learned, too, that in many foreign countries, yours for instance, people no longer die of the diseases that plague us. Medicine has erased many of the scourges that ravish my country."

Chlöe was fascinated. Even the words he chose were so different from the man she had known two years ago. It was a metamorphosis.

"Did you learn," her voice was taunting, "that women are human beings too?"

"Chlöe!" Slade shot out a warning she ignored.

"I have known," General Lu-tang turned to look at her, his eyes glittering and bright, "a few women who are the equal of a few men." His eyes smiled now, and he nodded his head almost as though in a salute. Chlöe knew he was trying to pay her a compliment, and she felt a thrill rush over her. "I saw women working along with men, if that is what you mean. But no. Women are not the equals of men. I do think we Chinese," and she could tell he meant men, "have perhaps been uncharitable in our behavior toward women. We have tended to treat them as animals, as vassals. We have not taken their intelligence . . ."

". . . nor their feelings . . ."

He nodded again. ". . . into consideration. So perhaps I do feel more charitable toward women. But I do not think women are our equals. Nor would I want them to be. They are here to help provide for our comfort and pleasure. But," he waved a hand and grinned at her, "we might begin by thinking of *their* comfort and pleasure sometimes too."

At this Slade laughed loudly. "General, I suspect you are voicing something that most men believe, but we—meaning in the West—don't have the guts to say aloud."

Chlöe turned to face her husband, who was not looking at her. Did he believe what he was saying? Could he possibly mean that?

"You allow women too much freedom in the West," said the Chinese. "They do not know their place." He did not look at Chlöe as he said this.

"You don't believe in equality, then?" She tried to keep her voice level, angrier at Slade than at Snow Leopard.

"China is not ready for democracy," the general declared. "It must be brought out of its middle ages gradually. I think Chiang Kai-shek is using empty words to curry favor with the West when he calls China a republic. I would like to see my country a republic, eventually. A democracy in which all *men* have equal opportunity. But it must happen slowly. I do not believe Chiang believes his own words. He has termed himself generalissimo and wants to have as much personal authority as the Manchu emperors had."

He warmed to his subject.

"This was once the foremost civilized, sophisticated country in the world. I would like to see some of that recaptured. I do not want it divided up by foreign powers. I think your country," he nodded toward both of them, "and England, and Germany, and France and Belgium, these countries have helped to ruin my land. They introduced opium so they could become rich. I myself smoked it for many years. Someday, it seems only fair, your country may be awash in opium because your own warlords want money. They will not care any more about their own people than they cared for mine. There are some people who care only about money and power, and they must be destroyed. But if there is—how do you call it?—poetic justice, someday your country and England will be destroyed—as much as mine has been—by opiates that dull one's senses, make one weak, make one kill for a bit of it. It will wreck your civilization too."

"Is that a prophecy?" asked Slade, who was taking copious notes.

"No, of course not." The general shook his head. "I am not a seer. I am saying it would be only justice. Retribution. But then, it probably will never happen, for nothing in this world is fair."

"You want to kill drug warlords?"

"I am willing to kill those who endanger my people." He made it sound like a simple answer. "I want to kill Japanese who kill my people in order to have our land. I want to kill those of my countrymen who kill Chinese who speak their minds. I want to kill those Chinese who wish to subjugate my people even further. I want to annihilate people who kill children and women and who pillage the countryside for the sheer pleasure of hurting, raping, and killing."

"Raping?" Chlöe forced him to pause. "Why, General, I thought you considered women part of the spoils of victory."

Slade glared at her.

But the general softened his voice and looked at her steadily. "Perhaps once I did. But I like to think we can all grow. I should hate to spend a lifetime absolutely positive that the world is flat only to discover, when it comes time to die, that it is round and I have lived mistaken all my life. I should hate to become so old that I could not change. And evolve. Is that the word?"

She couldn't help smiling. "Yes," she said, "that's a very nice word."

"Chiang Kai-shek and his cohorts undermine these values I have come to believe in. China can never regain its greatness as long as it sells itself cheaply to foreign countries. We must wrest ourselves from under the yoke of imperialistic nations and fend for ourselves if we are to achieve self-respect. Chiang has abandoned Dr. Sun's so-called democratic revolution. He does not admit this, but he wants China's masses under his thumb. He does not permit people to speak their minds. As soon as they do, he executes them. He cares more about China's taking its place with the nations of the world than about the people themselves."

"Well," Slade said, "the Communists and you agree on those points. Why not join forces with them?"

The general shrugged. "Just because we are against the same things does not mean we are for the same things. I do not believe communism can work. We are not all equal. Communism does not take human nature into consideration. If you will notice, I said I believe in equal opportunity for all. I do not think all are equal. I have more brains, more foresight, more education than most. I am a leader. Some men can never be leaders."

"What about women?" Chlöe interjected. "Do they never have the qualities for leadership?"

"Get off your one track," Slade said, his voice evidencing anger.

But Snow Leopard answered her. "Of course not. Once in a while a woman ruler comes along, like the dowager empress. Like Queen Victoria. But they are more accidents of birth or marriage. They are not real leaders. For instance, a woman—like yourself— who is not born of royalty and does not marry into it can never become a leader."

Chlöe couldn't argue that point about the two women he mentioned. And she certainly couldn't imagine herself a leader of the stature they were talking about.

"The fundamental problem before China today is Japan," Snow

Leopard continued. "I do not know why Chiang is so blind. He thinks his only enemy is the Communists."

"Oh, come now," said Slade. "Isn't it that Japan has outgrown its territory and needs to expand?"

"You are all fools,' he proclaimed. "If Japan is not stopped now, you, too, will be the brunt of its imperialism, you and the other Western nations."

Slade laughed. "Do you know the size of Japan and of the United States? Impossible. Japan's no threat to us."

"Do you know the size of Japan and China?" the general asked. "And look what a threat it is to us."

"Well," Slade countered, "they say they want only the province of Manchuria, that it's empty and largely unpopulated. They need more space. Perhaps they'll stop there."

Snow Leopard laughed a harsh laugh. "Your country must either adopt a neutral attitude and not aid Japan in its conquest of my country, or—if you are intelligent—you will help us to defeat this nation which will try to take over the world."

Chlöe thought perhaps Snow Leopard hadn't acquired such a degree of sophistication after all. He thought that Japan's attacking his country made all the world vulnerable to its attack.

"I must differentiate, of course, between the use of imperialism by Japan, which wishes to take over my country, and the Western powers' imperialism. The latter just wish to take advantage of us, not take over our peoples and government."

"I'm not sure there's much of a government to take over," Slade said. "Chiang and the Reds fighting, no cohesive central government . . ."

"The foreign nations are accepting Chiang's government at Nanking."

Chiang had recently moved the capital from Peking to Nanking, the ancient capital, and there he and Mei-ling, with government moneys, were trying to turn that ugly city into a place of modern beauty.

Hovering by the doorway, in the shadows, Chlöe saw a lovely young woman. How long she had been there Chlöe didn't know, for she had just noticed her. Obviously, so had Snow Leopard, for his eyes flitted toward the young woman, who could not have been much beyond girlhood, and he clapped his hands.

"Enough," he said, standing. "Tomorrow we shall continue."

He was going to spend the night with the young woman,

obviously. Chlöe wondered what the young woman thought about Snow Leopard. What she felt about him. And if he made love with passion, with tenderness, or if he just rushed through it, his pleasure quick. She wondered if once he was satisfied he would toss the young woman aside, or if he would keep her next to him all night.

For the first time in more than a year she did not dream of Nikolai.

# CHAPTER 41

The sky was bleached blue. The sun, still dancing down the mountainsides, had not yet hit the valley. Chlöe stood by the edge of the narrow river—more of a creek really—watching the shallow water tumble over rocks, hurtling toward some unknown destination.

Chlöe wondered if the young girl was still in Snow Leopard's tent. By her feet at the river's edge was a small, fragile-looking purple flower. She stooped down, touching its velvet softness, rubbing her fingers across its petals. Her nails pinched the stem. Standing, she brought the flower to her cheek.

"I never thought to see you again." His voice was low, behind her.

She turned, crushing the flower in her fingers. "Nor I you."

He was leaning against the big tree whose leaves overhung the river, his arms crossed over his chest. "It matches your eyes," he said, nodding to the petals in her hand.

She smiled at him, not knowing what to say.

"Why do you act as if we have never met?" he asked.

Chlöe looked away, embarrassed. "We have spent many days traveling to find you," she finally said. "My husband has been looking forward to meeting you. If he knew you were Snow Leopard, that you're the one he thought . . . well, he would be too angry to interview you. I thought it best to keep your identity secret, so that my husband is open to what you have to say." Now her gaze met his.

"You didn't tell him that . . . that I . . . that we . . . ?" His dark eyes widened, and his voice reflected surprise.

She turned from him again, to face the river, and he left the tree, walking toward her so that he could hear her answer. "I'm afraid I did break my promise to you and told him the truth. He's the *only* one I did tell the truth to, though. I knew I was breaking my vow to you, but I also wanted to preserve my marriage. I think there should be no secrets in the marriage bed."

She heard him give a low laugh.

"I did tell him the truth."

After a moment's silence Snow Leopard said, "Ah! He did not believe you, is that it? He could not imagine that a man would refuse the opportunity to bed such a beautiful woman?"

He thought her beautiful? Before, he'd told her she didn't appeal to him. She nodded, pleased at his compliment. "Yes. I guess something like that. It took him a year to get over the idea that someone else had . . . had had me. He has hated Snow Leopard with a vengeance. And I would like him to like you."

"Why?" he asked, his tone indecipherable.

"Because . . ." Now she turned to look at him. "Because I like you. Because I have always been grateful to you."

He digested that in silence, leaning down to pick a long blade of grass and stick it between his teeth. Then he laughed. "But it is I who have been grateful to you. You saved my life. Also, had I not met you, I might never have begun my journey. Perhaps I'd never have traveled throughout my country, never have become what I have become, or am becoming. I would probably never be fighting the Japanese for the reasons that I am. I would not be," his laugh became self-conscious, "whatever it is that I am now. Every step that I took I have wanted you to know about. I have wanted to let you know that I am no longer a barbarian. I have wanted you to know that my opinion of women *has* changed because one affected my whole way of thinking. I am glad you have come back so that I can tell you that. I had no way of knowing if you were still in my country, or how to find you. I spent two weeks in Shanghai last year, thinking I might meet you."

"I spent much time in Wuhan last year," she said, amazed at his words.

"Why are you not home, with children?" Neither of them thought it an impertinent question.

"My children, all three of them, are dead." So was her voice as she told him.

"I have dead children also," he said. "It happens in my country."

"Yes." She turned away from him and stared across the river. "Sometimes I hate your country. It is a cruel land."

"What you think cruel is just part of life to us."

"But," she said, her voice almost a whisper, "so much of your life is death."

"I think that is from a Western perspective. Most Chinese do not know what the word *happiness* means. We exist. And that has been enough. One seldom sees happy peasants. What I call passive contentment is the most they feel in life. A positive feeling of happiness about one's existence is rare. If we have enough to eat and are not in physical pain, that is life to us. If we can laugh once in a while, and have full bellies, we are content. We think life is good. If not all our children die, or not too many of our children are daughters, we think fate has dealt us a kind hand." He said, "Come, let us have breakfast. Go awaken your husband, and come to my tent."

"Wait." She caught at his arm. "Do you still kidnap trains?"

He looked down at her hand on his sleeve and laughed loudly and merrily. "Of course not. Do you think I am still a barbarian?" He walked off toward his tent, his arms swinging at his sides.

I can't believe it, she thought. Can he have done all this, changed so much, because of our time together? This man who held women inferior made her feel important again, more so than Slade had ever done, or even Nikolai. Not since Cass had a man made her feel so important. If she accomplished nothing else, Snow Leopard let her know she made a difference to one other human being, a marked difference. And to someone who might be a part of the future that would change China.

"No," General Lu-tang said, "I do not condemn cruelty as you phrase it, justice as we call it. Of course I'm vengeful. The enemy destroys my people; I shall destroy him. We are not, after all, the only country that is this way. The world has never been free from wars. As I study history, it often seems that the more 'civilized' the country, the more often they go to war."

Chlöe shuddered. Inflicting pain was something she had difficulty condoning or even comprehending. Or vengeance. An eye for an eye.

"America is one of the most violent of countries," the general said to Slade.

Chlöe interrupted them. "How can you say that? We fight wars only to defend ourselves or our principles. We . . ."

". . . spend Saturday afternoons at movies watching Westerns," Slade said, "watching cowboys shoot Indians or Pauline falling out of a train. I agree." He nodded at Snow Leopard. "We thrive on anything that's violent. Look what we did to Indians, how we gobble up news of executions. Look how we honor soldiers who kill exorbitant numbers of the enemy, Sergeant York for instance. The more killed, the more heroic." Slade looked at the general. Chlöe could tell that Snow Leopard fascinated him.

The young woman of last night waited on them, bowing as she tiptoed backward, always facing Snow Leopard until she reached the flap of the tent. He never once looked at her. Chlöe wondered if he even knew the girl's name. She was sure they had bedded together the previous night. She tried to study the young woman, but couldn't do so unobtrusively.

He was splendid looking. Not handsome in a conventional way, certainly. His skin was smooth, even though he must be in his mid-thirties, about the same age as Slade. Yet Slade looked older. She hadn't realized it before. She watched both men as they talked, and she realized Slade had gray threads running through his hair that she hadn't noticed before. There were wrinkles beside his eyes, and his mouth was tense, taut. She hadn't taken the time to look at him objectively for years. And what was it now? . . . They'd been married six years. He was thirty-four.

Snow Leopard hadn't a line on his face. She'd heard that Chinese didn't grow hair like Caucasians did. Did he have to shave? She had seen a few elderly Chinese with scraggly beards and thin mustaches. But not many. She wondered if he had hair on his chest, or if it was bare, like a baby's. His wrists were almost feminine, they were so graceful, yet she thought, Here's a man, and doubted that he'd ever questioned the male part of himself. She imagined he'd always been sure of himself, always known who he was.

"I want China to be able to afford what Western nations can, yet I do not think I want us to be like a Western nation. You are too mercenary. You measure worth by how much money you earn. What has that to do with the inner man?"

"Certainly you have men who measure their worth by how much money and power they can amass," Slade said.

The general nodded. "Of course. But those are in no way the

measure of success of a human being. It is the inner qualities that count. China is basically a nation of families. Our lives center around our families. It is this center that has held our nation together."

"Do you have a family?" Chlöe asked.

Snow Leopard smiled. "We all have families. However, I renounced mine so that I am free to pursue a larger goal." He leaned back against the pillows.

"Would it interest you," he spoke to her, "to hear the story of my life? Would it lend you insight into who I am and what I fight for?"

Before Chlöe could answer, Slade said. "That'd be terrific."

But Snow Leopard's eyes had not left Chlöe's.

"Would *you* like to know what kind of man I am?"

Slade was digging in his pockets for a pencil.

Chlöe, elbows on the low table, leaned her chin on her hands, fingers wound around each other, and gazed at the Chinese.

"Yes." Her voice was low. "I would like to know why you are . . . you."

Snow Leopard laughed. "Are you going to make me famous?"

"You bet," answered Slade, who didn't realize he wasn't part of the conversation.

Weeks later Chlöe took great pleasure in describing General Lu-tang in a letter to Cass and Suzi. It was a letter that she thought Slade might never see, but that perhaps half a million other people would.

> Up in the mountains of the northeast is perhaps the most fascinating man in China.
>
> Like Chiang Kai-shek and Mao Tse-tung, he wants to free China from the Western imperialism to which it has been chained for a hundred years. Like Mao Tse-tung, he wants to improve the lives of the peasants, the nearly half a billion Chinese who labor like animals.
>
> But none of these men is alike.
>
> General Lu-tang does not burn with the inner fire of idealism, thinking he has the answers for his countrymen. He has no firm vision for the future. He fights to change China, to give his people a better life. Each day he works toward it. Sometimes killing, it is true.
>
> General Lu-tang has contempt for Chiang Kai-shek, calling him a power-hungry general who refuses to acknowledge the Japanese threat. Mao Tse-tung says the same thing.

*While Lu-tang may not have contempt for the Communists, he claims they are naïve, with no comprehension of human nature. He is a self-styled warlord who, amazing for this country, has actually had military training and led battles.*

*He was born thirty-seven years ago, the second son of a wealthy landowner who believed in education for all his sons. Lu-tang, inspired by legends of his people who had fought over the mountains of Shantung, dreamed of courageous deeds, of fighting for his people.*

*All of his story I did not get from him. I walked through the tent village where he headquarters, and later—on horseback—he took Slade and me to the larger town where he grew up. There I talked with many who had known him as a reckless, adventurous young man. Smiles accompanied reminiscences of his youthful exploits.*

*He dreamed of a military life despite the fact that his father thought soldiering the lowest of occupations, claiming that soldiers only destroyed and never built. When he could not dissuade his son, the father used his considerable political influence to enroll Lu-tang in the new Shantung Military Academy. Lu-tang is one of the first Chinese to have been introduced to modern military training, which means, among other things, that he did not go into battle accompanied by musicians. It meant also that he learned how to use rifles with fixed bayonets.*

*Already an accomplished horseman, Lu-tang distinguished himself by leading skirmishes against warlords who threatened his province, and others who tried to put down the revolution begun by Dr. Sun Yat-sen. By the time he was twenty-five, Lu-tang was a brigadier general in the Shantung army, three years before the League of Nations granted his Chinese province to Japan as part of the spoils of war.*

*Thanks to his family's influence and to their wealth, as well as to his own heroic deeds, his political fortunes rose steadily. He became Shantung's Director of Public Safety, a position, he says, of no import or responsibility, but one that brought gold and influence to him. He laughs, dark eyes sparkling—so unlike the eyes of the majority of Chinese—when he says, "I was an official. And there were two things certain about all officials. They were corrupt. And they smoked opium."*

*When I asked if either of these had been true of him, he answered, "Both."*

*I looked at this clearheaded, dynamic man and said, "First, tell me about opium."*

His eyes clouded. "Westerners do not understand. So many of us grew up on opium. In this region, opium is smoked as commonly as tea is drunk. It begins early. Parents calm irritated or boisterous children by spreading opium on sugarcane and letting their children suck on it. By the age of one, we are addicted. As I grew older, like all other boys, I began to smoke it. I never had to steal or kill for it, though." I gathered many others did.

"And corruption?"

"Plunder of public funds was . . . a duty to one's family, a right. One entered politics only to enrich oneself. It was what I had been taught."

He'd first been married when he was fourteen, he told me. He'd had, at one time in his twenties, four wives and "I don't know how many concubines." He built a palatial home, where they all lived in what he says was "harmony." I have to wonder.

"I had," he said, "everything anyone could desire. I had wealth. I had poppy dreams. I had power. I had many descendents. I was respected. I had the prospect of a prosperous future. But I had a fatal flaw. I liked to read, and reading made me aware of the larger world. It made me realize what small lives I and the people around me lived.

"I looked around and saw villages being attacked, heard of peasants being slaughtered mercilessly. I sat, in my poppy haze, dreaming of saving these peasants. I realized, too, that this so-called revolution was a zero for most of my countrymen. The overthrow of the Manchus made no difference in their lives. They were still in the dark ages.

"I read that China had never, in its four-thousand-year history, taken its place among world nations. I thought to myself, It cannot all be done at once. First my people must be freed from the fear of starvation, of disease, of death . . . fear even of other Chinese. And I decided I could help, but I knew that to dedicate my life to that end, I must give up everything that would take my energies away from the goal. I must give up all that made my life comfortable and drained me of energy.

"It did not happen quickly, but I gave up all my wives and concubines. I provided a home for them, the house and grounds where we had all lived, and I pensioned each one with enough money to care for them, perhaps even to attract a new husband. All my children are cared for financially. . . ."

"All your children?" I asked. "How many have you?"

He shrugged his shoulders. "I don't remember. Later, I sent for my eldest son, whom you have met—he guided you here. I cannot burden myself with children."

I tried not to impose my values on this man who voluntarily gave up all his children when my own heart was breaking for the children I'd lost.

"Now." He laughed. "I did not seem like a candidate for a revolutionary, did I? A wealthy man weighed down by ownership, a corrupt official like all other officials, an opium addict?

"I knew that I must relinquish not only my family but rid myself of opium addiction. I had seen others try, always in vain . . . seen the sweats, the hallucinations, the physical pain. I knew it would not be easy, but I knew I could not be beholden to that habit and reach the goal I set for myself."

He proved, however, to be a man of steel. Not convinced of his own self-discipline, Lu-tang found his way to Chungking, far west of his home, thousands of miles up the Yangtze. Here he booked passage on a British steamer bound for Shanghai, a voyage that would take a month. No opium could be brought on board a British boat. As it sailed downstream, the night sweats, the nightmares, the frazzled nerves, began. He finally lay unconscious on the floor of his cabin, fighting his pernicious practice.

"It was the hardest battle of my existence," he said, clear-eyed, confident. "I began a new life."

I sat looking at him as he talked, unable to imagine what it must have been like, withdrawing from a habit that ruled him.

He then gathered together an army of soldiers and began to repel marauders from the villages in his home province. He admitted to having to tax the peasants to provide the necessities of life for his soldiers, but others told me he was a Robin Hood. He became revered rather than feared, defending ever larger areas, always more villages. When famine struck the northeast, as it sometimes does all parts of the Orient, his villages always had food even if he had to steal and plunder from others—perhaps just enough to keep them from the starvation that wiped out millions of others—but enough.

Yes, millions. It's like the national debt, simply beyond comprehension. The figures are meaningless to us, so alien to any experiences we may have had.

When I asked him why he thought he changed so drastically, he answered, "I traveled. I studied. And I wondered why a foreigner *called me a barbarian. I knew in my belly that I could no longer stand by and be part of a system that allowed so many people to die or exist marginally. I want to awaken and save my people.*

*"I used to think my people were in the fields and villages of this province. But now I think they are all Chinese."*

*I looked for a long time at this tall, golden man with his appetite for knowledge and his stirrings of compassion. Yet I sensed also a streak of cruelty. When I mentioned this he nodded at my accusation and said, "I am just."*

*Different countries use different words for the same things, I thought.*

*"I have learned what love means," he told me.*

*"I thought," said Slade, "that you'd rid yourself of the women in your life."*

*The general waved his hand, brushing aside the idea. "Westerners are so limited. You are the only ones, you know, with the concept of romantic love. I do not mean love for a woman.*

*"Desire, yes. I have not given that up. I have no desire to be a monk. I satisfy my desires quickly so they do not get out of control. But that has nothing to do with love. I mean love for my countrymen."*

*"Isn't that an abstract kind of love?"*

*He looked at me, and I had to explain what abstract meant.*

*He thought for a while. "Perhaps," he finally said. "If necessary, I will die for China. I do not know about anything else. But die for a woman? Never. We Chinese are not so foolish. I may die trying to free my people and to awaken them to their possibilities. I might possibly give my life to save my eldest son. I have risked my life many times in battle and probably will again. I might die to save a friend . . . Love for a friend is worthwhile. Would you?" he demanded of Slade.*

*"I guess I'd give my life for my country," he answered. "I don't know about a friend."*

*"And your family? Would you give you life for your wife?"*

*Slade waited a moment. "That's not fair, General. To ask me that in front of her. But probably. In being willing to give my life for my country, I'd be doing so in order that a way of life I believe in could go on. So that my family can live in the freedom I find necessary for existence."*

*"But then we are again abstract," said the general. "And, after all, how do we know what we would die for until we are tested? I*

*think I would die for a friend because I like to think I am that kind of person. But how does one know until the time comes?"*

Of course Chlöe did not include in her letter the sudden realization that she did not love Slade enough to sacrifice her life for him.

> *General Lu-tang has no clear vision of what he wants for his country. He is not dedicated to a cause like Mao Tse-tung. He is not interested in power, as is Chiang Kai-shek. He does know he wants to rid Shantung and all of China of Japanese invaders. He does know he wants his fellow Chinese to learn that their lives can be better and to help them work toward that. But he is still searching for answers.*
>
> *My husband and I came away more impressed with General Lu-tang than with either Chiang Kai-shek or Mao Tse-tung, despite the fact that he thinks violence and revenge are the way to solve problems. When I disagreed, he laughed, those dark eyes of his glittering, and asked, "What is the way, then?"*
>
> *"Reasoning," I answered.*
>
> *The general doubts there will ever come a time when most problems can be solved by reasoning.*
>
> *I want him to be wrong.*

# CHAPTER 42

"No wonder you're tired," said Chlöe. "You haven't taken a vacation since we've been married, unless you count that trip to see Mao and General Lu-tang last year as one."

"Well," said Slade, "maybe we should take one. Nothing much to report right now, no stories breaking. No matter what any of us writes, America loves the Chiangs." His voice evidenced his depression.

"Let's go someplace we've never been," Chlöe suggested. "How about Japan?"

"I can't take more than two weeks."

Chlöe shook her head. "Forget it. I know what we'd do in

Japan. See everything we could, and you wouldn't relax for a minute."

Slade thought about that. "You're probably right, but I'd like to go anyhow. How about if I promise not to search out any interviews, if I promise not to work at all? We'll go to Mount Fuji and stay in one of those inns I'm always hearing about. They're supposed to be fantastic."

"When?" Chlöe did feel a tinge of excitement. She'd long wanted to visit there.

"I dunno. How soon can you be ready?"

"Tomorrow?" She laughed.

Slade grinned. "I'll see when the next ship sails."

Chlöe imagined it would be a second honeymoon. No work, he promised.

And there were elements of that. They held hands at the railing as Shanghai faded from view and, again, as Yokohama appeared on the horizon. Slade slept with his arm around her, something he hadn't done in years. After they'd taken the train through the green rice paddies and the fertile farms up into the mountains, Slade's usual exhilaration reappeared.

Chlöe thought the inn where they stayed quite the most charming place she'd ever been. Though furnished in a spartan manner, it was delightful. The futon on which they slept, on the floor, was rolled up during the day. A fresh flower, just a single one, swam in the bowl the maid brought in each morning. One day an azalea, another an immense chrysanthemum, a third day a white rose, its outer edges tinged with cerise. Chlöe thought it more effective than a dozen flowers.

A sliding door of small-paned translucent rice paper opened onto a balcony with its breathtaking view of Mount Fuji. A full moon silhouetted the snow-capped peak. From the gardens below came the scent of roses.

One night when they made love Slade didn't hurry at all. But the next day he slept until early evening. When he awoke he had a coughing fit.

"I'm okay," he reassured Chlöe. "Must've picked up some bug I can't shake."

"If you feel better tomorrow, I've heard of a group that's going to climb partway up the mountain. The view's supposed to be glorious."

But in the morning Slade told Chlöe to go without him. He'd sit on the balcony and imagine he saw her climbing.

"At noon I'll wave," he said.

She tried to feel guilty for enjoying the climb while Slade lay exhausted back at the inn. But she couldn't. It was too beautiful to ever forget. Though the ascent was gradual and the path smooth, they made it only a third of the way up the mountain. The view was, as she later tried to explain to Slade, incredible.

"I thought I'd gone to heaven," she told Slade. "Up there, above the rest of the world, I saw how beautiful it all is. From up there everything below looks perfect. I tried to figure out what I felt, and all I could come up with was exquisite joy."

She fell into bed, after a dinner of sushi and sashimi, sleeping as deeply as Slade did. She didn't know he'd slept all day too.

Near the end of the ten days they spent at the inn, Slade's energy did return, though one night when he coughed he spit up blood.

Chlöe insisted he see the doctor when they returned to Shanghai, but the doctor thought it nothing to worry about. It had happened only once. The doctor thought Slade would feel better now that winter had arrived.

For a while he did, though he wouldn't cut down his furious pace. He traveled down to Canton, but when he came back he took to bed, too exhausted to do anything but get up in the middle of the day and go to the office for a few hours.

Daisy came over one noon, on her lunch break, and said, "Do you know Lou's worried about Slade?"

"I am too," Chlöe confessed. "But I don't know what to do. He's been to the doctor."

"Have you thought of getting out of China? Going back to the States?"

Chlöe sighed. "Whenever I mention it, he refuses to discuss it. He says this is where the world's changing."

Daisy took a big gulp of her drink. "Talk Slade into going home. He may have one of these damn China bugs. Get him out of here."

"Tell Lou to try. He never listens to me."

Daisy shook her head. "I think he tunes you out because you're really too much woman."

"What in the world does that mean?" Chlöe wondered.

"Maybe nothing." Daisy shrugged.

"Talking of too much woman. Is that what keeps Lou from doing anything about you?" She'd never been that direct about the two of them before. "Do you scare him?"

"Well, I've given up my frenetic life with the travelers passing through," Daisy admitted, "and settled down. I'm not seeing anyone but Lou, if that's what you mean. I just had to get my head straight. It only took me about a decade."

Chlöe couldn't quite decipher what Daisy meant. "Have you gotten over that love affair back in the States?"

"What love affair back in the States?" Daisy raised her eyebrows.

"You once told me you'd loved only one man and he wouldn't have you. I took for granted it was before you came here, that that's why you *did* come."

Daisy shook her head, melancholy reflected in her eyes. "Honey, the only man I've *ever* loved is Lou Sidney."

Chlöe cocked her head in surprise. Then why had Daisy slept with so many men? Why did men make jokes about the stars on Daisy's ceiling?

"Does he know that?" As though his knowing might make him love her in return.

"Of course," Daisy replied. "He loves me too and always has. But it doesn't solve anything at all."

"Why not? It seems to me you're together all the time."

"Yeah. Well." Daisy stood up. "Not everything is simple in this world, my dear. Maybe not anything is simple. I've got to get back to the consulate. If Slade won't leave, maybe he should consult another doctor. Lou is sure he's not well."

"I think Slade would agree he's not well. It's been going on for at least six weeks. He never shows how he feels, of course, but I think he's a bit worried. I'll see what I can do. I long to go home myself. I haven't seen my family in years." Or Cass and Suzi either.

"I haven't seen mine in a dozen," Daisy said, "and I don't care if it's another dozen." With that, she was gone.

When Slade came home, he said he wasn't hungry. He'd been saying that too often lately. Su-lin had taken to preparing him herbal teas. They didn't seem to make a difference, though he drank them, gagging on the taste of some, savoring others.

After dinner he said, "I think I'll go to bed with a good book."

But when Chlöe entered the bedroom half an hour later, planning to talk with him, he was sound asleep.

In the morning she said, "Let's go home. Nearly seven years is long enough to go without seeing family."

"I don't have any family except my sister and her six or seven kids. That's not for me, Chlöe. You homesick?"

She nodded. "I'd like to go home."

"To Oneonta? I thought you hated the place."

"Well, back to the States. Certainly Cass could get you a stateside assignment."

"C'mon," he said, "you're worried about me. Hon, you heard the doctor. Look, I don't like it either, but it's not going to hang on. If I'd just stop coughing and spitting up pus or mucus or whatever."

She hadn't known he did that. At least it wasn't blood again.

"How about consulting another doctor?" she suggested.

He was silent for a minute, and then admitted, "I've been thinking about it. I could go see that naval doctor."

"Let me come with you."

"Afraid I won't tell you the truth?"

"Yes."

"Okay. You make the appointment."

The naval surgeon, Dr. Cummins, examined Slade thoroughly. "I'll tell you what I think. You have TB."

"TB?" Slade's voice cracked.

"Yes, tuberculosis. There's no real treatment, Mr. Cavanaugh. Bed rest. Salubrious climate."

"That rules out Shanghai," Chlöe said.

"Yes. Go to the mountains. Go to the States. Get out of China."

"TB?" repeated Slade. "How'd I ever get that?"

The doctor shook his head. "We don't know the answers to these things. One can get any damn thing in China. So many people. So much dirt. So many diseases. So little sanitation. My recommendation is to catch the next ship home."

"Is it contagious?" Slade asked, his face ashen.

"Again, who knows. And I can't be sure that's what it is. You need X rays. And even then we might not be sure."

"If I refuse to leave Shanghai?" Slade's voice was brittle.

"Why would you do a stupid thing like that?"

No answer from Slade.

"Well, take to bed. Stop running around. Cut out your traveling. Don't get out of bed for any reason other than going to the bathroom. Might clear up in six months that way."

"And if he goes home, back to America?" asked Chlöe.

"Same prescription. They'll probably send you to a sanitorium in the mountains, where the air's clear and clean. About the same length of recuperation time."

"And if I don't do any of these things?" Slade asked.

The doctor looked at him. Finally, he answered, "You could die."

"I don't want you to die," Chlöe said as she put a quilt over him.

"Look, the doctor said bed rest for six months whether I'm here or there. So what's the difference? There I can't earn a living. Here I can."

"How, if you're bedridden?"

"You'll be my eyes and ears."

Chlöe sat down in the chair she'd pulled up to the bed. She reached for his hand, but it lay limp and cold in hers. "Why? Why do you refuse to help yourself, or let me help you?"

"Dammit, I am helping me. I've taken to bed. Can you imagine me taking to bed for six months, for God's sake? Do you think I'm not going to go out of my fuckin' mind?"

"Slade . . ."

"Look, I want to hear no more about this. I'm not leaving Shanghai. We'll talk to Lou. He'll know when there are stories that need to be covered. He'll clue you in. You can go, take notes, bring 'em back, and fill me in on details, and I'll write the stories from right here in bed. Rig me up a bed table I can type on."

She went up to Harbin, and over to Chungking, up to Peking several times. And not just Lou but members of the press club took to stopping by, not only to chat with Slade for a few minutes but to tell Chlöe the latest news or that a story was breaking in Manchukuo or Sian or wherever it might be. She spent most of each month on trains, in saddles, in cars, on the backs of hay wagons, on foot.

Each time Chlöe returned from a trip, whether it was of two days' or several weeks' duration, she thought Slade looked worse. Even staying in bed and exerting himself in no way, his energy level was becoming lower all the time.

The only time he disobeyed the doctor's orders was Wednesday afternoons, when he insisted on getting up from bed, dressing in his nattiest clothes, and taking whatever articles he or Chloe had written down to the office to cable to Chicago.

Chlöe argued with him. "For heaven's sake, I can do that. That's the least part of it."

"Allow me this much dignity, will you?" He summoned all his strength to stand erect.

He'd be gone until nearly evening, arriving home exhausted, taking to bed, and always having a coughing fit that lasted for hours, spitting up phlegm and, once in a great while, blood. Bloodred blood, in clots.

Dr. Arbuckle had confirmed the naval doctor's diagnosis—TB. If Slade refused to leave China, or at least Shanghai, all any doctors could do was suggest bed rest. And they told Chlöe not to sleep in the same bed, or even the same room, with him. They had no idea whether it was contagious. She was to wash her hands after handling anything he touched. So were the servants.

She thought he had become little more than a skeleton.

She also felt like a traitor.

She hated herself.

She watched her husband waste away before her eyes and had never felt more fulfilled in her life. She was infused with energy all the time, except when she entered Slade's darkened room. She attended the consular functions with a different viewpoint, and now minded them not as much. She was back in the social whirl, not so much as a participant as an observer, yet felt more a part of it than she ever had before.

The foreign population of Shanghai again considered her a heroine. Taking care of her ill husband and doing his work too.

Chlöe hoped that word from other journalists wouldn't get back to Cass. Slade insisted Cass not know he was ill.

But as the months dragged on, Slade showed no signs of recuperation. The six-month mark since the naval doctor's diagnosis had long since passed. His wasted body lay beneath the sheets and he could hardly exert enough energy to feed himself. He stopped getting up to go to the bathroom.

One evening in the early spring of 1931 Lou brought a cable to Slade from Cass. "Ship leaves San Francisco tomorrow. Should be in Shanghai within the month. Will we recognize each other? Plan to stay a month. Expect you to show me China. Give love to Chlöe."

It was over, then, she thought.

"What are you going to do?" Lou asked. He knew Cass had no

idea. They'd all worked hard to help Chlöe, to keep from jeopardizing Slade's job.

"Actually, I feel relieved," she admitted. "This way of living can't go on forever, trying to hide Slade's illness. Cass has to know sometime. And God, I'll be so glad to see him. He's one of the most important people of my growing-up years.

"A month," she said. "I guess I won't tell Slade until it's nearly time. I don't want him to worry."

One afternoon, ten days later, Chlöe walked into Slade's bedroom to find him asleep, breathing so heavily it sounded like snoring. She pulled a chair up beside the bed, waiting for him to awaken, pouring herself a sherry first.

She was still there, wondering if she should send for the doctor, when Daisy arrived. Slade breathed heavily and rapidly until she thought he might burst, and then suddenly stopped. The breathing ceased. A full minute with no breathing at all. Then it came in rapid, deep gasps.

"He's dying," she said.

Daisy put her arm around Chlöe. "I'll stay with you."

When Chlöe did send for the doctor, he shook his head sadly. "There's nothing more to do, my dear."

For the next three days Slade floated in and out of consciousness. When he was alert, he reached out for Chlöe's hand, his eyes frightened. He tried to smile, but all Chlöe could see was the tightened skin around his bones, like a sunken skeleton. His breathing became labored, as though all his muscular energy was being used in the struggle for air. It pained Chlöe to hear him, to watch the life leaving the man she'd lived with for nearly eight years.

She looked at him, holding his bony, clammy hand, and wondered if they'd ever really known each other, if they'd ever really shared the deep parts of themselves. They'd never ever had a talk about their togetherness. Those months before Nikolai, after Snow Leopard, she'd tried . . . tried to make contact, but he had closed up. Had they ever been more than two people living in the same space?

His eyes fluttered open and he whispered something. She leaned over, trying to hear. But he was gone, his breathing tortured, fighting for air.

His final breaths came as rattles. His fingers clutched at the sheets, while his eyes, open, stared at the ceiling. One more deep breath, and his chest stopped heaving.

# CHAPTER 43

She looked down at the unblinking eyes staring at nothingness. Leaning over, she closed his eyelids, thinking his skin was like parchment, dry and translucent.

Where have you gone? she asked silently, wondering where her tears were.

She unfurled his gnarled fingers clutching the sheet, so that when rigor mortis set in she would not have to pry the fabric from his rigid grasp.

In no way did he resemble the good-looking young man she'd fallen in love with just eight years earlier. Suddenly his wasted body jerked. Just one spasm, but she jumped and heard herself cry, "Christ!" Gooseflesh crawled down her back.

She remembered the day his arms, full of yellow roses, surrounded her, and he'd told her they were going to China. It had sounded like such an adventure. The adventure that had cost her two unborn children, her beloved Damien, and now her husband. Some part of her heart echoed, And don't forget Nikolai. Nikolai too. Sinking into a chair, she let out a ragged sigh.

"A son," he'd whispered just days before he died. "I'd have liked to leave a son." It was the only intimation he gave that he knew death was imminent.

She shouldn't have listened to him. Months earlier she should have insisted, should have forced him to return to America and the doctors there.

Chlöe walked out onto the verandah and sank onto the wooden swing, swaying back and forth, gazing out at the river.

"I'll go home with Cass," she said aloud.

Home?

Where was home? She'd felt more a part of China than anyplace else. Yet, God, she hated it here. Hated its robbing her of the people she'd loved. Hated the dirt and the poverty and the hopelessness.

She felt so alone.

I've been alone for a long time, she thought. There had been only moments when she hadn't carried loneliness around within her—years maybe. It was not just Slade's dying. The acknowledgment that it had been Slade's living that created her loneliness stunned her.

Once he had asked her, and only now she realized he hadn't been joking, "You enjoy this, don't you, this being a heroine? You are reveling in my having become Chlöe Cavanaugh's husband. The husband of the woman who sacrificed her body . . ."

She understood, now, that she had been deaf to the tone of his voice then and blind to the accusation in his eyes. Or had she wanted to be blind and deaf? She had walked over to him and put her arms around him, but he'd stared down at her with such a look that she withdrew, feeling the pain like a physical blow as he turned from her. That's when the loneliness had begun, she thought.

Except for that brief time with Nikolai, it had never abated. Not even with Ching-ling, because she knew Ching-ling had many things to do, tasks that were paramount to her, ideas that needed to become realities.

Loneliness, she thought, must be the realization that you aren't the most important person in the world to someone. Someone you love.

Just then Lou's head popped through the doorway.

"What can I do?" he asked, walking over and reaching down to take her hands in his.

"The eulogy," she said. "You knew him better than anyone." Better, even, than I, she thought, filled with sadness.

Slade was buried in the Methodist cemetery, he who had been raised a Congregationalist and claimed that ultimately he believed in no God. But it was an American piece of ground, and Chlöe didn't know where else his body belonged. The whole American, and much of the European, contingent turned out for the funeral.

Afterward, Chlöe wanted to go back to the house alone, close the drapes, and lie down in the dark. She wanted the emptiness to go away, wished the headache that had started early in the morning would stop throbbing.

She wanted to go back to America, to Oneonta. Have her mother wait on her as she'd done when Chlöe stayed home from school with measles or tonsillitis. Feel the cool washcloth on her forehead and her mother sitting, with the shades drawn, at the foot of Chlöe's bed, telling her stories or reading to her until she fell into a feverless sleep.

She wanted to leave China, to leave death and loneliness.

"What are you going to do?" Daisy asked the next morning. She was gulping tea, ready to rush to the consulate. Chlöe watched Daisy gobble down a huge breakfast, herself unable to swallow anything.

"Go back," Chlöe answered, aware she hadn't said *go home*. Maybe Cass would hire her. She knew he'd make a place for her somehow. Somewhere.

Daisy reached her hand across the table and touched Chlöe's arm. "Would you like me to stay with you a few days? I mean, of course, I have to work, but in the evenings . . . Would you like that?"

"Oh, I would, Daisy, but I doubt I'll be very good company."

Suddenly they were interrupted by shouting and wailing. The gate banged closed and, looking out the open window, they saw Su-lin hurrying along the path toward the house. They waited. But no sign of Su-lin and no further noise.

"Probably merchants," Chlöe guessed. "Su-lin has her own way of turning people away."

Daisy smiled. "Okay," she said, and stood, running a hand through her unruly curly hair. "I'll be back for dinner, how 'bout that? I'm not coming back to be entertained. I'll bring a book and can read if you want to be alone. Or I've very strong shoulders. They don't mind being cried on."

"I don't think I'm going to cry," Chlöe said. "I did that while I watched him waste away. I have no tears left."

Daisy leaned over, kissed the top of Chlöe's head, and was out the door.

In less than three minutes she returned. Chlöe was still sitting, her elbows resting on the table, her hands still wound around her cold cup of tea as she stared out the window.

Daisy stood in the doorway. "Chlöe."

Chlöe looked up.

"I think you'd better come out to the gate." Her eyes were blank but there was a tremor in her voice.

Behind them Su-lin's voice was strident. "No. No need bother. Just trash."

Daisy's eyes met Su-lin's. She jerked her head toward the door. "C'mon, Chlöe."

Chlöe sensed a tug-of-war between the two women. She could tell they knew something she was unaware of. Daisy reached out and took her hand, leading her through the hallway, out into the already bright sunlight, to the old wooden gate. She pulled it open and stood back.

In front of it was a very pregnant young Chinese woman, pretty by any standards, and two young children, both girls, neatly dressed and standing slightly behind their mother.

Chlöe looked quizzically at Daisy.

The young Chinese woman put her hands on the shoulders of the little girls and pushed them forward.

"You buy?" she asked, her voice as soft as her eyes were beseeching.

Again Chlöe glanced at Daisy, whose veiled green eyes betrayed no sign of emotion.

"No." Chlöe shook her head. The woman was well dressed, her gown of silk. She did not look like a beggar but like a comfortable Chinese city housewife, perhaps several steps above the average. The little girls were really very pretty, she thought. The smaller one must be about three, judging from the size of her. The older might be five or six, a beautiful girl. Certainly, the woman was not near starvation. Chlöe had seen women standing on street corners trying to sell their children. She knew they'd be bought by factories and brothels and had always averted her eyes. And her heart. But this woman didn't look destitute.

"Come into the kitchen," she said, opening the gate wide. But the woman stood there.

"You no buy? Take, then. Good girls. You take them. For free." She pushed the older one forward slightly, and the girl stared at Chlöe with wide, luminous black eyes.

Chlöe turned to Daisy and said in English, "She doesn't look poor. They're well dressed and obviously well fed. She's what, about seven or eight months pregnant? Why does she want to get rid of them?"

Daisy said, "The father is no longer at home."

Oh, Chlöe thought. Abandoned. "I can give you a little money," she said to the pregnant woman. "Or do you need work? Where's their father? Your husband?"

The black eyes were unfathomable. "Dead." So was her voice.

"I'm sorry," said Chlöe. "My husband is too." And then when the woman and her children continued standing, not moving, not talking, Chlöe asked, "Have you no relatives?" Maybe she could give her enough train fare to get back to a town, a village, though this did not look like a village woman.

"I can no longer feed them," the woman finally said. "No longer any money." Her blank eyes remained fixed on Chlöe.

"Perhaps I can find work for you. I have many friends—"

"I do not work for you!" The woman's voice evidenced anger as her eyes at last flared with life. "I sell you children."

"Perhaps . . ."

"They children of your husband."

The words hovered there, slithering in the air that became sultry and heavy. It snaked in coils between them.

Chlöe felt Daisy's hand on her shoulder.

"No," she said. "My husband's dead. He's been sick for a long time." She looked at the woman's swollen belly. Slade couldn't be the father of this woman's child. He'd been too sick seven months ago. Eight months. A year. Slade hadn't had energy or desire for longer than that. "You must be mistaken."

"Wednesday afternoons," the woman spat out. She reached out and put her hand on the older girl's head. "This one, when you in Canton."

Chlöe's breath caught in her throat. That's when she herself had become pregnant the first time. This couldn't be. While she and Ching-ling and Nikolai were fighting their way through gunfire, before she'd had time to be aware of her own pregnancy? Right after Slade had left her to return to Shanghai? Right after he'd impregnated her he had sown the seeds for this child? Impossible.

"She's lying. Or she's mistaken." Chlöe turned to Daisy. "Of course she is."

Daisy's arm encircled Chlöe. "No," she murmured into her ear. "It's true."

Chlöe's head jerked. "What do you mean, it's true?"

"I've known for years."

Chlöe started to sink, but Daisy held her in her arms.

"You've known? You mean it *is* true? Oh, my God!"

She turned her head and looked at the Chinese woman with the two beautiful little daughters and the unborn child swelling her belly and reached out for the heavy oak door. With all her might she slammed it in their faces.

Sinking to her knees, she looked up at Daisy. Daisy knelt down beside her and put her hands on Chlöe's shoulder. "Oh, my dear. We hoped you'd never know."

"We?" Daisy began to spin around and around and Chlöe couldn't focus on her. "We? Who else knows? Everyone?" Her throat burned. She couldn't swallow.

"Only Lou, I think. Only we two."

Chlöe pressed her hands against her forehead, trying to control the vertigo, trying to force the jagged pain out of her head. "Why didn't you tell me?" Her voice cracked. "Jesus Christ, why didn't you let me know?"

"It would have served no purpose." Daisy sounded defensive.

"Oh, God." Chlöe sobbed and began to pound her fists against the heavy studded door. Blood dribbled down her knuckles. "It's all been a lie," she cried, and at that moment understood she had never hated as she hated Slade now. While she had lost three children, he was creating ones with another woman.

# *CHAPTER* 44

Daisy stayed until Lou arrived.

The sun blinded her, so Chlöe pulled the drapes and sat in the cool darkness of the living room, not moving. Her elbows rested on her knees; her hands cupped her face. She hadn't changed her position since Daisy dragged her in, leaving Chlöe only long enough to order Su-lin to send for Lou. Su-lin clucked a strange noise and gave Daisy a look of disgust.

Over and over Chlöe kept saying, "It's all been a lie."

Only vaguely did she hear Daisy whispering in the background, softly closing a door. Then she heard footsteps crossing the room.

Pulling a chair close, Lou sat down and gazed at Chlöe, reaching out to take her hands in his.

When she realized who he was, she said softly, "You knew?"

He nodded imperceptibly, his fingers smoothing themselves over the backs of her balled fists.

"You know what hurts most?" She knew her voice sounded as though she was crying, but her cheeks were dry. "I've been thinking." A huge sob escaped her. "It's not the infidelity. It's not the actual act of his making love to another woman." She'd been thinking of herself and Nikolai. That had forever changed her relationship with Slade. Or it had forever been changed and that's why she and Nikolai had ever been. Could ever have been.

"It's the lie. Fucking . . ." She had never used the word before, not even in her thoughts. "Fucking in itself isn't grounds for divorce. It's the mental, the emotional unfaithfulness. It's thinking you have something special with someone and then finding out it wasn't what you thought it was at all. Maybe never was."

Lou started to speak, but now she pressed his fingers tightly and continued as though all she'd been thinking for the last hour and a half needed to be said aloud. Her words rushed out in little breaths, the sounds stinging her palate as she forced them out. She swallowed so hard it hurt.

"I mean, I thought we had something that we didn't share with anyone else. And it's not true, is it?" At last her eyes met his. "I thought the pain of not having children was something we shared. But he's been a father all along. You've known, haven't you?"

Lou reached out and put a hand on her shoulder. She brushed it away.

"Not at first," he said, his voice soft. "I just knew there was someone. I . . ."

"Have you been feeling sorry for me all these years?"

Lou took her hands again, mute.

"It's not even as if it was casual, is it? One woman after another? No wonder he didn't need me that year. Or anytime else, I expect. Oh, Jesus, Lou." Chlöe freed herself from Lou's hands and stood up. "Did you know he wouldn't touch me for a whole year after I'd been kidnapped? Wouldn't believe me when I told him that really—truly—nothing had happened. But even if something had— even if I'd lain in Snow Leopard's arms for three nights, even if I'd enjoyed it, Slade made me feel untouchable. Made me feel dirty at the thought of another man's touching me, for Christ's sake, and here he was out screwing her, that woman, and he made me an untouchable!" Her voice rose. "What a hypocrite. What a goddamned hypocrite." She laughed shrilly. "Oh, the irony of it all!

"How dare he?" She began to cry now, yelling, perhaps hoping the dead Slade could hear her. "He was out fucking that woman, creating babies while he wouldn't touch me." She glared at Lou as though he were the guilty one.

"It must have started, oh, dear God . . ." Now she came back and, sinking to the floor beside him, buried her head in his lap. "Oh, Lou, it must have started the first year of our marriage." Convulsive sobs racked her. She felt his fingers gently patting her head. He reached into a pocket and brought forth a handkerchief, handing it to her.

She cried.

And cried.

And cried.

Finally, she blew her nose loudly, her sobs turning to ragged deep sighs until at last she began to breathe, if not normally, at least evenly.

Looking up at Lou, she asked, "Do you think he loved me?" thinking, he couldn't have.

Lou didn't answer.

Finally she squeezed his fingers. "Lou? Talk to me. Please."

His smile was sad. "Chlöe, my dear, I'm trying to think of what to say. How to answer your question *and* alleviate your pain."

She put her cheek against the back of his hand. "He loved me when we first married. I know that. When did it stop? What happened?" It wasn't the last three years she was trying to understand. Nor the time since the Blue Express. It was how to explain a six-year-old child, conceived before they'd been married a whole year. A daughter who must have been conceived within weeks or days of her own first pregnancy.

"I can't answer your question, Chlöe." Lou's voice was so quiet she had to strain to hear. "I suspect you were too much for him."

She jerked her head up, her neck rigid. "That's what Daisy said too. What in the world does that mean?"

Lou shook his head. "I'm not sure. Daisy and I've discussed it over the years."

Discussed Slade's not loving her? Oh, dear God.

"Ego, as well as other things, is bound up with love," he went on. "You'd known each other just a week or so when you married? Chlöe, he was already famous then. You know I covered the European war too, and though I never met him over there, I heard about him, read his flamboyant though inevitably accurate accounts. I was also always hearing of his exploits with the ladies."

"But it wasn't ladies," she thought aloud. "It was one."

Lou looked down at her.

Oh, she thought. Not necessarily. He thinks I'm naïve.

"Chlöe, I've thought you've never known how beautiful you

are, never been aware that when you enter a room, everyone stares. I'm sure Slade was one of those who was captured by your beauty. Men like to have other men think beautiful women love them. You know, of course, that fortunately women don't usually judge a man by his looks. But it's not true of us, of men. I imagine no man at all who has ever looked at you has not fantasized you in his arms, in his bed."

Chlöe's mouth slackened. Was he trying to make her feel better, give her back some faith in herself? Certainly he couldn't be serious. She remembered Slade's saying, one night as she was dressing in front of the mirror, on their way to some dance, "You're not really beautiful at all, you know." She had glanced over at him, laughing.

Lou went on. "Slade Cavanaugh and his beautiful wife. All he needed to enhance his glamour. Oh, my dear, if you could only have been that, his beautiful wife. Slade Cavanaugh's wife."

Her puzzled eyes silently questioned him.

"If you'd not been all else that you are. If you weren't so vital, so intelligent, filled with such joie de vivre, if you yourself weren't so talented with words, weren't always the center of attention."

"Are you telling me," she asked, "that it's my fault Slade turned to other women?"

Lou shook his head no.

"I think I'm saying his ego couldn't handle you. You were the first time he wasn't center stage. I was around once when he was introduced as 'Chlöe's husband' and I saw the look in his eyes. I think it," she knew he meant the long liaison with the Chinese woman, "was because he never doubted his power there. He was the focal point of her life. Once he said to me, 'No matter what else in life, I know Chin-Chen is *always* waiting for me. She is not out at a party, or laughing with someone else. She is not going off on her own. She is home, taking care of our children, and the *only* important question in her life is when will I be there. Yet she never makes demands on me. Never makes me feel guilty when I don't appear. And when I am with her, only what pleases me is of importance to her. She is a real woman.' "

A real woman?

"What I'm trying to say, my dear, is that it wasn't your fault. You were simply more than Slade bargained for. He needed someone who was no competition, someone who faded next to him. Chlöe, you never fade next to anyone, not even Ching-ling. Had you been beautiful and slightly vapid, beautiful and not terribly intelligent, beautiful but not have such joie de vivre, beautiful but not so competent . . . but then, no, I don't suppose even then. Slade probably needed to have more than one woman. His ego needed that. Chlöe, it had nothing to do with you. It kept him, you see, from intimacy. And Slade couldn't handle intimacy. Most of us—I mean men—can't." Lou's voice was wistful.

She was having trouble letting all this sink in. She had never seen herself as Lou described her. She thought she'd been along for the ride, bumpy as it had been.

"Daisy says you don't know you have that power. Maybe I'm doing you a disservice, telling you this. Part of your great charm, probably, is your not knowing it. But, Chlöe, you do have it. And it scares most men shitless. Only the very strong can take on a woman like you, even if those average ones of us might dream of you."

Chlöe's mouth hung open. She couldn't possibly be the one Lou was describing.

"What do you want me to do?" Lou asked. "How can I help you?"

Chlöe was still staring at him. She heard herself sigh. And she thought, I wish Cass were here now so I could go home with him. I want out of this. I can't stand any of it. It's a nightmare and I'll wake up any minute. But she knew Cass wouldn't arrive for another ten days or so, and she had to get through that time. Then she'd leave. Get out of this damn country. Forever. This goddamn land that had robbed her of all most women considered their due. Now, she realized, it had also robbed her of innocence.

"I don't know, Lou," she answered. "I've got to think. Right now I want to be alone."

"Call me anytime, whenever I can help, or just to be here. Daisy will be back tonight."

Chlöe reached up a hand and put it on his arm. "Lou, I know it's none of my business. But you and Daisy, why . . . ?"

"Why haven't we married?" Lou pressed his lips together in a thin line, and Chlöe saw pain reflected there. His eyes did not meet hers as he stood and shrugged, his shoulders sagging. "I was wounded during the war." His voice was barely audible. "I'm impotent, Chlöe. I'm goddamned impotent."

And he was gone.

She sat where she was for several hours, numbed. It's all too much, she told herself.

Slade's slow death had been bad enough. Looking down at his spiritless body was as much as she'd thought she could take. With his dying, she realized, her whole way of life would vanish. Yet she realized she wasn't the first twenty-nine-year-old widow. She was still young enough to make a life for herself.

She had never resigned herself to the fact that she could never again be a mother, never nestle babies in her arms, never . . . Stop it!

Now, all but sitting on her doorstep, were his children and his— his what? Mistress, concubine?

Her fists balled so tight her fingernails cut into her palms. Flexing her fingers, she took a deep breath.

Now . . . Daisy and Lou. Bearing his burden for over ten years. Impotent? How must a man feel with the knowledge he could never . . . Did it mean desire was dead too? If not, the torture he must feel wanting Daisy . . . and Daisy. Poor Daisy.

Chlöe stood up, exhausted.

"I'm going for a walk," she called out.

Su-lin, who must have been just outside the door, rushed in. "Call for rickshaw."

"No. I want to walk."

"I come with you."

"No." Chlöe turned to look at Su-lin, reaching out to take her hand. "I'll be all right. I really will. I want to be alone."

"What for? Not healthy to be alone."

"I need to think."

"What think about?" pursued Su-lin.

Chlöe sighed. "I don't know. Everything. Maybe nothing. I'll be back before dark."

It was not yet noon.


It was twilight when she returned home. Only then did she realize Su-lin had been following her all afternoon, trailing blocks behind, but probably always within view.

"I think maybe you not come back," Su-lin explained, relief evident on her round face.

She stood in the doorway while a servant brought Chlöe her dinner. Absently Chlöe raised the bowl to her mouth and began shoveling the food in with her chopsticks. She hadn't eaten all day.

She rocked back and forth as she ate, saying nothing to the hovering Su-lin.

When Chlöe finished, Su-lin reached out, took the bowl from her hands, and turned to go.

"Wait. Su-lin, what will happen to those children?"

Su-lin made a gurgling sound in her throat. Chlöe wondered if it were a sob. "Too young for brothels. Sold to factories, like my babies. Maybe train as servants or prostitutes. If new baby is girl child, mother will probably smother it with pillow or throw it in river."

"Good God," whispered Chlöe, recalling her trip along the waterfront with Ching-ling.

Su-lin shook her head. "Is done all the time. Better to smother than be sold, I think. Better to die immediately than work until drop dead in factory at twelve, thirteen. Better to die right away than be used by men in whatever ways they want. Not so bad to die right away. Never know anything." She padded away to the kitchen. "Only mother sad then," she muttered.

Chlöe heard men calling to each other on the river, saw lights twinkling as barges floated by. She heard voices of children laughing and screaming with delight at some game.

Walking up to the bathroom, she put on her nightdress and, leaning her back against the wall, looked down at the dragon winding itself around the claw-footed tub. She slid down the wall to a sitting position, hugging herself as she looked into the dragon's eyes.

Chlöe began to weep, tears she could not stop, great, uncontrollable gulping sobs. At three in the morning she went tearing through the house, to Su-lin's room, shaking her awake.

"In the morning," Chlöe cried, "as soon as it's light, go find that woman. Bring her here. Tell her I will take care of her and her children. She is to come live here. Do you understand?"

Only then did she sleep.

# CHAPTER 45

The pregnant woman, along with Slade's two daughters, moved into the guest house, with its one bedroom. Since the little stone building was off to the side of the big house, Chlöe did not even have to see them, she told herself. She instructed Su-lin to make sure they were fed, and she herself told the woman that when it came time for the new baby, she would send for a doctor. The irony was not lost on her. This woman—for days Chlöe could not make herself say her name aloud—did not want her children if she had no way to feed and house them. This she could not do without Slade's support. And Chlöe had lost three, three whom she had wanted badly. Now they were living under the same roof, so to speak. That little three-year-old had been conceived in the year Slade would not come near her, censuring her for his believing she gave her body to save other lives, while all the time he was making love to this Chinese woman. Regularly. She knew it wasn't just Wednesday afternoons. She knew now that it must have been many evenings when he had pleaded work, or when he said he and Lou and Daisy went to the greyhound races. He probably ran over there after lunch some days, perhaps even for lunch. Maybe he stopped off on his way to the office mornings.

Perhaps when he'd sent her off to Peking or overnight to cover stories he had moved in with this woman and their daughters. She wondered if he'd ever come fresh from making love with this—this other woman—and made love to her. And, if so, had he done it because she aroused him too, or he thought he'd better, so she wouldn't suspect anything?

Had he played with these little girls, acted like a father to them, taken them to watch the sailboats on the lake in the park, or to fly kites on windy days? Had he sat them on his lap and told them stories? He must have taken them presents, for all three of them were nicely dressed. Had he laughed with them and told them they were his darlings? Had he lain next to the woman, after a surfeit of lovemaking, and held her in his arms, talking with her?

She knew she was torturing herself with these questions that so haunted her. He had had a liaison with—and now she forced herself to give a name to the woman—Chin-Chen almost as long as they'd been married. While she and Nikolai and Ching-ling had been battling bullets in Canton, Slade had been creating . . . what *was* the name of that eldest one, the little sloe-eyed beauty?

As she was thinking, she came upon the little girl sitting in the midst of the pampas grass, crooning to a doll. The girl looked up at Chlöe and smiled a shy, bright smile, and before she realized it, Chlöe stooped down and asked her name.

"Jade."

Jade? That must have been Slade, Chlöe thought. She noticed the one arm of the doll hung askew, and asked, "Is your doll's arm broken?"

Jade solemnly nodded her head.

"Come, I'll fix it," Chlöe offered. The little girl jumped up, the doll in one hand, and reached up for Chlöe's hand with the other.

The touch jerked up to Chlöe's heart, and she stifled a sob, putting her hand around the little girl's, hoping she wasn't holding it too tightly. In the house she found a needle and thread, and swiftly sewed the doll's cloth arm back on.

"Here." She held it out to Jade, who thanked her with impeccable manners, and turned to leave. As she reached the door, Chlöe called, "Wait," reaching a hand out into the air to detain her. "Would you like a sweet cake?"

Jade's eyes showed no response. "Yes," she said politely. "That would be very nice."

Chlöe ran to the kitchen and found two cakes. When she returned, Jade was seated on a chair, her ankles crossed primly. She said, "My father was going to teach me to write my name."

Chlöe stared at her and tried to decipher what she was feeling.

"You were my father's number one wife, is that not true?"

Number one? Did that mean he had married Chin-Chen? She really didn't want to know.

"What shall I call you?" Jade wiped crumbs from her lips. "May I call you auntie?"

Oh, God in heaven. Chlöe nearly laughed, but it would have been a bitter laugh, so she controlled it. After all, she didn't have to take her anger out on this little girl. "No," she said. "I do not like that."

"What would you like to be called?" Jade stood, now that she had finished her cake.

"I don't know. I'll think about it."

"Can you read?" Jade asked.

"Yes," Chlöe answered, standing. "I think you had better go now. I have some work to do." She had nothing at all to do, but she wanted to be alone. The girl was unsettling her.

Jade walked toward the door before turning around to say "Thank you very much." And then she skipped out, little dancing steps.

———

The next day Chlöe found herself standing in front of a store window, looking at a toy sailboat. I don't want it, she told herself as she entered the shop. Yet she purchased it, excited as she hurried home, urging the rickshaw boy on. She set it on the table in the dining room and kept it there as Su-lin served her lunch. Su-lin made little clicking sounds, which Chlöe didn't recognize.

After lunch, boat in hand, she strolled over to the guest house. It was very quiet. She knocked on the door and started to turn to go when she heard no sound from within. As she turned, the door opened, just a crack, and Chin-Chen looked out. She waited for Chlöe to speak.

"I thought," Chlöe felt awkward, "maybe Jade would like to go to the park with me and we could sail this boat."

Chin-Chen stared at her, but all Chlöe could see was the swollen belly, where Slade's child grew larger each day. Damn, she thought, why did I come over here? It's like rubbing a cavity in an aching tooth. Am I just trying to torment myself? She wished she could turn around and run away where she could never see this woman and these children again.

But Chin-Chen turned into the house and called, in her pretty singsong voice, and Jade came running, laughing when she saw Chlöe and the boat. Chin-Chen nodded and said to Chlöe, "She would like that. My other daughter, Plum Blossom, would like to come too."

Chlöe hadn't counted on that. One was more than enough. Both of Slade's children? But she said, "Yes, of course."

Plum Blossom and Jade. None of this Chin-Chen, Su-lin, Chingling. Had these been Slade's choices? And how had he acted when they were born? Had he been present? Was he pleased and proud when he looked at them?

The two girls ran ahead of her, laughing and uninhibited. Jade was protective of her little sister and reached out to pull her back from a careering rickshaw. As they approached the park, the very one where Chlöe witnessed the beheadings her first day in China, Jade drew her sister back and reached for Chlöe's hand. Again, her heartstrings knotted in a feeling she did not understand.

These could be my daughters, she thought. Slade's and mine. But then she realized they could not. Their slanted eyes, their olive skin, their round faces. Though their hair is like mine, she thought. Or mine is like theirs. Straight and black. They were beautiful children. She could tell, when they saw the lake, that they had never been to the park before. Slade probably had never taken them any-place where he could be recognized.

Chlöe led them to the edge of the lake and, unwinding the string from the sailboat, pushed it into the water, letting the breeze take care of the rest. Two large mallards swam beside it, honking. Jade laughed loudly, clapping her hands, while Plum Blossom looked perplexed.

Jade took great pleasure in guiding the little boat until, eventually, she gave the string to Plum Blossom and admonished her to be gentle. She spent time teaching her little sister how to handle the string so that it controlled the boat. They were both entranced with the large birds that were so tame. Next time, Chlöe thought, I'll bring bread crumbs.

Next time?

As they walked home, Jade again put her hand in Chlöe's and asked, "Do you know how to write my name?"

"Yes," Chlöe answered. "I do."

That night, having located green ink, she wrote the character for Jade.

I will give it to her in the morning, Chlöe mused, smiling in anticipation at how pleased the little girl would be. And I will tell her mother that they can stay in the guest house even after the baby is born.

Yet, she realized, I will not be here much longer than that. I am going home with Cass. And he should be here in a few days.

Cass. He doesn't even know Slade is dead.

Cass.

It would be eight years in three months. Eight years since she'd married Slade. Eight years since she'd left for China. Eight years since she'd seen either Cass or Suzi or her family. Little had she known then what fate had in store for her. She never should have said yes to China. And she never should have said yes to a man she'd known for only one week. Oh, God, how stupid youth is! How blind I've been!

As she headed for bed, she thought, That's why I went to Nikolai's arms. She must have known deep down she wasn't the first priority in Slade's life, and probably never had been. She imagined his Chinese family had precedence in his thoughts . . . in his life. How could he have afforded both of them? He must have earned more money than she'd ever known to have supported his Chinese family and her too.

She slept until late in the afternoon; she could tell by the slant of the sun's rays. What awakened her was a ruckus at the gate, shouting, and someone knocking loudly on the great door.

"Where's my girl?"

She bounded out of bed, a cry of delight on her lips. It could only be Cass. Oh, Cass, dear Cass, was here. At last. A mantle of safety swept across her whole being. He would take care of her. He would help her get home. He would see she was safe. And she began to run, nearly tripping over the stone dog beside the doorway.

When she reached the gate, Su-lin had already opened it. Standing in front of the door, larger than life, his temples quite gray but looking for all the world exactly as she remembered him, stood Cass, his arms wide open as if waiting for her to thrust herself into them. Waiting to hold her and say, "Chlöe, my dear girl. My dear dear girl."

She burst into tears as his arms enfolded her.

"Hey, that's no way to greet someone who's been thinking of nothing else but seeing you for the last five weeks. Come, come, let me look at your beautiful face and see if I'd even recognize you!"

She pulled back, wiping away the tears that streaked her cheeks, smiling at him, reaching for his hands and not letting them go.

"Oh, I have never been so happy to see anyone in my entire life."

"Well." He grinned. "That's worth coming halfway around the world for! Now, how do I let this coolie know I want the bags in here?"

Chlöe turned to call out to the boy and then told Su-lin to see that the bags were taken to the extra bedroom, the one Slade often used as his office, where he kept his typewriter.

Cass laughed his booming laugh that Chlöe recalled loving so well. "You all sound like you're speaking Greek to me. How'd you ever learned that, Chlöe? I should have known you would."

"I've been here nearly eight years, after all," she said. "How could I not learn the language?"

Yet there were many who had been there longer and still refused to learn Chinese.

She pulled Cass into the house, her eyes feasting on him. God, it had been so long since she'd seen anyone like him. A beautifully cut silk suit, his stocky body emanating energy. So—so American! Oh, to be going home and seeing men like this every day. He looked efficient. She guessed even the Westerners who had lived here so long lost some of that animal energy Americans seemed born with.

Once in the living room, Chlöe said, "A drink?"

"Gin and tonic, if you have it," Cass said, looking around. "You've made this a lovely home, Chlöe. You're in the Chinese section?"

She laughed. "The whole country is the Chinese section," she said, making a gin and tonic for herself too. She didn't often drink.

"Of course." Cass nodded, accepting the glass. "Chlöe, my dear, you're a sight for sore eyes. You look as though China agrees with you. But you don't look like the young girl I knew."

"I'm nearly thirty," she said. "That's why."

"It's more than that," he said, walking out the door to the verandah. "Can we sit out here? And wait for Slade? Will he be home for dinner? It is nearly that time, isn't it?" He sat on the swing and patted the place next to him.

But she didn't follow. "Slade's dead," she said.

The glass fell from Cass's hand, splintering on the stone floor. He stood up and walked over to her, gazing into her eyes.

"He died six days ago," she said, her voice reflecting no emotion.

"Was this sudden? An accident?" He looked as though he were ready to put his arms around her but at the sound of her voice hesitated.

"No," she said. "Let me pour you another drink and I'll tell you about it. He'd been sick for a long time. Over a year."

"What was wrong?" He followed her back to the living room, watching her as she poured him another drink.

"Tuberculosis," she answered, leading him back to the swing outside. "Here, sit and hold my hand while I tell you about it."

She did not tell him about anything but the illness. He did not ask questions, but sat holding her hand with his left one and drinking his gin with his right. He watched her as she talked, her voice even and unemotional.

"I want to go home with you," she said when she'd finished. "I want to get away from this damned country that has robbed me of so much. I wish your ship were leaving tomorrow. I am so glad— so glad you don't know how glad I am—that you're here." He put an arm around her and she let her head rest on his shoulder. She closed her eyes and thought, I'm safe again. After all these years, I'm safe again.

# CHAPTER 46

Watching Cass react to Shanghai reminded Chlöe of her own initiation into the Orient. He was wide-eyed about everything he saw.

She discovered she was having far more fun seeing Shanghai through his eyes than she ever had before. She introduced Cass to the reporters' hangout—the Chocolate Shoppe—and he spent several afternoons there, talking with journalists from around the world. He immediately took to Lou Sidney.

After spending an afternoon talking to Lou, Cass returned to Chlöe's and, finding her on the verandah with Jade and Plum Blossom, flatly stated, "I think I knew. Someplace in my gut . . . a feeling I ignored."

Chlöe looked up from the Chinese paper book she was reading to the little girls. It was wonderful to have him around, to suddenly hear his voice, to look up and see him there. She wondered how she could feel so happy with all the recent tragedy and discoveries. She had not yet told Cass why Chin-Chen and the little girls were there. Or who was the father of the expected baby. She would tell him all that on the ship on the way home.

She closed the book, patting Jade on the head, and said, "Tomorrow. Come back tomorrow. That's all for now." As the girls scampered away, she stood and asked, a smile playing across her face, "Should have known what?"

"Lou just told me what you've been doing for the last year, that it wasn't Slade writing those stories. It's been you. And you know what?" He laughed. "I told myself his style was changing, a more human element was creeping in, that straight reportorial and political analysis had been overtaken by human interest. To readers in Chicago, China has become a reality rather than a far-off place whose policies and peoples it's never understood." He walked over to her and put his hands on her arms. "And here it's been you . . . hiding the fact that Slade was sick. You, running off to Peking and Manchuria and wherever else. What a wife you've been, my dear." He pointed at her. "What a woman!"

Chlöe felt blood rushing to her cheeks, warm with pleasure. "Ready for a drink?" she asked.

Cass glanced down at his watch. "The sun *is* over the yardarm, I see. Of course. But," he followed her to the living room, "you're not getting off this easily. It's true, then, you've written everything for the last year?''

"Not quite," Chlöe said. "About eighty-five percent. Slade and I'd talk together about what was happening and where the stories were. I have to give a lot of credit to Lou and the other foreign journalists. They fed me stories, they'd even seek me out and whisper where a story would be breaking. I took it as a token of their esteem for Slade that they wanted to help. Lou Sidney has been, since the very first day we arrived, a wonderful friend.''

"Not only to Slade, I gather." Cass took the drink and walked back to the coolness of the verandah. "He admires you and is very fond of you."

"I love Lou," Chlöe said. "He's a friend without equal." She followed Cass but did not sit next to him on the swing, choosing, instead, the settee opposite. "Well, excepting you."

Cass leaned forward. "Show me China, Chlöe. I didn't come this far for just a glimpse of Shanghai. Introduce me to the Chiangs, to the people and places you know. Let me see it all for myself.''

Chlöe leaned back, one arm resting along the top of the settee. She sipped her drink, glancing over the glass's edge at the man who had taught her so much back in her college years. She remembered thinking how wonderful it would be to have Cass for a father, to be under his tutelage. Now he was asking her to guide him.

"Just this morning I heard that Madame Sun will probably be returning to China," she said, "though I don't imagine the circumstances are much to her liking. I would like you to meet her.''

Cass sat back, rocking the swing, sipping his drink as he waited for Chlöe to continue.

"Despite all the stories we sent back, I'm not sure how much you really know about China."

"Well, thanks to Henry Luce, Americans love Chiang. I gather you and Slade don't. In fact, most of the journalists stationed here don't seem to favor him. In America he's becoming a folk hero, he and that beautiful wife of his.''

A smile played along Chlöe's lips, but her eyes reflected none of it. "I guess I won't try to brainwash you. You've read everything we've written, I would imagine?''

Cass nodded his head. "Every single word of it.''

"But you haven't published every word of it.''

"That's my prerogative with any reporter," Cass acknowledged. "You people in the middle of things can't ever seem to see the larger picture. I also sell papers in order to make money. What people aren't interested in, they won't read. They ate up the generalissimo's wedding to Mei-ling."

"Ah, yes," Chlöe said. "The Americanization of China, thanks to its American-reared first lady. Is that it? And she is, after all, a Christian!"

She liked looking at him, talking with him. It had been so long since she'd felt this safe with anyone. "Anyhow, Chiang refuses to let Peking be the capital of China anymore. Anything that was Manchu. This is the new China, he says. Needs a new capital. So he's moved the capital down to Nanking."

"Which is where?"

"Upriver from here a few hundred miles. Not the prettiest of cities. But he and Mei-ling are using the taxes of China, emptying the coffers to remake Nanking as the capital of this Celestial Kingdom. I haven't seen it in years, but I'm told I would hardly recognize it. He's let the rest of the cities stay slums, but is redoing Nanking as a showcase.

"In order to lure my friend Ching-ling back to China, hoping no doubt to win her approval and thus Dr. Sun's followers, he has spent what I hear is a million dollars—American, that is—to build a mausoleum to Dr. Sun."

She crossed her legs, locking her fingers around a knee.

"I was there, in his room, when Dr. Sun died, when he asked if he could be buried on the Purple Mountain near Nanking. So Chiang has built this mausoleum, which I hear is a monument to bad taste, and is planning a gigantic ceremony, moving Dr. Sun's remains from the West Hills in Peking, where Dr. Sun would never rest easy, to Nanking. He's sent Ching-ling's youngest brother to fetch her in Berlin so that she'll be present at the ceremony. No doubt the newsreels will whir and the rest of the world will think Ching-ling approves of her brother-in-law."

Cass sat nodding his head, smoking his foul-smelling cigar, rocking back and forth in the swing.

"Would you like to go to the ceremony and meet Ching-ling? I think, with a man of your stature as a guest, that I can arrange an interview with the Chiangs. I have met Mei-ling any number of times and was, after all, a guest at their wedding. They know of my friendship with Ching-ling but they also need the foreign press. I would like to see my dear friend Ching-ling again. It has been far too long." And, Chlöe thought, get word of Nikolai. She had heard nothing from him, ever. And nothing *of* him in well over a year. "I'd like you to meet her too. She's the most remarkable woman I've ever met. Perhaps the most remarkable person."

Cass's eyes were alight with excitement.

"Will you make arrangements, then? I feel like a kid. I want to see it all. It's another world, isn't it? I don't know why I haven't come before, instead of crossing to Europe every year."

"You probably were afraid I'd tell you our three years were long since up and I wanted to come home."

He glanced at her, narrowing his eyes. "I wonder if that's true. Suzi said it wasn't fair to leave you over here so long."

"You haven't really talked about her, you know. And I get letters from her less and less often. Out of sight, out of mind sort of thing? She hasn't mentioned this man she's been in love with for so long. God, it's been years. Tell me, why aren't they married?"

Cass took his glasses off and stared out through the willow at the river. He didn't say anything for a while, and then he said, still gazing into the distance, "It's me. My fault. The man's old enough to be her father."

Chlöe waited. But he said no more.

"So?" she prompted.

He looked at her. "So? Isn't that enough? She should have a family. Grant's forty-seven. He doesn't want a second family. His two kids are nearly grown. Also, he lives in St. Louis."

"Do you mean to tell me that's reason enough, your objections, to keep Suzi from marrying him? She mustn't love him very much. Does she see anyone else at all?"

"She used to. But she says no one can compare with him. No. She spends all her time at work, which, of course, is a benefit to me. I do worry about her. Her life seems very narrow. And yet I love having her live at home."

"My God, Cass, can't you hear yourself? What are you doing to her, and to yourself? It sounds like you can't bear the thought of your beautiful daughter in bed with an older man, that's what. She's almost thirty. I wouldn't quite call his being forty-seven old enough to be her father."

"Practically. I'm only three years older."

"Don't you love her, for heaven's sake?" Chlöe's voice took on a combative tone. "Cass, I can hardly believe this of you. You're robbing Suzi of happiness she could be having."

"Chlöe, he'll be dead long before she is, leaving her a widow in the prime of life."

"Jesus God almighty, Cass." This made Cass sit up straight. He had never heard Chlöe talk like this. "She might as well be a widow now, for all she has. She's in the prime of life now. What does she *do* with her life?"

Cass looked at her as though he'd never thought about this. "She works."

"Just like you? Come on, Cass. She's still young. How can you let yourself wield so much influence over her? Don't you care about her happiness? For heaven's sake, give her your blessing to do anything she wants. Even if it doesn't make her happy, she has a right to try it. Oh, Cass, let's stop talking of this now. It feels like chalk scratching on a blackboard. I don't want to be angry with you."

He cocked an eyebrow and stood up, walking over to her. "Is that what you are? Angry with me? I don't want you to be either. Next to Suzi, you're my favoritest woman."

She smiled and, reaching over, took his hand. "Tomorrow I'll make arrangements for a trip. If we're going to Nanking, you ought also to see Peking. It's not like any other Chinese city. Probably not like any other city anyplace."

He squeezed her hand. "I'd like to see countryside as well as cities. But, while you're planning our itinerary, how about me pouring us drinks?"

She smiled up at him.

"Despite some rather awesome faults, you're one of *my* favoritest people in the whole world. And you have arrived here at a time when I *need* you. Thanks for just being."

"I like to be needed." He raised his glass. "I like that very much. Especially by you."

# CHAPTER 47

"Chiang is very clever," Ching-ling said. She was looking into Cass's eyes, but she was holding Chlöe's hand and absentmindedly stroking it. Chlöe thought her friend looked haunted, as if she could stand a good meal and some tranquility. "He had crowds meet me every-place."

"Chiang Kai-shek arranged for crowds to meet you?" Cass asked. "That doesn't make sense to me."

Ching-ling shook her head. "The last stop in China for the Trans-Siberian is in Harbin. I was astonished to see crowds waiting for me. Flowers were pressed upon me. For a moment I thought it really was for me. But how did they know I was coming? No, Chiang is milking my return for all the publicity he can get."

Cass, obviously as fascinated with her as was everyone who came into her presence, leaned forward, his elbows on his knees. "You'd think after your statement from Berlin he would choose to ignore you."

Ching-ling's smile was melancholy. "Do you think the press of the world is bothering with me? Even though my stay in Moscow disillusioned me completely about the Bolsheviks, the Western world is so enamored of Chiang and my sister that they see me as a Red zealot and ignore me."

"I'll run this interview verbatim," Cass assured her.

Ching-ling shrugged. "That may be, but who will read it? They're so in love with these new leaders, they don't even believe in all the atrocities. They don't understand or care what is going on here."

Cass nodded. "That may be," he agreed. "To most Americans, China might just as well be another planet."

Ching-ling turned to Chlöe and reached out to hug her. "And to think it is an American whom I feel has become my true sister."

"I've worried so about you," responded Chlöe, basking in the nearness of her friend.

"You're going to leave China, aren't you?" Ching-ling looked into her eyes. "Now that I've returned you're going to leave. Is that true? I feel it in my bones."

Chloe nodded. "I have no reason to remain here. I want to go back. I want to go where it's clean and there aren't ravaging diseases and where there's no war. I want to see my family."

Ching-ling nodded. "I feared that. I was afraid I would lose the only sister I feel close to." She squeezed Chlöe's hand. Then she turned back to Cass. "Well, ask me what you want and I'll answer as well as I can."

"Would your husband have been pleased with the ceremonies today?"

Ching-ling's laugh was brittle. "Eighty thousand square meters of marble? That big sign on the arch as you enter, proclaiming PHIL- ANTHROPIC LOVE. The long tree-lined corridor with that inscription of his, saying 'The world belongs to the people.' And all those steps leading up to the mausoleum?"

"To say nothing," Chlöe interrupted, "of all those cupolas and that iridescent blue roof."

"It is ugly," Ching-ling agreed. "They've made a mockery of all Dr. Sun's sayings, scattering them around on the walls and put- ting his flag on the ceiling. He would rather be buried in an un- marked grave and have his beliefs put into action than have all this fuss with empty words. My brother-in-law is merely trying to curry favor with those who started the revolution. He does not believe these things. I shall continue to speak out loudly against him when- ever anyone listens."

"That doesn't sound wise to me," Cass counseled.

"Wisdom is not how one lives one's life. At least not how I live mine. I would rather die and be true to what I believe than live a lie. I do not want to silently witness what that man and his Green Gang are doing to China."

"Do you think he's the Green Gang's puppet?" Cass asked.

"Whether he is jerking the puppet strings or they are is imma- terial. He is out for personal glory and power and cannot get either without the backing of his thugs. None of them cares a whit about China, only what they can pocket or who they can control. They *are* controlling the Western powers now, though your country will not believe that. The West doesn't think any Orientals are smart enough to pull the wool over their eyes."

It was true, Chlöe thought. Americans thought of Chinese as coolies or as thugs in tong wars in San Francisco.

"Here," Ching-ling said, "take this down as a direct quote. There have been betrayals and a complete distorting of the Nation- alist movement. The greatest blot upon China is that this shameful counterrevolution is being led by men who have been intimately associated in the public mind with the Nationalist movement. These men are trying again to drag China along the familiar road of petty wars for personal gain and power."

Later, Chlöe asked Cass what he'd thought of all the people he'd met that day. They were sitting in Chlöe's hotel room, she scrunched up on the bed with a pillow behind her and Cass sitting in the one straight-backed chair. He was drinking scotch. It had been a long and tiring day.

He thought before he answered. "I can't help but be impressed with the Chiangs. She is gracious and exceedingly beautiful, though not so much so as her sister. The Soong sisters are astonishingly good looking, aren't they?"

"So you've fallen in love with them too?" Chlöe hugged her knees.

"Chlöe, I *am* a man, and one who enjoys looking at beautiful women. However, these are not just lovely-looking women, there's something magical about them, magnetizing. But I find something not quite sincere about Madame Chiang. She lacks warmth, though makes up for it with graciousness. She's always onstage. She doesn't know what the word *suffering* means, does she? Yet it is written all over Ching-ling's face. And I get the idea it is not just her own private suffering, but she bears the cross for all of China. Both women are exquisite.

"What I found most interesting, in a country where romantic love is next to unknown, is that Mei-ling loves her husband."

Chlöe cocked her head. "You think so? It's strictly a marriage of power joining hands. He had two wives, you know, and numerous concubines. It's still rumored that he has many women."

"Nevertheless, I think his wife is in love with him. And he kept looking for or at her all the time. Of course, she serves as his translator, but he doesn't need that with his own people. He seemed, I thought, to seek her approval with each step."

"Hmm, that's interesting. You think he needs her?"

Cass shifted in his chair and crossed his legs. "What will Ching-ling do now?"

"She told me she's going back to her home on the Rue Molière in Shanghai. She has not been happy away from China."

He put his glass on the table. "I'll wake you early," he said, standing. "Doesn't the train for Peking leave at the crack of dawn?"

"Ten is the crack of dawn?"

"Oh, well. I'll still wake you early."

"Peking may no longer be the capital of the Celestial Kingdom, but its aura of grandeur is without compare," Cass said. "No place in Europe can equal it. Maybe Athens, but not even Rome."

"It *is* impressive," Chlöe said, glad to be sitting after their tour. They'd taken it all in—the Forbidden City, Tian An Men Square—

all the places she'd first seen with Nikolai and Slade as they whiled away their days waiting for Dr. Sun to die. They sat in one of the Russian tearooms Nikolai had so enjoyed, and she told Cass of that winter six years before.

She hadn't realized that she'd lost Peking and was talking more of Ching-ling and Nikolai until Cass interrupted her.

"Was he in love with you?"

Chlöe's train of thought broke. "Who?"

"The Russian. Zakarov."

She wasn't ready to tell him yet. She would, in time. She wanted to share these things with Cass, but up in Lu-shan, when they were alone. Not when she wanted him to concentrate on Peking.

"At that period he didn't have the time for love." The balalaika's strings tightened Chlöe's heart as she remembered the evenings they sat here, talking long into the cold night.

Cass smiled as he sipped his vodka. "That's not what I asked. You've gotten very good, you know, at not answering questions directly."

Chlöe found herself slouching in her chair, her fingers wrapped tightly around her teacup. "Oh, Cass, my life has been so strange here. So much of it I didn't even know about. Funny, not to know about your own life, isn't it? I'll get around to telling you."

He reached across the table, his palm up. She smiled and put her hand into his. His fist closed around it. "Chlöe, my dear. You can take all the time you want, but know that I'm here, or wherever, when it is time. And that I care. I care a great deal."

"Maybe I'm afraid of boring you. I mean, what is one insignificant life when millions are starving or dying because of floods or pestilences or in war?"

"No life is insignificant. And certainly not yours. At least, not to me."

"Has your life ever been valueless or meaningless to you?"

Cass thought a moment. "I wondered, after Jane died."

He'd never talked of his wife, and Suzi had been so young when her mother died, she could scarcely remember her. Chlöe sat watching him, seeing his eyes revert to a time and place she could never go. "I loved her. From the first minute I laid eyes on her, when we were both seventeen, I loved her. There was never a minute that I didn't love her. She was the most wonderful human being imaginable. She filled my life with light."

"So no other woman has ever been able to compare?"

His eyes came back into focus. "Something like that. But it was a long time ago."

"And there've never been other women?"

"Chlöe, Jane died when she was twenty-six. So was I. I'm fifty years old. I'm relatively normal and, at least as far as being a male is concerned, healthy. Of course there have been other women. Many of them, over the years."

"But none you wanted to marry?"

"None I wanted to marry. That's right. It would have to be someone very special."

Chlöe said, "Let's get out of here, okay?" She stood up, not even waiting for him to finish his drink. Lately she found life infinitely confusing. "Let's walk, and I'll tell you about other interesting things. I haven't told you about what *I* think of Mao or of Snow Leopard."

"Snow Leopard? The one who—raped you? I have tried not to even mention that, but I've wondered what kind of scars it left. Are they still raw?"

"Let me talk about him politically first," she said as they went out into the hot, dusty sunshine. "I wish I knew where he was. He's someone I'd like you to meet. But I've no way to contact him. He could be anywhere, anywhere there are Japanese to fight. Sometimes I think he is the sole hope for this country."

"I thought that was General Lu-tang." When she didn't respond, Cass added, "You like neither Chiang nor Mao."

"I don't like Chiang, that's certain." She walked briskly despite the sultriness of the afternoon. "I don't know how I feel about Mao. I've a feeling he's too intellectual to be a leader. I think he's idealistic, and not quite in touch with reality. I don't see him as a leader of a country. I like many of his ideas. When we saw him at his mountain fortress, he claimed women and equality are part of his vision of China, yet I found him rather chauvinistic, in the sense I thought he used women for his own means."

She began to talk of her experiences, not only with Mao and General Lu-tang, as she now called Snow Leopard, but also escaping Canton with Ching-ling and Nikolai all those years before, and how she helped them in Wuhan. But she never touched on her feelings about losing three children, or mentioned Slade's unfaithfulness, or her own with Nikolai, or anything close to her heart. Cass observed her throughout all this, his eyes searching for some expression in her eyes or her voice, but he found none.

When they reached their hotel, she said, "Remember, we're dining with the American ambassador tonight. He won't be here in Peking much longer. The embassies have to move down to Nanking. As you can tell, Nanking can't compare with Peking. I don't think any of the foreign embassies will appreciate the move."

"You said you had a surprise for me."

"I do." She smiled. "We're leaving tomorrow and heading toward my favorite place in the whole country. I'm going to take you to Lu-shan before we go home."

"Lu-shan?"

"You'll find it a magical place."

# CHAPTER 48

Lu-shan was not the same, though its mystical quality was intact. Bearers still padded up the narrow mountain trail in their bare feet, and the sedan chairs swung crazily out over the hairpin turns, but changes were in the air. Dozens of men labored at the bottom of the mountain, beginning to build a road so that cars could ascend its heights.

When they reached the top, long after the sharp cool air hit them at the halfway mark, Chlöe knew this was the last time she would come to Lu-shan. The Chiangs were building a summer home up here, to please Mei-ling, so that she could escape the hot summers of the Yangtze Valley. They were sitting on the rocky promontory overlooking the valley, the spot that was Ching-ling's favorite. They could see for hundreds of miles. Cass reached out for Chlöe's hand, and she turned her gaze from the valley to him as he stated evenly, "You don't hate China."

"No? Then what do I feel? Do you know what this country has done to me?"

"I think you love it," he said, smiling. "That's why you get so upset. You don't want this country that has become so much a part of you to be destroyed when you see its potential."

"I don't love it," she said, taking her hand from his and lying back, her hands pillowed under her head.

"You won't fit in back in the States, d'you know that?" When she didn't answer he said, "I've an idea I've been tossing around this past week. Come home with me and see your family. Visit with Suzi. Stay with us in Chicago a bit. But come back to China. Come back and be . . . be 'my man in China.' "

He let it hang there.

"What you gave to those stories," he continued as she stared at him, her mouth agape, "that you wrote for Slade was humanity. People didn't read just hard facts, they saw and felt. The Chinese became real. They became heroic people. Chlöe, you love them. You *care*. Come back here and write whatever you want. You won't have to cover the stories all the other reporters do if you don't want to. I'll give you carte blanche. Travel around. Give Americans the chance to believe in the Chinese people, see them in a different light than they ever have. Come," he reached out his hand again, "work for me."

Chlöe sighed, thinking, I don't want to stay here. I want to go back to America. She looked at Cass, his auburn hair streaked with gray, as were his eyebrows and his sideburns. More distinguished-looking than handsome. Always imposing, grand really. She remembered how impressed she'd been when Suzi had first introduced her to him. He'd emanated power. He still did, though on this trip she saw, for the first time, the enthusiasm generated by the little boy in him. He took no pains to hide it, to act blasé. He who had mingled with presidents and other heads of state, whose social circle included the chairmen of the Detroit motor companies, those who headquartered in Grosse Point, and governors and senators. Though he always wore a patina of sophistication, he had never lost his immense enjoyment of whatever he was doing. Chlöe turned on her side, leaning on an elbow, and said, "Cass Monaghan, you may possibly be the nicest person in the whole world."

"What brought that on? Offering you a job?"

"Just looking at you. I think I've thought you were *one* of the nicest ever since I first met you. God, how long ago was that? Twelve years?"

He nodded. "I remember when you were just a little girl."

"Little? I wouldn't call seventeen little."

"Young, then. Very young. Now look at you."

"No," she said, leaning her head back against the pillow of her hands and staring up into the sky. "Tell me. Have I changed so much? Am I no longer the girl you knew? What's so different?"

He was silent for so long that she turned her head to study him. He was looking down at her. "I don't know," he said finally, "that I can answer you. In some ways you are the you I knew and loved as my daughter's best friend. Even then I saw the potential in you."

"The potential for what?" she interrupted.

He shook his head. "I'm not sure. But I knew you were never going to be like others. Even then you were destined not to travel any of the conventional paths. I sensed it. I hoped for it. I wanted to throw you into the lion's den, for I knew you'd emerge, bloodied perhaps, but unbowed. I knew the lions could never devour you, that you would grow from the process. . . ."

"You wanted me to jump into Slade's den, didn't you?"

Cass smiled. "I plead guilty. Was I wrong? You're not sorry you did, are you?" When she didn't answer, he nudged her. "You're not sorry, are you?"

Now, she thought, now is the time to tell him. Tell him how Slade started having an affair before they'd been married even a year, how he had two half-Chinese children with another about to be born, how he had refused to touch her after the incident of the Blue Express. And should she tell him of Nikolai too? Of loving a Russian Communist whom she hadn't seen in more than three years? That she'd slept with him before she even knew of Slade's Chinese woman? What would Cass think of her then?

"My answer will take a long time."

"Fortunately, we have days." He looked over the wide valley, and leaned back against the tree.

She told him everything . . . all about Slade and the truth about Snow Leopard. Told him about Nikolai and that her heart was thousands of miles away, she didn't even know where. Though as time passed, the sharpness of Nikolai did too. It was as though he, too, had died, for she knew they would never see each other again. It wasn't that she yearned for him, though she kept him in her heart. She thought she had done with mourning for him. Ching-ling said she didn't know where he was. Chlöe told Cass all about it—about everything, about the two little girls and the pregnant woman back in her house. She left nothing out.

When she finished, she found herself crying, tears streaking her cheeks, standing up, her back erect against the tall tree, looking out across the valley flooded with late afternoon sunlight. Cass was still seated where he'd been when she began the story two hours before.

When he realized she was done with it, that she had stopped the monologue, he stood up and walked over to her, gathering her in his arms, whispering, "Oh, my dear, I had no idea. I didn't know."

They spent the next two days walking the paths along the mountaintop, stopping to pick lavender and yellow wildflowers that grew in the shade, talking of everything and of nothing. Most of the houses were vacant, for many of the missionary families had been sent home. This was not a safe time to be in China. One or two of the houses were occupied, but it would be another year before the influx of Chinese would begin. These stone houses were too small for those taking over the reins of China. Chlöe and Cass had Lushan almost to themselves. Themselves and the birds.

They found two books in the cottage where they were staying, both in English. One was the poetry of Walt Whitman.

"Surprising that a missionary would keep his poetry." Cass smiled, opening it to read to Chlöe in the lamplight. " 'I celebrate myself . . .' " He looked over at her. "Do you mind if I read to you?"

She shook her head.

She closed her eyes and listened to his voice, its deep, rich baritone winding itself around her. When he finished, she said, without even realizing she'd been thinking it, "I wish I'd been Jane."

The room was silent, so quiet that for a second she thought the world had ended. She opened her eyes to find him staring at her across the room in the lamplight.

"For my part," he said, his voice low, "I'm glad I never was Slade. I could never have done to you what he's done."

"I know," she said. "I know you couldn't."

"I don't know when I've ever had more perfect days than we're having here. You've made me forget the rest of the world exists. I don't know how Slade could ever have wanted anyone other than you." He got up and crossed to her.

The lantern flickered shadows across Cass's face, and she reached out to brush her hand along his cheek. His hand wound around hers, and she reached down to kiss it. She felt his grasp tighten and then he let go. Now when she looked at him she couldn't read his eyes.

"I want the next three days to drag by," she said. "I want this never to end. I don't want to go back to the real world."

He didn't even smile at her.

She stood and leaned down to brush her lips lightly along his cheek. "Good night," she said, for she was afraid something she'd done had broken the spell under which she'd felt.

He still didn't answer. She left him sitting silently. As she neared the door he blew out the light.

Something had happened, was happening, she thought as she stood by her window, staring out into the moonlight. There was no sound, no rustle of breeze, no cry of birds, no breathing. Though the high mountain air was chilly, she stood naked by the window, her hands on the windowsill, leaning out, inhaling the smell of pines.

It was several minutes before she became aware that he was standing in the room, watching her. She turned around, seeing only a shadow by the door. It was at least a minute before she heard him ask, "Chlöe?"

She raised her arms, holding them out to him. In a second he crossed the room. She felt herself pulled into his embrace, felt his kisses on her neck, on her eyelids, felt herself being carried to the bed, felt his mouth upon hers, his tongue gently touching her lips as he began to pull at his clothes. Then his tongue on her nipples, his hands on her body, and she pulled him to her, kissing him with an abandon she hadn't felt since Nikolai, feeling her body come to life under his touch, trembling with passion at his kisses.

Cass made love with a mixture of tenderness and passion Chlöe had never experienced. He brought her to shivering ecstasy time after time, making love to her as not even Nikolai had. He touched her in places no one had touched, his tongue exploring places she hadn't even known were there. She moaned with exquisite pleasure, hoping he would never stop.

But eventually he had to. He lay on his back, panting, and reached for her hand. They lay next to each other until she heard his breathing become even, and then she rose to her knees, beginning to do to him what he had done for her. The only thing he said was "Christ God almighty!" And she thought, Yes. That's what it is.

They lay entwined in each other's arms, breathing each other's breath, kissing each other with long kisses. Cass's hands were urgent yet tender, his kisses were hard while his lips were soft, his body fit against and into hers as though they had been made for each other.

They tried more positions than Chlöe imagined possible, all of them exciting her until she had no energy left and lay under him, saying at last, "Cass."

He rolled from her onto his side, his arm across her, and they slept until the cool, clear light of morning awakened them, and then they made love again, gently, leisurely, and Chlöe said, "Is it possible I've died and gone to heaven?"

Cass laughed loudly and uproariously, but it didn't break his rhythm, and Chlöe thought, Ah, a man who can laugh in the midst of making love. At last. The evenness of his in and outness brought her to a shaking climax, to a sob that came from deep within her as he moaned and she knew that he, too, had come.

They walked through meadows, following a sparkling stream as it wound through the forest, and picked flowers. They smiled and said nothing whatever that made sense. They stopped to kiss each other, and when they returned to the little house for lunch, they took one look at each other and headed for the bedroom instead.

They spent two days like this, laughing in and out of bed, holding hands, reading to each other, kissing each other as they made omelets or fried rice. Chlöe had never been so aware of her body. It was alive, electric.

" 'I sing the body electric . . .' " Cass quoted Whitman.

On the day the bearers were scheduled to return, as they lay in bed in the morning, Cass said, "I rescind my offer."

"What offer?" Chlöe asked, aware of nothing but his body, of being close to him, of the lovemaking they were starting. She leaned up and kissed his nipples, running her tongue across them, running her fingers down the insides of his thighs.

"Don't stay in China. Please, darling Chlöe, don't stay in China. Come home and marry me. Or marry me and come home. Come live with me and be my wife. Come let this continue forever."

# CHAPTER 49

"Just as I was getting excited by the idea of becoming a famous reporter," Chlöe said.

"You know what pains me, don't you? When I realize how I've

contributed to Suzi's unhappiness over the years. Ironic, isn't it, that I become the victim of just what I've made her the victim of?"

"Age, you mean?" Chlöe cocked an eyebrow.

"Of course. I've stood in judgment of her and Grant, then I fall in love with someone my daughter's age. There's no other word than ironic."

Chlöe smiled. "How about poetic justice?"

Cass nodded. "That too. I shall go home and spend the rest of my life trying to make it up to her. I'll hire Grant away from St. Louis. Make him *my* managing editor!"

"I have to admit I never thought that an older man would be the best lover imaginable."

"Am I?" His eyes smiled, teasing.

She shook her head. "Without peer. Cass, you're so expert, I bet you've spent your life in bed." She turned to laugh at him. "Now, don't tell me. I don't want to know. I just want you to know I've never spent five days like we've had. And the last three have been spent mainly in bed. Right now I feel like that's where I want to spend the next fifty years."

"In bed with me?" He got up from the chair where he'd been sitting and walked over to put his arms around her, leaning over to kiss her neck as she stood at the stove.

"In bed with you. Or standing up with you. Or sitting on you. Or lying in the woods with you. Wherever. But making love with you. I suddenly feel I can't get enough of it. Enough of being touched by you, kissing . . ." She turned her head to kiss his cheek. "I feel craving, and oversexed, and ecstatic. I feel alive. Something I haven't felt in years. Maybe I've never felt this way."

"I've always loved you," he said. "You know that. Next to Suzi, I've loved you the most. I thought you were a second daughter. Now I'm in love with you, head over heels crazy in love with you."

He reached across the table and put his hand on her arm. "Marry me, Chlöe. It may not be fair to you, because I'll die long before you. But I think, I really think, I can make you happy for whatever time we have. I want to erase what Slade's done to you and show you how much fun marriage can be."

"How do you think Suzi would react to my becoming her step-mother?"

"How anyone else feels is irrelevant to me. All I know is I want you by my side. Right now I feel I *need* you by my side for the rest of my life."

"I'm not going to say no. But I'm not quite ready to say yes. Will you let me think about it? I mean, we have all this time ahead of us. It's not that I don't love you. I do. I've always thought you're wonderful. You're one of the first people, maybe the first, to make me think—"

Cass interrupted her. "My God, if you have to rationalize it!"

She reached over to him. "Hey, I've just come out of a marriage that, well, I don't know what it was. Where I felt betrayed, where I was ignored so that I was thrown into another man's arms. That's not quite fair of me, is it? Though I do think had Slade not rejected me for so long, I'd not have fallen in love with Nikolai. I'd never have let myself be put in those circumstances. Anyhow, I've just gone through weeks of hating men. . . ."

"Because of this Chinese woman in Slade's life?"

Chlöe nodded. "Of course. I don't like the feelings marriage gave me. I don't like the idea that my feelings and attitudes toward life were colored by what he did to me. Maybe I want time to find out who I am, if I'm anybody except somebody's wife. You know, ever since you suggested I be your 'man in China,' I've been tossing it over in my mind. I know China. I've been your China hand here for over a year already. Now, I rather like the idea of trying something strictly on my own."

"Hoisted on my own petard!" Cass said, and hit his forehead with his fist.

"Not necessarily," Chlöe said, reaching for his hand. "You tempt me in many ways. To accept your first offer and be on my own. And didn't I hear you say you could predict fame?" She smiled at him.

"A woman reporter who brings the real China, the human Chinese, the truth as she sees it, to Americans? Someone with your—not only writing ability—but ability to cut through the external crap, the superficialities, and get to gut level?" Then he stopped, his eyes searching hers. "I'm talking myself out of having you, aren't I?"

She shook her head. "No, but you're making me weigh things. On the other hand, Cass, I do love you. I love you in so many ways, more ways than I've ever loved anyone."

"But romantic is not one?"

"Don't do that to yourself or to me," she said, her voice brittle. "I'm thinking out loud, not rejecting. Cass, I shall never ever reject you. I shall always be part of your life if you want me there. I just don't know in what way. Romantic? What do you think this last week has been? The most romantic week of my life, the stuff movies are made of. You've made me feel like the most exciting, desirable woman in the world.''

"You are," he interrupted.

"You've made love to me and taken me to heights I never even dreamed of. Oh, Cass, you are the greatest lover the world must ever have known, and that's including Rudolph Valentino.''

He laughed. "That's because you've made me feel like a boy again.''

"No boy could make love the way you do," she said, leaning across the table to kiss him. "God, just touching you and I'm ready to go back to bed.''

"Too late," he said. "The bearers will be here in a moment.''

"I know. But I want you to know, I'm thinking of both your offers. The two best offers I imagine I'll ever have in my life. It's just the one may be too soon after Slade's death and all I've learned because of it. I'm not sure I'm ready for another marriage. But I'll come back with you. I need to get out of China, if not forever at least for a while. I need a vacation, and we can spend the month on the boat making love every night—and maybe all day long— can't we?''

"I've rather been envisioning a lifetime of that.''

"Sounds good," Chlöe said, standing. "And not just that, Cass. Talking with you, listening to you, just being near you is wonderful. I don't want you to think, if I opt for this second offer of yours, that it's just because you're so good in bed." She laughed and leaned down to kiss his cheek.

"I don't really care what your reasons are," he said. "Just come let us share our lives.''

They heard the bells signaling the arrival of the bearers at the mountaintop. Chlöe looked around. She knew she would never come back to her magic mountain. Never recapture the happiness she had experienced here once with Ching-ling and Damien and this time with Cass. Three of the people she loved most in the world. The only one of her children she had ever known. The woman, and the man, who had influenced her most in life.

They told the captain of the downriver steamer that they were married so they could share what passed in China for a stateroom. They were the only Westerners and were left to themselves. Chlöe observed the energy Cass put into everything, even looking at the ever-changing shoreline, watching him as coolies strung ropes around their shoulders and pulled them from either side of the river, through the narrow rapids.

"In China everything is manual labor, isn't it?" he said.

Chlöe nodded. She'd become so used to it she forgot what any other way of life might be like. She liked the way his eyes shone with excitement. She studied his strong profile, the jutting jaw, the aquiline nose, the bushy eyebrows. Even his glasses did not detract from his appealing look. They were part of him, and she hardly saw them.

I think I may just do it, she thought, smiling as Cass leaned over the railing, watching the long ropes the coolies pulled, listening to their chanting. I don't care about being famous. Funny, that had hung in the air, dangling in front of her, ever since he'd said it. To be someone. Not just someone's wife. But someone in her own right. Yet as she looked at him, enjoying himself so immensely, as his enormous appetite for life rubbed off on her, she thought, Maybe he's what I want.

And no matter what he thinks, I don't love China. And China doesn't need me. Maybe Cass does. He could be happy with a woman again. With me.

She reached out and put an arm around his waist. He looked over at her, grinning, and put his hand on hers, his gaze turning back to the river.

Tranquility washed over Chlöe. It lasted exactly fifty-two hours.

# CHAPTER 50

"I had to hire a wet nurse," explained Su-lin, holding the tiny infant. Chlöe had forgotten babies could be so small. "She vanished before the baby was a day old. Didn't even say good-bye. Just left baby and girls."

The two little girls peeked shyly from behind the bamboo clump, Plum Blossom holding tight to her sister's hand. Jade's eyes were large, round, questioning. Was there fear there, Chlöe wondered, or just uncertainty?

There was fear inside her, that much she knew. Cold, implacable fear. She tried to ignore the gooseflesh that lingered, having jumped to the surface when she'd learned the news. What was she to do with these three children—these children of her husband's?

She turned to search for an answer in Cass's eyes but found as much bewilderment there as in her own heart. As Su-lin held out the baby, Chlöe shrank back.

"It won't bite," she heard Cass whisper.

"When did this happen?" Chlöe asked, letting Su-lin plump the little boy in her arms. God, a baby felt so good, smelled so—so like a baby. Its almond eyes seemed out of place with such pale skin. She wondered if Jade had looked like this when she was born.

"Eleven days, it's been," said Su-lin. "I helped her. It was close to morning."

Chin-Chen didn't want the girls or the baby in her room that night, so Su-lin brought them all to the house and let the girls sleep in Chlöe's bed. She took the baby into her and Han's bed. In the morning when Su-lin went to Chin-Chen, she was gone. Her clothes were gone, and there was no sign of her, nor any sign she'd ever been there.

The baby cooed against Chlöe's breast and her lips brushed the soft downy hair on his head. He might have been mine, she thought.

She saw two little figures move beyond the pampas grass, saw the girls, still holding hands, come out of hiding and walk toward her. Jade stopped about six feet from her, her liquid eyes meeting Chlöe's, holding her gaze. After a moment, Chlöe handed the baby back to Su-lin and held her arms out to the girls. Plum Blossom rushed into them, but Jade hesitated. "Are we to call you auntie or number two mother?"

Cass watched silently, the outsider.

Later, after they all dined together and Chlöe rocked the baby to sleep, and after she tucked the little girls into bed, kissing each of them on the forehead, after Jade had thrown her arms around her neck and said, "I am glad you came home," after all that, Chlöe sat with Cass.

"I feel I've gone through an emotional wringer today," she said, kicking off her shoes.

"I too," he said, going to the sideboard and pouring himself a drink.

"I could use one too," Chlöe said. "Something stiff." He poured her the same scotch. Straight.

She took it from him and got up to walk out onto the verandah.

It was hot. The sticky humidity of all Shanghai summers. It was nearly August, the month and the weather that had taken Damien from her.

"That was a heavy sigh," Cass said, behind her.

She stared out at the night-lights on the slow-moving junks that floated on the river. Whole families lived on them. She heard voices in the distance, laughter, someone calling out.

"I wonder if the unexpectedness of it all—life, I mean—is what keeps us getting up mornings. We never know what the day will bring. Our plans never work out, do they? No matter what. Something always comes along. I think the most amazing thing about life is its surprise. It never, I mean never, has turned out as I expect it to."

"Are you complaining or philosophizing?" He put his arm around her and she leaned her head on his shoulder.

She didn't answer but said, "You may possibly be the most comforting person in the world. Just having you to lean on makes me feel able to cope."

He said nothing. He was inordinately quiet tonight, she thought. She ached with tiredness and turned her head to kiss his cheek. "I'm ready for bed. Want to join me?"

He turned, with his arm still around her, and led the way to her bedroom. Sensing she was too tired for lovemaking, he watched her undress and lie naked on the bed. Then he turned off the light and lay down beside her, not touching her, not even seeing her in the dark, but listening to her breathe. He said, "We *could* take them with us, you know."

When she didn't answer, he said, "You know that, don't you?"

In the morning she awoke as the roosters crowed, before dawn. And she thought, No, we can't. You've already said you don't want to start a family. You're fifty years old and these are three little children. The burden of three children would ruin whatever it is you feel for me. It wouldn't be good for a marriage.

She reached her hand down between his legs and stroked him gently. He murmured something unintelligible, but his arms came up and went around her, pulling her to him, and she kissed him, gently at first, until she felt him come awake and then she rolled on top of him, kissing his eyes and his ears and spreading her legs wide as his hands came up to her breasts. I don't want to give this up, she thought, her mouth hungry for him. This feels so damn good, I don't want to let him go, and then she stopped thinking as their lovemaking took on a frenzy, an urgency, a wildness. Almost a danger, she thought. It excited her.

Once she thought he said "Goddamn you," but imagined she had misheard him. Until it was all over, until they lay panting beside each other, until their ragged breathing quieted, and then he said it again. "Goddamn you. You're going to stay, aren't you?"

A few minutes later he took her hand gently and said, "Forgive me. I didn't mean it. I didn't mean goddamn you. I meant goddamn it all. Not you. I meant—mean—goddamnit. I've lost you. Just when I almost had you, I lost you. Before I even had a chance, huh?" And she was surprised to see the pain reflected in his eyes.

When he left two weeks later, he said, "It's a standing offer. Should I live to be one hundred, it's a standing offer."

"Guess for the time being I'll have to opt for fame." She tried to smile.

"I can at least tell myself you're still part of me," he admitted. "Part of the *Chicago Times* anyhow. I'll send you a monthly stipend, but don't stint. Anytime you need or want to take a trip, cover a story, see what the Japs are doing, find out what the heartbeat of the real China is like, don't hesitate. I'll phone your parents. They probably won't understand. And I'll urge Suzi and Grant to get together and even volunteer to wear a tux to give the bride away."

"Cass." She put her arms around him, pulling him closer in order to kiss him. "I have had the happiest months with you. You took me from tragedy to ecstasy. You made me forget my pain and see life with hope. You made me feel beautiful and exciting and desirable. Shhh, don't say anything. Let me finish." She put her head against the roughness of his tweed jacket and thought she might cry. "I think you are *the* most interesting man I've ever known. And the kindest. The most understanding. I love you. I really do. I have always and ever loved you. I shall always love you. Always. You are the most important person in the world to me."

"No," he said, "those kids are. But keep in mind I need you as much as they do. We could all live a life together. I'm willing to give it a try."

She shook her head, tears welling close to the surface.

"Tell Suzi I love you, will you? Tell her I love her too and I hope she and Grant will be as happy as we've been this summer. Tell my parents why I can't come home right now. Not about Slade, don't tell anyone they're his. Just say, oh, just say I'm involved with

Chinese orphans!" She tried to smile as tears started down her cheeks.

"Let me know what I can do to help," he said. "Whatever, wherever, whenever . . . I'll do it." He gathered her in his arms as they heard the steamship's horn blaring.

What do I do? wondered Chlöe. I don't know a thing about raising children. Between the wet nurse and Su-lin the baby was taken care of, so she was able to turn her attention to Jade and Plum Blossom. The three-year-old chatted all the time, her pudgy round face wreathed in smiles, though when she didn't get what she wanted she could pout and be silent, once even stamping her foot. Chlöe laughed at her though, so the little girl giggled and was soon over her discontent, hurling herself into Chlöe's arms.

Jade, however, was more serious. The night after Cass left, she asked, "Will you teach me to read?"

The next day Chlöe purchased a half-dozen elementary books, trying to remember how it was that she had learned Chinese. She remembered Mr. Yang, whom she hadn't seen in years. She wondered if he was still alive, for he had seemed old to her when she had first met him, what, nearly eight years ago? But she called the rickshaw boy and she and Jade climbed in, Jade clutching the books Chlöe had given her, and went in search of the man who had taught her so much.

Mr. Yang looked no older than when she had first met him. He no longer wore the silken gowns she remembered, but dressed in ill-fitting khaki pants, a sign of modernity and of the revolution. She wondered how such a Confucian scholar as he was adjusting to the changes of the last few years, but they did not speak of that.

"I would like you to teach this little girl to read," said Chlöe, pleased that he immediately remembered her.

"And to write," piped up Jade. She smiled and her dark liquid eyes captivated the old man, Chlöe could tell.

"I remember so well our times together," Chlöe said. "I hope you will educate Jade as you did me."

Mr. Yang bowed, as was his habit, and said, "I should be honored. But she is young to learn, isn't she?"

Ah, Chlöe thought. If I'd brought him a six-year-old boy he would not have said that. "She is very bright," she said, not knowing whether she was telling the truth. "And I will help her at home."

So, in the evenings, Chlöe sat with Jade, after Plum Blossom and the little boy, still unnamed, were in bed. The girl moved into the circle of Chlöe's arm, the lamplight shining on her silken black hair, and ran her finger across the written characters. Chlöe smelled her, the freshness of her right after her bath, and held her close as they read together.

After Jade went to bed, Chlöe stood watching her and Plum Blossom, her heart full. Then she went to Su-lin's room to take the baby from his cradle, rocking him on the verandah swing, until she nearly fell asleep, loving his smell too. Li, she thought. I shall call him Li. It's almost American. Lee.

The next day when Lou came to visit, as he did nearly every afternoon, he said, "I'm thinking of going up north, nearly as far as Manchukuo. Want to come?"

"What's happening up there?" Chlöe asked.

"There's a famine the likes of which the world has never seen," Lou answered. "It's in its second year. People are dropping dead like flies."

"I haven't even heard about it," she said.

"I know. That's why I'm going. I have word that over two million people have already starved to death."

"Two million?" She sat up straight. "Two million people starving to death? That can't possibly be."

"That's what I thought. Why don't we go see?"

"Don't look, Chlöe, just don't look," Lou urged as they walked along Changchun's streets. "There's nothing we can do to help."

She had spent yesterday throwing up. Nothing in her worst nightmares could have prepared her for the actuality. It was a land of naked horror.

Unseeing eyes stared out of faces that resembled skeletons. Some of the men dragged themselves along the streets, but most of them lay moaning, unable to summon forth energy enough to stand. Most of the women and the children had long ago been sold—or died.

"What really tees me off," said Lou, his lips set in a straight, severe line, "is that the rich are not starving but getting richer."

Dr. Robert Ingraham shrugged his shoulders. "What did you expect?" he asked, but it was a rhetorical question.

Lou had managed to get himself and Chlöe attached to a team from the China International Famine Relief Commission, financed by Americans. It was a group that dashed from one area of China to another, trying to alleviate famine caused by drought or by floods or by locusts. This time three amazing men headed the relief work, and all of them were exhausted. Bob Ingraham, a medical missionary, said, "I thought I'd seen the worst there could be. But I hadn't."

They were all risking their lives, for the people were typhus-ridden as well as starving.

Lou continued, as though talking to himself. "These peasants have sold not only their children but their land. Wealthy landlords zoom in like vultures and give them four or five days' worth of rice for land that's been theirs and their family's for a millennium. The rich have shipped their wives and families south, where they still live in the lap of luxury. While Rome burned, Nero fiddled. Well, China has its fiddlers too."

Suddenly a bony hand reached out and clamped itself around Chlöe's ankle, nearly tripping her. It was one of the rare women they'd seen, a woman lying in the midst of other bodies, holding a bundle to her breast, her face so sunken it more nearly resembled a skeleton than a human being. Her lips moved, but Chlöe could not hear her. As she started to lean down, Lou's hand grasped her arm. "Don't, Chlöe," he whispered. "Don't get near any of them. Don't get something awful and die on me here or I'll feel too guilty to go on living. I suggested this trip, after all."

She brushed away his hand and knelt down, trying to hear the woman, whose eyes barely focused. All she could understand was "please" and "save." With those words the woman's grip on Chlöe's ankle abated as her hand slid to the ground. The woman's eyes wavered and became lifeless.

"I've watched too many people die in this country," Chlöe said, talking to herself. "Too many people in my lifetime." And then she heard it, the faint wail from the woman's breast, from the bundle lying on top of her. Despite Lou's warning, Chlöe reached into the filthy rags, knowing before she saw it what she would see there.

It couldn't have been more than a few days old, if that. How that scrawny dying woman could have given birth, Chlöe couldn't imagine.

Lou saw it too. "Leave it," he said. "It doesn't stand a chance."

Chlöe stared up at him, not believing this was the Lou she had known so long and so well. The baby wailed faintly. Her hands reached out for it, disentangling the dirty cloths from the dead woman, feeling the coldness of the infant as her hands touched it. Maybe it was dying too. Perhaps Lou was right, but she couldn't just leave it there.

Dr. Ingraham reached out his hands, and she put the baby into them. He kept shaking his head. "It doesn't stand a chance as long as it's here where there's nothing to eat."

"I'll get on a train tonight," Chlöe said.

He looked at her and smiled. "Well, I suppose saving one life is better than nothing."

If the one life was someone you loved. She looked at the baby and thought it could have been one of hers. If someone had been able to reach out and save Damien . . .

"Hey, Chlöe," shouted Bob Ingraham, "come here."

Among the litter of dead and dying bodies crawled a child, certainly not more than eight or nine months old, not making a sound, so skinny that its ribs stuck through its skin, its stomach protruding like a bowling ball.

Lou put a hand on her arm to hold her back. "Chlöe, look, I understand how you feel, but these kids haven't a chance to grow up normal. Their brains have probably been affected by malnutrition, they'll have physical and psychological deformities that can never be surmounted." His voice had a pleading tone to it. "Let them die, Chlöe."

She held back for a moment, letting his words sink in and then threw off his hand. "I have to, Lou. I have to try. Just because you think I'm defeated before I even try doesn't mean I shouldn't try."

She heard him sigh and then he said, "Well, the least I can do is help you, then."

Dr. Ingraham said, "There can't be any more pitiable sight than watching somebody die right in front of you because there's no food. You can see every bone in their bodies. Look at the dead children, their crooked bones, their legs and arms no bigger than twigs, their tummies swollen not only from malnutrition but because they've been fed bark and sawdust, anything to keep alive. Funny, isn't it? Even in the extremities of such painful dying, a person fights to hang on. The women, what few women there are, just lie there, as though patiently waiting for death. Some of them have killed their kids so *they* don't have to suffer, yet can't take their own lives. You know, there's no one left with the strength to bury all these dead."

"Look at the buzzards." Lou pointed at the sky darkening with vultures.

"Bob," Chlöe said, "let's walk through this mess and see if there are other children."

"Bless you, Chlöe," he said, handing the nine-month-old to Lou as Chlöe carried the infant.

"Aren't these enough?" Lou asked. "What the hell are you going to do with more kids?"

# CHAPTER 51

It was not the last time Lou was to ask that question. Over the next four years, every time a baby was left by her gate, every time a mother came begging for Chlöe to take her child, whether it be a newborn or five years old, neither Chlöe nor Su-lin turned any away.

The chaos that was China in the 1930s led to more and more children in Chlöe's establishment. For establishment it had become. But it did not stop her far-ranging activities on behalf of the *Chicago Times.* For this she received help from two women who had been in China more than twenty years but of whom she had never heard.

They were teachers from a Methodist mission in Changshu, on the river between Shanghai and Nanking. They appeared at her door one day, two women in their early to mid-forties, each of them holding Chinese babies whom they had brought with them on their journey.

"We heard of you," said the pale blonde one, her eyes bluer than any eyes Chlöe had ever seen, "and hoped you might add these two to your collection. We're on our way home—"

The other one interrupted, "Home? Seems funny."

"I'm Dorothy Milbank," said the blonde one, "and this is Jean Burns. These were left with us at the mission, which is closed now. We're heading back to the States and thought . . . we hoped . . ."

Chlöe opened the gate wider. "Come in," she said, thinking to herself, How many more? For she saw the handwriting on the wall.

"When you sigh like that, I know it's more than you want, isn't it?" asked Jean.

"Sorry. I didn't even know I was doing it. Sometimes I feel it's more than I can handle. I have thirty-three children now. What's another two? I've rented the houses on either side of me and my servants and I manage, but . . . I also have to work to make enough money to feed this brood. It sometimes seems more than I'm capable of."

There was silence. And then Dorothy's tentative voice asked, ever so faintly, "Jean?"

And so Jean and Dorothy came to live, taking care of the children while Chlöe participated in the cauldron that was boiling all over the country.

She rushed to Manchuria when the Japanese seized that northern territory. Though Cass ran her account on page one, it was at the bottom right, not the lead story. Other papers throughout the world either ignored the invasion or carried it near the back of their papers. The League of Nations said they'd "investigate," but nothing ever came of that.

The Chinese, those who heard of it, and not many more heard of the invasion than had heard of the three-year famine that thankfully ended the same year, were outraged that Chiang Kai-shek did absolutely nothing, not even reprimanding the Japanese. His concentration was against the Communists, whom he saw as *the* threat to his power.

In 1932 Japanese businesses in Shanghai were attacked by rioters urging a declaration of war with Japan. They called for Chiang's resignation. Chiang followed his normal pattern when attacked. He withdrew. This always caught his assailants off guard. He and Mei-ling flew to their retreat in Lu-shan, taking the army with them. The army camped at the base of the mountain and no one could even approach the generalissimo. His deputy took over the reins of China only to find the treasury's coffers empty.

Big-eared Tu and his Green Gang saw to the bankruptcy of China, so that within a month Chiang was recalled to Nanking. He made his brother-in-law, T.V., vice premier and finance minister. T.V. made China solvent by negotiating immense loans from America, loans to industries in which the Soongs had large holdings. He and Mei-ling courted Americans well.

Chlöe saw Ching-ling only if she went to her house on the Rue Molière, for Ching-ling did not leave her home. It was not safe for her to do so, nor did she wish to participate in the country China had become.

Japanese were murdered or disappeared with no trace. On January 24, 1932, the Japanese Navy steamed up the Hwang Pu River, claiming they had come to protect their nationals in China. Even though Chiang's armies—reputed to be over two million men—vastly outnumbered the Japanese, he made no move to defend Shanghai until a week later when he sent a small contingent of fifteen thou-

sand men to Shanghai. Only one third of them lived to tell of it.
By March 3, six hundred thousand Shanghainese were homeless,
over twelve thousand were dead. All shops and trade of any kind
were at a standstill, and nearly a thousand businesses and factories
had been destroyed. Shanghai was paralyzed.

During that two-week period and shortly thereafter, Chlöe and
her friends acquired seven more children.

Around this time Daisy shocked Chlöe one afternoon. "I'm
leaving," she announced.

"What do you mean, you're leaving?" Chlöe stopped pouring
tea.

"I'm getting out. I've asked for and received a transfer. I'm
going to the embassy in India."

Chlöe realized her mouth wouldn't close. "Daisy!"

Daisy looked at her.

"What will I do without you?"

"Chlöe, for God's sake, I'm thirty-eight years old. I've got to
make some change in my life. I'm not too old to have a baby . . . if
I get far enough away from Lou, maybe I can get on with my life
instead of being like a phonograph needle stuck in a groove, unable
to move forward. I'm sick of it. What—you've been here how many
years?"

Chlöe had to stop and think. "Nine years."

"Well, I've been here fourteen. Being a secretary and translator
at the consulate fourteen years. Letting my life be stuck. It's not in
a groove, it's in a rut. I'm going."

Chlöe sat down, leaving the tea unpoured. "Does he know?"
She already felt a sense of loss.

"No." Daisy shook her head. "I'm going to him now."

Chlöe thought of Cass and their time together at Lu-shan, the
things he had done to her there. "You know, even though he's
impotent, there are things he can do . . ."

Daisy's laugh was bitter. "Do you think there's anything we
haven't tried? But it's no good, darling. I want out or I'll go
bonkers."

The day before she left, Daisy came to Chlöe. "Give me one of
your children, Chlöe. Let me take one of them out to safety. Let
me have someone else to think about. Let me be a mother."

———

Chlöe didn't see or hear from Lou for two weeks. When he returned, they never mentioned Daisy. But some life went out of Lou. It was as though he had to push himself to get through each day.

Unknown to the rest of the world, down in the mountains of southeast China, in the provinces of Fujian and Jiangxi, twenty thousand men, a couple of hundred children, and twenty-six women broke through the weak Nationalist blockade. Chiang's soldiers had gone home because they had not been paid for over a year. These were the Communists Chiang claimed to have eradicated. On October 16, 1934, they began a march that would take them 368 days and six thousand miles, a march to a part of China, the unpopulated northwest, that would free them from Chiang's continual harassment. It became a journey that changed the lives of one fifth of the world's peoples, though no one involved even imagined the scope that the march would take on. One of the important things that happened on this march was that Mao Tse-tung was elected to lead the Communists. Though no one even suspected it at the time, for the vast majority on the journey were young men, every one of China's leaders in the second half of the twentieth century participated in this march.

It took months for word to spread that an army of eighty thousand was traveling through China's most rugged terrain—over the mountains, across the rivers, and through the plains of China. Not even military strategists could predict that in order to get to the northwest from the southeast they would choose such a circuitous route that defied logic and baffled the Nationalist Army.

Japan, meanwhile, marched through the northern province of Chahar, making Sherman's march through Georgia tame by comparison. It merged its latest triumph and acquisition with the provinces of Hopei, Shantung, Shansi, and Suiyuan, fencing in Peking, which stood like an island surrounded on all shores.

Chiang's reaction, in 1935, was to offer the Japanese a friendship treaty. Return the Chinese lands it had taken and China would boot out all the Western powers, turning over to Japan all those territorial concessions and businesses that the Western powers now held.

However, the Japanese Army had tasted victory. They wanted the land, and they also wanted to subjugate the Chinese people. Treaties were too tame. They wanted all the riches that China had never mined, the riches that the West had exploited for so long. They wanted everything.

Foreigners left China in droves, consular officials sending their
wives and children back home. Japanese warships at the entrance
to the Hwang Pu were not reassuring.

More and more Chlöe stayed in Shanghai proper, which was
still the vice capital of the world . . . where for a few yuan a man
could have a young girl or boy, doing to them whatever he wished.
Sometimes the children were never seen again. Or, for a few yuan,
you could arrange for someone to disappear, to have someone's
Achilles tendons severed so he could never walk again, or arrange
an accident so he could never lift again, thus robbing him of a way
to earn a livelihood. Or you could arrange kidnappings, murders,
any sort of sadistic act that the human mind can come up with.
Vengeance and pleasure cost the same—a few yuan.

Chlöe became more and more protective of the children, especially Slade's. Between her and Su-lin they spoiled the baby, Li, to
pieces. At four he was chubby, smiling, sweet. Plum Blossom, with
her sunny disposition, prattled on constantly, playing with Han.
They ran around the yard inventing games, hiding in the pampas
grass.

But it was Jade who stole Chlöe's heart. She should hate this
child and what she represented, but Chlöe found herself thinking of
the young girl when she was away from home, searching for her face
and sober eyes when she entered the gate. There was an elfin quality
to Jade, who was ten by now. Her nose was always in a book, and
she accumulated knowledge like a sponge. At this age she was beginning to think abstractly, and Chlöe found her a delight.

And Chlöe told her of faraway places and of China's history,
and its geography, and talked with her for hours at a time, while
Jade, sitting across from her, watched the fire, and the shadows, and
the faraway look in Chlöe's eyes.

# PART IV
## *1935–1939*

# CHAPTER 52

"A beggar," said Su-lin, disgust evident in her voice, "insists on seeing you. He calls you 'Madame.'"

We barely have enough food for ourselves, thought Chlöe. Well, what's one more? "Did you take him to the kitchen?"

Su-lin shook her head. "It is not food he wants. It is you."

Chlöe felt too tired to get up. "What makes you think he's a beggar, then?"

"His clothes." Su-lin sniffed. "He smells like a horse." She tapped her fingers on the table at which Chlöe sat. "Let me send him away."

She knows better, Chlöe thought, and couldn't help smiling. She knows all too well I never turn anyone away. But if it's not food, what does he want? Su-lin welcomed only those with children. There were never too many children for Su-lin.

"Show him in." Chlöe sighed, thinking the world was getting to be too much for her. She'd spent the day roaming the streets, looking for a way out of the stranglehold in which the Japanese now held the city. If it were just herself and the other women, she could manage. But the Japanese required ration stamps. And she had none for the children.

No one was allowed to either leave or enter the city. The Japanese were polite, and smiled, but outside the city—especially after dark—gunshots could be heard, people trying to circumvent the prison Shanghai had become.

They would let her and her alone out, the Japanese lieutenant told her. Not into China, but on a ship bound for Japan or America. She was, after all, a U.S. citizen.

Su-lin said, "He refuses to come in. He awaits you at the gate."

Chlöe looked at her watch. It was after nine. No one called her to the gate this late at night, and it was never men who begged her to take their children. She reached into the drawer of the lacquered table and took out the small pistol that Cass had insisted on leaving, tucking it into the pocket of her sweater. She had taken to doing that at night. These were strange times.

In her cotton shoes she padded across the courtyard, aware of the odor of chrysanthemums and of the chill air of the moonless night. Standing outside the gate, clothes ragged and dirty, a scarf across his face, stood the tall man. They could not see each other's faces.

"Madame Cavanaugh?" He talked slowly, enunciating clearly. "It is I." He unwound the scarf from his face but she could not see him. "I have come to take you away from Shanghai."

She moved closer and looked up at him. "General Lu-tang?" It was a gasp. Snow Leopard, here?

"Pack as little as you need." He spoke softly but forcefully. "We must hurry if we are to meet my men by dawn."

She stared at him.

He reached out and put a firm hand on her shoulder. "Do you not understand?"

"Come," she said. "There's no one to see you. Come in and let me offer you a cup of tea."

His voice was impatient. "This is no time for amenities. This is war. No one is safe in this city that is surrounded by the enemy."

"I know," she said. People did disappear.

"My men and I are heading to the far north. I have come to take you with us."

Chlöe laughed in spite of herself. "Are you going to kidnap me again?" And then, realizing he was serious, she repeated, "Do come in." She turned, and he had no choice but to follow her.

As they entered the house, Chlöe nodded to Su-lin. "It's all right. He's no beggar. He's someone I've known for a long time."

A long time. It was nine years since he'd kidnapped the Blue Express. Seven since she'd last seen him, when she and Slade had gone up north to interview him. She turned to look at the face she would have recognized anywhere. That face like no one else's, the high cheekbones, the jut of the jaw, the sensuous lips that were now drawn tight. The only sign of the passage of time were crow's-feet around his now-bloodshot eyes.

Glancing around the room, he observed, "So, this is how foreigners live." He moved over and ran his fingers along the smoothness of the dark table and sat in the deep-cushioned chair. "Pack," he said, "only what you absolutely need."

"No. I can't." She found to her surprise that her hands had knotted together. I want to, she thought. I want to get out of here, away from being surrounded by Japanese, away from worrying how the children will eat, away from pleading eyes. Not only Su-lin but Dorothy and Jean expect me to care for them. They always think I'll come up with ideas.

"You have no children and no husband. You are free to leave."

How did he know all this?

"I'm not free." But for a moment wished she were.

He raised his eyebrows in question.

"I have forty-six children, all under twelve years of age, for whom I'm responsible."

"China has too many children." His voice was flat. "There will always be more children. That woman, the one who met me at the gate, she can care for them. Do not sacrifice yourself for children who have no future. Children who are not yours."

She looked at him. "Children *are* the future. I would rather you took one of them than me. I can take care of myself. They can't. And that woman—where I go, she goes. I love these people."

He sat, his legs sprawled wide in front of him. "I think," he said, "that many years ago we talked about love. It, like sanitation and philosophy, is for the affluent."

"I think not," said Chlöe, "or you would not be here, risking your life for me. You are putting another person ahead of your own safety, General. That is an act of love."

"I have wondered," and he permitted himself a small smile, "what has impelled me to such an uncharacteristic act."

Chlöe smiled in return. "It's called humanity."

"Whatever it is," he rose and moved several steps toward her, "it is wasting time to talk about it. Are you telling me you refuse to be rescued?"

She nodded. "I would appreciate being rescued, leaving this city that now terrorizes me. I would love to get away from the Japanese. I want to take my children far away—to safety. But I will not leave them, General."

His black eyes pierced through her.

"I do," she continued, "appreciate your thoughtfulness. In fact, I'm rather overwhelmed to realize you've even thought of me and have come so far out of your way."

"You saved my life once." They stared at each other. Then he bowed almost imperceptibly and, turning on his heel, walked from the room.

A man she hadn't seen in years offered to rescue her from this war zone and she turned him down? She knew he jeopardized his own life to come into Shanghai. Somehow he had infiltrated the enemy lines. He had come hundreds of miles south to make the gesture and would risk his life leaving as well.

She thought back to the first time she'd met him, when he'd told her he would spare lives if she would offer herself to him. Even then she had not been afraid of him. In the end, he had given her dignity.

The next afternoon at five, a toothless old woman knocked at the gate, asking for "the Madame." She thrust forth a dirty hand in which was wadded a piece of paper. She waited, her gums clapping together, as Chloe read:

*Have your children ready by midnight. Impress on them that they must make no noise. Pack only what each can comfortably carry. They will travel for many miles. Give this woman 50 li.*

It was not signed.

Seven hours in which to feed forty-six children and to get them ready to march when they would not even be ready to stay awake. Seven hours! Seven hours to change their lives.

Chlöe ran into the house, telling Su-lin to give the old woman fifty li.

"Fifty li?" exclaimed Su-lin.

"Just do it. Then find Jean and Dorothy. Feed everyone as quickly as possible."

Su-lin stared at her, her mouth hanging open.

Chlöe tossed her head. "Just do as I say." She wouldn't tell her yet and didn't want the cook to know. Didn't think anyone should know. She suspected it should all be done in utmost secrecy.

"Bed them all down the minute they've finished eating." Might as well let them get a little sleep. It would be better than none at all. She'd have them make bundles of their clothes, ones that could be slung around their necks. Of course, there were those too young to walk, and many too small to walk even to the city's border. She sat down at her desk. Make a list, she thought, of everything I can think of. After she'd done that she looked up, staring into space.

She put her head in her hands and wept with relief.

# CHAPTER 53

Every dawn the wagons that carried nightsoil littered all roads from the city. The hundreds of men who collected the excrement and refuse of China's largest city fanned out on the paths and dirt roads toward the outlying farms, where their cargo would be used as fertilizer.

The Japanese let them through, waving them on quickly so that the stench would soon pass. At precisely the same hour, in the time right before night became day, of the hundreds who earned their living carrying shit, thirty-two found their wagons missing. Each swore he'd been gone but a moment, into someone's garden, into the servants' quarters, wherever. But when they returned to their putrid wagons with yet another jar of foul-smelling refuse, they had disappeared.

That afternoon, around the countryside, scattered all over the western roads, thirty-two nightsoil wagons were found, each one far from the others.

Of the forty-six children, not one was heard to cry out, not one emitted a sound for the five hours it took to carry out the escape. Many vomited, however. And the women did too, except for Su-lin. The stench was unbearable.

Chlöe, huddled in the dark as she was pulled over paths worn smooth from years of bare feet padding along them, retched into the straw.

The cart stopped. She could tell the bearer had laid down the bamboo poles that rested on his shoulders. Could she move yet? Hands pawed at the straw covering her, and she felt herself being picked up. The still-dark sky was pale on the horizon, and she couldn't unbend her knees. Snow Leopard held her.

He had pulled her cart himself, like a coolie. She straightened her left leg and, holding on to the general, put her other foot onto the ground. Prickles of pain swept through her but were gone in a moment.

Snow Leopard's eyes scanned their surroundings before he said, "We must walk to the river."

They came to the wide, muddy river, yellow in the hazy morning sun, now edged above the horizon.

Snow Leopard turned to her. "The Japanese keep close watch on the river, so we can't take a barge down it. We will take sampans across it, timed irregularly, and they won't be able to tell whether we're fishermen or hawking vegetables. In order for nothing to look suspicious, this will take several hours. On the other side the rest of my men await."

Chlöe could tell by the sullen expressions on the faces of his men that they did not happily participate in this exodus.

"Are none of these men fathers?" she wondered, not knowing she had said it aloud.

Snow Leopard looked down at her. "Probably all of us are."

She arranged for Jean and Dorothy to be on the first sampans, each carrying two of the smallest children, so that they could organize the children on the other side. Reassure them. She'd stay on this side, she told Snow Leopard, until they'd all left safely.

Several began to whine . . . tired, hungry, uprooted. They looked across the river and could not see the other side. She could see disapproval in the soldiers' eyes. The general issued orders in a quiet voice, shoving a sampan off with a gentle push, waiting until it was out of sight before permitting another one to leave, pointing it up-stream. Boatmen with long poles silently glided from the reeds that hid them, their eyes unfathomable, bare from the waist up even in the morning chill, never saying a word.

"I've promised them a day's catch of fish on the other side," Snow Leopard explained.

"And some li too, I'd imagine," Chlöe said. The fishermen were endangering their own lives . . . If the Japanese discovered . . .

"No." He shook his head. "No li."

Then why? she wondered. And how had he arranged all this so quickly? It was the first time she had ever seen speed and efficiency in operation in all her years in the Orient.

His eyes met hers. "I will go now so that I can make all ready for leaving. You will come last. Then we shall know that all are safe, and we shall be ready to ride."

The sun was high in the eastern sky before all the children had been ferried from the south bank. When they were gone, the junk that had taken Snow Leopard appeared, and Chlöe climbed aboard.

On the other side of the river, only Snow Leopard was waiting for her. There was no sign of the others. He was astride a big black horse, looking down at her with that imperious air of his. He did not dismount. Instead, as she climbed from the junk, her feet and ankles wet in the riverbank's mud, his horse pranced and neighed. Coming close to her, a smile lighting his eyes, Snow Leopard leaned over and reached for her hand.

He swung his foot free of the stirrup and pulled her up so that her wet cotton-shoed foot could slide into it, then slid her up in front of him. Indicating the high pommel of the saddle, he said, "You can hold on to that," and he was off, his horse rearing so that she slid back against him.

What she felt so close to Snow Leopard was not the man but safety. As the horse's hooves beat the ground, it galloped like a dervish, blurring the world around her. All she felt of her surroundings was a flash of air. Her whole body relaxed, and she began to cry . . . silent tears that Snow Leopard could not see, for they dried on her cheeks as the horse hurled its riders into the wind.

Moments later they pulled to a halt and she saw more than two hundred men on horses. Saddled in front of forty-five of them were the children. Her eyes sought and found Su-lin, Jade, Dorothy, and Jean mounted on horses of their own. At the end of the line of horsemen were several dozen donkeys, many of them carrying litters whose curtains were drawn. Concubines, thought Chlöe. They always need women, I guess. Did they share these? Or were these Snow Leopard's? Had they been kidnapped or were they here voluntarily? She didn't want to think about it. It was none of her business, she told herself. And who was she to stand in judgment of the man who was saving her and her children?

After the children were bedded down that first night, Snow Leopard came searching for her, nodding his head to indicate he wanted to speak with her alone.

Chlöe followed him to the campfire in front of his tent.

"You must follow our rules." He sat, squatting on his haunches in front of the fire.

"Of course."

"We have money. When we take food from peasants, we pay them. I may have to negotiate with local warlords, but there should be little trouble since we mean no harm. Our journey will probably take two months."

"Two months? Where are we going?"

"You are not going that far. We should reach Sian in six weeks, more or less."

"Sian? I've been there."

He nodded. "It is a city where you and your children will be safe. Though it is in the north, it is still far from the Japanese. If Sian becomes unsafe, you can find transportation south to Chengdu and from there either to Chungking or Kunming." He hesitated. "My men are not pleased to have children to slow us down and to feed."

That was obvious.

"Will any of them rebel, like that man who tried to kill you before?"

Snow Leopard's eyes narrowed. "I learned from that incident." In the firelight she saw the flash of white teeth. "Democracy sometimes has odd beginnings."

"What do you mean?" she asked.

"At such times, when I have a reason for doing something that they probably do not understand, I explain my motives to them and invite discussion."

"And if some disagree?" Chlöe didn't think this was the way most armies were run.

"Sometimes I am open to alternatives. When I am not, after deliberation, I suggest those men return to their homes and leave us. Or, as in this case, there were close to seventy-five who refused to come south to rescue a woman, even though she saved my life. I appointed a leader and sent those men ahead of us to Yenan."

"Yenan?" She stretched her legs out.

"North of Sian," he told her. "It is where the Communists are gathering after the Long March."

"Ah, so they've been found." The Shanghai journalistic community, now so isolated from any news, had not heard that. Thinking of that group of people, she realized Lou would have no idea where she and the children had disappeared to. "How did they get there—to Yenan? It's thousands of miles from where they were last heard of, down south."

"All I know," Snow Leopard answered, "is that they are gathering in Yenan. If we can find them, my men and I will join them."

"So, you've become a Communist?"

"No." His voice was harsh. "But right now China's enemy is Japan. The Nationalists sit around trying to figure where the Communists have disappeared to and ignore the Japanese gobbling away our northern and eastern boundaries. Chiang sent fifteen thousand soldiers against the Japanese in Shanghai, yet amasses armies of hundreds of thousands, waiting to hear where the Reds are."

"How do you hear all this?" she asked, chagrined to know so little.

He did not answer but said, "My men think it is a burden to have half a hundred more people. It slows us down each day and is no small thing to buy enough food daily for so many. You and your children will find yourselves hungry—not starving, but hungry. Tell your children not to complain or cry."

Chlöe studied him and raised her knees, hugging them. "General, these are children under twelve years old. At least two dozen are five or under. They cannot understand those orders. Babies cry because they're uncomfortable—hungry or wet or in pain. They cannot help crying. Were you never around your own children at such times?"

"No." He stood up. "When they cried, I sent them away, with their mothers."

"And did you think that automatically stopped their crying?"

Snow Leopard didn't answer. After a while he said, "My men will carry the children on their horses, but we do not wish to be slowed down. When we stop overnight, you and the other women will see that the men are not disturbed. The children are not to wander around.

"We are traveling in such a manner to avoid skirmishes and fighting anyplace. We desire to save our ammunition, our horses, our energies, for the Japanese. Therefore, you should all be safe. But if I give any orders, no matter how sudden, see that all the children obey them immediately."

He looked across the dying fire at her and smiled, "That applies to you too."

Chlöe laughed. "I have some rules too."

He cocked his head, waiting.

"These are little children. You must stop every two hours to permit them to relieve themselves. Ten minutes is all I ask. Your men must *not* punish them. Tell me or one of the other women and we'll attend to it. You must stop at midday to feed them. Their stomachs are too small to last all day without food.

"I do not want to delay or deter you. I am eternally grateful to you, General, and we shall do whatever we can to be as little trouble as possible."

He nodded.

"One other thing," she said.

His eyes met hers.

"Tell your men to leave my girls alone." She had seen the way Fen-tang, the general's aide, looked at Jade, his eyes following her every move. "My oldest is ten years old. I don't want anyone touching my girls. I know your men are used to the spoils of war . . ."

Snow Leopard waved a hand as though to silence her. "I have not permitted that for a long time. There are concubines for their use. But I shall tell them."

"Tell them I'll kill whoever touches any one of my girls." She stood up, her legs apart, her hands on her hips. "Or my boys, for that matter."

# CHAPTER 54

They stayed away from any but the smallest villages, where the peasants were happy to sell them grain and vegetables.

Su-lin suggested, "If we cook for these men, they will not be so angry."

"Cook for two hundred men and fifty children?"

Su-lin grinned. "Cook for two people easy. Cook for ten not difficult. Cook for fifty, pretty too much. But once used to that, what is two hundred more? Whatever we cook is better than what they cook for themselves. They bring concubines to satisfy the men's hunger of one kind, but they did not bring cooks for the other kind of hunger."

Each man was supposed to cook for himself.

"What do you think?" Chloe asked Dorothy and Jean.

"How are we going to tend fifty children and cook too?" Dorothy asked.

"You care for the children while Su-lin and I cook." It would be pleasant to have the men stop glaring at them, have their resentment lessen toward the children who rode in front of them on their saddles.

When Chlöe mentioned the idea to Snow Leopard, he nodded. "Full bellies make a difference. But you—you should not cook. You are a lady."

Ironically, his words made Chlöe suddenly feel guilty not to know how to cook. Su-lin could tell her what to do and she'd learn how, albeit for two hundred and fifty at a time.

"Mother?" They had years ago settled on a name for Jade to call her. Chlöe taught her the English word *mother*. It was not a name the girl had ever called her own mother. It was not a name any child of her own would ever call her. Every time Jade said it, the word touched Chlöe's heart. Every time.

"Mother," Jade said again. "I would like to help."

"Of course. We can learn to cook together." She put an arm around the girl.

Amazingly, the stew that Su-lin concocted was delicious. Made from rice and sweet potatoes, turnips, several chickens, and some herbs, it met with unanimous approval. Though perhaps not the hungriest of men had sufficient to eat, it fed everyone.

Their days and nights took on a routine. And, as time passed, the dynamics of the trip changed. Chlöe wondered if it had begun with Su-lin's cooking. Instead of dozens of little campfires, instead of the men busying themselves with housekeeping chores after a day in the saddle, instead of shoveling unappetizing food they'd cooked for themselves into their hungry mouths, the soldiers sat around, smoking and talking, joking—from the sound of their laughter—as Su-lin, Chlöe, and Jade prepared their meals. They all ate together, forming circles, sharing humor with each other, and eventually sharing mealtimes with the children.

One night as she walked, always within sight or sound of the camp, a shadow emerged from trees on a ridge. For a moment fear raced across her chest, but it was Snow Leopard.

"I watch you," he said, "and wonder where you go."

"I don't go anyplace," she said, pleased at his company. "I just walk."

He paced his stride to hers. They didn't speak for a while.

Finally, she said, "Your men are very kind to my children. I appreciate that."

He nodded, his arms swinging as they walked. "Yes. It is unexpected. No one is complaining of our pace. We have run into no troubles. They no longer think you are a—what do you call it?"

"Jinx?" She laughed.

"Yes," he said.

"Why do you not let the other women, those in the sedan chairs, why not let them come eat with us? They can help us with dinner too. How awful to be shut up in those all day and kept apart all night."

He laughed. "They do not lack company at night, and they have a servant to fix their meals. They would rebel at having to cook."

Did he send for one each night?

"Well, they are welcome with my women and me," she said.

"Men do not lose tempers nearly as much if we bring these women with us."

He seemed to be trying to apologize to her.

"Your customs need not be defended," she said.

"It is our way."

She found nothing to say to that. She guessed it had been Slade's way too.

They walked along in silence. Then, surprisingly, he asked, "Do you believe in the American God?"

She stopped. "Why do you ask that?"

"I do not believe in a god," he said, "but I believe in a code of ethics. I understand that in America you are not considered ethical unless you believe in a Christian God. That puzzles me."

She had never thought of it that way.

"Well," she thought aloud, "I don't think a god tells me what is good or evil or tells me how to act. I think that comes from within."

"From where within?"

"From my conscience," she answered.

"Is your idea of good or evil absolute?"

"What do you mean by that?"

"I mean," he talked slowly, "if something is wrong for you, do you consider it wrong for all mankind?"

I don't know, she answered silently.

He went on. "If something is not your way, if it is not the American way, then do you consider it wrong?"

"No." She shook her head. "But I think most of the Americans and British I've met in China do." They ridiculed the customs that were not theirs. "They want things done in foreign countries, in other cultures, just the way they do at home. They are very sure they're right. I don't think they can even imagine learning anything of value from . . . from a culture so . . ."

"Are we so . . . so backward?"

Chlöe didn't answer.

"And you are not that way?" he pursued.

Chlöe laughed. "I feel very lucky when I think I'm right. I used to think I knew right from wrong, good from evil, but the older I get, the more confused I become. I cannot say that practices of nearly half a billion Chinese are wrong because they are the opposite of what I learned as a child."

They had not resumed walking but stood in the darkness, the moon behind clouds.

"You are not like other Americans."

"No, that's not quite true," she said. "I may not be like other Americans you have met. But I am very like many other Americans. I am much the same as human beings all over the world."

"You do not inflict your values on us like the Western powers have tried to do for a hundred years."

Sighing, she said, "I think the world is big enough for different beliefs and different values. We are all united by humanity, General. You and I . . . you are saving us. We are all one in some ways. You and I, and your soldiers and my little children, we are all part of each other, of a common denominator—"

"Denominator?"

"Humanity, General. All over the world we are united because we are human beings, with the same drives and needs and desires, if not the same way of going about getting them."

He hesitated, thinking. "So, you think all people are tied by common bonds and that they are good?"

"No, I do not think all people are good. Nevertheless, some humanity links us. I think love is the overwhelming redeeming—"

"We talked of love a long time past," he said. "I thought then it was only for those with the leisure for it. However, I look at my men with your children, and I . . . I find within myself the need to fight for my country. I think perhaps my view of this favorite word of yours was too narrow. I thought it was limited to a man and a woman. I still do not think that is worth dying for, but I see you practicing love with these children of yours and I have hope not only for China, but for the world."

Chlöe smiled. "Don't overrate me, General. I can't save the children of the world. Only those who have been given to me. The children of the world are our tomorrow, yours and mine."

"That young girl," he said. "That Jade. I would think she is yours."

"She is," Chlöe said. "She did not come from my body, but she is my daughter. She is the hope for the future."

"She is your immortality?" he suggested.

Chlöe stared at him, though she could not see his eyes in the darkness.

"General, you never cease to surprise me."

"I see, too, that given a chance, perhaps your kind of love for mankind could replace the violence when it comes to persuasion."

"I don't believe in violence under any circumstances," she said. "That much I know."

Snow Leopard did not converse with her every evening, but he tried, at least once a day, to see if she and her children were in need of anything. Not one of the children became sick, except for occasional mild diarrhea, which was a constant in China. Jean thought God was on their side. The saddle sores became calluses, their skin became leathery and wind-beaten, and they slept soundly nights.

So soundly that at first Chlöe thought the cry was the wind soughing. It swept down out of the Siberian steppes at night, whistling across the plains, dust blowing so hard they could hardly see in front of them. Sometimes it shrieked.

It was enough to awaken her. She lay there, thinking it now sounded like a whimpering puppy, and turned over. But it was not the wind, she realized. The wind had died down, as it always did near dawn. Again, the whimpering animal sound, one of fear and pain. She opened her eyes wide and lay looking up at the stars. Nothing. A wounded animal, perhaps. She rolled over.

Jade's quilt, next to hers, was empty. Chlöe sat up. The girl had probably gone to the bathroom, crept beyond all the sleeping bodies to relieve herself. But that sound. Not even a whisper now, but the memory of it haunted Chlöe. Where was Jade? She sat there for endless minutes, waiting for the girl to return. When she didn't, Chlöe arose.

The hair on the back of her neck stood up. Something was wrong, she knew. Where *was* Jade? She shivered, both because of the cold and the trickle of fear that played in her gut.

She looked around, unable to see far in the dark. Even the sentries that patrolled the perimeters of the large group were out of sight. As her eyes became accustomed to the night, she picked her way among the sleeping bodies, heading for the outer rim. She stood, waiting for the sentry to pass by. They patrolled every half hour, she knew.

If one had just come by, it would be an eternity until he returned. That shriek that had become a mewling cry preyed on her. Had no one else heard? Was it her imagination, her dreams? She stood there, hearing nothing.

And then she began to walk, discerning shapes blacker than the night . . . a clump of trees, just three of them standing sentinel over the landscape. Beyond them a small barn from whose owner they'd bought millet for their dinner. She headed toward the trees, but nothing was there. Bare dirt. She looked around, able to see nothing else on the horizon, whose eastern edge was now pale with the hint of dawn.

A noise came from the barn, not quite a scream, not a wail, but a voice . . . almost like a cat. She ran for the barn, whose door was open. The farmer would never have left it that way, inviting the elements to destroy his harvest.

She ran faster than her feet had ever carried her, thinking, I shouldn't call out . . . I must be quiet, not knowing what she expected to see, but afraid of whatever it was. Gasping for breath, she stood in the doorway, her eyes searching through the dark.

There on the dirt floor was the curve of a naked back, humping back and forth, up and down, while the body under it struggled, while the girl cried, but a cry so low and so in pain that it sounded like breath had gone out of the body. Chlöe knew. For just a moment she stood still, riveted to the spot.

Standing by the door was a snub-nosed shovel. Chlöe grabbed it and dashed toward the figures on the ground. Raising the shovel in the air, holding tight to its handle, she brought the shovel itself down with a fury that released more energy than she had ever used.

A crack rent the air as the man screamed in agony. She raised the shovel again and brought it down upon his back. And again.

Raised it yet again before the small voice cried, "Mother?" Chlöe stopped, her breath in gasps.

She knelt down to see Jade's face, tear-streaked. The man lay motionless on top of her, ragged moans emanating from deep within him. Chlöe tossed the shovel aside and pushed at him, but he would not budge.

Oh, Christ, she thought, he's inside her. She stood and, leaning down, pulled at him, tugging as the limp body made unintelligible sounds of agony. As she shoved the man off Jade, the girl curled up in the fetal position, crying uncontrollably. Her clothes were ripped, and bloody scratches covered her. Chlöe gathered the girl in her arms, rocking her back and forth, crying with her, murmuring over and over, "Oh, darling."

Moments later Snow Leopard arrived. Chlöe didn't even have to see the rapist's face to know it was Fen-tang, whose spinal cord she had broken. She had seen the look in his eyes whenever Jade passed by him.

# CHAPTER 55

Panting from running, Snow Leopard sized up the situation in an instant. Not looking at Chlöe, he bent down to touch the wrist of Fen-tang.

"I told you to keep him away from her." She rocked back and forth with Jade in her arms, barely controlling her fury.

Drool slobbered from Fen-tang's mouth as his eyes rolled in his head.

"He was inside her," Chlöe said, her voice wobbling. "I don't care if I killed him."

At last Snow Leopard looked at her. "He is not dead."

"Well, he should be. Or castrated. That's what he deserves."

Snow Leopard looked around, pointing at the shovel as he stood up. "You hit him with that?"

It seemed obvious.

"You probably broke his back."

"Good," she said. "I hope he suffers the rest of his life. I hope he's incapable of ever again doing such a dreadful thing. The scars this young girl will carry . . ."

"Get out," Snow Leopard's voice was cold steel.

Chlöe looked at him.

Jade's eyes were wide with fear. She clutched Chlöe as though she would never let go.

"Get out of here," he repeated.

Cradling Jade's head in her arms, Chlöe whispered, "Can you walk?"

She helped Jade to stand. Blood oozed down the girl's legs. Her ripped trousers lay in a shredded heap next to Fen-tang. The two of them made their way out of the barn, Chlöe all but carrying the limping Jade. In the early dawn, the entire camp watched them in silence. She put Jade's arm around her shoulders so she could more easily escort her.

Jean came rushing up to them, her arms outstretched, her voice an anguished wail. "Oh, Jade, dear dear . . ." She reached for the young girl's free arm and, together, she and Chlöe carried Jade back to her quilt.

The girl clasped her hands between her drawn-up legs, crying soundlessly, her body shaking convulsively.

"Where's another quilt?" Chlöe heard Dorothy's voice.

Then in the silence came the sound of gunshot. One shot ringing across the flat land from inside the barn.

Snow Leopard appeared, his gun still smoking in his hand, his arm hanging at his side. His shoulders sagged and Chlöe could tell even from this distance that though he gazed out at all of them, he did not see them.

The tension in her body coiled itself tighter as she realized he'd shot Fen-tang. For the first time she realized she'd all but killed him, and Snow Leopard finished the job as one would a wounded horse. Fen-tang could never walk again. He would have lain there slowly dying.

If he'd let me, she thought, I'd have done it. I could have shot bullet after bullet into him. Her rage was not lessened by Fen-tang's death. She looked down at Jade, so small and fragile, the blood caking on her thighs, shivering as though she could never stop. And now, just now, did her cries take voice.

The next two days Jade rode in a sedan chair with one of the camp women. She was too hurt to walk or to sit astride a horse. But by the third day she insisted on joining Chlöe and the others. She had not talked once in all that time. At bedtime she curled herself into Chlöe's arms and slept there all night, not budging.

She wouldn't go near any of the men.

And Snow Leopard did not come near them at all.

The men ate Su-lin's food, but though the children still rode on horses with the soldiers, there was no more laughter after dinner between the two groups.

"They're angry at us," said Dorothy. "They think if it weren't for us, Fen-tang would still be alive."

"Of course," Jean agreed, irritation in her voice. "It's true. If it weren't for women being so attractive, we wouldn't get raped! I get sick of this attitude. They act like it's our fault."

"Our fault!" Chlöe, who had not done with her anger, raged. "I wonder if Jade will ever trust a man again, if she can ever forget that incident. Our fault!"

A week later the soldiers again resumed talking after dinner with the young boys, but would have nothing to do with any of the females. They played games with the boys, and made it very clear it was not the children they resented. It was women.

"It's their loss," Jean muttered.

But it was more than that.

When Snow Leopard did not approach her after nearly two weeks, Chlöe sought him out one evening. In that time he had not talked to her, nor had Jade spoken.

Winter was in the air, and neither she nor her children were dressed for it.

"How much longer, do you think?" she asked as though there were no rift.

He did not turn his head to look at her.

Finally, in a monotone, he answered, "Three, four days. Not long."

Ah, that close. What a relief.

She made no move to leave but stood watching the back of his head as he sat on a large rock.

Finally, when he did not acknowledge her presence, she said, "General—"

He interrupted her. "Because of you I have killed two of my closest friends."

"That's not fair," she said. "It's not my fault."

After a while he said, "No." He nodded his head imperceptibly. "It is mine."

He still did not turn to look at her.

Stars dotted the winter sky.

"I thought you told me long ago that I saved your life. When you kidnapped us, that friend—as you call him—planned to murder you!"

Silence again. Then slowly he turned to face her, one hand resting on his left knee, the other arm hanging beside him. "But if I had not threatened to have you, if I had not acted selfishly—thinking only of my own pleasure—of dallying with a Western woman instead of . . . then he would have had no cause to think of killing me. You would not have had to save my life."

"That's not fair!" she cried.

"Did someone teach you that life is fair?" There was no inflection in his voice.

Yes, she thought. School did. My parents did. I thought it was supposed to be.

"If I had not decided to be gallant and rescue you—and your children . . . if I had led my men straight to Yenan, as I should have, Fen-tang would still be alive."

"It's not your fault! You told your men not to touch my children, I heard you. He disobeyed you! It's not as if he hadn't been warned . . . and besides, you killed him as an act of love, I know that."

"Love?" Now his voice rose, and she heard anger in it. "I am sick of that word of yours. I shot him from pity. He could never walk. I could not let him suffer as he was."

"And I?" she challenged. "I have to see Jade's suffering every day. Every minute. She hasn't talked since. She can't let go of me. If I get up during the night to go to the bathroom she has to come with me. She's to be pitied too. She may never get over that."

He spat out, "That happens to women all the time. It leaves no scars! It is not worth killing a man for!"

She hated him at that moment. Hated him with all the fury she'd felt for Fen-tang. Hated him for all the women who had ever been raped, for all the men who thought women had no feelings. Hated him for not understanding, for hating her. She hated him and all men.

It was nearly dawn before she fell asleep.

As they rode through the large gates of the high walls surrounding Sian, it began to snow.

Snow Leopard left most of his army camped five miles from the city, while he and four of his men accompanied Chlöe and her group. After leaving the children, he and his few men would bring back supplies of food to those waiting out on the plain.

In Sian they found the Methodist mission with little trouble. But there were not forty-five available beds.

"After all this," sighed Dorothy. "Now what?"

Snow Leopard looked at Chlöe.

Everyone looked at Chlöe.

"There's an orphanage here, isn't there? Run by nuns?"

"There was," said Mrs. Butler, the superintendent. "But they've moved the children down south to Chungking, I believe."

Perfect, thought Chlöe. "Where is it?"

"I can see what you're thinking," said Mrs. Butler. "But how would you feed yourselves? Even if they left beds, there's probably no bedding."

"Somehow we'll find food," Chlöe answered with an assurance she didn't feel. "Certainly you can help for a few days?"

"Of course," responded the gray-haired woman. "We'll be glad to do whatever we can."

"Then let's go find this place," Chlöe said, picking up her pack.

"Leave the children here. We'll feed them their supper while you look the orphanage over. I don't think it will be large enough, for the nuns didn't have that many children. There were just three women, all those years."

Chlöe smiled. "Well, there are four of us." She turned to Snow Leopard. "Will you go with me? Will you stay until the children are settled?"

He nodded. He had talked to her little since the Fen-tang incident. Whatever he said, it was more than Jade voiced.

Snow was falling in large flakes now, making the noises of the city muted. To Chlöe, Sian did not look as it had when she'd been there with Nikolai, on their way to Ulan Bator. But then, she had not looked at it in the same way. She had been concentrating more on Nikolai.

Snow Leopard left his men with the children and other women while he and Chlöe took off to find what she hoped would be the abandoned orphanage. It sounded too good to be true.

Yet it was.

The Catholics must have been in Sian for many years, judging from the solid stone edifice not too far from the ancient Drum Tower.

There was no sign of life, yet after Chlöe reached up to pull the heavy bell, they heard soft footsteps within. The door creaked open and a single eye stared out at them.

When Chlöe explained who they were and that they were looking for housing for nearly half a hundred children, the door swung wide. Staring at them was a woman who couldn't have been more than five feet tall, wrinkled, her skin as translucent as parchment, dressed in a very soiled and very tattered nun's habit. "I have prayed for you," she said, "prayed to God to be of further use."

Within four hours the forty-five children and four women were housed, albeit without sheets or quilts or food, in the old Catholic orphanage. Chlöe had no doubt at all that food would somehow be supplied. "Tomorrow," she told Snow Leopard, "I'll find the hospital and tell them our plight. Something will turn up."

"I shall leave you, then," he said.

"What will you do, continue north to Yenan?"

He nodded. "The other half of my men are no doubt there already. We shall join the Communists to fight the Japanese. When that battle is over, we shall turn our thoughts to what is going to happen within our country."

"I envy you," she said. "You'll hear the stories of the Long March, and you are going to be part of the future of China."

He looked around. There was no one else in the vast empty stone courtyard.

"You and I have not eaten," he said.

"I'd forgotten. We were so busy with everyone else."

He reached his hand out to touch the sleeve of her jacket. "I will buy you some food and tea. Come."

It was the first friendly overture he'd made in weeks.

They found a restaurant not far from the orphanage, nearly empty at this late hour.

"Are you going to take care of these children all your life?" he asked once they were seated and had ordered.

Chlöe shrugged her shoulders. "They won't need me all their lives. I shall take care of Jade, Plum Blossom, and Li. As for the others, General, I do not know what is going to happen. I have a job too. An American job, you know. Maybe when I'm sure the children are safe here, I'll find my way to Yenan so I can interview the Communists. I'd like to be the first journalist to get their story."

She had not thought of that before. Suddenly, she knew it was something she *had* to do. It might be one of the biggest stories ever to come out of China. Why hadn't she thought of it that way before? There had been next to no information about the Reds for a year. Now they suddenly reemerged thousands of miles from where they were last seen. How many were there? What were they doing? Going to do? What had the trip been like? Was Mao with them? Who was their leader? How were they going to fight the Japanese *and* Chiang Kai-shek?

She hadn't even asked one of these questions on this whole trip. Now they poured into her head.

"Oh, General, I wish I were going with you!"

"Why? To tell the Communists' story to the world?" There was contempt in his voice. She remembered he did not approve of the Communists' ideals.

"To tell this part of China's story to the world!"

He leaned across the table, his elbows on its edge and his voice tinged with what she recognized as anger, and he asked, "Why do you care so much about my country?"

She sat back in her chair. "I don't know, General. I thought at one time I hated it. I have every reason to hate it. It has robbed me of my children and my husband . . . and my innocence." She thought for a moment. "All I know is that it has become a part of me. I don't think I love it." There was that word again. "I get angry and frustrated with it. Sometimes it fills me with rage. Yet, when I've had opportunities to leave, I have not been able to. Perhaps being angry at it only ties me to it more closely. I do not know why I care so much about your country."

"Go home," he said. "It is not your cause. There is going to be much bloodshed before all this is over. Go home to your safe country. Free yourself from our cause." He signaled a waiter for the check.

Chlöe looked at him. "That sounds very nice. But how can I free myself when I am so bound up with it? Not only that, General. I am going to find Yenan myself before too long, and I will make front-page headlines by interviewing the men who marched across China for a year. I will show the world there is a different China from Chiang's."

He looked at her in silence for a minute.

"Are you so famous and so important that you can do that?"

"I think so." She smiled. "I really think so." Or at least Cass is. Cass and his newspaper.

Snow Leopard stood up and looked down at her.

"You are very perplexing. I do not even think I like you, yet I jeopardize all that I believe in for you. I do not like the kind of woman you are, for you are not soft like Chinese women. I kill because of you. My life has not been the same since the Blue Express. If that taught me one thing," his eyes crinkled into a smile, "it has been to never kidnap another train."

She stood up too, unable to fathom whether he was insulting her or being nice to her, and followed him from the restaurant.

As they walked down the snowy street, he said, "Before my men and I leave tomorrow, I shall return to see that you have food for your children. It will be evening, for I have business to attend to in the city before we leave. We shall not leave for Yenan until the following day."

"You need not concern yourself with us. We shall make out just fine." Where, she wondered, did this confidence come from?

"I shall come by before dark tomorrow."

He left her at the door, and she stared after him as his shoes left prints in the snow.

What a puzzling man, she thought. I have never felt the same about him two days straight.

In the morning, fourteen bushels of rice were delivered before dawn. Chlöe wondered if Snow Leopard could have worked that quickly.

# CHAPTER 56

He didn't show up until twilight the next day. But a doctor did. Chlöe didn't even have to go to the hospital. The doctor came to them in the form of an American, a silver-haired woman named Esther Browning.

"Mrs. Butler told me you'd settled in here," the doctor said, reaching out to give Chlöe a firm handshake. "You're going to have a hard time."

She didn't look as though that should faze anyone. "Thought I better have a look-see at the kids. Any sick ones?"

"Colds. Sniffles. Some mild diarrhea. Nothing unusual for China."

"You came from Shanghai?" Dr. Browning handed a sack to

Su-lin. "Brew me some tea, will you?" She spoke Mandarin grace-fully. Her movements were quick, and her small frame reminded Chlöe of a bird about to take wing. "We'd better see about feeding this many kids." She looked around the large vestry in which they stood. "This could be converted to a dorm room, couldn't it?"

Chlöe hadn't yet had time to make any plans. "Good idea," she said. She hadn't had a chance to more than greet the doctor.

"You alone here, with that Chinese servant?"

Chlöe shook her head. "I have two friends with me. Amer-icans."

Dr. Browning reached into a bag and took out a cigarette, lighting it by scratching a match with her fingernail. "Why do we Americans have this obsession for China? Don't answer. That's rhe-torical. Well, is this your destination?"

When Chlöe nodded, Dr. Browning continued. "What they need right now is quilts. How many are there?"

Before Chlöe could respond, the doctor moved through the doorway and started walking down the hall. Chlöe followed.

"God, they're all little, aren't they?" she finally said. "What's the oldest?"

"Ten."

This time the doctor looked at Chlöe and waited for a response.

"My daughter." Before she realized it, Chlöe—in a breathless rush—told her about Jade's rape. "She hasn't talked in weeks," Chlöe said.

The doctor tossed her cigarette on the stone floor, grinding it under the heel of her boot. "Where is she?"

Chlöe took her to the room she and Jade, along with Plum Blossom and Li, shared. It was hardly eight feet square. Only Jade was there. The other two children had gone to find the rest of the group.

For a long time the doctor stood in the doorway and looked at Jade, huddled against the wall. She turned to Chlöe. "Leave me with her, okay? Then we'll all sit down—not her, but your two women friends and you and me—and plan what to do."

Another deus ex machina, thought Chlöe. From out of no-where, a savior.

The doctor left an hour later, saying, "I shall return before dark. I think I'll spend the night here, with all of you. We can make plans. Give me your maid. You don't have any men, do you? Too bad.

Well, we'll collect some food. You can learn where to go later, after we get things organized."

She just took over.

It was late afternoon, a gray day with the clouds low. It wasn't snowing, but it might as well have been for the way the damp cold went through them. Twilight was approaching, so Chlöe thought it must be about four-thirty, and they'd been so busy all day she hadn't had time to wonder where they might get quilts. There was no money. They'd left Shanghai quickly. And besides, she thought, what did that have to do with it? There was no money left in Shanghai either.

The bell at the big gate clanged loudly. Chlöe looked around. Su-lin was out with Dr. Browning. The bell's discordant tolling did not stop.

Snow Leopard stood there, alone, his horse behind him.

He held out an armful of fur. "Here," he said. "If you want to interview Mao and hear what happened on this Long March of the Communists so you can tell the world of Chinese heroism, you need warm clothes. These are worn with the fur side inside. I hope the boots are large enough. Chinese women have smaller feet than you do. Be ready in the hour before dawn if you want to accompany us."

He held out the clothing, but Chlöe stood there, her mouth agape. "I can't leave," she said. "We're not even settled. I have to stay with the children."

I can't leave Jade, she thought.

"You'll need warm clothes wherever you are." He plopped them in her arms, and she staggered under the weight.

He looked across the armful of clothing at her, his eyes not flickering, solemn. Almost angry, she thought.

"Your men hate me. I thought you would be glad to get rid of me."

"My men do not understand the death of one of their comrades over a woman. They do not understand women traveling with us unless they are . . . they are in the sedan chairs."

"No," she said, holding the clothing out to him. "I cannot go."

He smiled at her, but she did not think it a friendly smile. "Then you will not tell this story to the world? I thought you could inform the world of what others than Chiang are trying to do. You can't do this, after all?"

She pulled the clothes back toward her chest, her arms tired from holding the heavy leather and furs.

He was goading her, trying to manipulate her.

"Oh, General." She laughed, and now his eyes warmed too. "How can I resist your offer? Let me see what I can do. If I can leave all these children. How long would I be gone?"

"I do not know how long it will take you to get this story to tell the world."

I don't know either, she thought. Will Mao even give me an interview? He wants the world to know too, doesn't he? "How long will it take to get to Yenan?"

"It depends on the weather and if we are stopped. A week, perhaps. Ten days."

A month. She should certainly be back in a month, she thought. "I'll ask my friends and the doctor." She knows Sian better than we do. Can forty-five children and three adults get along without me in a strange city? And she laughed to herself. What can I do that they can't?

"The hour before dawn," he said, turning toward his horse.

His erect stance reminded her of the way Ching-ling stood. Regal.

He sat on horseback when she opened the door to peer out into the darkness. Large wet flakes fell slowly. How long had he been waiting? Beside him stood a tall, mottled gray horse, snorting in the cold. Snow Leopard's face was surrounded by the dark fur that lined the hood of his heavy jacket. Snowflakes stuck to his eyelashes.

The world was hushed.

He was silent as he turned his horse and began to trot along the street, only the clopping of the horses' hooves making any noise.

Gradually the sky lightened, turning first a steel gray, then pewter, until it became pearl gray, and the flakes were fewer and farther between. Any tents at the camp had been stricken. As soon as the men saw Snow Leopard, those who were not already mounted jumped on their horses. The sedan chairs were at the rear. Chlöe wondered if the ladies even went into battle.

Now Snow Leopard stopped his horse and turned to her.

"You will ride at the end of the line, behind even the sedan chairs. My men think you are my woman, and will accept you on that level and that level only."

Chlöe started to protest, but Snow Leopard galloped to the head of the line of men, leaving her to weave her way to the tail. The army began to move. No one paid her the least attention. She waited until the dozen sedan chairs swung by, following several feet behind them. He was doing this to humiliate her, she thought. That he had offered to let her accompany them must have been a moral dilemma for him. He cared more about telling their story to the world than about getting rid of her. It must gall him to have to accommodate her at all.

She was glad to have the furs. Her hands would already be frozen had she not had these mittens. She pulled the scarf across her face so that only her eyes were visible in the vast, barren landscape. The snow stuck to the frozen ground, but the brown earth and its stubbled dead plants impeded their passage.

They did not stop to eat at midday.

In late afternoon they came to Lochuan, where Snow Leopard's men bartered for food and Chlöe watched chickens being slaughtered, heard pigs squealing, the wail of dogs, the braying of donkeys. Anyone who could eat dog, she thought, was akin to a cannibal. In the distance the loess hills rose against the darkening sky.

They camped shortly beyond the town that night, setting up their tents in the dark. Snow Leopard rode back to get her.

He nodded his head. "Come to my tent. And keep your head down."

She followed him, but she did not lower her head.

He jumped off his horse and strode into the already erected tent. He pulled off his gloves. Outside the tent, a servant was brewing tea. A large bearskin rug covered the dirt floor.

Without looking at her, he said, "I believe you will be embarrassed at the conditions under which I brought you." Whatever they were, she thought that any embarrassment on her part would please him. "The only feelings my men understand for a woman are desire. In order for them not to resent you for Fen-tang's death . . ."

"I didn't kill Fen-tang!"

He ignored her outburst and continued. "I have to let them believe that I desire you, that you are my woman. They understand that. Therefore, you will eat and sleep in here. You will not wander around the camp or show yourself. You will act as though your main concern is to please me. Do you understand?"

Is he enjoying trying to humiliate me? she wondered. She would not let him. Instead, she cast her eyes down and demurely said,

"General, I am in your debt. I shall do as you please and thank you for permitting me to join your army." Damn him, she thought. But I won't let it upset me. I'll get the story of the decade, thanks to him. Besides, he has been too good to me too often. He is still angry about having to kill his friend. I shall not anger him more. She knew she was safe in his tent. He had never desired her. In fact, he had said, "I don't even know if I like you."

They ate in silence. There was none of the stimulating conversation she remembered from the last time she shared a tent with him, so many years before. There was no banter, no laughter, no exchange of ideas. Once the meal was cleared away, Snow Leopard pulled on his furs and went out into the night. She sat, listening to the sounds of a camp getting ready for sleep. Had he gone to one of the concubines?

When he returned in the dark she heard his movements, realizing he had lain down on the bearskin rug where she sat. Soon she heard his even breathing and thought he had fallen asleep. But he said, "Do not go wandering around when you must relieve yourself. Do it right beside the tent."

She crawled outside in the darkness and did just that. When she came back inside she felt for the rug and lay down on it, her feet grazing Snow Leopard. He did not move, so she knew he must already be asleep.

As she felt herself in that state between consciousness and sleep, she heard him say, as though to himself, "I have lost my senses," anger in his voice.

# CHAPTER 57

January 1936. Yenan, China.

"It is a significant coincidence," Mao Tse-tung told me, "that in this far northern province history replays itself. This area corresponds almost exactly to the birthplace of China. It was thousands of years ago, but here was the very place where the Chinese people unified themselves."

Then he laughed. "Do you know Chiang Kai-shek has offered a quarter of a million silver yuan for my head—on or off my body?"

*Mao Tse-tung has emerged, after the Long March, as the un-equivocal leader of the Chinese Communist Party.*

*He remembered me from the brief time my husband and I visited him nearly eight years ago in his mountain retreat to the south. Six thousand miles to the southwest of where he is now. Six thousand miles over some of the toughest and most remote terrain on the face of the earth. Six thousand miles that thousands of men and twenty-six women walked, climbed, swam, slid, and sometimes crawled over in 368 days. A feat without parallel in all of mankind's history.*

*Mao told me he is willing to end the ten-year-old civil war. He will even accept Chiang Kai-shek as his leader if Chiang will agree to stop hunting Communists and turn his attention and his armies against the encroaching Japanese.*

*How had I—an American woman—come to this remote north-west headquarters of the Chinese Communists?*

*I came on horseback, on foot, and on mule. Following stream-beds, I and my companions—non-Communist Chinese, led by Lu-tang, a famous general from the far northeast who has devoted the last decade to fighting the Japanese.*

*It was not difficult, once we reached Yenan, to gain an audience with Mao. But first I was interviewed by Chou En-lai, a handsome, intelligent, charming, heavily bearded (for a Chinese) man who speaks excellent English (and fluent French). He stands between Mao and the world, it seems to me.*

*Chou invited me and my companion, General Lu-tang, to dine that evening, with him and Mao. Mao is different than he was when I last saw him. But then, I am different also. He still has the seeming simplicity of Chinese peasants, but he is not simple. He is an edu-cated man who writes poetry and puzzles over the universe's ab-stract questions. He can be coarse and vulgar at the same time he is a pedantic historian and philosopher. Careless about his personal being, he is reputed to be a stickler for disciplinary detail. His fellow officers consider him a military and political strategist of genius pro-portions. He says it will be a long war. That it will last for years.*

*"Do you know," he said, leaning across the table at dinner, waving a chopstick in my face, "that rape is now punishable by death?" He was showing me that his idea of equality between the sexes was no idle threat.*

Mao had informed Snow Leopard that if his small army was to join the Communists in fighting the Japanese, all must obey the

same rules. Chlöe did not write that after hearing this, Snow Leopard's attitude toward her began to change.

> Mao and Chou En-lai live like the rank and file of their army. Mao
> says he owns only two uniforms and his bedding. Like all other Red
> soldiers, the only adornment on his uniform is the standard two red bars.
>   In the weeks I've spent in Yenan I've never seen him anything
> but pleasant, yet tales abound of his wrath and his ability to make of
> any human being a mass of quivering jelly.
>   He believes man can solve his own problems, and that he can
> help men to solve their own problems.
>   His eyes mist when he remembers dead comrades and the cause
> for which they died.
>   "Do you know," he asked me, "that at this very moment my
> country faces one of the most severe famines of all history? (No, I
> didn't.) Over thirty million people are existing on bark and earth. Do
> you know why? Taxes have been collected sixty years in advance.
> Unable to pay exorbitant rents and the interest on loans, farmers
> have abandoned hundreds of thousands of acres of land. The greedy
> landlords take over the land, but it lies idle. The countryside is bank-
> rupt. The people starve. We," and I gathered he meant the Com-
> munists, "will see that no one dies of starvation. We shall dam rivers
> and prevent floods, eradicate cholera, typhoid, malaria . . ." I thought,
> Big dreams. Impossible dreams. Yet dreams are what change the
> world. So, maybe . . .
>   "Right now, though, it is our external enemy we must attack.
> Japanese imperialism is not only the enemy of China but also of all
> people of the world who desire peace. We expect friendly nations to
> at least not help the Japanese and remain neutral. It is probably too
> much to hope that any nation will actively help China resist the
> invasion and conquest."
>   I had to ask him, "If China is able to defeat Japan, how will that
> solve the age-old problem of foreign imperialism that Chiang fosters?"
>   He smiled. "A strange question coming from an imperialist."
>   "Do not confuse me with my country," I said. "Because I am
> an American does not mean I always approve of its policies."
>   Mao looked at me and answered. "If China defeats Japan, it
> will mean that the Chinese masses have awakened, have mobilized,
> and have established their independence. Therefore, the main problem
> of imperialism will have been solved."
>   He lit a cigarette. He smokes constantly.

Chlöe lay down her pencil and stretched her fingers. Was anybody at all, including Cass, going to give a damn what an unknown Chinese Communist in the hinterlands of a remote region of China thought?

She shivered in the cave she shared with eight other women, all of whom were survivors of the Long March. Three had given birth on the trek. Being pregnant while marching up mountains and through rivers was not easy, they'd told her. Two of the women had been forced to leave their infants with peasants along the way. Neither was sure her baby had survived. The third gave birth on the great grasslands of western Szechwan and insisted on carrying her baby every step of every day of every month thereafter. The baby survived, nursing at its mother's breast as Chlöe wrote.

The men and women did not share caves.

It was late and Chlöe was tired. She had been sitting, bent over her notepad, her eyes fatigued by the flickering of the candlelight. Not only were her fingers stiff, her back ached.

She reached for her coat and, standing, walked from the cave into the night air. Lights from the few houses down in the valley twinkled in the brisk winter night. She hugged herself despite the fur against her body.

A million stars. Aloud, she said, "I can catch one just by reaching out."

"Catch what?"

She turned abruptly, the voice in the darkness startling her, even though she recognized it. He stood not six feet from her.

"A star," she answered, wondering how Snow Leopard had appeared so quickly, as if from nowhere. Only the women's cave was in this section.

"Catch a distant star?" He laughed, not moving.

"Aren't they beautiful?" she said.

"They're always there."

"That doesn't make them less beautiful. Don't you notice them?"

He hesitated before answering. "Always."

They were silent for a few minutes. Then he asked, "What do you think of him?"

She didn't have to ask whom. "I'm not sure," she answered, having unsuccessfully tried to answer that question several times before. "His ideas are similar to Ching-ling's." And to Nikolai's.

"Ching-ling?"

"Madame Sun Yat-sen."

"Ah, yes."

After a while he said, "You have not answered my question."

"I know." She pulled her hands back inside her sleeves and the fur felt warm and soft. "He seems to be China's hope, and yet something in me fears him."

"I agree. It's that he's too positive his way is the only way, his ideas are the only worthwhile ones, and I am afraid of someone who is so positive he's right."

"It's called missionary zeal," she said, remembering that long ago Cass had said much the same thing.

"Once the Japanese are defeated—"

"Will they be?" she interrupted.

"Once the Japanese are defeated, what may he not do to achieve his ends?"

"Like you?" She stared over the valley, not looking at him.

"No. I am safer. I am an optimist but not an idealist. Chiang is evil because he kills other Chinese who stand in his way. Given the opportunity, Mao will too, even though he condemns the Nationalists for doing so now."

"You really think so?"

Snow Leopard didn't respond.

"Mao and Chou En-lai, too, seem very impressed that a general of your stature is joining their cause. The welcome mat was certainly spread out for you."

"I am joining the fight against the Japanese."

"They seem to welcome what Chou called your military insight."

He laughed. "I have never lost a battle. Strategy is my strong point. I know before they do what moves the enemy will make just by looking at the land and knowing who commands the enemy troops."

Chloë was impressed. "You won't know the Japanese commanders."

"I will study the terrain, however."

"Maybe the Japanese do not wage war like the Chinese."

"Like you are not like Chinese women?"

She smiled into the night. "I doubt that all Chinese women are alike."

"You are not like any of them, of that I am sure." His voice was so low she had to strain to hear him. "You are not like any woman anyplace."

There was silence. After a minute she turned toward him, but he was gone.

The wind whistled down the gorge.

"The people," Mao said, "must be given the right to organize and arm themselves. This is a freedom which Chiang Kai-shek has denied them. Students are beginning to prepare themselves politically. The intellectuals will march—perhaps in Tian An Men Square—to awaken the peasants. The masses have not yet got their freedom, cannot be mobilized, cannot be trained and armed. When the masses are given economic, social, and political freedom, their strength will be intensified and the true power of the nation will be revealed."

I learned that Mao's four slogans had, at first, been opposed by experienced military men. However, on the Long March these tactics became the basis of all Red victories.

One: When the enemy advances, we retreat!

Two: When the enemy halts and camps, we trouble them!

Three: When the enemy seeks to avoid battle, we attack!

Four: When the enemy retreats, we pursue!

Sounds simple, doesn't it? I mean childlike simple. Perhaps that's part of its success.

I learned that the province of Kiangsi had been completely controlled by Communists as long ago as 1930, six years ago. Land was taken from the "greedy" warlords and redistributed, taxes lightened. Unemployment, opium, prostitution, child slavery, and compulsory marriages were eliminated. The lives of peasants were greatly improved.

Why had I not heard of this? I asked.

Because the Nanking government had not permitted one single foreign journalist into the Communist province. True, mass executions of landlords were carried out on a grand scale. This Mao openly admitted. "Revolution is not a tea party," he said.

I guess not.

The Long March was a daring voyage of indomitable heroism and tenacity, victory, misery, renunciation, fidelity, and a bright exaltation (and exultation). The thousands of young men and women enjoyed eternal confidence in their expectations and an astonishing enthusiasm—a radiance—that would not tolerate any thought of conquest or defeat . . . not by other men, or by the vicissitudes of Nature, not by any god or by the death of comrades. This was a heroic odyssey unlike any other in recorded history.

Close to 80,000 men of the Red Army and thousands of peasants began one of the outstanding feats of humankind. In three days more than a year, less than twenty thousand of them completed the trip. On foot they crossed mountains that were thought to be inaccessible; they crossed China's mightiest rivers, and some of its most dangerous rapids; they crossed the vast uninhabited grasslands. The Nationalist forces, when they could discover the line of people many miles long, bombarded them from the air and attacked when they could find the ground forces.

From all reports, Chiang's soldiers found no local welcome and must often have wondered why they were attacking their fellow Chinese on their own territory instead of the Japanese invading their land.

The Nationalist Army was outmaneuvered at every point. When Chiang's men thought the Reds had no choice but to go north, the Communists turned west. When the Nationalists were convinced they had them cornered in a valley, a hundred thousand Chinese climbed mountains that had never been scaled before, slipping and sliding— inching—through narrow passes and up steep precipices. Over a hundred thousand human beings, clinging to the sides of mountains, holding on to trees and each other, challenging the elements, escaping from the enemy which, this time, was their own people rather than the armies of the Rising Sun.

One of the most stupendous of human feats will, I am sure, one day become famous for its sheer unbelievability. On the western Tatu River is a centuries-old iron suspension bridge, and here sixteen iron chains are slung between the perpendicular cliffs on either side of the churning river, holding up a bridge that is the only way to cross the river for hundreds of miles.

At the northern edge of the bridge the Nationalist Army awaited the Reds at machine-gun point. They had removed the wooden planks so that the Communists couldn't walk across it. However, with hand grenades strapped to their backs, thirty Red volunteers swung hand over hand across the iron chains that suspended the bridge.

The enemy fired, and three soldiers dropped into the swirling rapids below. But twenty-seven made the crossing. The Reds re-planked the bridge and the hundred thousand plus made their way north.

By now there was little to eat and no villages presented themselves. The marchers devoured wild berries and roots, but so many people quickly diminished natural resources. They ate their horses and boiled their shoes and leather belts to soften them. By these methods their strength survived and they could again climb mountains.

The grasslands. As they told me of this immense area of western China they rolled their eyes heavenward. Seas of wet grasses, perilous marshy swamps where many a comrade disappeared in deceptive ooze. Mantzu tribesmen who hated strangers and whose queen threatened to boil alive anyone who helped these trespassers.

Along the way thousands of people dropped out. They went home to families, or revolutionary fervor died in the unexpected rigors of the journey; they died in battles and from illnesses. The sick and infirm were left in villages. Many could not keep up the pace.

It was six thousand miles of arduous walking over some of the most inhospitable terrain on the face of the earth—through rain and snow and sweltering summer heat, through driving winds (frigid from the mountainous cold or dusty furnaces from the shimmering heat of midsummer), through locusts and mosquitoes and near starvation.

They marched to the far northwest, to Yenan, where cliffs line the deep gorge made by the rushing river. And in the cliffs are caves, where the people dwell and where there are a hospital and military headquarters. These caves are cool in summer and protected in winter from both the elements and Chiang's bombing raids.

Next month the army plans to move east to engage the Japanese in battle. The Communists have subordinated all other goals to that of opposing Japan's aggression. They even offer to cooperate with their most hated enemy, landlords, if the landlords will join their struggle against the Nipponese. They are banded together for the survival of their country.

Their invitation to be joined in this struggle for the survival of China has been met by Chiang's determination to exterminate the Communists from Yenan, and from life ("the extermination campaign," the Nationalists call it). Meanwhile, the Japanese take over increasingly more Chinese land and subjugate ever more Chinese people. Both they and Chiang look westward. Chiang at the Communists and the Japanese at all China. One is forced to wonder if Chiang ever looks east.

Chlöe Cavanaugh

# CHAPTER 58

I have to get back to Jade, Chlöe thought as she shivered awake. I have left her too long.

She also knew she'd gotten the story she came after, one that no other journalist had. Mao had spent every one of the last six nights telling her his life story, his beliefs, his philosophies. His plan for China.

From dozens of people she heard tales of the Long March.

Now it was time to leave.

She wanted to see if Dr. Browning had worked wonders and if Jade was speaking. A tinge of guilt slid across her chest. She knew she should never have left the girl in such a traumatized state. Yet she also knew what a once-in-a-lifetime opportunity this had been.

What bothered her was the inordinate amount of time she spent thinking of Snow Leopard, glancing up every time someone approached, hoping he'd be outside her cave again at night. But he had not returned.

His attitude puzzled her. Ever since he'd shot Fen-tang he'd been angry at her. He'd said China had too many children, irritated at her for refusing to leave Shanghai without them. However, he'd become a father figure to the children until the Fen-tang incident, when he'd withdrawn from them all.

Chlöe knew he spent most of his time now drilling not only his soldiers but ones whom Chou En-lai assigned to him. She'd heard his guerrilla tactics were without equal. Suddenly she longed for Lou. By talking over her questions with him, she'd always been able to clarify her thoughts.

She heard other women beginning to stir in the cave's darkness, their internal clocks telling them all that morning had come even if there were not yet signs of daylight.

It came unexpectedly. Home. "I want to go back to America," she said aloud.

She had not even allowed herself to think that since the children had come to her. Not even when the Japanese took Shanghai. Now the yearning flooded over her, and she was surprised to feel a tear stinging her cheek.

If I could make sure the children are safe, she thought. I could take Jade and Li and Plum Blossom to Oneonta and then come back to the others.

But she knew with certainty that she did not want to come back.

Maybe she could figure out a way to get all forty-five children to the United States.

Well, she would leave Yenan today. She would ask for a guide and head south toward Sian, to Jade. And to a way to cable her story to Cass. She could write more about Mao and the Long March when she had time. She had enough information to fill a book, she thought, wondering where she'd get the energy.

Chou En-lai told her he'd supply a guide to the next village south, and there she could find one to take her to the next, and so forth. He also told her, with that half smile of his, "We have capabilities of cable here. We can send whatever you want to Chungking, where they can send it on to Canton, and to Hong Kong, then on to America."

She spent the morning taking care of that and, with relief, packed her few belongings. She was glad once again of the fur coat and heavy boots Snow Leopard had insisted she wear.

She must find him, thank him. Say good-bye to him.

But he beat her to it.

His eyes were angry when she looked up to see him standing in the cave's entrance.

"You were not going to tell me?"

"Yes." She put the last article in her little bag. "Of course I was. I just decided to leave this morning. I was going to find you after lunch . . ."

". . . After lunch? While I was on the drill field?"

"I couldn't leave without saying good-bye, without thanking you."

"I will be your guide, not so far as Sian but to the next village south."

She laughed. "You don't know the way any better than I do. We passed along the road to here at night."

"I have made arrangements already. I can be back here by tomorrow night."

"Really, General, you're needed here. . . ." Yet she did not want to protest enough to change his mind. He never ceased to surprise her.

He shook his head. "We are not planning to infiltrate the enemy lines for another three weeks, nor do battle for a month."

That was their strategy, she already knew. Send men behind enemy lines, pretend to be villagers while silently smuggling guns to the townspeople, instilling in them the courage to resist, to hack the enemy to death when battle began. From inside. And, so far, the enemy had not caught on.

She and Snow Leopard took off after lunch, with a canteen of water and a knapsack of food, with Snow Leopard's rifle tied to his saddle, his pistol in its holder, grain for the horses, and began their descent from the high cliffs of Yenan. The next village south was half a day away.

For the first several hours they did not talk. She followed him on the narrow path that wound through the mountains. By the time it broadened, late winter afternoon had turned to twilight, and Snow Leopard turned to wait for her. They rode side by side as large white flakes sprinkled their shoulders and began to cover the path.

She noticed him glancing from side to side along the rocky path.

"We had better find a cave," he said.

She had begun to worry about getting lost in the snowy darkness. At the same moment they each saw the dark hole against the gray hill.

Within moments Snow Leopard found a few twigs and had a fire built at the entrance to the cave. Chlöe tethered the horses to bushes, thinking if they had an ounce of sense they could easily pull the bushes up and set off. The fire sent shadows dancing against the walls. The cave seemed to go back forever, endless, and that frightened her. She walked close to Snow Leopard and his fire.

"I have some meat dumplings and noodles," he said. They were leftovers from lunch. Back in Yenan that would be their supper tonight too.

"Sounds good." She smiled. He would not let anything happen to her, that much she knew.

He turned to look at her, staring at her a moment before turning back to the fire, dishing the food into a tin plate, which he handed to her. Joining her on the log, he ate from the pan in which he had warmed the food.

"The wood will not last long," he said. "The fire is dying." Wood was scarce all over the country, loggers having denuded the country of trees centuries before.

Snow Leopard got up and left the cave, returning in a few minutes with his saddle quilt. There was only the one. "It is going to be a cold night," he said, tossing it to her.

She was not tired. It probably wasn't even seven o'clock, but there was nothing else to do.

"Put the quilt under you to keep the damp chill of the cave away."

She spread it out and lay down, pillowing her hands under her head, ostensibly staring into the fire but really observing him. He stood at the cave entrance, leaning against it, his arms folded across his chest.

"I have been trying," he said after a while, "to find words."

"Words?"

"Let me speak." He put his hands behind him and walked a few steps, looking at the floor. "It is not easy for me. I have been thinking and rethinking words to say to you for many days, and many weeks, and many years." He turned to look at her in the firelight. "It is not often just one person changes your life. But in my life it has been you." He held up his hand in a gesture meant to keep her silent. "If you interrupt me, I may never get around to saying what my heart needs to say."

My heart? Chinese did not talk this way.

"Many years ago when I kidnapped the train, when you saved my life—which was threatened only through my own arrogance—and we spent those nights talking, you awakened something within me. You showed me there was more in the world than I had ever imagined. When we separated, I could not forget you. You were a woman, and you taught me many lessons in a few nights. I had never thought a woman worth listening to before. Yet I could not forget *anything* you said."

He walked over and stood staring down at her. She couldn't see his eyes. "You sent me on a journey of self-discovery and of discovery of the world. You are responsible for my renouncing my way of life—my wives and concubines and children. You led me to renouncing opium, to seeing the world on a larger scale, to realizing my country. And to the understanding that my people must be awakened, that they should not be allowed to live any longer as animals, but that they should be able to stand up and be counted as people with thoughts and feelings and passions. Yes, passions. For, through you, I have become a passionate man. I care!"

Sitting down beside her on the quilt, he laughed. "In short, you have ruined me!"

She looked at him, astonished at his words.

"You have ruined me as a warlord, as a man who can lead his own life in contentment. You have made me dream to save my country, to become brothers with my countrymen."

Now he turned on his side and sprawled beside her, his elbow resting on the quilt, his chin in his hand, staring into her eyes. "You have made every other woman impossible for me."

Then he was silent. She met his gaze, reaching out her hand to brush his quickly.

"You made me yearn to learn foreign customs. You have made me want to know love. I have learned it for my fellow human beings, but I have not been able to evoke it for any woman whom I have bedded. It is just an act. I tried," he laughed aloud, "to kiss a woman once, but I did not know what to do with my lips. It was nothing. As all my relations with women have become. In the old days, at least their bodies appealed to me. My hunger was instantly satisfied by any pretty woman. But the hunger you awakened in me has never been satisfied, and I need to tell you that before we part."

"I thought you did not find me desirable," she finally said, not letting herself reach out to touch his face.

"What gave you that idea?"

"You told me, back when you'd kidnapped me, that you did not find me desirable. That a white woman did not appeal to you."

His voice was not a whisper, but she had to strain to hear him. "If I told you that, I lied. From the moment I saw you, I have wanted you. I have wanted you all these years. I have wanted you so much that all the other women I've had have been as nothing. I have," his smile was more a grimace, "not even bothered with a woman in over three years, for they leave me hungrier than ever for something that I don't understand."

The fire crackled.

"Why are you telling me this?" she asked. She was aware of his maleness, of his closeness.

"Because you should know that what I once considered a lowly woman has been of utmost importance to me. You have changed the direction of my life and my habits and my dreams."

He was so close she felt his breath and wondered if he could hear what he was doing to her heart. Certainly he must hear its pounding.

"Lately I dream that I am going to die in battle. And I do not mind. I think it honorable to die for a dream, in helping my country throw off its yoke of servility. I dream sometimes that I shall die fighting the Japanese, and that I shall be part of the process of freedom. If I had never met you, I could not think that way."

She reached out to put a hand on his jacketed arm. "You will not die. You are going to live to make a difference to China. I know it."

He put his hand on hers. The fire dancing before her was as nothing compared to the heat that shot up her arm.

By the dying embers she saw his shining face. Taking his hand in hers, she brought it to her lips, kissing its palm gently.

"That is a kiss," she said.

"I *know* what a kiss is." He smiled. "It is lips touching. . . ."

She did not let go of his hand, and her eyes did not leave his. "No, it is not just touching. It is what happens when lips touch. See, this is different from the first time." She ran her tongue across his palm. His hand closed around her chin in a caress.

His head was directly above her. She reached up, pulling his mouth to hers. "Do what I do," she whispered. "I will teach you how to kiss." Her tongue darted into his mouth and she heard his intake of breath. He gathered her into his arms, pulling her up to him. His mouth did not leave hers.

When they pulled back, she laughed.

"I did not do it right?" he asked.

"Oh, I think you're going to do very well," she said, "but I am laughing at our trying to be close with all these furs between us." She wanted to feel his warmth, wanted to kiss his cheeks and his eyelashes, and run her tongue down his neck. She wanted his hand on her breast before she remembered that Chinese men did not find breasts attractive.

He reached over and began to untie the thongs of her jacket, helping her remove it. "Come, mine is large enough for us both," he said, pulling her close to him so that she could feel the roughness of his shirt as he enfolded her in his heavy coat.

He held her like that for several minutes, and then he asked, "Are you afraid of me?"

"You have saved my life over and over. How could I be afraid of you?"

"But now," he said, "when we are close like this? When I want you?" His laugh was low. "I have always wanted you. But I have never been used to pleasing women. And I want to please you. I do not know how."

"You are doing very well." She sighed. "Try kissing me again, or didn't you like it?"

For answer, his mouth was upon hers hungrily. She took his hand and put it on her breast, running her tongue along his lips, finding her body responding to his desire. When he finally stopped kissing her, she said, "Lips are not the only thing to be kissed." She pulled away from the warmth of his coat and, crossing her arms, pulled off her sweater, and then quickly undid her brassiere. She lay back upon the blanket as he stared at her. "Kiss my breasts," she said. "It is something I like very much."

He leaned over, and she said, "Bite me, but very gently." He did. And she wanted him badly. She had not had a man in five years, and his lips upon her body made her wild with desire.

She reached for the buttons on his shirt. He jerked his head up and looked at her, standing up to take off his clothes. She stood too, twisting out of her shapeless Chinese trousers. He reached out a hand, saying, "Stop. Let me look at you. Chinese women do not look like you."

She stood for a moment, like a statue, glorying in his studying her, and then she walked toward him slowly. He sank to his knees as she approached, and she said, "Bellies are for kissing too." He grabbed her, hugging her stomach to his face, kissing her wildly, nibbling her flesh, reaching up for her breasts, pulling her on top of him as he sank to the quilt.

"Wait," she whispered. "Don't hurry." And she leaned over to run her tongue across his nipples, laying the length of her body along him, spreading her legs wide, kissing his neck as his hands clasped her buttocks.

The fire died out. In the darkness she searched for his mouth again, kissing him, feeling his tongue, gently yet urgently pressing against hers. As she raised herself against him so that he could kiss her breasts, she could feel his tongue giving life to her desire, the passion igniting deep in her belly.

She rolled off him, onto her back, and he followed her. She wound her legs around him, pulling him into her, feeling the smooth thrust, the power, the ecstasy that she had nearly forgotten. They rocked back and forth, his hands under her, pushing her against him so that they were one.

Later, when they lay next to each other, she reached for his hand, holding it between them. She could not help asking, "Is this the way Chinese make love too?"

He squeezed her hand tightly. "I have never made love before."

# CHAPTER 59

In the morning, there was more than a foot of snow. But they didn't discover that until after they made love again. Snow Leopard did not willingly let her leave his arms.

"After this is all over," he said, "I will come to you."

"What if I am not in Sian?" she asked.

"I will find you. I will always know where you are."

She laughed, reaching her arms around his neck. "How will you do that?"

"My heart has become a compass, always pointing its way to you."

"Kiss my heart," she said softly.

He ran his tongue across her breast. "Chinese women do not have breasts like yours," he murmured. "They are more like boys. Your breasts are beautiful." He caressed her, looking at her body. He grinned. "I am glad you taught me to kiss."

"I wonder why it is not a Chinese custom. Kissing has always been part of Western civilization, I think. It's terribly nice, don't you think?" She stretched to kiss his ear.

"Perhaps it means I am now in an advanced stage of civilization?" He laughed.

"You don't know, do you, that I was just a tiny bit disappointed that you didn't want me when you kidnapped me? No, I didn't really *want* you, or at least I didn't let myself think so. But I wondered if Chinese and Americans made love the same way. It was not scary to me. I did not think I would dislike what you did to me. You did not frighten me."

He looked at her, amazed. "But you would not have kissed me then, would you?"

She had to think about that. "I don't know. It would have depended. You made me feel important."

He held her so close and so tightly, she could hear the beat of his heart.

"I will come to you after this war with the Japanese is over and together we will make a life." He grinned. "Even with forty-some children. We'll go to Kunming, where it is beautiful and peaceful."

"When the Japanese are defeated, you will be back to fighting as to which Chinese, and which philosophy, will rule China. I think you would be better than either Mao or Chiang. I do not think you belong in Kunming. China needs you."

"You do not?"

She thought a moment. "I want you, it is true. But I do not need you as China does."

"Your wanting me is enough for now. The future will take care of itself. Promise me you will stay in Sian long enough for me to fight battles for a few months and then come to you. Now that I have you, I want to be with you. Until then, promise to wait in Sian until I can come and we can make plans together."

"I will wait," she said, "until you come."


Going down the mountain was tedious in the deep snow. At the foot of it was a small village, and there they found a guide who, for an exorbitant fee, agreed to take Chlöe to the next village. It would be nightfall before she could arrive, because she and Snow Leopard had been so late starting.

"I'll ride hard and will be back in Yenan before dark," he said. It was not yet noon.

With none of the men she had gone to bed with, not with Slade, or Nikolai, or Cass, had she felt such unity. She did not stop to examine her feelings. She just watched Snow Leopard turn his horse and ride up the pass, disappearing around the bend hidden by the big rock. He did not turn to look back. A part of her was going off to battle for China, while the part of her left standing there was returning to her children. Her Chinese children. She would not return to America after all.

Perhaps, she thought, I feel this way about him because I have become more Chinese than American. Because I have needed only a Chinese lover to become Chinese. Now I have what other Chinese have. And she thought, Next time I will ask Snow Leopard for a Chinese name. I will let him give me a name. Suddenly, she was filled with overwhelming sadness that she could not bear his child. Could not have a Chinese child.

"But I do have Chinese children," she said aloud, eager now to return to Jade and to Plum Blossom and Li. She had spent so much time worrying about Jade's trauma and her silence that she had hardly given a thought to the other two. Following the guide as he mounted his mule and began to trot, Chlöe thought, I love them too.

Yet it was Jade whom Chlöe felt was her own, often feeling about her as she now did about Snow Leopard, as though the girl were an integral part of her.

Snow Leopard. She could still feel his hands on her, feel his tentative kisses, feel his tongue on her nipples, remember his swift thrust inside her, and she wanted to lock him in, to never let him leave. God, it had been so long.

Her mind rambled as the guide set an even gait. My mother would be so shocked, she thought to herself. I've made love with four men. And yet in so many ways I've had a sexually deprived life. So many years since a man had touched her, since those ten days with Cass up at Lu-shan, right after Slade's death.

Now, suddenly, Snow Leopard. Part of her had come to life again. Part of her that she hadn't realized she'd buried. She closed her eyes and felt his naked body against her again, felt the smoothness of him, the warmth of him next to her.

Her horse halted.

The guide had stopped. He pointed in the far distance, where Chlöe could barely discern a village, mud-colored as was the earth, covered with inches of snow.

"I leave you here. There is an inn there where you can stay the night. Ask for the man with the clubfoot. He will guide you to the next village."

Chlöe dug deep in her fur coat and drew out some coins to pay him. "Thank you," she said, bowing her head in courtesy.

"It is nothing," he said, reaching for the money. Then he turned and, kicking his mule, took off.

Chlöe approached the village, quiet in the late afternoon except for a rooster crowing. She laughed. Roosters crowed all over China at the strangest times. They never waited for dawn.

It was a nondescript village, as were thousands all over China, dark in the snowy winter. There was no sign of life except for a man who rode toward her on a large gray horse. He was bundled in a greatcoat, but she thought he rode more erectly than a peasant and decided he must be a soldier. The nearer they got to each other, the more easily she could see the rifle slung across his saddle.

They drew close to each other and she greeted him with "Ni

*hau."* In response to his determined questioning, she told him she sought comfort for the night and the man with a clubfoot to guide her to the next village. He stared at her, a thin mustache straight above his rigid lips.

He said something she did not understand as he picked up his rifle. Though he did not aim it at her, he gestured that she should ride into the village ahead of him. Perhaps he did not realize she was a woman, Chlöe thought. She was bundled up so, one could hardly tell.

Once inside the village there was no sign of life. Fear insinuated itself down her spine. The man said something again. Spat something out was more like it, but she still could not understand. He rode around in front of her and, by gestures, indicated she should dismount. She did.

Raising the gun at her, he nodded his head to indicate that she should precede him into the inn.

Inside, seated at a table, with only a candle to light the entire room, sat a uniformed man with a bottle of beer. His legs were sprawled out, a pistol lay on the table near his hand, and when he smiled at Chlöe she noticed a front tooth was gold. Chinese could not afford gold teeth.

The two soldiers spoke, and suddenly Chlöe thought, They're Japanese. I think they're Japanese. Oh, dear God.

The soldier at the table spoke to her in broken Chinese. "You are a woman?"

She nodded. "I am an American woman."

He stood up and approached her, staring in surprise. Raising his hand, he pushed back the hood of her jacket. Her hair cascaded around her shoulders. He peered at her, running the back of one finger down her cheek.

"Where have you come from?"

Not Yenan, she thought. I cannot give that away. "I am lost," she said. "I am trying to get to Sian."

He looked at her sharply and returned to his seat at the table, drinking from the bottle. "I did not ask where you are going to. I asked where you are coming from."

"I am coming from Shanghai," she said.

He looked at her and stood up again. "I asked where you are coming from that you are up here in this little mountain village."

Be sharp, thought Chlöe. Keep your senses, girl. Don't let down your guard. "I don't really know," she said, trying not to let her nervousness be reflected in her voice. "I left Shanghai many weeks ago, and I have wandered from village to village. The last one told me if I followed the path, I would come to a village with an inn and perhaps I could find a guide to take me south."

He walked over to her, an inch or two shorter than she, and peered into her eyes. "I will ask again. What village did you stay in, and where are you coming from?"

She shook her head. "I don't know."

His hand whizzed through the air, and she felt a sharp stinging blow on her cheek. Involuntarily, she raised her hand to it.

"I really don't know where I was last night," she said, trying to control her voice. "I am not lying to you. I don't even know where I've been today."

He returned to his seat and, sprawling into it, said, "You speak Chinese like a native."

She didn't respond.

He called something, and yet another soldier rushed in. After an exchange of several words, the new soldier, a young boy, nodded his head, which she took to mean that she was to walk ahead of him. They walked down a dark, narrow hallway, and when they came to an open door, he shoved her in, clamping the door shut behind her.

It was too dark to see, but she felt her way around the room, only to discover there was no furniture at all. She sat down on the floor. Fortunately, she could not feel the cold through her layers of clothing. She heard no sounds.

They'll let me go, she told herself. When they realize I am not a Chinese. When it begins to dawn on them that I am an American, and Japan is not at war with the United States. Of course they'll let me go. Thank goodness the one in charge understood some Chinese. In the morning she would explain to him . . . What would she explain? What could she tell him?

In the morning she discovered it was a small band of only five Japanese, but with rifles and ammunition, and they had terrorized the village. Chlöe was marched outside at dawn, and there she saw the bodies of a dozen villagers lying in awkward positions like stick figures. Somewhere in the distance she heard weeping.

She had not eaten since noon of the previous day. The Japanese offered no food or water. Yet everything in her stomach came up. She vomited as she looked at the dead. One of the women held a baby. It looked as though a bullet had gone through its head and on through the mother's heart. There was no blood on the baby, none at all. Just a hole above the left eye. The mother still held it, clasped against her breast, where blood *was* spattered.

The Japanese captain—or whatever he was, he was in charge—was looking at her, one eyebrow raised. When she turned to meet his gaze, he smiled at her.

"I am an American," she said.

He nodded. "You can ride."

The captain mounted his horse. The villagers paraded after him and, behind them, Chlöe was permitted to ride. Two soldiers brought up the rear as the other two rode along either side of the column, calling out to slow walkers, once zinging a whip through the air though not grazing anyone. They marched until midday, when the soldiers stopped to eat. No food was offered to the prisoners. Nor water.

Chlöe's lips were so dry they cracked. Her fellow prisoners had no warm clothes and no shoes. Ribbons of red trailed them as they walked through the snow. No one talked.

Late in the afternoon it began to snow again, and an old man sank into a snowbank by the side of the path. "I can't go on," he muttered. A middle-aged woman leaned down, pulling at his arm.

But a crack resounded in the thin air, and the old man reeled to the ground, blood spurting from his chest.

Ten minutes later they came to another village, where there were no villagers, no animals, no nothing. The prisoners were herded into the inn, and there the women were put to cooking. Turnips and cabbage soup. Chlöe had never tasted anything better in her life.

After they'd eaten, the captain came into the room, where the prisoners were crowded around the fireplace, trying to absorb any warmth they could.

"Come with me," he said to Chlöe.

She followed him to the small room he had commandeered as his office.

Without turning to look at her, he shut the door and said, "Take off your pants."

She stared at him.

"No."

He jerked his head around to look at her. "Perhaps you do not understand. You are my prisoner. You will do as I say."

"I am not your prisoner. I am an American, and Japan is not at war with America."

"Who Japan fights has nothing to do with your being my prisoner. You are a woman. And I have a gun. Take down your pants."

"I will not." Could he tell she was afraid, or was all he heard the anger in her voice?

Slowly, he walked to her, bringing his arm back and, with all his might, striking her so hard on the side of her head that she fell to the floor.

He shouted, and one of his soldiers ran in. The captain, fury in his voice, rattled off some unintelligible sounds that made the soldier smile as he knelt over and grabbed her hands, pinning her to the floor. The captain kicked her hip. He leaned over and pulled down her trousers. With a flick of his knife he cut off her underpants. The young soldier held on to her hands.

The captain loosened his belt, letting his own trousers fall to the floor. But without even kicking them off, so that they dangled around his left ankle, he knelt with a leg on either side of her. She heard the soldier holding her arms laugh.

With a quick thrust the captain entered her, and pain seared through her. She screamed and tried to kick, but he was too strong. He drove into her, jamming himself in and out with a painful rhythm, until she saw the glazed look come into his eyes right before he moaned. He fell on top of her for just a minute, and then he straightened up, laughing at her before he spat at her, his spittle grazing her cheek, seeping into her eye.

Pulling his pants up with him, he stood, and saying something to the soldier who still pinned her to the ground, he walked to the door, calling out. With the light behind them, she saw the three other soldiers line up outside the door.

One came in without closing the door. He spoke to the soldier holding her, who released her arms as the other grabbed them. The young soldier, who had pinioned her arms, dropped his pants and climbed on her. She felt him thrust into her, wiggling back and forth, grinding into her—and then it was all over. In less than three minutes. She wanted to kill him.

They took turns. When they were through, after they had left, she reached down to touch herself, to pull her own trousers back on, and felt the sticky ooze of blood.

The whole thing could not have lasted more than fifteen minutes.

I won't let fifteen minutes change my life, she thought, her hands balled into fists. Five men in and out in fifteen minutes. I'll be goddamned if I'll let that change my life.

But she could not stop crying.

# CHAPTER 60

The soldiers didn't rape her again. They took turns with a different woman each night. None of them screamed. Chlöe realized they must be used to such treatment.

She was kept apart from the Chinese villagers. Now and then, as they passed by a farm, the soldiers captured more prisoners. Once in a while Chlöe heard a shot in the distance.

Any time Chlöe tried to speak to one of the Chinese, a soldier interrupted, hitting not her but the Chinese. She soon stopped trying.

Ten days of marching brought them to a large encampment, hundreds of tents and one mud-brick building, all covered with netting, over which were tossed branches and leaves. It was the first time Chlöe encountered camouflage. Mao's men could study this valley from mountaintops, or fly over it, except that they lacked planes, and never see it.

By now the ranks of prisoners swelled, even though a number of the original villagers had died along the way or been shot if they became too infirm to travel. They were ordered to stand single file in the icy mud. They waited. And waited. It was over an hour before a stocky Japanese with rimless glasses and epaulets on his shoulders strode from the headquarters building. He wore jodhpurs, and his uniform was trim, unlike any Chinese soldiers she had seen. He stood, hands on hips, surveying the prisoners. Chlöe was the only one on a horse. She thought she should have slid down to stand among the others so that she would be less noticeable. The soldiers had never even suggested she walk or attempted to confiscate her horse.

Chlöe had tried to ascertain what direction they were traveling. The sun was hidden daily under skies leaden with winter. She thought they'd been heading northeast, which made sense. That's where the Japanese strongholds were.

The commander waved his arm into the air, pointing at the

prisoners, and several soldiers ran forward, rounding them up and pressing them toward two of the large tents near the headquarters. Chlöe began to follow, but a soldier halted her, shaking his head to indicate that she was not included. She sat where she was, on her horse, hoping this Japanese commandant understood she was an American and, as such, should not be treated as a prisoner of war.

The field was cleared of prisoners, and she alone was in the center of it, mounted on her horse, her fur hood wrapped around her head, her jacket protecting her from the wind that sprang up. There was no one in sight now except the commandant and his aide.

He stood, still with his hands on his hips, looking at her across the parade ground, until he finally turned to his aide, said something, and then strode back inside the building. The aide approached her, indicating that she should dismount and follow him.

The building offered Chlöe the first warmth she had felt in weeks. She followed the aide down a wide hall and into an office, spartanly furnished but clean. The commandant stood with his hands clasped behind him, staring out the window into the darkening afternoon.

He turned to look at her. "You are an American, I understand."

She breathed a sigh of relief. "I am."

He gestured toward one of the straight-backed chairs opposite his desk. "Let us have some tea," he said, clapping his hands smartly. His Mandarin was impeccable.

An orderly appeared, and the commandant ordered tea.

Chlöe sat in the chair. Civility after the brutality she had witnessed.

"Permit me to introduce myself." His manner was courtly. "I am Colonel Sakigawa." He lit a long cigarette in a longer holder. "And you?"

They might have been at afternoon tea.

"I am Chlöe Cavanaugh."

He smiled, and his teeth were even and very white. She noticed that while his face crinkled into a smile, his eyes remained like steel.

"What," he asked as his orderly brought in two cups of steaming tea, "are you doing in China?"

All her stories went out the window. "I am trying to get to my children in Sian."

He inhaled deeply, blowing smoke rings, studying them as he asked, "And what are your children doing in Sian?"

"Trying to escape the Japanese armies." She burned her tongue on the hot tea, but inhaled its fragrant, delicate aroma. "This is lovely tea."

He nodded. "I am very particular about my tea." He looked at her. "That really is not the answer I was searching for. Why are you and your children in China? Are you a missionary, is that it?"

"No." She opted for honesty. "My children were starving in Shanghai, so we left there, heading toward Sian. Three friends are with me. I have"—she paused briefly—"over forty children with me. We run an orphanage, and there was no food in Shanghai. So we decided to head west. I separated from them, trying to find a short-cut, and am hoping they are safe in Sian. I was trying to get there when your soldiers found me."

She did not tell him they'd raped her. She did not think that would bother him.

He held out a package of cigarettes, but she shook her head. "I do not think you were lost. But it does not matter."

"You must let me go," she said. "I have no part of your fight with this country. I am an American citizen."

He studied a fingernail as though it were fascinating. "How long have you been in China?"

"Many years."

"Yes. I thought so. Your accent is perfect. Madame, I consider you a prisoner of war. As far as I am concerned, you are Chinese. You have lived here for a long time and obviously your sympathies are with the Chinese. You *are* our prisoner. You may have a tent of your own, as I understand Westerners crave privacy. You may have that as long as you do as you are told. You shall be treated with every consideration if you behave. We shall be leaving here soon, and I shall expect your cooperation."

Chlöe said nothing.

The privacy Westerners craved began to drive her nuts. She was allowed out of her tent twice a day, a soldier walking to the latrine with her, standing observing her every minute. One morning, as they walked the well-worn path, Chlöe gasped. Buried in the ground, up to her neck, was a young woman, her eyes filled with panic. The dirt around her neck was recently spaded. What in the world . . . ?

Chlöe stopped, starting to kneel down, but the soldier butted the end of his rifle against her back. White with fury, Chlöe turned to face him.

"Take me to the colonel," she said.

He paid no attention to her, prodding her on toward the latrine.

God, were they going to let that woman die there? Was she going to suffer a slow death, dying of hunger and thirst, buried alive in the ground, unable to move? Dear God in heaven. Are You there? Are You looking and listening? The colonel must not be aware of this. He's civilized. I've got to get to him, Chlöe thought. He'll save her. He's not like those soldiers of his.

When the soldier who brought her thin gruel every morning arrived, she told him she needed to see the colonel. He nodded.

Nothing happened.

By midafternoon she could stand it no longer and, against the rules, opened the flap of her tent. She could see the head of the woman still buried in the earth. What did her eyes look like now?

Chlöe walked out of the tent into the thin sunshine and headed toward the headquarters. Two soldiers immediately rushed up to her, their rifles pointing at her.

She raised her arm and brushed away the rifle aimed at her chest. She didn't think they would kill her and have to answer to the colonel. She strode toward the building as though her heart were not pounding with fear. More than fear, she felt anger.

A soldier guarded the door, but she marched past him as all three of the soldiers now covered her with their guns. She wasn't trying to escape, they weren't going to shoot her, she told herself.

Down the hall she sailed, slamming open the door to the colonel's office. He glanced up from his desk, where he'd been studying papers, raising his eyebrows.

"What is the meaning of that woman?" Chlöe asked. "That is defying the Geneva convention, that is inflicting merciless, cruel treatment on a human being. Do you know what's happening, Colonel? A woman is buried up to her neck by the path to the latrines. I know you can't be aware of it. Put a stop to it. Please, come with me and see. You'll be as horrified as I. Please, Colonel. Come right away."

He leaned back in his chair, gazing at her. Then he murmured something, and the three soldiers withdrew, closing the door behind them.

"Mrs. Cavanaugh, do sit down," he said, his voice moderate.

"No. I want you to come see this heinous crime. I want you to punish whoever's responsible for this!"

He sighed. "Are you going to become a problem, Mrs. Cavanaugh? The soldiers obey my orders. They do nothing without my express orders."

Chlöe did sit down. "*You* ordered this? Oh, Colonel, how could you?"

"She tried to escape." He said it as though his actions were thus justified.

"Then shoot her. Do something quick, humane. Don't do this!"

His smile now lit his eyes. "Ah, but this way everyone can see what happens when such a situation arises. Tomorrow you will see her again, and the horror will dissuade you from disobeying us. There is no horror to shooting. Just a nice clean shot, something that is expected in war. You, along with the others, should learn from this, Mrs. Cavanaugh. And from that look in your eyes, that self-righteous fury, I'd say you are going to try to think of a way to rescue her, or shoot her to relieve her misery. Don't, Mrs. Cavanaugh, or a hole will be dug for you."

There was no threat in his voice. He sounded as though he were making pleasant conversation.

"You prisoners will be heading north within the next few days. A train awaits in the next town to take you to Taiyuan, where there is a prison camp. You will not be treated so understandingly there or with the courtesy I have extended you."

"Courtesy!" she spat out. "Solitary confinement! Two inedible meals a day. Women buried in the ground. Rape! Courtesy, you say! Colonel, you are a barbarian!" She remembered the last time she had called someone a barbarian.

He was not intimidated, but laughed. "Western women are such bothers. What you really need is a good beating. Japanese women know how to behave."

"I'll bet. Any spirit is beaten out of them. You don't like women, you like robots. You—"

The colonel interrupted her. "You will return to your tent, and you will not rush in here again. You have been warned. Tomorrow morning when you follow that path again, study that woman and learn what happens when we are disobeyed, either as men or as the enemy."

"It seems they are one and the same in the Orient," Chlöe blurted out.

"You are reckless about your safety."

"I would rather die than live like your women do!"

"Be careful," he said, his voice hardening, "or that can easily be arranged."

"And then you'd have the entire United States on you."

He laughed. "Don't be a fool. They don't even know where you are. You say you've been lost. You've disappeared. No one knows where you are. You are not safe because of your nationality, Mrs. Cavanaugh. You exist at our whim. I shall not warn you again."

No food was brought to her tent that night.

But the next morning, when the soldier led her along the path to the latrine, the buried woman's eyes stared vacantly and her tongue hung out of her mouth. Chlöe hoped she was unconscious. Or dead. She had never hoped anyone was dead before. She prayed, If she is not dead, let her die quickly.

Three days later a caravan started for the train that would take them north to the prison camp. They marched. This time Chlöe did not have a horse, and was permitted to mingle with the Chinese, who treated her with suspicion. Nights they slept in cold caves, the men and women herded into them together, with soldiers guarding the entrance. There were no lights. The only meal was at midday, when the soldiers stopped to rest.

The soldiers marched them until they dropped, leaving those who faltered in the mountain passes, knocking them out with the butt end of a rifle. The husbands and wives of those who could no longer go on tried to stay behind with the infirm, but the Japanese prodded them on. Sometimes they shot the dropouts, clean through the forehead, and smiled when a wife wailed or a husband beat his head against a rock.

One morning the youngest prisoner, a seven-year-old girl, was found dead and bloody. Chlöe knew she'd been raped repeatedly. Her drawers were lying on the ground beside her frozen blue body.

By the time they reached the train station, the first week of March, the smell of spring was in the air. Boxcars waited at the depot, and many of them already were loaded with prisoners. All of Chlöe's group were herded into one car, so tightly packed they could not sit or lie down but were forced to stand erect. They had all lost weight on the trip, and Chlöe had to keep holding her pants up so they would not fall off the wasted body hers had become.

The train did not budge. They were offered no food or water.

They stood all night. And then, with the first streaks of dawn, the engine choked into life, steam hissing into the air. With a jolt the train began to move, swaying with its heavy load. The car stank with the odor of excrement, urine, and vomit.

It was still early, though the sun was rising quickly, the first sun they'd seen for weeks, and now it was making the car a hellhole. Suddenly there was shouting, cries ripping through the air as the engine's brakes exploded, sending the prisoners crashing to the front of the car. Bursts of gunfire filled the air.

We're being rescued, Chlöe thought. Someone's attacking the train.

And she knew as surely as if she could see outside the car that it was Snow Leopard. She knew it with certainty.

# CHAPTER 61

They came roaring down from the hills, over five hundred strong. They came riding with rifles, with pistols, with bayonets. They came with grenades and knives, and with cries that would have set a banshee's teeth on edge.

They were careful where they aimed, avoiding the boxcars. They aimed only at the engine, and once it stopped, the Chinese soldiers were all over the train, climbing to the roofs of the cars, standing with their guns aimed at anyone who might try to run away or to challenge them, bombarding the two cars where the Japanese soldiers were gathered. One car was behind the engine, and the other was the caboose. Within seconds the Chinese aimed a machine gun into the car behind the engine, spraying glass as Japanese soldiers, fumbling for their guns, fell out of windows and crunched down on the floor, trying to avoid the bullets.

One Japanese managed to fire point-blank at the approaching Chinese, hitting the leader in the thigh. Though he grabbed his leg, it did not stop him for a second. He waved his arm, and the men behind him jumped from their horses, covering the car as though they were ants, crawling up its sides and into the doors at either end, spraying gunfire randomly.

Snow Leopard, clutching his leg, jumped from his horse, and with a heroic effort and the help of two soldiers uncoupled the first two cars of the train. The Chinese pushed the cars, the second one now full of dead or dying Japanese. When they were two hundred or so feet from the boxcars filled with prisoners, the Chinese soldiers fell over themselves, getting away before two bombs, within seconds of each other, exploded, disintegrating the two cars into splinters.

Then Snow Leopard turned his attention to the cars filled with prisoners. His soldiers had eliminated any Japanese in the caboose. The air was gray with the smoke of gunfire.

With hatchets the soldiers chopped down the doors, Snow Leopard peering, his eyes alight with a kind of craziness, into each of them, into the dark gloom, watching as the freed peasants spilled out into the daylight. Chlöe was in the fifth car. She burst into tears when she saw him standing outside the doors, searching for her. When his eyes found her, he closed them for just a moment. As though he were saying thank God, yes, thank God. Though she knew he wasn't, he might as well have been.

There was no smile in his eyes as he came limping to her, grabbing her hand, paying no attention to the hundreds of other prisoners streaming into the fields. He put his arms around her, holding her close, as she whispered, "I knew it was you."

"Of course," he said, his voice husky. "I told you I would always know where you were."

"I mean," she said, her head clasped against his chest, for he held her as though he would never let her go, "as soon as I knew we were being rescued, as soon as I heard the shouts, I knew it was you."

He nodded, and said again, "Of course." People swirled past them, breaking into freedom.

Snow Leopard pulled Chlöe on his horse, holding her tight against him. "We shall destroy the Japanese railhead, and then we shall lead these people back to their villages."

"It took us weeks to get here," said Chlöe.

"War is never quick," he said, his arms around her as they rode slowly at the head of soldiers on horseback and the ragtag group of freed peasants. "We know of a place nearby where there is a running stream, and you can wait there until we do battle in the town. We shall be back by sundown."

Her hand rested on his leg, and it was then she felt it, the thick, coagulating blood. "You're wounded," she said with a start.

"I've had other wounds," he said. "Soldiers expect it."

"You can't go into battle in this condition."

Snow Leopard met her words with silence. Whether it was because she was the first woman who tried to tell him what to do, or because he was in pain, she couldn't tell.

"Do what you must," she said, and his arms around her tightened.

"I always do what I must," he said.

"Thank goodness," she whispered, but he heard her and brushed his lips through her hair.

When the town had been cleared of Japanese and Snow Leopard could organize the prisoners he discovered there were three hundred twenty-seven, over two hundred fifty of them having come from other places than Chlöe's group. None of them knew from what direction they had come, or where their villages were.

"Come with us," said Snow Leopard, and most of them nodded. Yes. They had to go someplace. They were filled with an implacable hatred, willing now to go anyplace where they could seek revenge on this enemy they hadn't even known existed. They wanted to chase the enemy away, and to kill him. Kill with their bare hands, for vengeance seethed from their very pores.

They did not have time now, but later they would mourn the loss of their ancestral grounds, worrying about who would take care of their dead. It would not sink in until later, and by that time Chlöe would be long gone and not fully aware of what war and its aftermath did to people.

She herself hadn't faced being raped . . . five men she didn't know using her like an animal, treating her not as a human being but simply as a vessel in which they deposited their maleness. Nothing more. She did not let herself think about it, but buried it under layers of consciousness, hoping never to have to confront it. Telling herself it was behind her.

It wasn't.

Though she and Snow Leopard slept out in the field with the other hundreds, he pulled her close to him, not caring what others thought of his actions. She curled against him all night, listening to him moan in his sleep, with the pain of the bullet in his leg. When they awoke, he was hot with fever.

"We must get you to a doctor," she said, her voice filled with concern.

"There's no doctor for hundreds of miles," he said.

"Your leg's infected. We must get the bullet out. Look at it." He'd had to cut a hole in his pants leg. Chlöe put hot compresses, from water she insisted on boiling, on his swollen leg, but Snow Leopard would not hear of slowing down.

"I can ride," he said. "Staying here won't help."

The soldiers on horseback set as slow a pace as they could so the straggling walkers would not be left behind. But Snow Leopard and Chlöe, along with three dozen other soldiers, rode ahead. "There," Chlöe pointed at the numerous tents, "that's where we were kept. They buried a woman there, all but her head, and just left her to die. It was awful. Unbearable." But she *had* borne it. They all had.

Snow Leopard, lying on a quilt, laid out a battle plan. He marshaled all his energy to explain to each one of the soldiers exactly what to do.

"Don't kill the colonel," said Chlöe. "Bring him here."

Snow Leopard nodded. He understood vengeance.

The Japanese, playing cards or dozing in the afternoon, were surprised. They were dead within ten minutes of the Chinese attack. Except for the colonel, who had been working alone in his office. When he heard the gunfire, he reached for his pistol and stood behind his desk, shooting at the men who opened the door. He killed only the first one. The next two grabbed him by the arms and took him back up the hill to where Snow Leopard and Chlöe awaited them.

The minute the Japanese saw Chlöe he knew how he would die. She ordered the soldiers to dig a hole.

"It's fate, don't you think, Colonel?" she asked. "In my country we have a saying, 'What ye sow, ye shall reap.' I am not doing it for the reasons you did, to teach a lesson. I am doing it because I don't want you to have a—wasn't the word you used *clean?*—death. Anyone who did what you did deserves to suffer the same fate. Here, sit down and wait. Watch them dig that hole, Colonel."

Snow Leopard, lying on the quilt, watched her. Watched as she had men lower the colonel into the hole so that only his head was aboveground. And then Chlöe knelt beside the colonel, beside the mound of dirt the soldiers had shoveled from the ground, and slowly, by handfuls, dropped the earth back into the hole, surrounding the colonel, who did not once flinch. Chlöe did it slowly, so slowly that it took over an hour to fill the hole. And then she sat back, hugging her knees, studying the Japanese.

"All the time that remains to you, I hope you will think of that woman you buried, and know how she felt. Know that if you had never done such a thing, your fate would not be as it is."

"All is preordained" were the only words the colonel uttered.

They rode on for a mile before stopping for the night, where there was shelter under trees, and wood enough to make a litter for Snow Leopard. He fell asleep immediately.

Chlöe put her arms around him, but she could not sleep. As soon as she closed her eyes she saw the face of the buried woman. She saw the staring, vacant eyes and the tongue hanging out of her mouth. She saw the colonel, alone in the dark, imagining his slow death, envisioning the fright, the thirst, the claustrophobia. She told herself he deserved every bit of it. He probably had done this to women—perhaps to men too—dozens of times. He had never taken the time to imagine how it would feel. Now he would know. Now . . .

She tried to think what it would be like to die slowly, to starve, to die of thirst, to be unable to move, to go stark raving insane. . . . And she tossed, unable to sleep.

When the stars began to fade, she found Snow Leopard's pistol and, mounting her horse, rode back the mile they had come. Her eyes, accustomed to the darkness, saw the head beside the road.

She slid down to the ground and walked over to the colonel. It was not light enough to know whether he saw her. She knelt down and said, "Colonel?"

"It is you." His voice was flat.

"I have come to make it clean."

"Yes." And then, "Thank you."

She pulled the safety on the pistol and stood back from him. They both heard the click. Her arm stiff, she took aim, saw only the dark shape of the head, none of his features. And pulled the trigger.

The shot reverberated through the hills, echoes bouncing from one to another.

Jumping onto her horse, she trotted away, wishing she could gallop, but unable to see the road clearly enough in the time before dawn.

When she returned, Snow Leopard was still feverish but reached for her hand and said, "I heard. And I am glad. It is what I did for Fen-tang. Your Japanese deserved to die, but there was no reason to be inhumane."

"Why didn't you say that to me yesterday?"

"It was your vengeance, not mine. It had to come from within you. And I am glad you did what you did. Otherwise, you would have trouble sleeping the rest of your life."

He pulled her to him with the little strength he had and kissed her. "I am glad you taught me about kissing." His smile was weak.

"I am glad too." She pressed his hand to her breast, then raised it to her lips.

Late in the afternoon they were forced to stop. Snow Leopard was delirious. They moved him to a quilt on the ground and Chlöe could tell he was burning with fever. She examined his leg, horrified at the foul-smelling area that was red with swelling, thick pus running from the gangrened wound.

Oh, God, she thought. He's not going to be around to lead China after all.

She walked away from the soldiers and found a grove of trees, where she sank to the ground and cried. Cried and cried.

She sat by his side all night, holding his hand. Near morning he awoke, conscious, his hand moving within hers. He smiled at her. "What ye sow ye shall reap, isn't that what you said? And I said, long ago when I was so sure of myself, that a woman was never worth dying for." He reached for her and she pulled herself close to him. "It has been worth it."

Her arms around him, she said, "You're not going to die. China and I need you too much." She touched her lips to his.

"To have discovered love when I did not believe it existed makes it all worthwhile."

Tears fell down her cheeks.

"Sometime, *if* there is an afterlife, our dust may mingle." His voice was fading. "Until then . . . Odd, isn't it? We met because of a train. And now to die because of a train." He lay in her arms, his eyes closed. "To die in your arms, with your tears on my cheeks, with your lips on mine . . ."

She put her mouth against his again, feeling his last surge of life against her.

"You are not like anyone else in the whole world," she whispered. But he was gone.

They buried his body high on a ridge.

Now she wanted to be the one to kill any Japanese who might get near them. She had taken Snow Leopard's rifle as her own. She wanted to kill, to kill all the Japanese. She wanted to punish them, to annihilate them. She wanted to scream at them and claw their eyes out. She wanted to run her nails down their arms and see blood drip. She wanted to—

Ahead of them, down in the valley, was a campfire. The soldiers with her stopped. Someone volunteered to find out whether they were friend or foe. Chlöe said, "I'm coming too."

They looked at her silently. She could tell none approved. It didn't matter. As long as none of them stopped her.

She and Chin-li, the volunteer, slid down the hill, crawling through the thick undergrowth for more than half an hour. Twilight became night by the time they reached the fire. Sitting around it were eleven Japanese, one of them talking, gesturing with his hands, while the others listened, laughing now and then. They were unaware of how close danger was.

And there, staring at Chlöe although she knew he couldn't see her, was the captain whose soldiers had originally captured her. The captain who had raped her, treating her as though she were not human. The captain who had granted his soldiers permission to use her as they wanted. The captain who she was sure had already forgotten the incident. The captain who she was sure had used women that way all his life. The captain who, with his men, had raped a different woman each night of their journey. The captain who was searching for the armies hidden at Yenan, she imagined. The Japanese who was out in the mountains of northern China searching for ways to subdue the land and all its peoples as he had a few women.

If she'd had Snow Leopard's rifle with her, she'd have taken aim for the center of his forehead and pulled the trigger. He'd never know what hit him.

An hour later, when she and Chin-li climbed back up the hill, the soldiers in their group had decided it was best to wait until the Japanese were asleep. Right before dawn they'd attack. In the meantime they'd find their way through the forest and wait near the Japs, permitting themselves a little sleep first.

Chlöe did not sleep. She lay staring up into the darkness, thinking, I don't want them dead. That's too easy. Too clean.

They captured the Japanese, swiftly and silently in the sleepy hour before daylight. Chlöe singled out the captain and the four men whom he had permitted to use her. The others were shot. Chlöe stood staring down at the men who had raped her. She looked around at the soldiers behind her. "Is any of you a medic?" she asked.

One young soldier stepped forward. "I have assisted in operations."

"Castrate them," she said, her voice cold. "Do not let them die if you can help it."

Castrate them so they will have to live out their lives unable ever to do to a woman again what they did to me.

The feeling of their invasion into her body came back to her, and she vomited into the dark dirt. Let them live unable ever to have a woman again.

The young Chinese soldier sharpened his knife on a stone. Three others held the captain.

"Kill me," he pleaded. "I'd rather be dead."

She smiled, looking directly at him. "Exactly."

She stood and watched it happen, listening to screams rending the air, watching as the young Chinese cut off the Japanese men's testicles. After each operation he sewed up the man with coarse black thread. Chlöe watched it five times without flinching.

She felt no pain, no guilt. No exultation either. "Let them go. We don't need them as prisoners."

Whether they died as a result of infection, whether they survived to kill more Chinese, did not matter to her. She had evened the score as much as she could. She thought now she would be through with being raped.

She did it for Jade too.

She did it from uncontrolled hatred. She did it with malice and took satisfaction from revenge. She understood now how someone could gain intense pleasure from slowly garroting an enemy. Or beheading them.

That night she dreamed of the white pear blossoms in the side yard at home.

Home. Oneonta.

"I want to go home," she said aloud, as she had nearly six weeks before in a cave in Yenan.

# CHAPTER 62

"You are nothing but a bag of bones," exclaimed Su-lin, shaking her finger at Chlöe at the same time that tears ran down her cheeks.

From down the long, dark hall that ran off the courtyard came a shout, and Chlöe heard the pounding of feet along the cold tiles. As Jade entered the courtyard, a single ray of light hit her and she stopped, staring at Chlöe, who held out her arms to the girl.

But Jade just stood in the doorway, her mouth twitching, her hands balled tight into fists. And then she whispered, "I thought you were never coming back," before rushing toward Chlöe and throwing herself into the waiting arms. "Oh, Mother, Mother."

They were all crying. Chlöe, Jade, Su-lin.

"What's all the racket?" called Dorothy, and then, when she saw, tears filled her eyes too. "Oh, God, Chlöe. We were afraid . . ."

Chlöe nodded, reaching out an arm to encircle Dorothy too. "I don't even know how long it's been. So much has happened."

Jade clung to her, refusing to let go.

"It's been over two months," Dorothy said, wiping her eyes with the sleeve of her jacket.

"It's been sixty-nine days," Jade said, a catch in her voice.

Chlöe laughed as Plum Blossom and Li came tearing down the hall, followed by Jean, who was carrying an infant. Chlöe stooped down to encircle them in her embrace while Jade's arms wound around her neck.

"My goodness, you're skinny," cried Jean as the baby burped on her shoulder.

Su-lin moved away from the circle, saying, "I shall prepare some food."

Jade said, "I told them the only reason you weren't back is you were a prisoner of the Japanese or you had lost your way."

Dorothy laughed at the insanity of such an idea. Chlöe looked up at her beautiful daughter. "It's true," she said. "I was a prisoner."

A silence fell over the group.

"I'll tell you about it after I eat something, and after I get my fill of looking at you. Do you know how beautiful you all are?"

All the way back to Sian she'd been thinking that if Dorothy and Jean had things under control, if they felt they could manage alone, she'd take Jade and Plum Blossom and Li and go home. The Christian missions might be willing to support the orphanage, and Sian, for the time being, seemed safe. Certainly much more so than Shanghai had become.

But world affairs conspired against her, for the world's affairs were taking place in Sian. Chlöe's first inkling was awaiting her in a cable from Cass.

STORY FROM YENAN SOCKO. GLAD YOU'RE OUT OF SHANGHAI. CONTACT CHANG HSUEH-LIANG, HEADQUARTERED IN SIAN. HE'S IN CHARGE OF ARMIES FIGHTING JAPS AND REDS. MUCH LOVE. CASS.

He, of course, knew nothing of the past two months of Chlöe's life. He'd insist I come home if he knew, she told herself. But, instead, she wangled an interview with Chang Hsueh-liang, better known as the Young Marshal. Before meeting with him, however, she set out to discover all she could about the man directing China's armies in the northwest. What she found out intrigued her.

But first she heard the unbelievable news that Chiang Kai-shek was negotiating a treaty with Japan. Chiang volunteered to force all Western nations and their concessions out of China and turn over all of their commercial and territorial rights to the Japanese. In this way he hoped to stop Japan's further aggrandizement into his country so that his attention could continue to be focused on eradicating the threat of the Communists.

The Young Marshal, an intelligent, sensitive man who had grown up surrounded by corrupt and mercenary warlords, directed Chiang's northern armies. "I shall not rest," the Young Marshal told Chlöe at the end of her interview, "until we as a country are united in our fight against the aggressors. The Japanese now have five provinces of China, and I shall work to free them."

"Will the enemy come as far as Sian?" asked Chlöe.

The Young Marshal shrugged his shoulders, lighting a cigarette, which he held between his thumb and forefinger. "Tell your American press to warn your people that they, too, are in danger from the Japanese. Unless they help us, they, too, shall be at the mercy of the enemy."

Chlöe, who wasted no love on the Japanese, smiled to herself. The little islands of Japan were in no way a threat to the enormous United States of America.

Chiang Kai-shek, later that year, announced an "annihilation campaign," wherein all his forces would be directed toward the elimination of all Communists in China. He flew to Sian to relieve the Young Marshal of his command, reassigning him to duty in a remote southern section where there were, as yet, no Japanese and far from the northern stronghold of the Communists.

When the Young Marshal and a fellow sympathizer, General Yang, tried to reason with Chiang, the generalissimo flew into a fury and slammed the door, directing his driver to the Lishan Hills hot springs a dozen miles north.

As Chlöe wrote of what then happened, she remembered that she and Nikolai had stopped to bathe there before their long Mongolian trek. She did not know that the story she would send to Cass sparked more interest than her meeting with Mao. To the world, Mao did not exist. Chiang Kai-shek was China.

> Early in the morning, after a night wherein the two generals wrestled with their consciences, they took action. If they allowed Chiang Kai-shek to go ahead with his annihilation campaign, they knew they would be sent south and rendered powerless, that their cause against the Japanese would be lost. General Yang said to the Young Marshal, for perhaps the tenth time, "Let us hold Chiang Kai-shek hostage." At last the Young Marshal agreed.
>
> It is well known that Chiang arises an hour before dawn to meditate. His false teeth were on a bedside table and he wore only his nightshirt. Apparently he was staring out the window into the cold predawn when shots were heard.
>
> Two aides rushed into his room, urging him to make haste. Leaving his dentures and wearing nothing but his nightshirt, Chiang followed them to the back door, where they boosted him up over the wall. He fell on the other side, bruising his ankle and hurting his back. There was nothing before him but a prickly hill. He climbed up the hill as fast as he could with a swelling ankle.
>
> Soldiers combed the spa and the hillside, knowing that Chiang could not have escaped. Four hours after they knocked down the walls to the compound, they discovered Chiang hiding in a shallow cave. A soldier pulled him out, shivering with pain, cold, and fright. He was carried down the hill on a soldier's back and folded into the waiting car.
>
> They drove back to Sian, where General Yang and the Young Marshal greeted him at their headquarters, permitting him to take to bed and sending for a doctor.
>
> Their mission was a success.
>
> The Young Marshal and General Yang issued a declaration demanding that Chiang reorganize his Nanking government to include

*all factions, including Communists; that he allow political gatherings of any type to take place freely; that the civil war stop; that all political prisoners be released; that citizens be allowed to demonstrate politically; that the will of Dr. Sun Yat-sen be carried out.*

*Friends were permitted to see him and they urged him to understand that the Young Marshal was not an enemy, but a patriot. His first thought should be for China.*

*Three days later Madame Chiang flew into Sian to be with her husband. She emerged from her Fokker trimotor in a mink coat, bundled against the frigid northern winter. Accompanying her were her maid and cook, for she trusts no one. As she was driven through the city gates from the airport, the body of the slain soldier was still nailed to the wooden gates.*

*If any of us ever underestimated Madame Chiang, and I admit I have been one, we should not do so again. Madame Chiang Kai-shek listened to the Young Marshal, and to Chou En-lai, who had come down from Yenan, and said, "From now on, all our internal problems must be solved by politics, not by force. We are, after all, all Chinese." She agreed to their demands.*

*The generalissimo was released. As a token of good faith the Young Marshal accompanied them back to Nanking.*

*Will Chiang be as good as his wife's words?*

Only time would answer that.

And Chlöe could wait no longer. Dorothy and Jean, albeit sadly, admitted they thought they could run the orphanage without Chlöe's help. They understood her need to go home.

She never dreamed the journey would take nearly two years.

# PART V

# *1939–1949*

# CHAPTER 63

It gleamed whitely. Chlöe thought she had never seen anything whiter. Nestled on its hills, surrounded by trees, lay the city by the bay. Among the white were pastels, and there was no smell. None at all, except—as the ship pulled to the dock—the odor of fresh bread from a nearby bakery.

"It's beautiful," breathed Jade from her side. "But I thought you said it was a big city. Where are all the people?"

Chlöe laughed and put an arm around the girl's shoulders. It was true. After even a country village in China, San Francisco's streets seemed half empty. It looked so clean, pure. It wasn't gray; it wasn't dun-colored; its buildings were not the same monochromatic brick color as its earth.

There was so much Chlöe wasn't even aware of. The World's Fair had opened in the spring in Flushing Meadows, New York. Germany had invaded Poland, and Britain and France had declared war against Germany in September, the previous month. Americans were humming "Three Little Fishies," "Mairzy Doats," and "Sleepy Lagoon." *Gone With the Wind* had taken America by storm, and would become the longest running and largest grossing movie in the world. Clark Gable reigned supreme as the King of Hollywood. And it looked as though America was finally pulling out of its nearly decade-long Depression. Franklin Roosevelt was the most popular president since his cousin Teddy. John L. Lewis was one of the most hated, and one of the most beloved, men of the country. Hated by those who thought unions were ruining America; most hated after Hitler and Mussolini, of course.

Jews were being slaughtered in Europe. One after another of the European countries was falling to Hitler's armies. America danced to Glenn Miller, Guy Lombardo, and Tommy Dorsey, danced the big apple and the lindy hop. College freshmen swallowed goldfish, schoolchildren still said the Pledge of Allegiance and meant it, and Lana Turner had just filled the silver screen with her sweater.

It was not uncommon for Americans to remark, while watching

Fox Movietone newsreels in the movie theaters, hearing Lowell Thomas's always-on-the-edge-of-disaster voice in the background, "Why do they bother with all this war junk? I get tired of it. I can never tell who's who anyhow. The Japs and Chinks all look alike." But they'd sit up straighter and smile if a picture of Mei-ling came on the screen. Proud that such a beautiful, intelligent woman had been educated in America, had converted her husband to Christianity, and was thus fighting for the right. They all knew they hated the Japs because Japan had invaded China. But they didn't quite understand why they were supposed to like China, unless it was America's proverbial propensity to side with the underdog.

They knew why they hated Hitler. But they couldn't come to grips with identifying with the Chinks and were glad when that part of the newsreel was over.

America was still innocent. Or was the word *ignorant?*

As she looked at the city so rapidly coming into focus, Chlöe remembered the last time she had seen it and the happiness brimming from her then.

Just then Plum Blossom and Li came running around the deck, where they had been playing hide-and-seek, shrieking with laughter. They joined Chlöe and Jade at the railing. Chlöe looked at the three of them. Such handsome children, she thought. The girls were raving beauties. Jade, at almost fifteen, already turned heads. A serious girl, she had never been filled with the sense of irresponsibility and giggles that possessed her sister.

"Will they laugh at my English?" she asked Chlöe again.

"Probably. But you mustn't let that bother you. They'll appreciate that you are trying. You mustn't ever let that hurt your feelings. Chinese people were very kind to me when I was trying to learn Chinese, but I could see them smiling behind their hands. Americans are not likely to be so polite. But they will mean no harm by it."

She wondered if she was telling the truth. Though she had written years earlier to her parents to say she had adopted three Chinese orphans, she wondered how they would react to these grandchildren. Would the children be ostracized? Well, she wouldn't worry about things she couldn't change.

She thought that on the transcontinental train to Oneonta she wanted first to stop off in Chicago and see Cass. It had been nearly nine years since she'd seen him. Though there had never been a month, all the years she was in Shanghai, that she didn't hear from

him. Not simply in a business way, but with a long personal letter
and a check for the orphanage. Telling her that Grant did become
*his* managing editor, and that he and Suzi were incredibly happy and
Cass was ashamed of himself for having acted as he had for so long.
He wrote from England and Paris and Munich, where he'd predicted—in 1935, the last she'd a personal letter from him—war. He
wrote love letters which she'd read over and over again, tucking
them into the drawer of her bedside table, rereading them randomly.
But they had all been left behind four years before, when she'd
escaped Shanghai with the children, when Snow Leopard had come
for them.

All she'd said when she sent the cable six weeks before was,
"I'm coming home," not even signing it. For all she knew he was
remarried.

She'd had no word of him or of her family. What if her parents
were dead and she'd not known? She hadn't even seen them since
she was twenty-one. Or might they not recognize each other? The
idea of living in Oneonta appealed to her strongly. Life had come
full circle. No crowds. Cleanliness. No war. No brutality. No dying
and abandoned children. No bound feet. No men using women for
momentary pleasure and discarding them. Well, not visibly doing it
in the streets anyhow.

At least they'd all made it alive together. It hadn't been easy.
From the day they left Sian, in early January 1937, it had taken
more than two and a half years to reach America.

As the train to Chengdu had pulled out of the cavernous Sian
station, Chlöe thought it might take a month, six weeks at the most.
But no travel in China was easy, and war had interrupted any services that might have functioned.

She'd hated Chengdu, where the people were suspect of white
foreigners and spat upon her. A city more crowded than Shanghai,
it seemed to her. Cold and dark, and for a month, a place she was
afraid she was doomed to stay in. The railroad to Kunming was not
functioning, and there was no sense heading east, downriver to
Chungking.

From Chengdu to Kunming is five hundred miles. They traveled
it by bullock carts, by camel, by foot, by donkey. They sometimes
went days without food.

They recuperated for six weeks in Kunming. Ah, Kunming! It
must be my favorite city in China, Chlöe reminisced. Called "the
city of perpetual spring," it was high in the mountains of Yunnan,

China's southwesternmost province. They took picnic lunches and sailed on Lake Dianchi. They stuffed themselves on the hot spicy dishes for which western China was famous. The children stared in bewilderment at the numerous ethnic groups who clung to their native dress, lending color and variety to Kunming that was nowhere else evident in China.

In sedan chairs they became part of a caravan heading to Hanoi, in the north of French Indochina. From there they booked passage on a junk heading to Saigon, a city that fascinated Chlöe. It could have been a typical Oriental city at first glance, but evidences of French influence abounded. It was a city of gardens, of beauty, of culture, of filth, of intrigue. The American consul there finally found Chlöe and the children accommodations on a copra ship, heading to Darwin.

In Darwin, at the very top end of Australia, they finally caught a bus to Alice Springs, and from there the train to Adelaide and on to Sydney.

No city could equal Sydney, she thought, with its harbor as a backdrop. It was also the cleanest city she'd seen in sixteen years. It didn't smell. She drank water from the tap and thought the sound of flushing toilets more beautiful than Mozart.

She dined on T-bone steak, French fries, and a green salad. The children stuck up their noses at such food. She took showers in the morning and at night and sometimes in the middle of the day. But there was no room for four people on any ship bound for San Francisco.

Finally, Chlöe took herself to the American embassy and there they recognized her name, saying, "We thought you were dead." Within a month they were on a cargo ship that wound around the Pacific. On the ship from Sydney she had stopped speaking Chinese to the children, forcing them to be surrounded only by the language they'd now need.

In San Francisco, after they'd all stared in awe as they passed under the newly erected Golden Gate Bridge, Chlöe noted that there were few people on the dock, so she guessed a cargo ship could be unloaded any—

And then she saw him. Saw Cass waving, holding his hat high in the air, trying to get her attention. He held an enormous bouquet of white flowers. Thank God they're not yellow, she thought. Oh, how had he ever traced her, how had he ever known when she'd arrive? That wonderful man. Just seeing him made her feel safe again. She hadn't felt that in so long. Tears slid down her cheeks.

She pointed him out to Jade, who had met him in 1931 but had no memory of him whatsoever. Jade held a hand over her eyes to shade the sun, squinting so she could see him.

"Do all American men look like that?"

"No, they're all different. In China you're used to everyone having black hair and black eyes. Not so here.

"Come on, children," she said, grabbing Plum Blossom's and Li's hands so they wouldn't get lost, but it was an hour before they could get down the gangplank with all the red tape involved. Her eyes were focused on Cass. He did not move, but she could tell he was smiling. He didn't rush to greet her. There weren't that many passengers, she thought. It's not as if it's crowded. Why is he just standing there? As her feet touched America, her eyes still on Cass about six yards away, she nearly tripped over an older woman.

"Excuse me," she said, barely looking at the woman, starting to run toward Cass, when she stopped cold. She jerked her head around to stare at the woman. Standing behind the woman was her father.

"Oh, my," she cried, and suddenly they were laughing and crying and hugging each other and Chlöe couldn't control herself. The children stood by in bewilderment.

"You're emaciated," cried her mother. "You're all skin and bones. Oh, darling, we thought you were dead." She burst into tears again.

Chlöe was too overwhelmed to talk. Her father kept patting her arm, making little tsk-tsk sounds, and said, "Mr. Monaghan paid for our train tickets, and is putting us up at the Drake Hotel. Fanciest one I ever saw."

"Fanciest?" said Mrs. Shepherd. "The only one you ever stayed in!" She daubed at her eyes with a dry handkerchief.

And then Cass's voice broke in. "You do look like hell, but you're a sight for these eyes."

"Oh, Cass." Chlöe reached up to kiss him. "How wonderful of you. You dear man." And now she couldn't stop the tears as his arms surrounded her.

She heard her mother saying, "And these must be my new grandchildren?"

Oh, thank God. Thank you, Mother.

Cass had reserved a suite for her and the children, across the hall
from her parents' room and next door to his.

After Chlöe tucked the children in bed, she and Cass and her
parents sat in the living room talking until after midnight. She sat
between her parents on the sofa, holding their hands the entire
time. After they'd gone across the hall, Cass put his arms around
Chlöe, pulling her close.

"I nominate myself as the most selfless man of the year. I've
wanted you in my arms every minute, yet here you are surrounded
by all your family, thanks to me."

"I thought you might be married by now."

"Fat chance," he said, kissing the top of her head.

She thought nothing in her entire life had felt better than having Cass's arms around her.

He tilted her head back, his finger under her chin. "When
you're ready, I want to hear of every moment since you left Shanghai. I can tell by looking at you you've been through hell."

Chlöe shook her head. "It's been tedious and sometimes a bit
hairy, but it hasn't been hell. Hell ended, really, when I returned
to Sian from Yenan."

Cass looked into her eyes, and she saw her reflection in his
glasses. "I want to share it, hear it all," he said. "I want to know
the you you've become since I last saw you. I want . . . Oh, God,
Chlöe, I want you."

She smiled and said, "I suspect my parents are still puritanical,
but I imagine I could slip next door to your room for a few minutes
without anyone's seeing me."

Cass cocked an eyebrow. "A lovely idea, my dear." And without wasting another minute, he opened the door and closed it softly
behind him.

Chlöe looked in on the sleeping children and followed Cass to
his room. "I almost took the time to shower first but thought I could
use yours."

Cass reached for her hand. "Have you ever taken a shower with
anyone?"

Chlöe shook her head. "I must admit I never have."

Cass scrubbed her back and shampooed her hair and nibbled her
nipples. He washed each of her toes and her belly button and kissed
her wetly as the shower rained prickly beads of hot water on them.

He dried her with a huge soft towel and, taking her in his arms, tossed her onto the bed. Chlöe relaxed, letting his touches and kisses erase all thoughts from her mind. She gave herself up to feeling, to feeling Cass's caresses, and his tender kisses, and his tongue. She heard his murmurs, his words of love, and felt her body come alive, tingling with desire. She opened her eyes and saw the man coming toward her, lowering himself on top of her, felt him trying to enter her and she screamed, trying to raise her fists, to wrench her arms from the stranglehold the soldier had on them, tried to raise her knee to kick him in the groin, but all she could do was scream.

Cass reared back. "My God, Chlöe!"

He put his hand over her mouth to stifle her scream.

Her glazed eyes came into focus, saw Cass's concerned face, the shock in his eyes, and she began to cry, great gasping sobs that she could not stop.

Cass's arms were around her, cradling her, rocking back and forth, murmuring into her hair, "There, there, my darling. You're safe. You're here with me, and I'll take care of you. You're all right, darling."

Later, when she was able to talk, she told him what the soldiers had done to her. "I haven't told anyone before," she said, her voice still cracking. "I thought I'd forgotten it. It happened over three years ago."

"We'll work through this together," he said, his eyes filled with tender concern. "There's no hurry, my darling. We'll talk about it again—and about everything else that's happened to you. What matters now is you're safe and you're here." He put his arms around her. "Later we'll spend time alone, and we can vanquish these monsters that haunt and inhabit you. Oh, my dear, brave Chlöe."

She stayed wrapped in his arms until she could no longer keep her eyes open. "I mustn't leave Jade alone all night in a new country," she said. She'd tell him about Jade later. She'd tell him everything. Cass was the one person in the world in whom she could confide everything.

Well, maybe not about Snow Leopard. He was hers alone.

# CHAPTER 64

She took the children to Oneonta and stayed there through Christmas, which was as she remembered it. The children were greeted as war orphans—fashionable at the time, especially those from Europe. That Chlöe's three were a bit more exotic made them that much more interesting. Lee, respelling his name, took to America with gusto. Plum Blossom became shy and hesitant. Jade observed while the boys observed her.

Chlöe slept a lot. She drank an inordinate amount of water straight out of the tap. Life in America had changed so much in all the years she'd been gone.

However, three months was about a month more than she could quite take. She had regained her health and twenty pounds. She was able to smile easily. She was not only restless but told herself she needed to earn a living.

Cass sent presents to them all, but he did not come for Christmas. He called, as he did every week, and told her he wanted to, but he had never spent a Christmas away from Suzi and didn't wish to. He asked if she'd like to take the train and spend New Year's at the lake with him. "It'll be cold," he said. "Bring long underwear."

Chlöe laughed. "It can't be much colder than it is here." Her mother encouraged her. "Jade and I'll take care of the children," she said, putting an arm around the girl. "Won't we?"

Chlöe could tell that Jade was pleased to be treated as an adult, and she had loved Mrs. Shepherd from the beginning.

"I'll be back in a week," Chlöe said later to Jade, but that's what she'd said when she'd gone up to interview Mao and returned sixty-nine days later. "I think I'll try to get a job with Cass. We may all move to Chicago. But don't mention it to Grandma."

"Move from here?" Jade's voice was plaintive.

Chlöe put her arms around the slender girl. "You're tired of moving, aren't you? Well, maybe I can make us a home and have a job too. I have to earn money, darling. And I need something to do. I need a challenge."

Cass met her at seven-thirty in the morning at Union Station, a fur hat making him look like Chlöe imagined a cossack might look. His black Packard was waiting.

It was almost dark by the time they arrived at the cabin. Chlöe had fallen asleep and Cass's "Here we are" awoke her.

"It looks just as I remembered it," she sighed happily.

But inside there was newer furniture and it wasn't quite as rustic. But still oil lamps and no electricity, no phone.

"Here," Cass said as he brought in the suitcases. "Here's lamp oil and matches. Go around and find lamps, okay? I'll bring in more firewood, and it won't be but half an hour before we'll be cozy. I brought a couple of steaks and we can bake potatoes in the fire. Mrs. Donovan packed a pecan pie too. Oh, and in that box is wine. You might look for a couple of glasses." He kissed her and bounded back outside to the box of firewood.

Dinner was delicious.

Cass took pillows from the sofa and tossed them in front of the fire. Pouring each of them another glass of wine, he said, "Come on, woman, here where it's warm. Come, let me kiss you."

His lips were warm and tender, tasting of Beaujolais. He leaned his head back against the pillow, putting an arm around Chlöe's shoulders. "We're going to face some of these dragons of yours," he said, "but not tonight."

When they went to bed, Chlöe curled into his arms, but he merely kissed her forehead.

They took long hikes through the dark pines. Strolling under snow-laden skies, through fallen leaves, they saw tracks of several deer. They sat on the pier and watched the fish jump into the air, followed the flight of osprey swooping down for prey. They walked hand in hand in the cold winter sun, watching their breath curl like smoke. Then he stopped, turning, pulling her to him, kissing her and saying, "I feel I'm alive again."

He helped her feel that way too.

And he forced her to talk.

She told him about breaking the back of Snow Leopard's close friend, about burying the colonel, and of castrating her rapists.

"I've done things I never dreamed I could ever do," she said, her voice flat. "I regret being in positions where I had to do such things, but you need to know I'm not sorry I did any of them. Never once have I regretted any of those terrible acts."

She felt as though she were telling him of some stranger.

The color drained from Cass's face, and his eyes reflected anguish, but he never interrupted her. He did not reach out to touch her but sat quietly as she relived those years for him. And for herself.

The only thing she omitted was the night she spent in the cave with Snow Leopard. But Cass said, when she told him about Snow Leopard's death, "He loved you, after all, didn't he?"

She didn't respond but arose and looked out the paned window, into the grayness of winter.

They'd been up in Michigan for four days. The night before they were to leave, Chlöe said, "I told Jade we might move to Chicago."

Cass turned from putting a log on the fire and half his face was red, half in shadow. His sideburns were white now, though the rest of his hair was still the thick rust she'd always known.

"I need a job," she said. "I have to think of earning a living. Also, I need a challenge."

Cass laughed. "Chlöe, one would think you've had enough challenges to last a lifetime."

"I need a job," she said again. "You going to give me one? Anything will do."

He hugged her tighter, gazing into the fire, not responding for a few minutes. Then he said, "I don't suppose you'll consider that standing offer?"

"Give me some time," she answered, putting her hand on his knee. "I think I'm still in culture shock. I'm not yet adjusted to America. It's all so clean, everything's so easy, there's so much of everything on grocery shelves and in stores that it still seems obscene to me. I'm not quite ready to make any long-range plans. I need to adjust. But I can't just coddle myself. I have three kids to support."

He leaned over and kissed her cheek. "Chlöe, you can write your own ticket on my paper or probably any paper in the country. I told you you'd be famous. You do know, or did I neglect to tell you, other papers kept calling, wanting to carry your articles, until you were being carried in twenty-six cities around the country?"

She sat up straight, looking into his eyes. "No, you haven't told me that. How could you forget such a thing?"

He loosened his hold on her shoulders. "God forgive me, Chlöe, I don't know. Since that scoop about Chiang in Sian, these last three years, we haven't even heard from you. You might want to write some articles of how you and the children escaped Shanghai, of your adventures after that, your capture by the Japanese, those things."

She leaned back against him again. "Oh, I don't think so, Cass. I don't want to relive those times."

He kissed the top of her head and reached down for her hand. "It might help you to exorcise those phantoms," he said. "Get rid of those demons that have bound you up tight as a drum."

"Is that how I am?"

He nodded.

"I've lived for so long like this that I can't recognize it."

"Get it out of your system if you can." His arm around her shoulder tightened. "Write of it. You might be doing the world a favor to get an inside view of the Japanese and the Nationalists and the Reds. America loves heroic stories. Helping those kids escape, and bringing your three to America. Write a series of articles for my Sunday section. I imagine I can talk nearly all the leading papers in the country into carrying them too."

"Oh, Cass, do you think so?"

"Why not? You must have a lot to tell about Mao and what you learned about the Long March. Give us details of the Chiangs that Americans don't know. But, in particular, your journey home with three Chinese kids."

"But I need immediate money to live on."

"Don't worry about that. Come live in Chicago, near me, and write it. It might take a couple of months. Get an apartment, or a house in the suburbs, if that would be better for the kids. You can enroll them in school and let them get to know me. Maybe they'll convince you I'd be a proper father for them."

"You once told me," and Chlöe felt every fiber of her come alive, "that you didn't want a second family, not at your age."

"Ah," he smiled, "but then I was only fifty and now I'm older and wiser and have a different perspective."

She thought to herself, I do love him. Cass Monaghan is one of the nicest people in the world. It was not the first time she'd thought that.

"I want to do anything that will please you."

"I'll tell you what, then," she said, putting her arms around his neck. "How about our taking our clothes off and lying on that rug in front of the fire and seeing what will happen? I suspect that would please me."

They had not made love in nine years.

It was worth waiting for.

# CHAPTER 65

Cass urged Chlöe to take a house in a suburb like Oak Park so that the children could go to fine schools and make proper friends, but Chlöe wanted to live in the city itself. So he helped her find a large old house on a street with big maples, near a school he assured her was tops. He supplied private tutors for Jade, so that she could catch up with Americans of her age. On weekends he took them on picnics, or skating on a pond not far from their house, in a little park. In the spring he took Lee to a baseball game, and bought a swing for the backyard. He took them to movies, and on vacations up to the cabin on the lake. And he gave Chlöe the alone time she needed for writing.

Most of the country's newspapers did feature her series of articles, and she was asked to speak in numerous cities around America. What her articles reaped most of all were hundreds, and eventually over a thousand, inquiries from her readers about how they could adopt war orphans, how they themselves could give homes and love to children from foreign countries.

"Start an organization," Cass suggested, "that'll bring orphans from these war-torn countries to America. Keep the names of all these letter-writers, and between them and publicity, you won't have any trouble finding homes for these kids. It can be a lesson in racial and international understanding too."

Chlöe looked at him. "Cass, I can't possibly do anything like that. I wouldn't even know where to begin."

They were sitting in her living room surrounded by bags of mail.

"My dear, I have faith in you." He grinned. "Where there's a will . . . Let's see, among all my friends I must have someone who's raised funds and done that sort of thing who might help give you some insight. It would be a way to begin." He snapped his fingers. "Wilburn Bruce. He's just the one, top-notch. A prince. I'll arrange lunch one day next week with him."

"What would I do without you in my life?"

"I hope you never find out," he said, nuzzling her ear.

"I don't even know that I could *live* without you in my life," she said. "You've become so important."

"How important?" He was kissing her neck now, and his voice was muffled.

"Well, I'd been thinking now that my little family thinks you're part of it, it might be time . . ."

As she talked, he stood up straight, drawing away from her, searching her eyes.

Looking up at him, she began to smile. ". . . to make it all legal. But I guess if you'd rather I took on this job, this job that would take up too much time for me to be much of a wife . . ."

He reached down and took her hand, pulling her up so that they stood facing each other. "Well, I'll be damned," he said. "I think I'm being proposed to. Am I?"

She put her head against his shoulder, loving his closeness. "I think I'm ready, after how many years? Yeah, I'm serious. I've been thinking a lot about it lately. And I think I owe it to myself. You've become the most important person in the world to me."

He kissed her forehead and held her closer. "That sounds like a good enough reason to get married."

He bought the biggest, most elegant home Chlöe had ever seen. And kept his penthouse downtown too.

The children became, to their great delight, Americans. Jade Monaghan, Lee Monaghan, and Laura Monaghan. Plum Blossom now thought her name did not fit into American culture and asked if she could change it. She wanted to be called Laura. Where that came from no one knew, but officially she became Laura, though Chlöe and Jade never did call her that. She had been Plum Blossom far too long. The children called Cass Daddy.

The War Orphans Relief Organization took eight months of planning, and then Chlöe and Cass flew to China in early October 1941. They left the children in Chicago, when Mr. and Mrs. Shepherd volunteered to come stay in the big house.

China's war with Japan being full blown, they had to fly a circuitous route and enter China by flying over the Himalayas—already in flying legend being called "the hump"—from Burma into Kunming. It was China's only entrance or exit, for the eastern coast was now completely taken over by the Japanese—Hong Kong, Canton, Shanghai, Peking, now all in Japanese hands. The capital had moved from Nanking, ransacked and burned by the Japanese, up the Yangtze to Chungking. Generalissimo and Madame Chiang Kai-shek headquartered there, and Ai-ling and H.H. had been forced to evacuate their home and take up residence in Chungking also. Chlöe was surprised to learn that Ching-ling lived there now too. In fact, now that all factions of China were united against the Japanese, a family truce had been called, and the three Soong sisters worked together for relief of famine. Overjoyed to see each other again, Chlöe and Ching-ling spent an evening alone together. Ching-ling responded with enthusiasm to the idea of rescuing hundreds of children from starvation and of giving them homes. Chlöe assured her there were families in America willing to adopt them. Ching-ling approached her sisters, who also volunteered their help.

Chlöe and Cass brought 222 children back with them, into the waiting arms of Americans yearning for children of their own, or for children to add to their families, people who had an abundance of love and a desire to share.

The organization soon began to include rescued children from Western Europe. Chlöe and her organization found homes for all of them.

And major organization it had become. More than two dozen volunteers and three paid assistants now devoted their waking lives to this cause. They flew to China or to Europe or to Australia, where many of the Chinese children had been temporarily taken, waiting for transportation to America. They spent hours on phones. They traveled across America by train or by bus to deliver the children.

One evening in early February 1942, Cass said, "I need your advice."

Chlöe looked up from her desk in a corner of the library. "Anything wrong?" she asked.

He smiled. "No. But I can't make this decision on my own."

She put down her pencil and gave him her full attention.

"I had callers today," he said, adjusting his glasses, "who want me to run for the Senate."

She took a deep breath. "It's a wonderful idea."

"Do you think so?"

"Oh, darling, of course." She got up and walked over, sitting next to him on the sofa. "If there were more people like you in the government, I'd be less worried about the future of the world. Who were these people?"

"One was the governor."

"Do you want to?"

"I told them I'm sixty-one and that seems old to become a senator."

"It doesn't seem too old to be elected president. Cass, you have more energy than half the men your age."

"I'm not arguing that. But how would you feel about picking up and moving to Washington? You could," he reached out for her hand, "run your organization from there as well, perhaps better, than from Chicago."

"Of course I could," she said, then laughed. "You're already talking as though you're the winner."

"What about campaigning. Do you have time for that?"

She leaned over to kiss him. "I shall make time for it. I make time for anything I believe in. And I believe you'd be wonderful helping to run this government. Or anything else, I might add."

"I'd need more of your time than I've needed here. Yet, I don't want you to give this up."

"You forget. I also have more energy than most people. And I'm young! Darling, I'm twenty-one years younger. Wouldn't you have made time for *all* of it when you were forty? I'll just have to learn to get by on less sleep. Or become incredibly efficient."

She did both and not only moved her headquarters to Washington, but charmed the capital with her eloquence, her impromptu parties, her knowledge of the Far East, and her dazzling good looks. Congressional members who served on committees dealing with the Far East got in the habit of stopping at Senator and Mrs. Monaghan's late afternoons, before the parties and dinners that abounded every evening. They wanted to probe Chlöe's firsthand knowledge of the Orient and to ask her opinions. Together, the Monaghans were a fine addition to the nation's capital.

They both loved it, despite Cass's complaint, "I'm not used to being a junior anything or keeping my mouth shut. Sometimes both of those are hard."

"So don't play by the rules," Chlöe suggested. "You were the one who first taught me that. You don't have to worry about pleasing them. It's not as if you want this as a career. Don't keep your mouth shut."

So, he didn't.

He became known as the congressional maverick, as the "blunt, outspoken senator who can't be bought."

Washington seemed made for them. And they seemed made for each other. Despite the chaotic condition of the world, Chlöe had never been happier.

# CHAPTER 66

The end of the war did not end Chlöe's work. In fact, if anything, it increased it. Jade, who had just graduated from Georgetown with a degree in international studies, applied to the State Department for a job, but she did not want to return to China. She wanted to stay near Chlöe.

In her years in college she'd dated a few times, but after her dates had tried to paw her, she stopped seeing them. One young man whom Chlöe thought very nice, a young sailor in the V-12 college program, seemed to have an inside track for many months. Jade admitted, to Chlöe as well as to herself, that she enjoyed his kisses, but then one night after they'd been seeing each other every weekend for four months, his hand ran across her sweater, cupping her breast, and she broke into tears, refusing to see him again.

"For Christ's sake, let's get her to a psychiatrist," Cass bellowed when Chlöe repeated what Jade had confided in her. "*You* got over it."

"With your help. And I was in my thirties by the time it happened. Also, I wreaked my vengeance. I—what did you call it?—exorcised my demons."

But no amount of counseling would permit Jade to date again. She danced with men, she laughed with them at picnics or at parties or ice skating. But she vowed to herself that no man would ever touch her that way again. She saw that she was never alone with a man who might threaten her. Though she was affectionate with Cass and genuinely liked Grant and enjoyed her American grandfather, she refused any and all male overtures.

"All that beauty going to waste," Lee said to his sister one day.

Jade flared at him. "You mean I'm a wasted person if I don't belong to a man? My looks are wasted if some man doesn't go to bed with me?"

That shut him up.

Chlöe made six trips to the continent in 1946. Cass could accompany her on only one, as he could not leave Washington. Her trips were brief, and she always returned with dozens of children. Each time, she had to leave hundreds who wanted and needed parents. Chlöe and her organization had placed over a hundred thousand children with American parents. Her picture had been on the cover of *Time*, articles had been written about her and her organization in the *Saturday Evening Post* and *Look*. Together she and Cass made *Life*'s cover, being referred to as "Washington's most dynamic couple. Movers and shakers of the world. If it's a noble cause and you want to get something done, ask the busiest couple in the capital. Maybe in America."

Despite not having learned to keep his mouth shut as the junior senator from Illinois, Cass had just been voted into a second term by the largest majority any senator from Illinois had ever received. And for a man of sixty-seven he did a prodigious amount of work. Going into the Senate he'd already had a roster of friends who made the governments of the world spin. But the only strings he pulled were ones that would help Chlöe and her children. In the last year the War Orphans Relief Organization had expanded to international stature, since Australia volunteered to take homeless children from Europe, though not any Asians. They would have to wait another twenty years or more. Europeans who had lost their own children begged for homeless children.

Now, though most of her hair was still coal black, a blaze of gray, starting over the left side of her forehead, flowed back through her luxuriant locks. She thought it quite dramatic and became fond of it.

"You know," she said to Cass as she sat in front of her mirror, getting ready for a party. There was always a party or a dinner. "I feel my age."

"God, when I was your age, I thought the world was my oyster. Guess I still do. How about going up to the lake the day after Christmas?" he asked.

They always spent Christmas at Suzi's. Chlöe smiled. "Make it just you and me? Leave the kids out of it this time. I could stand some time just with you."

"Chlöe, my love, you always know how to get to me. The world may think a man my age is over the hill, but when you look at me like that, I feel eighteen. Let's come home early tonight, or, better yet, let's not go to the party at all."

She looked up at him and laughed. "I'm game, if you mean it."

He stopped tying his tie and looked down at her. She began to take off her earrings, giving him a teasing smile. "At least, let's be late. Unfashionably very late, and let's not give any excuse. Come here, you, and unzip me. I can't reach it."

He did as she asked, grinning at her. "How was I ever so

fortunate?" he wondered aloud. "Shit, I'm sixty-seven years old and I'm going to be late to a party because my wife wants to get laid."

"Are you complaining?" she asked, slipping her dress off.

"Bragging," he said as he unbuttoned his ruffled, starched shirt. "Let's do this every night at the cabin."

She stood in her slip, provocatively dropping the narrow satin straps slowly, smiling at him as she did so, and said, "Make me forget I'm getting older, Cass."

He did.

The week at the lake between Christmas and New Year's was as peaceful as any time Chlöe could remember. They sat and read in front of the fire, they walked through the thin layer of snow to their favorite places, watching deer drink at the water's edge. They talked of nothing important, and lay in bed late mornings, holding each other, making love slowly, drinking coffee while holding hands across the table. Cass did the cooking and Chlöe cleaned up. It was a time, Chlöe thought, of rejuvenation, of feeding her spirit so she could go on. Replenishing her soul so she could reemerge into the world and give some more.

Neither suspected it was their last time together.

As they were flying back to Washington, Cass turned to her to say, "You know, I don't feel well."

She saw the grayness of his face, saw the startled look in his eyes as one hand clutched his chest and the other reached out for her, and then he was gone. Dead. Just like that. Before the plane could land in Washington.

# CHAPTER 67

After the funeral Chlöe told Suzi, "We always knew it would happen before I was ready for it. We always knew I'd have years left, alone. But these years have been the happiest of my life, the most fulfilled. I guess anyone who has any years like these out of a lifetime should consider herself lucky."

She was surprised. No tears had accompanied Slade's death, even before she knew of his unfaithfulness. She could not let herself cry as she watched Nikolai's plane fade into nothingness. With Snow Leopard's death her seeking vengeance obliterated any tendency she might have had for tears.

She *had* cried when she lost Damien. Cried for weeks. And now, again, she found herself crying. Everyone commented on her bravery and stoicism at the funeral, but once that was over she could not seem to hold back the tears. Not that she tried. She let herself weep for the loss—for the emptiness that Cass's going would create within her. She wept for the loss of happiness and contentment. She wept because she would no longer look up to see those blue eyes twinkle at her. She wept because the support he always offered would no longer be available. She wept because now the world was less.

Though she threw herself into the work that awaited her, she had trouble sleeping, and in the evening—when Cass was not there to share his day with her and listen to her problems or successes— overwhelming loneliness encircled her. She had not known loneliness since the years she'd been married to Slade, and it was not a welcome companion. Loneliness brought the past back to her. Memories flooded her mind evenings when she lay alone in bed, memories not only of Cass and all they had done together, but of the people she had known and had not seen in so long. Nikolai flitted through her memory, and she began to think often of Ching-ling. Chlöe determined to fly back to China, just for a week—that's all she could spare—and see her friend. See if there was any help she needed. See if Ching-ling had lost hope. She must be in her mid-fifties by now. Chlöe had not heard from her friend in a long time. Was she still filled with idealism and fighting for what she believed?

Ching-ling was older, and pudgier. Perhaps not as physically beautiful as she had once been, but still had that serene air, that regal stance, the deep black eyes, the pulled-back hair. She was delighted to see Chlöe and insisted Chlöe stay with her "for your all-too-brief visit."

The Chiangs were back in Nanking, the capital that had been ravaged during the war and was still a city of rubble. Shanghai had not been destroyed despite its long occupation by the Japanese. But there were no longer foreign concessions. There was hardly any sign of Westerners. There was a vitality in the air, despite China's having been a war-torn nation for so many years, despite the chaos it was in now.

Ching-ling and Chlöe took long walks on the Bund, holding

hands. Ching-ling's life was still dedicated to her husband's principles, and she had not given up hope even twenty-three years after
his death. "My brother-in-law has sown the seeds of his own down-
fall, you will see. He has neglected the Chinese people in his own
lust for power, and the Chinese people are rising. They are rising in
the hills and the mountains, and Mao and Chou En-lai and all the
people will triumph. We will drive Chiang out of the country. We,
the Chinese people, are his enemy."

When Chlöe left a week later, she brought back to America
another fifteen children. There were thousands more Chlöe was determined to help, though it was still easier to place European children than Asians.

Back in Washington a message from the governor of Illinois
awaited her. She called him the morning after she arrived home.

"Chlöe," he said in that gruff voice of his, "I have to see you.
You want to come up here or shall I come down there?"

She looked at the calendar. "I can't leave again until Thursday.
I just got back from China yesterday and I have fifteen children to
do something about. Can it wait until then?"

"No, it can't wait. I'll get an afternoon plane," he said.

What the governor had to say shocked her so much she couldn't
have slept no matter how tired she was.

"I want to appoint you to fill out Cass's Senate term," he said
almost as soon as he sat down at the table and ordered a scotch on
the rocks. "And don't say no before you let me talk about it."

Chlöe looked at him, speechless.

"Okay, let's get to it," the big man said. "I have an idea we'll
need a couple of hours to talk this over. Only promise me you won't
give me a negative answer tonight, but you'll think about it."

She was able to force a small smile. "I guess I can promise that
much."

"You know I have to appoint someone to fill out Cass's unex-
pired term. It has another five and a half years to run. We've been
sitting up in the state house tossing around names, and I keep coming back to one. Yours. Now, wait, don't interrupt. I think it'd be
a nice claim to fame to be responsible for the first woman senator.
Who've we got in Congress? Clare Boothe Luce. Margaret Chase
Smith. She'll be a senator soon, I vow. Well, I'd like to beat them.
Appoint the first woman senator and let her be from *my* state."

"I appreciate this, I really do. I'm flattered—"

"Wait." He reached out and put his hand on her arm. "Lemme

finish my spiel. It's not just that you're a woman, though I admit I like that idea. It's because you're you. You're the most capable woman I know, and that means one of the most capable people I've ever met. You're already known. You're probably one of the most respected women in the whole country. You and Eleanor Roosevelt, and you're a whole lot better looking. You've got high visibility. I think you're someone who could get things done."

"Things *you* want done?"

That stopped him. He stared down at his glass and then took a sip. He looked up at her. "I don't demand that. I'm not trying to buy you. Your husband and I belonged to the same party, and have often thought alike. But not always. I don't ask any more than that of you. I want you to be your own person, live with your own conscience, though," and he grinned at her, "when we disagree, I'd like you to at least listen to my arguments."

She had to smile at that. "Sounds fair enough." She finished her drink, wishing she'd started out with something stronger than wine.

To be the first woman senator. Certainly it had appeal. But was she up to it? Could she do it? Would the other senators accept her? Did she want such enormous responsibility?

"I keep thinking," the governor said, "that it would be your posthumous tribute to your husband."

She had to laugh at that. "Don't give me that. Cut out the blarney and be sincere."

"Chlöe, is any politician sincere? I think I left that behind when I entered politics, though I started out as an idealist. I wanted to accomplish things for the people, for the state. But somehow ideals get perverted or lost along the way and one settles for practicality."

"I wondered what it was that I think we're losing as a country. So, it's ideals, huh?"

"Chlöe, there are times when I long for the innocence that was the America in which I grew up. The America that didn't know of wholesale slaughter, the America that laughed at Carole Lombard and William Powell. The kids who saved five cents to go to Saturday matinees. The more innocent times."

"Ignorant times, I'd say." She looked down at her hands, wound around the wineglass stem. "So, I'd have to lie if I became a senator?"

He was silent for a while. Then he said, "I'm not asking you to be anything other than yourself, Chlöe. But I am asking you to become the junior senator from Illinois, to fill out the five and a half years left to Cass. And I guess I would hope that you would then run for that seat on your own. You could build up some seniority for our state. I'd think the Senate would be idiotic not to make use of your Chinese experience. They could use you, Chlöe, and I have a feeling that if you'll accept, they'll be grateful to me, whether you're a woman or not."

She couldn't assimilate it all, and told him so.

"Okay, I knew that," he said. "And I know you're not emotionally ready to make any big decision, so soon after your loss. But I have to appoint someone within the month. Sooner, if possible. So, let me talk, because I know I've got just this one shot with you. And then I'll give you a couple of weeks to think it over. Just don't say no right off the bat."

The first woman senator! The second Senator Monaghan.

How did I come this far? she wondered. Yet, it was not an easy decision. She was still needed in the War Orphans Relief Organization. After all, it was her baby and had been for seven years. She didn't know if she could let it go, if she'd trust someone to take over the reins, to know as much about it as she did, have the contacts she did. She couldn't bear to see it fail, now when it was needed as much as ever, perhaps even more so.

She called Suzi and said, "Any chance you and Grant want a weekend in D.C.? I need your advice."

Ultimately, they told her they couldn't decide for her. Suzi observed, "I'm publisher of the *Times* now and you may be a senator. Chlöe, wouldn't we have laughed at the thought of ending up like this?"

"Well," Chlöe mused, "if you hadn't been my roommate, none of this would have happened to me. It's all your father. He sent me to China. And it was he who suggested this orphans' relief thing. Your father, my dear friend, has been a profound influence on my life, aside from giving me the most contentment I've ever known."

"Well, your life isn't over," Grant said.

"No." Chlöe was very aware of that.

Suzi leaned across the couch and put a hand on Chlöe's arm. "I admit after Daddy, another man probably couldn't cut it with you. There aren't many men to measure up to him."

"There aren't *any*," Chlöe said. "Your father has been the single most profound influence in my life. As a person, that is. I must admit my China experiences helped shape me too. But even when we were in college and I visited you up at the lake, I remember his telling me I could do anything I wanted except, perhaps, become president.''

"Maybe he was wrong." Suzi reached out to hug her and laughed. "Maybe you could do even that now."

Who knows? thought Chlöe. Maybe I could.

# AFTERWORD

When I was in high school, I discovered Pearl Buck's books. From that time on, China fascinated me. My interest in Pearl Buck waned, but never my interest in China. Over the years, I devoured books, both fiction and nonfiction, about China. In 1985 I spent the two most physically uncomfortable months of my life, wandering 3600 miles around China with my daughter Debra during a respite from her year of teaching English in a medical university in Xian. We had complete freedom to travel and do whatever we wished. Since then I have read well over a hundred books about China in preparation for writing this book. I cannot possibly remember or give credit to all those who have supplied me with background and incidents for this novel.

I must, however, single out several that have been of inestimable importance to me. Probably the single most valuable book is Sterling Seagrave's *The Soong Dynasty*. Others have been Helen Foster Snow's *My China Years*; Lois Wheeler Snow's *Edgar Snow's China*; Pearl Buck's autobiography, *My Several Worlds* (I didn't leave her behind, after all); Edgar Snow's *Red Star over China*; Hallett Abend's *My Life in China: 1926–1941*; Harrison Salisbury's *The Long March*; John B. Powell's *My Twenty-Five Years in China*; and Brian Crozier's biography of Chiang Kai-shek, *The Man Who Lost China*. Some of the incidents that happen to Chlöe really happened to Rayna Prohme (more later) and to the famous journalist Edgar Snow. Others actually happened to Hallett Abend, the *New York Times* China correspondent for many years, and to John B. Powell, who edited an English-language newspaper out of Peking.

As with my previous books, I have delighted in interweaving fact with fiction. The historical events are factual and really occurred. My description of places and conditions in China are true. Most of the characters are mixtures of reality and my imagination. Dr. Sun Yat-sen and his wife, Soong Ching-ling; Generalissimo and Madame Chiang Kai-Shek (Soong Mei-ling); T. V. Soong; Mao Tse-tung; and the Young Marshal were, of course, real. I have painted them factually according to my interpretation of the history I have read. All the books mentioned above have seen these people in the light in which I paint these characters.

Madame Sun Yat-sen died in 1981 (at age eighty-eight), and I have been as faithful to her memory as my research has allowed me to be. All the incidents concerning Madame Sun Yat-sen are based on actual ones. Only her conversations are not totally accurate, but they are as faithful to her as a person and to the events that occurred as possible. Ching-ling did move, after Dr. Sun's death, to Wuhan, which became for a while the center for revolutionary action. She did spurn Chiang Kai-shek's offer of marriage and remained a critic (and antagonist) of him her whole life. She did flee to Russia in the way I have described (and, though there was no Chlöe in her life, a beautiful young American journalist, Rayna Prohme, did become her most intimate friend and accompanied her on the 1927 flight to Moscow, where she became ill and died) and several years later returned to attend Dr. Sun's reburial in Nanking. Blinded, I think, by revolutionary zeal, though she never joined the Communist Party, she did become vice president of China under Mao and chose not to see that he was guilty of the same sins as the Manchus and of Chiang Kai-shek, subordinating all peoples to his drive for power. She has been called "the conscience of China." In fact, her close friendship with Rayna Prohme gave me the idea for this book. My Chlöe's personality has nothing to do with a real person's but her friendship with Madame Sun was suggested by Rayna's.

My main characters are fictional, although their genesis had some basis in reality. Nikolai Zakarov is based—his deeds, not his personality or private life—somewhat on Mikhail Borodin, who was even more influential in helping to instigate Communism in China than is Nikolai. Borodin actually spent time in Chicago, teaching English to foreigners and marrying an American, Fanya, in the early years of the twentieth century. Lenin did recall him to Russia in 1917 and sent him to China in 1922. When Chiang Kai-shek put a price on his head in 1927, Stalin called him home. However, as far as I know, his wife supported him in Russia *and* in China, though it is rumored that he had a twenty-year relationship with an American correspondent. The personal aspects of Nikolai, and his relationship with my fictional characters, come entirely from my imagination and in no way reflect on Borodin.

In Chapter 11, the details of the escape from the Sun's Cantonese home, through the passageway, are from Madame Sun's own ords as she described the escape that actually occurred in May 1922. Of course, my fictional Chlöe and Nikolai were not with her, but aside from that, all details of the escape and the events following until they reached Dr. Sun's gunboat are factual. I simply added my two characters.

The incident about the kidnapping of the Blue Express is based on a 1923 account reported in *My Twenty-Five Years in China*. The author was, for many years, the China correspondent for the *New York Times*. Snow Leopard, of course, is a figment of my imagination.

The Long March actually took place and several entire books have been written about it. All of China's rulers since 1949 participated in that journey.

After the Long March Mao Tse-tung was interviewed as I have described. Chlöe's interview of him is based on the one by the noted journalist Edgar Snow, who reported that interview after the Long March and Mao's first autobiography in his famous *Red Star over China*. My apologies for not giving him credit in the book and allowing my heroine to take his place in history. Slade's and Chlöe's interview with him in his mountain retreat, earlier, is based on descriptions of him *and* the retreat but had no real foreign journalist present.

Nikolai's and Madame Sun's escapes from Wuhan are largely based on fact. Two exceptions: Madame Sun did not leave the Trans-Siberian Railroad to meet anyone in Ulan Bator, but kept right on going. Borodin's entourage certainly did not include Chlöe, and it traveled in far greater style, but the other reports are true. While the individual conversations between the historical people are inventions on my part, everything else about them is portrayed based on historical accounts.

Dr. Robert Ingraham, a medical missionary mentioned in Chapter 50, did spend many years trying to help alleviate hunger in China.

When Chiang Kai-shek returned to Nanking after being kidnapped in the 1936 Sian incident, he made sure that forever afterward the Young Marshal never again walked freely but incarcerated him for the rest of his life—for the years that China spent fighting Japan, and for all the years that Chiang Kai-shek spent in Taiwan.

My fictional characters are not reflective of any living people. Probably all my major characters are reflections of parts of myself. That's one of the things that makes writing so wonderful. And so difficult. So agonizing and so joyous.

This book was begun in Eugene, Oregon, and written throughout Australia's Outback and in Mexico.

*Ajijic, Mexico*
*October 1991*

## ABOUT THE AUTHOR

Barbara Bickmore is a prodigious traveler and spent two months in China researching *Distant Star*. Her previous novels are *East of the Sun*, set in Africa, and *The Moon Below*, set in Australia. She is currently working on a new novel about Australia. Before moving to Ajijic, Mexico, where she now lives, she divided her time between New York and Oregon.